BETWEEN THE LINES

He sang as he worked. The deep, sonorous songs of the void—line nine. The chatter of the mechanics—lines two and three. The fast, rhythmic on-off state of the gravity controller—line four. And the heavy strength of the Bose engines that powered it through the void—line six. He didn't sing line one. That was the crew line, and this wasn't a happy ship.

"I've never heard of a linesman who sang before," said the crewman who brought him his third meal.

Neither had Ean. But then, most linesmen would never have described the lines as song either. He'd tried to explain it once, to his trainers.

"It's like the lines are out of tune but they don't know how to fix themselves. Sometimes they don't even realize they are out of tune. To fix them I sing the right note, and they try to match it, and we keep trying until we match."

His trainers had looked at each other as if wondering what they had gotten themselves into. Or maybe wondering if Ean was sane.

LINESMAN

S. K. DUNSTALL

ACE BOOKS, NEW YORK

An imprint of Penguin Random House LLC
375 Hudson Street, New York, New York 10014

LINESMAN

An Ace Book / published by arrangement with the authors

ISBN: 978-0-425-27952-6

PUBLISHING HISTORY
Ace mass-market edition / July 2015

PRINTED IN THE UNITED STATES OF AMERICA

10 9 8 7 6 5 4 3

Cover art by Bruce Jensen.
Cover design by Diana Kolsky.
Interior text design by Kelly Lipovich.

Penguin
Random
House

ACKNOWLEDGMENTS

Books like *Linesman* aren't produced by a single person—or even, in our case, by two people. A lot of people helped us turn this story into something we're proud of. Thanks to all of you.

Special thanks in particular to our überagent, Caitlin Blasdell, who took what we thought was a good story and helped us turn it into a much better one. To our editor, Anne Sowards, who helped us turn our better story into an even better one still. To copy editor Sara Schwager, who added all those serial commas in for us. (We'll do better next time, we promise.) To Bruce Jensen for the superb cover. Absolutely love it.

Thanks to our mother, who sat through so many dinner readings with us. You laughed in all the right places, loved the good guys, hated the bad guys, and generally made us feel we had a real story here.

It's scary sending your book out into the world to be read as a real book for the first time. Thanks, Dawn, for arranging it and for support in general. Thanks, Arthur, for reading it and for the feedback.

LINESMEN'S GUILD—LIST OF LINES
AND THEIR PURPOSES

LINE	REPRESENTS
1	Crew
2	Small mechanics 1—air circulation, heating, cooling, power. Overall comfort and running of a ship.
3	Small mechanics 2—tools. Interact individually with other lines for repair, maintenance, management.
4	Gravity
5	Communications
6	Bose engines (engines with the capacity to take a ship through the void)
7	*Unknown*
8	*Unknown*
9	Takes ship into the void
10	Moves ship to a different location in space while in the void

ONE

EAN LAMBERT

THE SHIP WAS in bad shape. It was a miracle it had come through the void at all, let alone come through in one piece. Ean patted the chassis that housed the lines. "You did good, girl," he whispered. "I know that, even if no one else does."

It seemed to him that the ship responded to his touch, or maybe to the feel of his brain syncing with hers.

The crewman who showed him the lines was nervous but polite. "We've waited two months for this work," he said. "Glad they've finally brought someone back." He hesitated, then asked the inevitable question in a rush. "So what's it like? The confluence?"

Ean considered lying but decided on the truth. "Don't know. I haven't been out there."

"Oh. But I thought—"

So did everyone else. "Someone has to service the higher lines," Ean said.

"Oh. Of course." But the crewman wasn't as awed by him after that and left abruptly once he had shown him the lines.

Ean supposed he should be used to it by now. But everyone knew the "real" tens—and the nines—were out at the confluence, trying to work out what the immense circle of power was and how it worked. Not that anyone seemed to have come up with an answer yet—and they'd had six months to investigate it.

When the confluence had first been discovered, the media had been full of speculation about what it was. Some said it was a ball of matter that exuded energy on the same wavelength as that of the lines, while others said it was a piece of void space intruding into real space. Some even said it was the original source of the lines.

Six months later, with the Alliance and Gate Union/Redmond on the brink of war, media speculation had changed. It was a weapon designed by the Alliance to destroy all linesmen. It was a weapon designed by Gate Union, in conjunction with the linesmen, to destroy the Alliance. New speculation said it was an experiment of Redmond's gone wrong. They were known to experiment with the lines.

Ean had no idea what it was, but he was sure he could find out—if only Rigel would send him out to the confluence to work, like the other nines and tens.

He was a ten, Ean reminded himself. Certified by the Grand Master himself. As good as any other ten. He sighed and turned to his job.

He worked forty hours straight, stopping only for the meals the crew brought him at four-hour intervals, immersed in the fields, straightening the tangled lines. Creating his own line of the same frequency, calling the fragments into his line, much like a weak magnet might draw iron filings. It was delicate work, and he had to concentrate. He was glad of that. He had no time to think about how he was the only ten left in the cartels available to do work like this because all the other cartel masters had sent their nines and tens out to the confluence.

He sang as he worked. The deep, sonorous songs of the void—line nine. The chatter of the mechanics—lines two and three. The fast, rhythmic on-off state of the gravity controller—line four. And the heavy strength of the Bose engines that powered it through the void—line six. He didn't sing line one. That was the crew line, and this wasn't a happy ship.

"I've never heard of a linesman who sang before," said the crewman who brought him his third meal.

Neither had Ean. But then, most linesmen would never

have described the lines as song either. He'd tried to explain it once, to his trainers.

"It's like the lines are out of tune but they don't know how to fix themselves. Sometimes they don't even realize they are out of tune. To fix them I sing the right note, and they try to match it, and we keep trying until we match."

His trainers had looked at each other as if wondering what they had gotten themselves into. Or maybe wondering if Ean was sane.

"It's because you taught yourself for so long," one particularly antagonistic trainer had told him. "Lines are energy, pure and simple. You manipulate that energy with your mind. You need to get that music nonsense out of your head," and he'd muttered to another trainer about how desperate the cartel master was to be bringing slum dogs into the system.

Ean had never mentioned the music again. Or the fact that lines had to be more than just energy. As for the thought that lines might have emotions, he'd never mentioned that idea at all. He'd known instinctively that idea wouldn't go down well. The trainers would probably have refused to train him.

His throat was raw. He drank the tea provided in one grateful gulp. "Do you think I could get some more tea?"

"At the rate you drank that one, you're going to need it." The crewman went off.

Ean went back to his work.

By the time he was done, the lines were straight and glowing. Except line one, which was straight but not not glowing, but you couldn't change a bad crew.

He patted the ship's control chassis one final time. "All better now." His old trainers would have said he was crazy to imagine that the ship responded with a yes.

He didn't realize how tired he was until he tried to stand up after he'd finished and fell flat on his face.

"Linesman's down," someone shouted, and five people came running. Even the ship hummed a note of concern. Or did he imagine that?

"I'm fine." His voice was a thread. "Just tired. I need a drink."

They took that literally and came back with some rim whiskey that burned as it went down.

It went straight to his head. His body, so long attuned to the ship, seemed to vibrate on each of the ten ship lines, which he could still feel. This time when he stood up, it was the alcohol that made him unsteady on his feet.

"I'm fine," he said, waving away another drink. "Ship's fine, too," slurring his words. He gave the chassis one last pat, then weaved his way down the corridor to the shuttle bays.

Of the quick muttered discussion behind him, all he heard was, "Typical linesman."

The music of the ship vibrated in him long after the shuttle had pulled away.

BACK on planet, they had to wait for a dock.

"Some VIP visiting," the pilot said. "They've been hogging the landing bays all shift."

The commercial centers on Ashery were on the southern continent. There was little here in the north to attract VIPs. Ean couldn't imagine what one would even come here for. Maybe it was a VIP with a cause, come to demand the closure of the Big North—an open-cut mine that was at last report 3,000 kilometers long, 750 kilometers wide, and 3 kilometers deep. Every ten years or so, a protest group tried to close it down.

Ean didn't mind. He sat in the comfortable seat behind the pilot and dozed, too tired to stay awake and enjoy the luxury of a shuttle he'd probably never see the likes of again. He'd bet Rigel hadn't ordered this shuttle. He fell properly asleep to sound of the autobot offering him his choice of aged Grenache or distilled Yaolin whiskey. Or maybe a chilled Lancian wine?

He woke to the pilot yelling into the comms.

"You can't send us to the secondary yards. I've a level-ten linesman on board, for goodness' sake."

Ean heard the reply as the song of line five—the comms line—rather than the voice that came out of the speakers.

That was another thing his trainers had said was impossible. He might as well have claimed the electricity that powered the ship was communicating with him. But humans were energy, too, when you got down to the atomic level. If humans could communicate, why couldn't the lines?

"I don't mind the secondary yards," Ean said. It would cut two kilometers off his trip home.

The pilot didn't listen.

"Level *ten* I said," and five minutes later, they landed, taxiing up to the northernmost of the primary bays, which was also the farthest from where Ean needed to go,

Ean collected his kit, which he hadn't used, thanked the pilot, and stepped out of the shuttle into more activity than he'd seen in the whole ten years he'd been on Ashery.

The landing staff didn't notice him. Despite the fact he was wearing a cartel uniform. Despite the ten bars across the top of his pocket. They knew him as one of Rigel's and looked past him and waited for a "real" linesman to come out behind him.

Ean sighed and placed his bag on the scanner. He *was* a ten. Certified by the Grand Master himself. He *was* as good as the other tens.

He'd been through customs so often in the past six months, he knew all the staff by first name. Today it was Kimi, who waved him through without even checking him.

God, but he was tired. He was going to sleep for a week. He thought about walking to the cartel house—which was what he normally did—but it was four kilometers from the primary landing site, and he wasn't sure he would make it.

Unfortunately, it was still a kilometer to the nearest public cart. A pity the pilot hadn't landed them in the secondary field, where the cart tracks ran right past the entrance.

The landing hall was full of well-dressed people with piles of luggage: all trying to get the attention of staff; all of them ignoring the polished monkwood floor, harder than the hardest stone; all of them ignoring the ten-story sculpture of the first settlers for which the spaceport was famous. At least the luxury shops along the concourse were doing booming business.

Ean accidentally staggered into one of the well-dressed people. Rigel would probably fine him for bumping into a VIP. The man turned, ready to blast him, saw the bars on his shirt, and apologized instead.

These weren't VIPs at all, just their staff.

Ean waved away the man's apology and continued weaving his way through the crowd. It seemed ages before the lush opulence of the primary landing halls gave way to the metal gray walls he was used to and another age before he was finally in the queue for the carts.

It was a relief to get into the cart.

Two young apprentices got on at the next stop. Rigel's people, of course. Who else would catch the cart this way? Their uniforms were new and freshly starched. They looked with trepidation at his sweat-stained greens and silently counted the bars on his shirt, after which they pressed farther back into their seats.

He'd been in their place once.

Four gaudily dressed linesmen got on at the stop after that. They were all sevens. Excepting himself, they were the highest-ranking linesmen Rigel owned. For a moment, Ean resented that they could take time off when he never seemed to do anything but work.

But that was the whole point of Rigel's keeping him here, wasn't it. Rigel's cartel may have had the lowest standing, and Rigel's business ethics were sometimes dubious, but he was raking in big credits now. The other cartel masters had sent their nines and tens out to the confluence. Rigel, who only had one ten—Ean—had kept him back and could now ask any price he wanted of the shipmasters who needed the services of a top-grade linesman.

"Phwawh," one of the new arrivals said. "You stink, Ean."

"Working." Ean's voice was still just a thread.

"Rigel's going to have words."

"Let him." He'd probably dock his pay, too, but Ean didn't care.

"And you've been drinking."

Ean just closed his eyes.

Cartel Master Rigel was big on appearances. His linesmen might have been ordinary, but they were always impeccably turned out, extremely well-spoken, and could comport themselves with heads of government and business. For a boy from the slums of Lancia, those standards were important.

The conversation washed over him. First, what they'd done on their night out; later it turned to the lines. Conversation always turned to the lines eventually when linesmen were talking.

"I went in to fix line five at Bickleigh Company," one of them said now.

Everyone groaned.

Kaelea, one of the other sevens, said, "I don't know why they don't get their own five under contract. We're in there so often, it would cost around the same."

"They tried that. Twice. The second time they even got a five from Sandhurst."

Sandhurst was the biggest line cartel. Over the past ten years, they had aggressively purchased the contracts of other high-level linesmen until now they had a third of all the nines and tens. Ean occasionally fantasized that one day the Sandhurst cartel master would see his work and offer Rigel a huge amount for his contract, too.

As if that was ever going to happen.

"I've been in there three times," Kaelea said. "You push and you push, and just when you think you have it right, it pops out of true again."

Sometimes Ean thought they were talking a different language to him. They used words like push and force when they spoke about moving the lines into place. He'd never pushed a line in his life. He wouldn't know how to.

His trainers had talked in terms of pushing and pulling, too.

"Push with your mind," the particularly antagonistic one had told him. "You do have a mind, don't you?" and he'd muttered to the other trainer that it was doubtful.

The first six months of his apprenticeship, Ean had wondered if he'd ever become a linesman. Until he'd learned that when they told him to push, they actually meant they wanted the line straight. He could sing the lines straight.

"It's probably a manifestation of your being self-taught," the not-so-antagonistic trainer had told him. "You push as you sing, and that bad habit is so entrenched now, you can't do it without singing."

Ean had never been able to break the habit.

He could feel the two apprentices in the corner listening as the linesmen talked. One of them was strong on line five, the other on line eight. Rigel didn't normally get anyone above a seven. Ean opened his eyes, but he couldn't see which one it was.

The trainers had told him you couldn't tell what line a linesman would be without testing, but sometimes Ean could hear the lines in them. The trainers had told him it was because he'd learned bad habits by not being trained in childhood, and that of course he could tell what someone was because he'd already seen the number of bars they wore. Ean didn't care. He would bet that Rigel had just got himself an eight. How long he would keep him—or her—was another question altogether. A higher cartel would poach him.

The conversation turned to the confluence. One of the sevens—Kaelea—had been out there to service the Bose engines, "Because the nines and tens couldn't do it, of course. They're too busy," and Ean hadn't needed his eyes open to see the roll of eyes that accompanied that. "It's . . . I don't know. It's huge, and it's . . . you can feel the lines, but you don't know what they are, and—"

He could hear the awe in her voice. But he couldn't tell what the lines were. Sometimes he could pick the level from the linesman's voice when they talked about the line. He hadn't mentioned that particular talent to the trainers either. They wouldn't have believed him, or they would have said it was another bad-training defect.

Kaelea had said "lines" rather than "line," which meant there was more than one line out there. What would have multiple lines anyway? A ship? A station? As Ean had pointed out to Rigel, he was good at picking lines. He'd at least be able to say if there were lots of different lines or just a few.

He'd like a chance to prove that he could find out, anyway.

"We make more money hiring you out while the rest of the tens are busy trying to work that out," Rigel had said.

That was true. Ean was busier than he'd ever been, and Rigel smiled more broadly every time he sent Ean out on a job.

Ean dozed after that.

One of the linesmen touched his arm. He blinked blearily, trying to focus.

"Are you okay?"

It was Kaelea.

He realized the cart had stopped, and everyone else was out.

"Come on, Kaelea," one of the other gaudily dressed people said.

"I don't think he's well."

"Leave him, or you'll be fined, too."

"I'm okay," Ean said. "Just really, really tired." He wasn't sure she heard him. Next time, he'd take more care of his voice.

He struggled to sit up and almost fell getting out of the cart.

"I'll help you," Kaelea said, waving off his protests, and led him up to the house. "My room is closer," and by now he was staggering too much to care. God but he was tired.

She pushed him down onto the bed and started to pull off his sweat-stained shirt. "I don't think Rigel saw you," she said. "You may not get a fine."

He tried to protest, but closed his eyes instead and was instantly asleep.

EAN woke, naked and sprawled out on the bed and couldn't remember how he'd come to be that way.

For a moment, he couldn't work out what had woken him either.

"He's a ten, you say?" The clipped vowels of the Lancastrian noblewoman made him think he was back home in the slums of Lancia.

He struggled awake fast. That was one nightmare he didn't want to return to.

"Definitely a ten." The oily tones of Rigel, Ean's cartel master, reassured him on that much at least. He was years past the grottoes of Lancia. "Certified by the Grand Master himself." Then his voice rose and cracked. "You can't be going to—"

It was all the warning Ean had before the disruptor beam slammed into his mind and ten lines of song came together in a discordant cacophony. His brain almost burst with the noise. He didn't even think. He turned the lines so they flowed back in on themselves down the line, back to the disruptor. The weapon disintegrated in a flash of heat and flame. He was only sorry to see that the Lancastrian lady had thrown it down before it had disintegrated. He would have liked to have burned off the hand.

A disruptor was a one-use weapon, made with a full set

of lines, created especially to destroy other lines. Ean had heard they cost as much as a small shuttle. Who could afford one, let alone use it? Who would even think to use such a monstrous thing against humans?

"He is a ten," the noblewoman agreed. She sounded almost surprised.

"Of course he is." Rigel was white.

Ean was pretty white himself. A disruptor would have killed anyone less than a ten, could even have killed him if he'd been a fraction slower.

"I've dealt with you before, Rigel," the noblewoman said. "Last time you sold me a five as a six."

Rigel did that occasionally, when he thought he could get away with it, and most people knew a Lancastrian wouldn't be able to tell the difference.

"I . . . Surely not." Rigel was back to his oily, obsequious best. He thought he was back in control.

Ean knew better. Lancastrian nobles may not know their line ratings, but they definitely knew revenge. He pulled on his pants and a pair of boots. He was in Kaelea's room. He didn't remember what had happened after they'd arrived. "So did you really want a ten, or just to teach Rigel a lesson?"

He was glad the gutter slum was gone from his accent. He spoke Standard now, could have come from anywhere in the Conglomerate. His voice, still hoarse, was better than it had been when he'd gone to sleep.

The noblewoman glanced at him and Ean saw for the first time the distinctive blue eyes of the Lyan clan. He forced himself to not wipe his suddenly damp palms down the side of his trousers. This wasn't just any clan. This was royalty.

The woman was smiling, actually smiling, at a slum creature like him. She wouldn't do that if she knew what stood in front of her.

"I did want a ten, but I wasn't planning on getting one from here," she admitted.

Rigel didn't get it, not at first. He opened his mouth and closed it again. "But he's a ten," he whispered, finally.

"If I'd died, I wouldn't have been, would I," Ean said. He understood Lancastrian revenge.

"But I would have offered her at least a nine." Not that Rigel had any nines.

Both Lancastrians shrugged.

"When I ask for a six, I expect a six," the Lancastrian noble said.

"But—" Rigel couldn't seem to stop the fish imitation.

Ean gathered up the rest of his clothes. "You obviously don't need me." He could see Kaelea hovering in the passage. "I'll leave you to it then," and made for the door.

"Hold," said the Lancastrian noblewoman. "I'll take him," she said to Rigel.

Rigel smiled his oily smile.

"Less the cost of the six I purchased."

The smile stopped, fixed. Then Rigel bobbed his head suddenly. "Of course, my Lady Lyan."

Lady Lyan. Only three women could call themselves Lady Lyan, and Ean bet this woman wasn't one of them. Any true daughter of the Lancastrian emperor would be tied up so tightly in protocol and security guards, she wouldn't be able to move. So who was this imposter? She must be one of the illegitimate children. There were rumors they were plentiful. Not that Ean cared, he supposed, but he hoped they would never come across true Lancastrian royalty or soldiers while he was working for the imposter. They were likely to all be killed.

"And I want the contract," Lady Lyan said.

The color faded again from Rigel's face. "But—" Ean could almost read his thoughts. No matter what Rigel said, Ean brought in 90 percent of the money right now. "Well, obviously that will cost more," Rigel said eventually.

"I don't like being cheated," Lady Lyan said. "I don't like my staff's dying because I give them tasks they can't do. Take the money and be glad I didn't destroy your whole cartel as I planned to."

Rigel made one more token protest, but Ean knew he'd already lost. The Lancastrian had done her homework. She knew how much it would hurt Rigel to lose his only ten, whether by death or by contract conversion. That was what she had come in today to do, and they all knew it. Ean was just grateful to be alive.

Even so, he was surprised Rigel didn't protest more.

Lady Lyan beckoned to Kaelea, still hovering in the hall. "Witness."

Kaelea looked as if she would turn and run, but Rigel beckoned frantically, too.

The exchange of contract took less than a minute. They all witnessed, then it was over.

If Ean was lucky, the Lancastrian noble would on-sell his contract today. Then, finally, maybe, he could get out into the confluence with all the other nines and tens. He didn't want to think about the alternative—stuck working for a Lancastrian. He'd sworn he would never have anything to do with Lancia again.

THEY left immediately, without giving Ean time to pack.

"Send his things on," Lady Lyan ordered Rigel. She looked at the shirt Ean now had time to pull on. "Except the uniforms."

The thought of Rigel's pawing through his possessions gave Ean the creeps. He was unlikely to get anything sent through. He considered demanding time to get his things, but he hadn't collected much in the ten years he'd been with the cartel, and anything of value was already programmed into his comms, which was in his pocket. Better to save his fights for important things, he decided.

His new owner had a private cart waiting. Not owner, Ean reminded himself. Employer. This woman might own the contract, but she was still obligated to pay him. And if she didn't— for who could trust a rich Lancastrian to abide by their contract if they could get out of it—then he could go to the cartel Grand Master for breach of contract. His contract stipulated minimum amounts, plus bonuses, and how frequently he was to be paid. He thought about the contract as they waited for the cart. It wasn't good pay.

His new owner—employer—must have been thinking similar thoughts. "Does Rigel pay everyone so badly?"

Only those desperate enough to indenture themselves into a twenty-year contract. Ean shrugged. A Lancastrian like her wouldn't understand how badly he'd wanted to become a linesman.

"You've been with him a long time."

Ten years two tendays ago. Ean had spent it repairing a military ship, the GU *Burnley*. He'd only realized the date because the captain of the *Burnley* had told him the ship was ten years old, too. Ean shrugged again. "You know what it's like when you're a kid and desperate to learn the craft." Not that he'd been as young as most. "Sometimes you'll do anything."

"With age comes wisdom, eh." His companion laughed. "I can relate to that. I'm Michelle by the way."

Which didn't help identify which Lyan she was, illegitimate or not, because every member of the Lyan household took a form of Michel as one of their given names. Still, it was clever. She had every right to use it although most of them would not have dared. This woman had guts, identifying herself the way she did.

"Ean Lambert," Ean said.

SURPRISINGLY, they made for the docks rather than the hotels, where the private cart avoided the landing hall altogether and went straight to a shuttle out on the edge of the field.

The name stenciled on the side of the shuttle was LAN-CASTRIAN PRINCESS—SHUTTLE I. Ean shook his head at the bare-faced effrontery.

They took off without having to go through customs.

In the confined enclosures of the cabin, Michelle leaned back with a sigh and closed her eyes. Ean used the time to study his new employer.

She was classically beautiful, with the heart-shaped face and high cheekbones typical of the women of the Lancastrian royal family. Rumor said they had paid a fortune to geneticists over the last two hundred years to develop those looks. Her lashes were long and black, curled over clear, unblemished, cream skin. The geneticists had definitely earned their money in this case. Except for the hair, perhaps, which was the royal family black, but Ean could see a slight wave instead of the expected regulation straight. Nor the deeper-than-expected dimples in her cheeks, particularly the right one. The emperor definitely wouldn't have liked that. Still, if Michelle was illegitimate, the geneticists wouldn't have been involved this generation, would they. Maybe some imperfections had crept in.

Ean smiled to himself, but it was a grim smile. Ten years ago, there was no way he could have studied even an illegitimate child of his regent this close. Michelle—and of course he would never have dreamed of calling her Michelle either—might own the contract, but there was no way Ean was going back to what he had been.

"What's so amusing?" Michelle had opened her eyes—so very blue—and was watching him.

Ean met the blue gaze. "Will you on-sell the contract?"

"I don't know." Michelle sat up as the bell chimed for landing. "We do need a ten."

So was there a job? And was it at the confluence? Ean hoped it was.

On-screen they could see their destination. A large freighter. Ean didn't recognize the model—it looked custom-built—but until six months ago, he had only worked on one- and two-man freighters and second-class company ships. Ships like this one in front of him were for the likes of House of Sandhurst or House of Rickenback.

The name painted three stories high on the side was LANCASTRIAN PRINCESS. The bay door they headed for had an enormous "1" stenciled on it.

The door in the freighter ahead irised open to let them in. The shuttle docked. The door closed behind them. This was definitely a private shuttle, and this was its regular docking pad.

Ean silently followed Michelle out into the ship proper.

The interior was luxurious. The softly textured walls and carefully placed lighting made the whole thing look like an expensive hotel. Everything was way above Rigel's standard. Ean couldn't even begin to calculate the cost of the fittings.

Even so, the ship had a military feel. It didn't help that the staff wore gray uniforms piped with black, and that every single one of them walked straight and upright. They all noticed Ean, and he could see that they filed whatever they had noticed for future reference.

Michelle led the way quickly through the center of the

ship to a room that looked like an office on one end but housed a comfortable set of three couches at the other.

One man was in the room. An older man. He looked up as they entered. "Misha. I found you your ten."

Misha was an affectionate form of Michelle, used among close friends generally. So this man—who wore the gray-and-black-piped uniform everyone else did—was a close friend.

"I found us a ten, too," Michelle said. "And I bet he didn't cost as much as yours did."

The uniformed man looked at him, and Ean was suddenly aware that he hadn't showered for more than two days, that his Rigel-cartel greens were sweaty and crumpled, and that he needed a shave.

"This is Abram," Michelle said. "He runs security and pretty much everything else."

Abram counted the bars on Ean's chest. "A genuine ten?"

"I couldn't kill him."

"So you hired him instead?"

"I didn't hire him," Michelle said, and her smile showed the full brilliance of the generations of genetic engineering that had made it, plus a dimple that same genetic engineering had probably tried to wipe out. She placed her card on the reader and brought up the contract. "I bought him."

Abram read the contract, then nodded slowly. "That would upset Rigel."

Ean thought it time to get back some control. He was a ten, after all. "If it's all right with you." He had to stop, because his voice came out thin and thready. He cleared his throat, and was glad the second attempt came out more strongly. "I haven't had time to clean up. I didn't get a chance to collect any clothes."

Abram looked at Michelle, who shrugged. "Rigel will send his things on."

Abram switched to Lancastrian. "We don't all have personal servants who have things packed in five minutes, Misha. His effects are unlikely to arrive before we leave."

"I'll replace them then." Michelle spoke Lancastrian, too. "I'd like that. He has a good figure under those stinking clothes."

"And so like you to know that already." Abram sighed and switched back to Standard. "I'll get someone to show you a cabin and get you some clothes," he told Ean, pressing a button on the screen as he did so. "Our other ten will be here at 19:00. We leave when she arrives."

An orderly in a gray-and-black uniform appeared at the door.

"Take Linesman"—he looked at the contract—"Lambert down to Apparel and get him a standard kit. I'll organize a room for him while you do." He looked at Ean. "We eat at 20:00. I'll have someone call you." He half turned away, hesitated. "Your voice. Is that normal?"

"Just strained."

"Take him via the medical center."

"Yes, sir."

Ean followed the orderly in silence. Abram was the sort who'd look up Ean's record as soon as he could. He—they—owned the contract now. Nothing was private to them. That little slip with the language wouldn't happen again.

The orderly—a tall, willowy woman who looked to be a little younger than Ean and whose name above the pocket said RADKO—was polite, but not truly friendly. Even so, she took time out to show Ean various parts of the ship. "Mess hall down there," she said. "Officers generally eat with the crew. Unless they're invited upstairs, of course." She looked sideways at him and for a moment Ean thought she was going to ask what rank he was. "Main lift well. Although most of us use the jumps, of course."

It was a well-run ship. The lines were clear and steady, their song bright and joyful in Ean's mind. Unusually, line one was the strongest. This was a crew who worked well together and looked after one another and their ship.

Or almost joyful, Ean amended. He could hear a slight off tone in line six. It was only minor, but it jarred because everything else was so perfect.

"And this is the off-duty area," the orderly said. Ean thought, from her tone, that it wasn't the first time she'd said it.

"Sorry."

"Officers have their own bar up on the fourth."

The bar on fourth was one bar Ean wasn't likely to end up in. He wasn't even sure he would end up in this one. Which left him precisely where? Stuck in his room, probably, given that they weren't on-selling his contract immediately.

"Here's Apparel." The orderly seemed glad to have arrived.

Ean stripped and stepped into the cubicle, where a grid of lights started at his feet and moved upward, building a perfect model of him. They didn't have tailoring modules in the Old-city slums. The first time he'd ever stepped into a cubicle like this had been ten years ago, when he'd started at House of Rigel. He hadn't known what to do. Rigel had had to show him.

When he stepped out, the orderly said, "Your kit will take twenty minutes. I'll bring them over to your cabin when they're done."

So at least he had somewhere to stay. "If you don't mind."

"Of course not, sir."

The "sir" was new, and as she led the way back to the newly allocated cabin, Ean thought he knew why. The soldiers' quarters—and he couldn't help but think of them as soldiers—were comfortable, but they were a marked contrast to the luxurious quarters that Lady Lyan—whichever lady she was—inhabited. Somehow, Ean had scored himself a cabin on the luxurious side of the cruiser. Some tens would accept that as their right. Rigel's people might be trained to handle it, but he—Rigel's only ten—had never experienced it.

"I'll get your clothes, sir," the orderly said, and loped off.

Ean left the door unlocked and went into the fresher. Michelle was right. He did stink. He soaped up, letting the needles of water wash the stink away. Eyes closed, thinking of nothing but the bliss of the warm water, the song of the ship flooded into his mind, still with that slightly off tone on the sixth line. Ean hummed a countermelody under his breath, trying to coax the line straight, but it was no use. Humming didn't work. He had to sing it.

The orderly was waiting when he came out, the freshly woven clothes in a neat pile in front of her. Standard issue included underclothes and shoes, Ean was glad to see. She handed him an outfit.

"Thank you. You don't have to wait on me."

"Of course not, sir. But there's still the medic." She pointed to a uniform placed apart. "That's the dress uniform. You'll be wearing that tonight if you're dining with Lady Lyan and Commodore Galenos."

Commodore Galenos being the casually introduced Abram,

Ean presumed. "Thank you," and he smiled his appreciation. "I know nothing about uniforms, ranks, and what to wear."

The orderly smiled back. "I didn't think you did, sir."

Ean was sure she didn't mean it as an insult.

"The medic's expecting you. To look at your voice and to check you over. He's already called to see where you are."

"Let me put these on first." Ean took the clothes into the bedroom. He had a separate bedroom, which he was sure wasn't standard military practice. He dressed quickly. His uniform was gray with the characteristic black piping. The only decoration was a tiny cloth badge woven into the pocket on his left chest and the name—LAMBERT—above it. Ean didn't count the bars on the badge, but he knew there would be ten. It was a total contrast to the pocket of his companion, which was covered with badges.

He came out, and the orderly left at a fast walk. Ean followed. "Radko. That is your name?"

The orderly glanced back. "Yes, sir," she said.

Ean wished she wouldn't keep calling him sir. "Thank you for all this, Radko."

"Just doing my job, sir." But she smiled and somehow the atmosphere seemed lighter as they made their way through the corridors to a well-equipped hospital. It was worrying that a ship this size needed a hospital so equipped. What was this ship?

The medic was waiting for him. "At least you've cleaned up some," he said, as he made Ean strip his freshly donned clothes and lie down under the analyzer. "I hear you stank when you came on board." He held up a hand to stop any comment—not that Ean had been going to make one. "Nothing travels faster than shipboard gossip. Not even a ship passing through the void."

"Even on a military ship like this?"

"Especially on a military ship like this." Which confirmed, once and for all, what type of ship he was on. Ean wished he'd taken more notice of politics suddenly. He didn't want to end up in the middle of a battle.

"What happened with the voice?" the medic asked.

"My own fault. Too much—" It sounded so lame. "I was singing." He wondered how the other ship was going. It had probably moved on by now. Ships didn't stay in port any longer than they had to.

"Hmm. Let me see you breathe."

For the next ten minutes, he peered into Ean's throat, X-rayed it, and finally gave him a drink of something warm. It soothed as it went down.

"The miracles of modern medicine," the medic said. "We can tailor your genes so that your voice is deep or high, but we still can't fix a strained larynx. Although"—he paused— "if it's truly damaged I can replace it with a synthetic one."

Ean shuddered.

"I thought not. If you continue to sing like that, maybe you should take some lessons on breathing and voice control. Have you been trained?"

Ean shook his head. Rigel had paid for lessons on how to speak with a faultless Standard accent, but there hadn't been any voice training with it.

"So you won't use your voice so badly that you strain it again, will you." It was an order.

"No, sir," Ean said meekly, and the medic let him go.

Radko escorted him back to his rooms and left him there.

He had two hours until dinner. Ean set the alarm on his comms—it wouldn't do to be late—then kicked off his boots and lay down on the bed.

He couldn't sleep. The off tone on line six buzzed into his brain and set his teeth on edge. After ten minutes he sat up, then stood properly—he wasn't going to be able to do this sitting down—got himself a glass of warm water from the sink in the bathroom, took a deep breath, and started to sing.

The line responded immediately. This was one beautifully tuned engine. It didn't take long. When it was done, Ean flopped back across the bed and didn't hear anything more until the increasingly loud, persistent beep of the alarm dragged him out of heavy sleep a hundred minutes later.

TWO

EAN LAMBERT

FOR A MOMENT, Ean lay there and thought about staying in bed.

The alarm beep grew louder, and he realized it wasn't the alarm at all but the comm. He pressed receive.

Abram's face came up. "Ean. Formal dinner tonight. Did Radko show you what to wear?"

Should he stand to attention? What rank was a commodore anyway? The hell with it. He'd been introduced as Abram, Ean would keep on thinking of him as Abram until told otherwise. He wasn't a soldier. "Yes, thank you. The uniform with the thinner piping and the fancier shoulders."

Abram smiled faintly. "That would be it," he agreed, and clicked off.

Ean dragged himself out of bed. He had seven minutes to get ready. If Abram thought it important enough to tell him what to wear, then he probably shouldn't be late. He showered in three, only wondering afterward whether showers were rationed on ship, shaved again—maybe he should depilate if he was going to be here awhile, a lot of spacers did—and dragged on his second new uniform for the day. Then there was only time for a quick comb-through of his hair—

thankfully, combs were part of the standard kit, too—and he was out the door with two minutes to spare.

He almost ran into Abram.

Michelle joined them at the lift. She wore a close-fitting midnight blue silk slit skirt that emphasized more success of the genetic engineering of body shape—and probably hours spent daily in the gym—plus a more-than-close-fitting white crop shirt that stretched across her chest, so fine it really didn't hide the breasts underneath, so short that as Michelle lifted her arm to work herself into the matching blue silk jacket she carried—also close-fitting—she exposed five centimeters of muscled abdomen.

"I can't believe you're wearing that," Abram said.

"This," Michelle said with dignity, "is the height of fashion for both men and women."

"For a formal dinner?"

The genetically enhanced smile flashed again. "At least three other people will be wearing shirts like this. Bet?" She held up a hand.

Abram's palm met hers. "I don't know why I'm so stupid," he said.

The lift stopped.

They stepped out into a room of richly dressed people and were instantly swamped. Rigel would love this. It was what he'd lived for, what he'd trained his people for but had never managed himself. At least, not at this level.

Ean saw two minor royals who'd been in the vids, a politician from Ganymede whose name he couldn't remember, and so much military braid he could have set up his own private navy. There had to be a hundred people in the room, probably more. Hadn't Abram said they were departing into space at 19:00 hours? He could hear from the ship lines that they had, so where had all these people come from?

How big was this ship anyway?

The glitterati wanted to talk to "Lady Lyan."

Ean slipped away. This was a lot of people calling Michelle Lady Lyan. Which meant that this woman really was one of the Emperor's children. Or that he, Ean, was right in the middle of planning for one of the biggest political conspiracies of the century. Or that there were a lot of gullible people out there. Get them far enough away from the center of power, and they'd believe anything.

There weren't many Lancastrians. Michelle, Abram, himself, plus three more men in uniform talking together over near the drinks table, watching their arrival. One of them said something quiet to the others, then made his way across. He'd be lucky to talk to Michelle right now. He'd be better waiting until the scrum had quieted.

But the soldier angled off and came straight to Ean.

"Linesman Lambert."

This close, it was easy to see his rank. The ship's captain. Like everyone else on board, he had a veritable pocket of badges. The name above the pocket said HELMO.

"Yes." What could the captain want with him?

"Nobody touches the lines on my ship except my crew."

He could argue that technically he was part of the crew. "Line six was off."

"We were aware of that. We were taking steps of our own to fix the problem."

They'd been taking their time about it. He thought about apologizing, but the captain didn't give him time. "Keep out of my lines," and turned and walked away.

That was one person he hadn't impressed. Ean collected a drink from a passing server and turned to survey the crowd. No one else came near him. He wasn't sure if it was the uniform—one richly dressed man handed Ean his empty glass—or if it was just that there were really only two centers of conversation. Michelle, of course, and a woman in a long blue silk dress that from a distance was almost the same color as Michelle's.

The woman's glossy brown hair was piled on top of her head in an elegant bun. Her green eyes were made up as a blue-and-green piece of art. A butterfly. With red spots. The red color was picked out again, shiny and glossy on her lips. She looked like a princess dressed up for a gala occasion. Then she moved and Ean recognized her.

Rebekah Grimes, from the Sandhurst Cartel. Sandhurst Cartel was the prime supplier of linesmen, known for their quality and service. They had twelve known tens at last count, and Rebekah was the best of them. Abram must have gone straight to the top. How much had he paid?

Ean moved closer.

"Just came in from the confluence," she was saying as he got close enough to hear her. He didn't hear the murmured reply, but when Rebekah answered, "You cannot imagine," Ean thought it might have been about the glory of the confluence.

"And how do you feel about this mission?" He was close enough now to hear the other speaker, a swarthy woman with so much gold jewelry he was amazed she could hold her arm up to take a sip of her drink.

"Excited," Rebekah said. "Delighted to be part of it. Happy to be working with people like this."

So she knew more about it than he did.

"And the other ten? You have worked with him before? Out at the confluence, maybe?"

"Other—" For a moment, Rebekah looked disconcerted. Ean was glad she didn't know everything. She recovered quickly. "I have worked with most tens."

Not this one, she hadn't. She probably didn't even know who he was.

Ean normally worked alone. Rigel had no one to pair him with, but jobs involving tens were usually single anyway. No one could afford two tens. He didn't often get to talk to other people of his own level. Not only that, this was Rebekah Grimes. He could learn a lot from her. He felt a flutter of anticipatory pleasure. Please let Michelle not on-sell his contract until they had finished this job.

The woman with the gold bracelets handed her empty glass to Ean. He reached for it with a sigh. It was the uniform. Plain and unadorned. This wasn't how he wanted Rebekah to see him—as a servant.

Michelle, whom Ean hadn't even seen come over, plucked the glass out of the woman's hand just before Ean touched it and passed it back to a real server. Radko. Ean looked around. There were more soldiers here than he realized—and most of them were carrying trays. No wonder she thought he was the hired help.

Radko smiled at him.

"Governor Jade." Michelle picked up two full glasses. She handed one to the gold-adorned woman, and one to Ean. "So you've met both our tens."

Ean quietly slipped his other, half-finished glass onto Radko's tray as well.

"Ean Lambert." Rebekah sounded as if she'd swallowed a lemon. She nodded regally and half turned to talk to Michelle and the governor. It seemed accidental, but the turn placed her so that her body was facing away from Ean.

She knew him. He made himself smile. "Rebekah." If she didn't want to talk to him, then he didn't want to talk to her. He nodded to the other woman. "Governor."

The governor had obviously decided to ignore her faux pas. She nodded graciously back. "So what do you think of our project, Linesman?"

Rebekah's smile was almost condescending. "This is your first real job, isn't it, Ean? Until now, you've been doing odd jobs, or so I hear. You haven't been anywhere near the confluence."

His jobs had been challenging lately. He smiled at the memory of his last job. He'd done well. He knew that. But it was interesting that the foremost linesman knew what he'd been doing.

"Linesman?"

Ean smiled at the governor. "Honestly?"

"Honestly."

"I don't know enough about the job to have an opinion yet," and thought he imagined the warm approval in Michelle's blue gaze.

"And so you should think that," said one of the men who'd come over with Michelle. He was in uniform—although Ean couldn't pick the world—and had been one of the first to swarm them when they'd stepped out of the lift. "It's dangerous. We don't know what we're playing with here. We shouldn't even touch it."

"That's why we have the linesmen," Michelle said smoothly.

"And didn't one of your linesmen get killed recently."

Michelle's lips tightened.

"That was nothing to do with the ship," Abram said, close behind Michelle as usual. "That was something else altogether."

"Still. It shows that we're meddling in something we're not supposed to be. Blow it up, I say. Get rid of the damn thing before it kills any more of us."

They had found something. Ean tingled with expectation. It might not be the confluence, but it was new and unknown.

"But Admiral," said Governor Jade. "Think what we can learn from it."

"Every crackpot in the universe will be thinking of that as soon as it becomes public knowledge."

If the representatives gathered in this room were anything to go by, everyone knew about it anyway.

Whatever "it" was. Since lines nine and ten were only used to travel through the void, and Abram and Michelle had recruited level ten linesmen, it was likely to be a ship. But what kind of ship could generate such a gathering of VIPs?

"It's a warship," the admiral said. "Will Redmond or Gate Union stay away once they know?"

The three major political groups—Gate Union, Redmond, and the Alliance—had been on the brink of war for years now. In the ten years Ean had been at Rigel's, he had seen the balance of power shift subtly, but surely, away from the old power, the Alliance, toward the other two groups. Over the past six months, he'd also had to fix a lot of warships, many of them built in the last twenty years.

Gate Union, in particular, was becoming quite powerful. The union had started out as a loose affiliation of worlds that had agreed to monitor and assign void jumps—after all, no one wanted to jump cold, that was deadly. They made up a network of sector "gates," tracking each ship, controlling their passage through. These gate worlds had become the major trade routes because all jumps went through their controllers. Fifty years before Ean had been born, they had formalized that loose affiliation into a political entity. Gate Union.

A lot of the cartels were covertly pro–Gate Union. The cartel houses were close to the gates—after all, the big money came from lines nine and ten—and the nines and tens were all on the ships that jumped through the void.

Ean realized, suddenly, that the Alliance had to be worried about that. Control the void, and you controlled shipping.

"That's why we are here," Michelle said. "To prevent Gate Union or Redmond getting anywhere near the ship. To protect and claim what is ours."

The gong chimed for dinner then, and huge doors slid open at one end of the room. "Admiral, Governor," and she walked in with them to the formally set dining tables now exposed.

Rebekah swept in behind them.

Ean waited until most of the others had moved in, then followed. Thankfully, another orderly was there to seat him. He was placed at a table halfway down. If Rigel's ranking lessons made any sense, that meant that he was halfway up the pecking order. Rebekah was at a table nearby; Michelle was at the top table, and Abram at the second table. Michelle's table was a riot of richly dressed color. Abram's table was all uniforms and fancy braid.

The woman on Ean's right wore a Balian uniform. He recognized it from the *Picasso*, which had been the first military ship he'd ever worked on. A massive warship, it had also been the first big ship he'd worked on. He had no idea of her rank, though, or her age. She was slender and looked fit, and her skin was flawless, but her eyes looked ancient, and the fingers that reached out to pick up her glass looked more like claws than hands.

The man on his left was a civilian. And Michelle was correct. The skimpy, see-through shirts were in fashion—for both men and women. Unfortunately, they required a perfectly sculpted body underneath, and this man was carrying some flab. The shirt hid nothing, and showed a roll of fat at the bottom.

"So what do you think of this ship they found?" the civilian asked.

Ean forced himself to look at the man's face. He probably couldn't afford one anyway, but he was never going to buy a shirt like that. He fell back on the answer he had given before. "I don't know enough yet to think anything."

The soldier on his right nodded. The military seemed to like his answers, at least.

"But you must have an opinion," the civilian insisted. His eyes were unnaturally bright, and his breath smelled of wine.

"Not really." Ean's voice was going again. He took a mouthful of the wine in front of him. What he really wanted was some warm tea.

The soldier laughed. "Give it up, Tarkan," she advised. "He's one of Lady Lyan's men. Of course he'll be discreet."

Tarkan was a formal title used on the three Gaian worlds. Rigel's etiquette coach had covered that much. The man was a landowner and a parliamentary minister. And if a Tarkan could end up halfway down the dining room, who in the worlds was on the higher tables?

"Admiral Katida," the soldier said, holding out her hand to Ean.

"Ean Lambert." They shook hands. He didn't add a title. They already knew he was a linesman.

"I know," she said, making him wonder momentarily if he had said it out loud anyway. "You worked on one of our ships. The *Picasso*. The captain was very pleased with your work. He'd had it in three times in three trips before that. Hasn't had to take it in since."

Maybe he should ask her captain to put in a good word with the captain on this ship. Ean smiled at her, and she smiled back. Her smile was more than warm, it was sizzling and held an invitation. She held his gaze until he had to look away. Right now, he needed another drink. This sort of thing didn't happen to Rigel's people.

Eyes lowered, he looked back to the Gaian on the other side. Naturally, he saw the shirt first, and raised his eyes a second too late to be really polite. He could feel the color rising in his face.

The Gaian smiled at him and pulled in his stomach muscles. He held out his own hand in turn. "Tarkan Heyington." His hand clasp was warm and a little too long.

"Delighted." Ean had to rescue this conversation somehow. He indicated the tables. "It's a diverse mix of worlds," he said. "Did everyone send a representative?" He thought that topic was safe enough.

"Every single member of the Alliance," Admiral Katida said. "Lady Lyan has done a remarkable job." She grimaced, and added, "I am glad I am not in charge of keeping this particular ship safe. If anything happens to us, it will start a galaxy-wide war. Lady Lyan has guts putting us all together like this. I'll give her that."

Ean thought of the harmless-looking freighter he had seen in the viewscreen. It didn't appear to have much protection. "People must have seen you arrive," he said. He'd probably seen some of them himself yesterday, on the long walk from the primary landing site to the carts. You couldn't hide that many ships, especially not ships carrying high-ranking government and military dignitaries.

"Of course people saw us arrive," Tarkan Heyington said. "We've been on the vids all week. But who would dare stay away from the party celebrating the impending nuptials of Emperor Yu's oldest daughter to Yu's close personal friend, Sattur Dow. Not I. I wouldn't dare."

It was rumored that Sattur Dow owned half the galaxy. Ean didn't know if the rumors were true. He did know Dow was a hard man, not someone he'd want his daughter to marry.

When Ean had been a boy—almost too young to remember but everyone in the slums remembered this—Sattur Dow had bought up Settlement City for the mining rights. He'd given the inhabitants two days to leave. On the third day, he'd sent in a demolition crew with explosives. By nightfall, a city that once held half a million people was a pile of rubble. The influx of refugees to Ean's home district had caused turf wars that had lasted years.

"Nor would anyone else here refuse to come to the wedding," Heyington said. "Except the daughter, of course. Who, rumor has it, is not happy about it at all. So—according to rumor again—she decided to take off and study the confluence, hoping that her father will get over this latest foolishness like he did last time."

Which solved, once and for all, the question of whether Michelle was one of the legitimate or illegitimate offspring.

"So are we going to the confluence?" Ean asked. Please let them be. He wanted so desperately to go. He'd just never have imagined Lancia would be the world to get him there.

"Of course not," Katida said. "Telling everyone she's studying the confluence gives her an excuse to get some tens. That's why we're here. There are four cartel houses on this planet."

Rigel's was the smallest and most insignificant, and Sandhurst wasn't one of them.

"But—" Tarkan Heyington held up a hand to forestall Ean's next question. Not that he had one. "The Emperor is determined this time. If the daughter won't come to him, then he will go to the daughter, and all of us will go with him." He shook his head admiringly. "Like the admiral said, she's got guts. Right under everyone's nose."

Ean looked around the room. "So are you all here for the ship or are some just here for the wedding?" And was Michelle actually getting married or not? There would be some guests you *had* to invite to the wedding—like Yu's grandmother, former Emperor Consort Jai—but he couldn't see her among the dignitaries, and based on her reputation, you wouldn't want her on a secret mission either.

"Oh no," Katida said. "Every single person here is hand-picked for this mission."

Except him, but he didn't tell Katida that.

Ean glanced up at the head table, to where Michelle was laughing with Governor Jade. The woman he had met today didn't look the sort who would come up with such a complex conspiracy. Or maybe she could. She'd been prepared to kill for revenge. Which was typical of a Lancastrian, even down to planning it out. "So when does the Emperor arrive?"

"Tomorrow. But we'll be gone by then." The Tarkan waved an expansive hand, nearly knocking Ean's wine over. "Sorry," as Ean rescued his glass. "At least, we'd better be. I'm sure he doesn't want that particular wedding to happen any more than his daughter does."

"Sattur Dow wouldn't mind," said another admiral from farther down the table.

Ean pondered the mix of people on board as he listened. If Gate Union took this ship out, the Alliance would lose a large number of high-ranking soldiers and politicians in one swoop. He hoped that Abram, who Michelle had said was responsible for security, was good at his job.

Even so, how long could it stay a secret? "People will suspect something." There were too many dignitaries, too many soldiers, for people not to notice.

"Haven't you been watching the vids?" Tarkan Heyington asked.

"I've been a little busy." He hadn't seen the vids in months.

"He's a ten, Tarkan," Katida said. "He has better things to do with his time."

"Should still watch the vids. Best indicator of public sentiment around. And driver of it. But I suppose a linesman doesn't have time for politics."

Ean shrugged.

"Let me give you some advice." And the Tarkan leaned close. "Linesmen do play politics. Especially the higher levels." He leaned even closer, so that their arms were touching. Ean could feel the warmth through the jacket of his formal uniform. He managed not to lean away. "That's why I've heard of that woman over there"—he inclined his head toward the table Rebekah was at—"while I've never heard of you, whom the admiral's captain is so taken with. It's not how you do the job, it's always about how you play the people."

Rigel had believed something similar. It hadn't got Rigel anywhere.

The Tarkan laughed. "Look at his face, Admiral. He doesn't believe us."

"There's a lot to be said for someone who thinks doing a good job is the only thing that's required." Katida sounded wistful. She gripped Ean's other arm. "Hang on to your delusions as long as you can."

It was time to rescue the conversation again.

He gently disentangled himself from them both on the pretext of taking another mouthful of wine. "So what—" His voice had mostly gone again. He took a second mouthful. "So what will the vids do when the Emperor arrives and finds us gone?" It was bizarre to talk about an undertaking like this in terms of how the media would react. Shouldn't they be discussing how Gate Union and Redmond would react?

"Well, the ones who predicted it will say they knew she'd run all along. The others will dig up something."

"Predicted it?"

"Public sentiment is 70 percent for her running, 25 percent against," Katida said.

"And the other 5 percent?"

"Undecided."

He'd seen opinion polls himself, but he'd never been intimately involved in one like this. That made it different.

"Getting that 70 percent was hard," the Tarkan said. "I tell you. I thought we'd be stuck at 50 for a while. Many people thought she'd stay to face her father."

"So you—" It was time for another mouthful of wine. Ean took a bigger gulp than he meant to.

The man on the Tarkan's left—another civilian—leaned forward. "Don't let him convince you he did it on his own. We all contributed."

"But 20 percent is a big swing." Ean thought it was safe conversation. Everyone liked praise.

The Tarkan snorted. "It was more like 50 percent altogether," he said. "It was only the last 20 that was hard."

It was appalling, but it was impressive. There had to be a better way than ruining one woman's reputation to get a group like this together in secrecy. Not that Ean had ever thought of the Lancastrian royal family as having a good reputation. He would probably have been one of the cynical 30 percent who'd believed the bad news already. Or was that 25 percent?

"What will you do if we find nothing?" All this secrecy, all this expense, for a ship no one knew anything about.

"That ship destroyed three Alliance ships," Katida said. "If the only thing we find is the weapon they used to do that, then it's worth it."

Ean had worked on a lot of military ships in the last six months. Gate Union, Alliance, Redmond. The ships were the same, give or take a few features.

The second-to-last ship he'd worked on had been a warship. The captain had met him personally and escorted him first to engineering, where line ten was holding together with little more than a thread, then up to the bridge, to the Captain's Chair, where what Ean thought of as the brain of the lines resided.

Not that his trainers agreed with that. They were simply lines of energy, they had reminded him, and attributing a brain to any component meant that he would never be able to fix them properly because he couldn't treat the whole thing as a constant line of energy.

Captain MacIntyre of the GU *MacIntyre* had been proud of his ship, which had been the first of the newly designed honeycomb models from the factories at Roscracia. After Ean had finished repairs, they had dined together, and after that, MacIntyre had given him a tour. He'd explained in detail how the honeycomb design allowed each sector to be quickly shut off and isolated in the event of a hit; of the titanium-bialer alloy that each sector was built from that could withstand the direct hit of a million-terajoule bomb; and how parts of the engineering section—inside the central honeycomb—were duplicated outside of it and could take the power from the shuttles so there was no single point of failure except for the lines, which were in the exact center of the ship, with multiple layers between them and the surface.

MacIntyre had been convinced no one could destroy his ship.

Either Alliance ships were a lot weaker than their Gate Union equivalent, or this new ship—which Ean still knew nothing about—was a degree of power greater than anything known. The way Katida said "destroyed three ships" implied deliberate destruction in a military sense. Ean looked around the room again, at the sea of uniforms and everyone discussing the find with animated expectation.

Were they going to war?

He was glad the next course arrived then. It gave him time to chew in silence and think.

There were ten courses. Small serves, but Ean was still full by the fifth. The people around him seemed to take it as their due. No wonder the civilians tended to be on the plump side.

The military, with a few exceptions, were more in shape. He had known an old soldier in the Lancastrian slums, so skinny his bones showed through translucent skin, who claimed to have been dismissed from the military for being overweight. At the time, Ean hadn't believed it—Old Kairo was so thin that, even as a boy, Ean had been able to encircle his skinny wrist with his forefinger and thumb—but now he wasn't so sure.

Conversation drifted on to other things. What it was like to be a linesman? He didn't know what it was like to not be.

Had he ever had a crazy ship? No, although privately Ean wondered if the last ship he had worked on might have been if it had been let go much longer.

The talk switched from there to general talk about crazy ships. *Strathcona*, whose crew had gone insane. *Davida*, a military ship Ean hadn't known about. "Her captain saved his crew, then disappeared into the void with her," Katida said. And of course, the infamous liner *Balao*, who had killed her passengers and crew by jumping with the lines wide open— or so it was commonly believed—subjecting them to the terrors of the void, so that they all died of fright.

Some people still believed it was sabotage.

"Now that is one weapon I'd like to have," Admiral Katida said. "Whatever it is that turns those ships."

The casual way she said it gave Ean the shivers. "You don't believe they truly did go crazy?"

"They're ships. Machines. A piece of equipment went faulty."

Ean bet the captain of the ill-fated *Davida* would have disagreed with her.

He disagreed with her.

Lines had . . . "personality" was the only word Ean could think of to describe it. He remembered one level-two apprentice who had accompanied Kaelea on a job and fallen afoul of the ship's cook. Kaelea swore the apprentice had done nothing wrong, that the cook had attacked him unprovoked. Whatever the cause, after the incident, line two hadn't worked properly in that ship's galley. Since line two controlled heating and cooling, the galley had been unbearable for weeks. The chef had blamed the apprentice, but Ean thought the boy had been too traumatized and too inexperienced to do anything. After Rigel's ineffectual attempts to fix the problem— and even he had enough linesmen to fix level two—the cook had resigned. The ship had never had any problems with line two since.

Katida must have seen something in his face, for she said, "Crazy is only a term because no one has a real explanation for the technicalities."

The man seated beside Tarkan Heyington—who was also a Tarkan, Tarkan Reynes, only more soberly dressed—put in with a laugh. "You won't convince him, Admiral. He's a linesman. They believe all ships are alive. Same way they believe all ships are female."

"Female ships are an old tradition," Katida said. "Brought in two hundred years ago to appease Redmond. The lines alone know why. Look where it got us."

Reynes laughed again. He had a comfortable laugh. "Why they wanted it, or why we wanted to appease Redmond?"

"Both. We spent two hundred years pandering to them, and they still kick us in the teeth by allying themselves with Gate Union."

People at the main table stood then, which signaled a general rise.

Ean joined the movement up and followed his dinner companions, wishing he'd paid more attention to politics. The people here were seriously concerned about Gate Union and Redmond. Yes, Gate Union was powerful around the gate worlds, but Redmond wasn't even a threat, at least not on its own. It was just a group of old-world planets that had been powerful in the early days of the expansion but had since regressed to secondary worlds. Maybe it was just their alliance with Gate Union that made people talk about them as a threat now.

Reynes joined him then, and said quietly, "You heard of the fire at Chamberley?"

Who hadn't? The biggest lines factory had been wiped out. New lines were coming in late. Every linesman had heard of it.

"An earthquake destroyed Shaolin last week. That's not common news outside this ship yet."

For a linesman, there was only one thing at either Shaolin or Chamberley. Line factories.

Ean had seen them on the vids. They were vast spaces, filled with massive vats, so large that workers used carts to drive around them. Over each of the vats was a grid full of tiny holes a millimeter wide, spaced at fifty-millimeter intervals. A thin layer of line compound was squirted onto a grid, which was then slowly raised. As the line material thinned, the nutrient in the vat created an energy flow between the two ends. A line.

Ean had just spent all night talking about political alliances. Chamberley was allied with Gate Union. Shaolin had been neutral. If the two sides went to war, all the lines coming out of Redmond now had to hurt the Alliance.

"So that leaves—" The old factories in the Redmond cluster as the only providers of lines for the foreseeable future. Plus the new one Redmond was building that everyone said was a total waste of money because Chamberley and Shaolin held the market. "An earthquake?"

"Apparently," Reynes said. His face and voice were expressionless, but Ean could still see the cynicism behind them.

"Thank you." For taking the time out to explain things to a total ignoramus.

Reynes smiled. "I'm sure you can repay the favor someday," and moved on to talk to someone else.

That was what politics was about, Ean reminded himself. You give me something, I give you something back. Even sexual favors—as Admiral Katida came to take his arm and draw him much too close as she took him over to meet a circle of military guests.

"This isn't going to go anywhere you know," he said, patting her hand.

She patted his hand back and didn't pretend to misunderstand him. "You're a ten," she said. "I sleep with every ten I meet."

Ean had heard about people who slept with linesmen—simply because they were linesmen—but Admiral Katida didn't strike him as a person who needed to do that. He couldn't stop a quick glance over to where Rebekah Grimes was surrounded by a dozen people. Surely not.

"Every single one of them," Katida said. "Except you, and the twins coming up at Laito Cartel."

At least she had some standards. The twins had just turned seventeen, or so Ean had heard. "Because they're so young?"

"Because no one's sure yet whether they are tens or just talented nines. Admiral Varrn," to the man she had been pulling him toward. "Have you met the Lancastrian ten yet?"

Ean followed numbly.

Varrn was a Caelum, with the genetically enhanced incisors made for survival on the Aquacaelum worlds. He bared his teeth in a frightening smile. "Naturally you would monopolize him first, Katida. Has she slept with you yet?"

What could he say to that?

"We were just talking about it," Katida said.

Varrn's neck seemed to fold into the muscle of his wide shoulders and into his chin. He shrugged and showed his teeth again. He looked like a shark wearing a dinner suit. "So what do you think of the alien ship, Linesman?"

Ean fell back on his stock answer. "I don't know enough yet to have an opinion. I want to see it."

"If we can get close enough without its killing us first. That'll be your job." Varrn turned away from him then. "An earthquake at Shaolin, Katida. Aren't many who could do that. Your people could."

Katida sighed and flagged down a passing orderly with drinks. "Not of that magnitude, and not without leaving a trace."

They all took drinks although Ean wasn't sure he wanted one. He'd drunk more in this one evening than he had in six months, and he wasn't used to alcohol right now.

Katida scowled down at her glass. "Not a trace," she repeated. "It could almost have been a natural disaster. I wish I knew how they did it."

Varrn laughed a wheezing, shark laugh. "I am sure that by the end of this year, you will know, and you'll be using it on the Outlier worlds." He then admitted, "Wouldn't mind the technology myself. Untraceable natural disaster. Be worth something."

Ean had a vision of sudden catastrophic earthquakes happening all along the Alliance problem worlds. He almost missed the tiny inclination of Katida's head. A deal had been struck.

These people dealt in big deals.

The rest of the night passed similarly. The initial polite conversation as two or more people came together was mostly about the ship. If Ean was there, they'd ask him what he thought, and he'd trot out his standard answer. Then the conversation would shift. To weapons or warfare or worlds;

and often ended with a nod or a handshake after some agreement Ean only partly understood.

Ean stayed with the uniforms. Rebekah stayed with the civilians. He did wander over to talk to her once, but she moved away before he got there. Which could have been accidental because he was sure she hadn't been watching him, but the timing was about as coincidental as the earthquake on Shaolin.

He was disappointed about that. It would be good to talk with another ten.

Admiral Katida rejoined him. "I expect she's not liking the competition."

Did they notice everything?

"I've a thick skin." He'd endured worse, a slum kid coming up through what was basically a middle-to-high-class caste system. Not that Rigel had been as bad as the others, but he'd still trained the slum out of him.

She patted his arm. "You have started making a reputation for yourself."

Any reputation he made was simply because the other cartel masters had sent all their tens out on a treasure hunt and none of the tens—or the nines—had returned from the confluence yet. This left no one except Ean to do regular high-level line jobs. Rigel had been smart keeping him back. Come to think of it, some of these admirals reminded him of Rigel. Ean wondered suddenly if he had underestimated the cartel master. Surely not. Rigel was a class-conscious snob and a bad businessman who cheated his customers when he could.

"Our princess has finally left. Shall we do it?" Katida asked, and added, when he looked at her blankly, "Lady Lyan has left the room. Let's do likewise. I'll show you my cabin."

He disengaged his hand again. "Not tonight. But I would like to go to bed. It's been a long day." A lot of other people seemed to think the same thing, for people were moving out even as he watched.

Tarkan Heyington was one of the few who appeared to have settled in for the night. He winked at Ean as they went past. Ean didn't know why he went pink.

The lift was crowded. No one else was going to his floor. Katida watched him touch the level. "You are honored.

Maybe I should go to your room. I bet your competition is placed with the other civilians."

If by competition she meant Rebekah, then she probably had the room they'd set aside for the ten, and they wouldn't have had anywhere to put him. The ship must be filled to capacity. They'd probably had a mad scramble to find him a room.

Varrn was in the same lift, and a dozen others Ean had talked to that evening. "Katida. You wouldn't get out the door on that floor." But Varrn and the others looked at Ean with more interest. Reassessing him.

Katida got out at the third stop. She looked at him. Ean shook his head and smiled. She smiled back and stepped into a good-natured—at least Ean hoped it was good-natured—wave of jeers and ribbing about being turned down by the ten.

The fifth floor was his alone. He stepped out into the quiet luxury and was suddenly exhausted.

Michelle and Abram were sitting on the couches in the central sitting-cum-workroom, drinking tea and talking. They both looked up at him.

"Katida was fast," Michelle said.

Abram laughed. "More likely disappointed. You turned her down?"

"Does everyone know she sleeps with tens?"

"It's a hobby of hers."

"There are few secrets this high on the tree," Michelle said. "Drink?" She indicated the pot.

Ean would have said no, but Abram waved him to the third couch and he wasn't sure if it was an offer or an order, so he sat and took a glass of tea with thanks. The warm liquid soothed his sore throat.

"We were discussing your contract," Abram said. So it had been an order. "It's unusually long."

Ean sipped tea and thought about how honest he should be. He'd just spent the evening talking with security from a dozen worlds. Half of them already knew who he was, and he'd bet Abram had spent some of the time between meeting him and dinner finding things out as well. In fact, now he came to think about it, they were speaking Lancastrian while he was speaking Standard. He switched to the language he'd been born to. Rigel hadn't tried to smooth the gutter out of it—Standard was all he cared about—but Ean had tried, and he had a good ear although sometimes it still slipped.

"Not really. Not for someone like me. I'm from the slums. My chance of getting into a cartel—" He shrugged. They probably had no idea just how difficult that was. They would have been automatically tested if they showed any promise. "I'd always been able to hear the lines."

"Hear?" Abram asked.

Ean hadn't meant that to slip out. He'd read all he could about how other linesmen interacted with the lines. Most of them described it as a pressure—some said against their body, some said in their mind—although one old-time linesman had compared it to a religious experience. None of them had ever said it was music.

"Feel," he amended, but he could see Abram knew that for the lie it was. "I wasn't trained. To me it was noise. You know how, when you don't have any parameters you make things up and by the time I was old enough—"

"So it's true that you sing to the lines?"

His untrained methods were the despair of Rigel's trainers. He tried desperately to bring the conversation back under control, and quickly. "I knew I was good, and Rigel's very aware of appearances. I knew he wouldn't just train me in the lines, he'd train me in other things as well." How to read and write and how to talk to a roomful of dignitaries, and how where you were placed in the seating arrangements defined your status. "If he trains you like that, he demands a long contract." Ean hadn't been aware of Rigel's standing with the other cartels back then, but he still wouldn't have changed anything. Rigel had helped him escape the misery of his childhood by giving him a job he loved.

"Rigel's from Dante," Michelle said.

Ean hadn't known that. Dante was the rubbish heap of the galaxy. Someone from Dante started even lower in the pecking order than someone from the slums of Lancia. No wonder he was so obsessed with status.

Even so, it still didn't excuse some of Rigel's questionable business practices.

He hadn't diverted Abram at all.

"If you sing to the lines, does that mean you are effectively out of commission until you get your voice back?"

"Not totally, no." He'd sung line six back on this ship, then had to admit that this was a well-tuned ship to start with. "Maybe some things."

Did that mean they would on-sell his contract before he even heard the new ship?

Michelle laughed, stretched, and stood up to take off her formal blue jacket. "The evening seems to have gone well," she said. She stretched again, almost catlike.

Ean was reminded just how obscene the shirts were. The tiny piece of almost noncloth made him extremely aware of the body beneath it. He looked away.

"The cloth is designed to make you look," Abram told him. "A clever piece of engineering, don't you think. Which reminds me," to Michelle. He dug into his pocket, pulled out his card, and dropped it onto the screen. "But only just," he said. "There were three others."

"Why do you think I said three?" Michelle said. "One thing I do know is fashion."

She knew a lot more than that if the people Ean had spoken to tonight were any judge.

A bell chimed on all panels. Ean didn't need Abram to say, "They're making the jump," because he could hear line nine clear and loud. They were in the void.

Ean stood up hurriedly. He'd only crossed the void once. From Lancia to join Rigel's cartel. Back then he hadn't understood the lines at all, hadn't known what to expect, and he'd been in his cabin when line ten kicked in. He'd thought he was going to be dragged through the void forever.

"I might go to bed," he said.

He was too late.

The high, clear notes of line ten moved through the deeper notes of line nine, tightened, then wrenched and went impossibly high and pulled and twisted line nine into another path. It only took seconds, Ean knew, but for him it lasted forever.

When it was over, he was kneeling on the floor, hands over his ears. Abram and Michelle were just beginning to react.

Abram reached him first.

"No." Because he could hear line nine still strong in his head. They were going to make multiple jumps. Nobody made multiple jumps that close together. Except a really good captain who knew and trusted his ship and wanted to hide where they went. Ean got that from line one, he didn't know how.

Abram didn't listen. He reached out and touched Ean just as line ten twisted the void line again. The vibration rattled through their bones, on and on.

When it was over—seconds again, but it felt like another lifetime—Abram pulled away and fell to the floor, dry-retching. Michelle put an arm across his shoulders.

"Don't touch him yet." Line nine was still clear and strong. But it was too late. Line ten twisted out again and tweaked them into another space and Abram, still vibrating from the last one, must have felt it. And so must Michelle, touching him.

After that, the noise subsided.

No one moved for twenty minutes, but after three jumps it felt like only seconds.

Abram eventually rolled onto his knees and from there shakily hauled himself up. "No wonder so many linesmen go crazy. Is it always that bad?"

Ean didn't answer. He lay on the floor and rested his face on his arms so that he didn't have to look at them. For a while tonight, he had dared to hope in a future that was more than just repairing lines. That he would be part of something new and exciting.

That wouldn't happen now.

Michelle accepted Abram's help up. "I've jumped with other tens. Even Rebekah Grimes once. On this ship. We were at dinner. She didn't seem to mind although she did notice." She came to stand over Ean and offered a hand to help him up. Her blue shoes were made of the same silk as her skirt.

Ean shook his head and got up the same way Abram had, by rolling over onto his hands and knees first.

"I'm going to bed." His voice was hoarse again, but what little there was shook with disappointment. He should have gone there straight from the function, whether the invitation to sit had been an order or not. At least then they would have just had him for insubordination; now they simply thought him crazy.

He couldn't even walk straight; and he could feel them watching him. He heard, and almost saw through line one, Michelle half step toward him and Abram put out a hand to stop her.

They waited until he was gone before they said anything, but his whole body was vibrating with the lines and he heard—clear as anything through line one—"Did you get the music?" before he deliberately blocked the lines out of his mind by repeating nonsense rhymes in his head.

THREE

✦

JORDAN ROSSI

THE CONFLUENCE WAS a perfect sphere 4,172.36 meters in diameter. Infinitely small on a galactic scale, yet if you asked most linesmen how big it was, they would say, "Huge as space, as big as the galaxy," and their voices would be full of the truth of just how enormous it was.

To Jordan Rossi, the confluence made him feel important and insignificant at the same time. It made him realize how vast the universe was and how small a part of it he was. The confluence was huge and glorious. It made him want to sing. It made him want to fall to his knees and dedicate his life to it. Every time he was near it, he was filled with something akin to joy and felt his heart would burst just being near the greatness of it.

Jordan Rossi hated it.

He'd always been a man who controlled his own life. From the five-year-old boy who'd insisted on taking the line tests, to the seventeen-year-old who'd *known* he was ready to be certified, all the way up to the powerful, influential ten he'd become. He'd been in control all the way. The confluence took that control away from him. Worse, he couldn't just walk away because the confluence wouldn't let him.

He stood at the viewing platform sipping a glass of wine—not generally allowed, but he was a ten, and who was going to stop him—and watched the nothingness that made it.

"What do you think it really is?" he asked Fergus.

Fergus had been his personal assistant for twenty years. They worked well enough together that when other linesmen came poaching, House of Rickenback always matched their offer and raised it, which made Fergus not only one of the longest-lasting assistants in any cartel but higher paid than many lower-level linesmen. He was worth every credit, if only for the way he could ferret out information from anyone. Not that Rossi ever intended telling him that.

It was the same question Rossi had asked every day since he'd arrived. Fergus had two standard responses—no answer, or a diatribe about its being a line sink, which Rossi always ignored. Fergus hated the confluence, too, but that was because he couldn't feel the lines and wanted to be back in the comfort of the cartel house rather than here on station.

Today, Fergus just shrugged.

A crowd of tourists flooded onto the viewing deck. A shuttle must have arrived. They recognized the uniform, saw the bars on Rossi's pocket, and left him room. One or two nudged each other and pointed him out. Rossi ignored them.

For most of them, this trip would be a waste of time. Even now he could see one disappointed tourist turning away with a disgusted, "That's it."

Rossi didn't care. If you couldn't feel the lines, Confluence Station was nothing but a spartan space station out in the middle of nowhere. Sure there were a few restaurants, and a nightclub—there always was when there were tourists and linesmen—but there was nothing else, and in two days, when the shuttle was ready to depart, most of the tourists would be ready to leave with it. Good riddance to them, too.

He was more interested in the linesmen who had arrived with them. This new batch was mixed. Two from Sandhurst, two from Laito, and four from Rigel. Rossi frowned at that. This was the second Rigel-heavy batch. Cartel Master Rigel was spreading his people much further than he should. Rossi was going to find the idiot who ran the service contract and have words.

The linesmen stood apart. They hadn't noticed him yet; they were too busy looking toward the confluence, awe on their faces. Not that there was anything to see.

Or anything showing up on the instruments the scientists loved so much, either.

Linesmen didn't use tools. They used their minds, that innate ability that scientists had speculated about for as long as the lines had been around. They didn't need instruments to know there were lines at the confluence.

The scientists weren't satisfied with that, of course. They'd sent in experts—as if anyone could be as expert in lines as a linesman; and their instruments—as if an instrument that couldn't even measure a regular line would be any use out here; and then the military had arrived with *their* instruments. As if any of it was any use when the linesmen couldn't even pick it.

In fact, the discovery of the confluence had reignited the old debate about what line ability was. Was it psychic, and if so, did humans have other as-yet-undiscovered abilities that no one knew about? Was it something natural that all humans had in some measure, like the ability to draw or to retain a tune? Or even a sixth sense they'd had since the first creature had crawled onto land but that had mostly died out because until recently—evolutionarily speaking—humans had no use for it?

Rossi wished the scientists and the military would all go away and leave the confluence to its true owners. The linesmen.

He'd suggested it once, and Dr. Apted, the scientist in charge, had the cheek to laugh at him. At him, one of the most powerful linesmen in the galaxy, if not the most powerful. Just remembering it now made his hand grip tight around the stem of his glass.

"That would be a joke," Apted had said. "All you people do is stand around and push thoughts at it. Which is doing a lot, isn't it."

"You have no idea how a linesman works," Rossi had told her.

"One thing I know." And she'd poked a finger at him, so hard and abrupt that he'd had to step back. "You people can't even work together. Each of you off thinking your own thoughts at it isn't going to do anything. Why don't you try working together?"

They did work together when they had to. But Apted seemed to forget that higher-level linesmen were rare and used to working alone. You couldn't share the burden of fixing line ten with anyone else. There wouldn't be enough linesmen to go around. With less than fifty tens galaxy-wide, working alone was the norm. Personally, Rossi preferred it that way.

Gate Union military representatives had arrived three months after the scientists. The military scientists were as bad as the nonmilitary scientists, but at least it had given Apted someone else to fight with and got her off Rossi's back. Although some of that might have been due to Fergus's doing his job of keeping people away and leaving the linesman to do what he did best.

Rossi didn't want to think about scientists or the military. He turned back to the confluence.

If it hadn't been for a ship going missing midtransmission, no one would have even known the confluence was there. But you could feel it, and there was something magical about feeling it for the first time. Just remembering it made Rossi's breath catch.

"Fool," he muttered to himself. Then the Sandhurst seven turned to look at him, and his breath caught again. The girl was tall and curvy, with a face that could have modeled meyanware. The way she smiled at Rossi showed that she knew it, too. She murmured something quiet to the other Sandhurst, the five, who turned to look as well. One didn't have to be a lipreader to know what they were saying. "Jordan Rossi. House of Rickenback."

Rossi inclined his head—the half nod granted to a lesser line—and turned back to the Plexiglas window.

"You want me to invite her to your rooms tonight?" Fergus asked.

Rossi was tempted. His habits were known. The cocky young thing would expect it. "No. I'm dining with that bitch Rebekah Grimes." He didn't know what she wanted, but she liked him as much as he liked her, so when either of them had to talk to each other, it was line business and important.

Cartel houses looked after the everyday business of training linesmen and managing their contracts, but the Linesmen's Guild looked after the welfare of the linesman. If a linesman had issues with their House, or felt their contract was unfair, they went to the Grand Master, head of the guild, who sorted it out for them. The Grand Master was the only official member of the guild—the cartels took care of most line-related issues—but there was an unofficial committee who advised him or her, and it wielded a lot of power. That committee consisted of Jordan Rossi and Rebekah Grimes— the two judged most likely to become the next Grand Master—and Janni Naidan, a behind-the-scenes manipulator who didn't normally come out into the open for line business but had as much power as Rossi and Rebekah.

The current Grand Master, Morton Paretsky, had collapsed with a heart attack soon after arriving at the confluence and hadn't regained consciousness since. Personally, Rossi wasn't surprised. Paretsky was a big man, and most of his bulk came courtesy of the perks provided to someone in that position. The big surprise was that it hadn't happened earlier.

Rossi planned to keep up his exercise and weights when he became Grand Master.

Meantime, Rossi, Rebekah, and Janni Naidan were doing all the work.

If Apted wanted to claim they didn't do any work, maybe she should have attended a few guild meetings. They still went on. And on. You couldn't get away from the damned things, even out here, where petty business shouldn't intrude.

Rossi turned back to the confluence. Sometimes, when he'd had too much to drink, he came out here and lost himself in the magnificence of it. It was the only time he could bear to lose control of his emotions like that. He finished his wine in one long gulp and handed the empty glass to Fergus. "I'm off to get ready for la Dame Grimes."

IT wasn't Rebekah Grimes who waited for him in the private dining room. It was Janni Naidan, the ten from House of Laito.

Rossi raised an eyebrow. "Whatever Grimes wants to talk about must be important."

"Or she's setting us up," Naidan said.

He knew what Naidan meant. Since Paretsky's untimely illness, la Dame Grimes had taken to sending other Sandhurst tens as her representative. House of Sandhurst had fully 30 percent of the tens, and they were actively recruiting. The day would come—soon—when that cartel tried to take over.

Not if he could help it.

Naidan was an abrupt woman, not given to small talk. "Linesman Grimes informs me she has taken another job."

He wished he could leave like that. Sometimes he thought the confluence was a drug, keeping them there.

"It must have been some offer." He poured himself a glass of wine, ignoring the disapproving look from Naidan. It wasn't for the glass he'd poured—she already had her own glass of finest green imported from Lancia—it was for the four glasses he'd had before he'd come.

"It was." Her face was grim. "Lady Lyan."

"Ah." He held the wine up to salute the confluence. There was something poetic about drinking Lancastrian wine when talking about a Lancastrian princess. "Did she want a ten?" Gate Union would do anything to get a spy onto Lady Lyan's ship, even to asking someone to pretend to be a lesser linesman. He hoped they wanted a six or a seven. Rebekah would hate that.

"Lyan is studying the confluence."

Rossi perused the menu set into the table so he didn't have to answer immediately. He keyed in his selection—Naidan had already chosen, he noted—pressed to order, and took another careful mouthful of wine, before he said, "Has anyone told Lady Lyan she's not welcome here?" She'd be stupid to come anyway. Lancia was affiliated with the Alliance. Gate Union and the Alliance weren't officially at war, but it was only a matter of time.

It felt as if half of Gate Union's military fleet was here at the confluence right now. Putting Lady Lyan in among them would have the same result as a horned rickenback jumping into a lynx sett. The lynx would have dismembered the rickenback before the foolish creature had even realized it had jumped into danger.

Although one never knew with Lady Lyan. She could do

some gutsy stuff. Maybe this was her way of kick-starting a war. Maybe Gate Union should be worrying.

He thought about the news vids he'd watched over the past two weeks. At least he still watched the vids. Some of the linesmen were so focused on the confluence, they even forgot to do that. "Isn't she getting married?"

To businessman Sattur Dow, if the media were correct. Even on the news, Dow had looked sour. If Rossi had been marrying Lady Lyan, he'd be looking much happier than that. Lady Lyan now, she could look gloomy. The man was twice her age, and he'd already buried three wives.

Funny that he always buried them, never separated.

If he'd been Lyan, Rossi would have been running very fast the other way.

Naidan dismissed those rumors with a flick of her hand. "Lady Lyan will get married when Lady Lyan wants to get married. Not when her father tells her to. But it is a problem because there are representatives from every Alliance world coming to her wedding. And if she comes here, they'll come, too."

So was she getting married or not? Emperor Yu arranged marriages for his children—both legitimate and illegitimate—for political expediency. It was hard to imagine what political benefit he could gain by marrying his oldest daughter off to a fellow Lancastrian, no matter how rich that Lancastrian was.

But it could get Alliance representatives together for some other reason. Like to agree on a preemptive strike against Gate Union.

Rossi savored another mouthful of wine and tried not to think of Lyan's curves. "We are talking Crown Princess Michelle Lady Lyan here?" There were three Lady Lyans, not to mention two Lord Lyans, and all of them had Michel in their name. Only the Lancastrians were stupid enough to name their children so similarly.

"The dangerous one, yes."

They were all dangerous, and Emperor Yu's children had fingers in every pie in the galaxy. Lancia was what had kept the Alliance together so long when it should have imploded from corruption and old age decades ago. But yes, Crown Princess Michelle was the most dangerous. And the most charismatic. And the most beautiful. Rossi let the confluence take him for a moment, thinking of that beauty.

He shivered and forced his mind back to the meeting.

"Exactly," Naidan said. "And she's coming here, probably with representatives from every Alliance world."

Rossi didn't envy Rebekah her job.

"So she comes, she looks, she goes."

Naidan snorted inelegantly. Rossi leaned back to avoid the delicate spray of wine that came out through her nose. This was one of the reasons she did backroom work, and people like Rebekah and he liaised with outsiders.

The first course arrived then, giving him time to regroup and reconsider while the waiter set the food in front of them.

The line cartels had always had a close association with Gate Union.

In the early days, when humans were just learning to use the lines, there had been no limits on the jumps. They lost five rich solar systems before they realized that ships coming out in the same space caused explosions that didn't destroy just the ships, it destroyed space near them as well. When they finally understood the cause, the worlds had implemented a booking system, overseen by a central bureau. At first it had been a loose consortium of worlds that had to work together for their own safety. Over time, those worlds had turned into the main trading routes, making them some of the richest in the galaxy.

Then, fifty years ago, the Alliance had tried to wrest control of the gates at Roscracia through political pressure. Some speculated it was because they realized the union of gate worlds had become a threat to their dominance. Others believed that they simply wanted their own part in the riches. Whatever the reason—the Alliance never said, and Rossi didn't care, but it had to be one of the stupidest political moves of all time—it had led to the official signing of the Gate Union Treaty, supposedly simply to reduce bureaucracy between the worlds, but everyone knew it was to cement power against the Alliance.

Nowadays, Gate Union's power rivaled that of the Alliance. Not only that, the recent treaty they had signed with Redmond meant that most of the line factories now came under Gate Union auspices as well.

All of them, Rossi reminded himself, remembering the earthquake at Shaolin.

Linesmen clustered where the lines were, because that was where the work was. Thus it was to their mutual benefit for the cartels to work with Gate Union.

The cartels considered the confluence theirs, which meant it was effectively also Gate Union territory. They wouldn't take kindly to the Alliance muscling in on it, and they'd expect the cartels to deal with it. That was obviously going to be Rossi's job.

His and Rebekah Grimes's. He poured himself another drink.

"I've seen the vids." He hadn't taken much notice of them, being too busy with the confluence, but he'd still recognized many of the dignitaries who had arrived for the wedding. "She has some powerful people with her."

Naidan snorted again. This time some of her wine sprayed onto his plate. He pushed his plate aside. "If Emperor Yu decrees a wedding, you can't not come even if you don't believe it will happen."

But suppose he hadn't decreed a wedding. Suppose it was just a way to get the power brokers into one place for a preemptive strike at Gate Union. Especially coming so soon after the Alliance had called their members to a special security council, ostensibly to discuss Redmond's preemptive attack on the Haladean cluster, a minor skirmish that no one should have even worried about, least of all the other Alliance partners. Especially given everyone knew that the Alliance couldn't possibly take on Gate Union and win.

But if Lady Lyan was coming here, then she could only be taking Gate Union on. Coming to the confluence was an out-and-out declaration of hostility. Even though the Alliance had nothing to win and everything to lose in the confrontation.

Maybe the Alliance knew that if Gate Union got any stronger, it would definitely lose. Doing it at this time, it had some chance of winning, or at least of forcing a standoff.

It was the kind of thing Lady Lyan would do. Bold, brassy, and totally unexpected.

Rossi leaned back in his chair. "Has anyone contacted Gate Union?"

FOUR

EAN LAMBERT

EAN WOKE NAKED, and for the second day in a row, he couldn't
remember where he was or how he'd gotten there.

He lay and stared at the unfamiliar ceiling. He was on a
ship. He'd been fixing the lines. No, that was another ship.
The lines on this ship were clear and good. Line one was
happy. Line six was . . . He closed his eyes. Line six was
good, but the captain wasn't happy with him, and he'd made
a complete fool of himself over line ten. He curled up and
pulled the quilt over himself, suddenly cold.

They owned his contract. They could ensure he never
worked as a linesman again.

He blinked hard, eyes gritty. Stupid to get emotional over
things he couldn't control. And he would work with the lines.
Nothing could stop that even if he wasn't part of a cartel.

He couldn't remember going to bed. He remembered
weaving his way down to his room like a drunk, stripping off
as soon as he entered the apartment, making direct for the
fresher because he wasn't sure if he was going to be sick or
just wanted to be clean. He remembered sitting on the floor
of the fresher, knees to his chin in the tiny cramped space,

long after the water cycle had finished. After that, he couldn't remember a thing.

Ean sighed and sat up. He didn't know what would happen now, but he'd slept away half the day cycle. Not a smart thing to do on the first day of your new job, especially not if you'd given your employers real cause to doubt your abilities the night before.

His formal clothes were on the bench built into the opposite wall. He looked at the precisely folded bundles with foreboding. He didn't remember doing that, and he had never been good at taking care of clothes.

Don't think about it. Act as if nothing happened.

He shaved, but didn't shower. If they were rationing water, they probably rationed it by the tenday. He didn't want to use up his allocation in the first two days.

Radko was seated on one of the couches in the living area. She jumped up as Ean came out. "Sir."

"Why don't you just call me Ean." He wondered if he was under arrest for injuring the two top-ranking people on the ship.

"Yes, sir."

Ean gave that one up for the moment. "So what happens now?" He didn't know what to do, where to go. And if he was under arrest, he probably couldn't go anywhere.

"Medic first," Radko said promptly. "Then food. Then I'm to take you down to the briefing room."

He followed Radko's long-legged stride down the corridor, trying to keep up, but he ached all over, and when a machine on line three flared into use, his bones vibrated with the feel of it.

Two people waited at the hospital, but the medic took him first. He felt bad about that. Radko leaned one booted foot against the wall and swapped insults with the sick men as he went in. He hoped neither of them was badly ill.

"Let me have a look at you," the medic said, and Ean stripped for his second medical in two days.

"Does this happen every time you go through the void?"

He wanted to lie. Whoever heard of a linesman grade ten who didn't travel? "This is my second trip."

"And did it happen the first time?"

"I . . . something. I'm not really sure. It was years ago. I was untrained. I didn't know what to expect." It hadn't been as bad as this. Maybe his tutors were right. Maybe you couldn't learn the lines as an adult. Not properly, anyway.

The medic was gentle, but Ean had to grit his teeth in order not to wince. As a boy, he'd been beaten by his father when his father smoked Juice until he'd learned to stay away from home after the Juice dealer had been through. It felt like that, which was stupid because he was unmarked.

"And your bones?" the medic asked.

"Bone-weary" was a term Ean had never thought had a literal meaning, but right now that was how he felt. As if his bones were too tired to hold him up.

The medic looked at his face. "I wish I'd seen what happened," he said.

He wouldn't have wanted to be there.

"You can get dressed." He helped Ean up, almost as if he realized Ean wasn't sure he could manage it himself. "I want to see you back here every day until I say otherwise. And I want to know all the symptoms. Including those you haven't told me today." He walked to the door with him. "And you'll do every jump under observation. I'll make sure Captain Helmo doesn't jump until you are here at the hospital."

Which was really going to endear him to the captain.

Radko left off baiting the other two spacers as he came out. Neither of them seemed the worse for the extra wait.

"Bring him back tomorrow," the medic told Radko.

"Yes, sir."

Maybe she just called everybody sir.

She led him out at the same fast pace. He struggled to keep up. "The mess is open all hours," she said, then stopped and looked back over her shoulder. "You should probably eat in the VIP dining room."

He couldn't take Admiral Katida or Tarkan Heyington right now. "All they'll do is hand me things to carry." Even if he had no right in the mess, he wouldn't have to be social.

A dimple showed. It looked like Michelle's dimple. "They would," she agreed, friendlier suddenly.

The mess was quiet at this hour. The chef cooked Ean up a huge meal, despite Ean's protests that he wasn't hungry. After the first mouthfuls, he realized he was hungry after all, and that it tasted good. Radko, seated opposite, ate a smaller portion of the same meal with gusto. If this was typical of the fare, then the crew were well fed. But then, he could have got that from line one. Or could he? Could you break the line down into specifics like that? Ean, strong enough now with food inside him, listened to the song of line one and tried to separate out anything to do with food.

The lines were clear in his head. Clearer than they had been yesterday. It was as if going through the void had switched something on and forgotten to turn it off again. Which was impossible, of course.

All he could get was something about Empire cake.

"What is Empire cake?" he asked.

Radko pushed aside her empty plate with a sigh of pleasure. "You've heard about that, have you?"

He half shrugged.

"And let's hope we're rid of this lot before it happens," Radko said. "Because I don't want them spoiling the tradition." She looked at him and blushed. "Sorry. I didn't mean—"

"Empire cake?" he prompted.

"The Crown Princess's birthday cake. It's divine. And only ever made on this ship. It takes weeks to prepare. Chefs were buying ingredients while Princess Michelle and Commodore Galenos were out hunting tens."

It was interesting that she called Michelle by her Lancastrian title. Or maybe not, because it was a Lancastrian ship, but off Lancia, she was generally known as Lady Lyan—all the legitimate children were known as Lord or Lady Lyan—because on many other worlds the title prince or princess was reserved for the ruler.

Her birthday must be close if the cake figured so prominently in the lines.

"It's more than just the cake," Radko said. "It's the tradition. We've all been with her a long time."

"Even you?" She didn't look old enough to have been anywhere a long time.

"Ten years in two tendays," she said.

Which meant she had to be at least his own age. "You came straight from training to here?"

"No one comes straight from training to here. I spent two years in general corps first, then three in Special Weapons."

Maybe older. She didn't look it.

Radko dimpled at him. Her dimples were exactly the same as Michelle's. Come to think of it, her eyes were the same shape too, if a lighter blue, and even though her short hair was honey brown, it waved in the same place Michelle's did. She glanced at her comms. "Finish your plate," she said. "You'll want to be at the next briefing."

He would? Ean finished his meal, and she showed him where to put the dirty plate. She was thorough, at least, at training him in all the right things to do. He just hoped he remembered it next time. After which she led him at a quick trot back to the briefing room, which turned out to be the dining room from last night. This time he could almost keep up.

There was one spare seat. Radko pushed him toward it, and he slid in just as Captain Helmo started speaking. Radko leaned back against the wall near him and lifted a boot to set against it in what he was coming to recognize as her characteristic waiting pose. Surely she didn't have to wait for him. Was he really under guard?

"A 4.15-kilometer circumference," the captain said, and the ship flashed on-screen. Ean promptly forgot Radko.

It was a sphere. The surface was a deep blue-black that should have blended with space and made it impossible to see, but the blue gave it just enough color. On the curve of the sphere, they could see the distorted reflection of another ship. It was so clear they could read the markings on the side. EMPIRE SUN, from the Haladean cluster.

"It's a perfect sphere," the captain said. "Our scientists say there isn't a single blemish."

The image changed to a Haladean warship. "The Haladeans sent two ships." Captain Helmo paused. "The images are of the first ship, taken from the second ship. The first ship is ten kilometers out, the second, thirty."

Even in port, the larger ships tethered hundreds of kilometers apart and let the shuttles go between. A big ship stopped mostly by inertia. Whoever had taken a warship that close to two other ships had a damn good pilot.

Two yellow lines showed under the image. One was three times as long as the other.

Two smaller shuttles, bristling with guns, detached from the side of the closer ship. A line at the bottom of the screen counted off the meters as the ship inched closer. More than one of the military audience members shuddered.

A third line appeared under the other two, and a counter started at ten and counted down as the ships moved forward: 9.9; 9.8.

At 9.7 kilometers, the sphere pulsed green. They watched the pulse come toward the shuttles. Both shuttles disappeared. The pulse kept going. Then, suddenly, the ship was gone, too. Still the pulse kept going. The kilometer line crept up. Past ten kilometers. Past twenty. Past thirty. The viewscreen glowed brighter and brighter green. Then everything went black.

"The ship was transmitting right to the end," the captain said quietly.

Michelle took up the story. "The Haladeans came to us."

Even Ean knew the Haladeans were at war with Redmond. They could ill afford to spare warships even to examine something like this, and they definitely couldn't afford to have them blown up.

"We—the Alliance—gave them ships in return for . . ." She waved an arm at the black screen. "We have five ships at a hundred kilometers out, all ready to jump at the slightest sign of a pulse."

"But what about the lines?" asked Governor Jade. "How will the linesmen help?"

"Every ship has linesmen up to at least level six," the captain said, and he could have been looking straight at Ean, or maybe Ean was just feeling guilty. "The linesmen on the Haladean ship identified the presence of something that felt like lines on the alien ship. They said that in the messages they sent back. Our own linesmen corroborated that when we arrived. They didn't know what level, only that it's greater than six."

Line nine was the void, and line ten twisted the void and moved whatever was in the void to a different place, but no one really knew what lines seven and eight did. Maybe this was where they found out.

No one knew where the lines had come from. They weren't human, that was for sure. All anyone knew from the history tapes was that the derelict ship they had been found on had changed ownership at least three times before it had arrived at the scrap heap at Chamberley, where a trader named Havortian had used his last credits to purchase it to repair damage to his own ship caused by a collision with an asteroid.

Havortian had a time-sensitive load and no money for real repairs, so instead of melting the ship down and using the metal to create a new outer hull for himself, he'd welded the newly purchased body onto his own cargo hold, made it airtight, and left to finish his job.

The weld was cheap and poorly done. A third of the way into the trip, the Havortians started to leak air. There was nowhere close enough to land before their air ran out. They were going to die.

According to legend, Havortian's nine-year-old daughter—a strange, solitary creature by most accounts—was able to communicate with the lines. When they knew they were doomed, Gila Havortian went around the ship saying good-bye to everything. She said good-bye to the lines, too, then had to explain why. The lines had asked her why the ship didn't just go through the void.

The linesmen and scientists laughed at the legend, of course, and said it didn't happen like that, but it was a nice story.

Ean believed it. Gila Havortian would have been untrained. Maybe she "heard" the lines, too. Maybe she even sang to them. He could well believe they communicated back to her.

Havortian became a rich man. His ship traveled the known sectors, taking days where other ships took years. Unfortunately, he wasn't a good businessman. The massive Chamberley Co-Op—which was prepared to use semilawful means to get what it wanted—soon took over his ship. Chamberley Co-Op spent money and resources trying to reproduce line technology. They replicated the mighty Bose engine they found with the lines within ten years, but it was just an engine without lines to control it. It was also slow, traveling at 0.1c in normal space. By then there were faster sublight ships.

That's where it would have stayed if Gila Havortian hadn't been obsessed with the lines. Only scientists were allowed near the lines, so she became a scientist. Only people who had been born on Chamberley were allowed to work at the Co-Op, so she faked birth records. She was known to have blackmailed at least three people who found out who she was, and it was rumored she had murdered another, but that was only rumor.

Gila Havortian bribed or blackmailed her way to become head of the laboratory. When she was placed in charge, she sacked all the staff and brought in her own carefully chosen set of new people. Physicists, mathematicians, chemists, geneticists, and xenobiologists.

She told them she wanted something replicated. She didn't tell them what. She didn't tell them how.

While her scientists were working on the lines, Gila Havortian plotted the destruction of the Co-Op in revenge for what it had done to her father.

She was fifty-nine years old when her lab worked out how to reproduce the lines. Havortian then set in place the destruction she'd planned and took herself, her scientists, and the lines and jumped to Redmond, where they set up the first line factory.

It opened the way to the stars. Humans spread out across the galaxy in a massive population explosion that was still under way five hundred years later.

In all that time, they had never met another intelligent species. Or a functioning alien ship. This ship was the first.

"Imagine a defense system like that," Admiral Katida said. "Can you outrun it?"

The captain seemed to be the technical expert. "Everyone has a jump ready. At one hundred kilometers, we have enough warning to enter the void if it triggers," he said. "Outrun it with our own engines, no."

Abram, whom Ean hadn't even noticed at the podium until then, said, "That is why this ship will remain one hundred kilometers away while our linesmen attempt to work out exactly what the lines are. After which, if we decide to approach the ship, it will be in a shuttle."

They could be killed. Ean hoped Captain Helmo was right

when he said they'd have time to escape back into the void if the ship pulsed again. The way his luck was running lately, he'd probably be on a shuttle heading straight toward it at the time. Still, even if he died, at least he would have been involved in something different. Something big.

He caught the movement as Radko shifted slightly against the wall. Maybe.

But he was on the ship now. They couldn't send him back, and even if they thought his lines were strange, surely they wouldn't waste a ten. Maybe they'd even send him in first, in case the first shuttle got vaporized.

"Let's see it again," Admiral Katida said. "And I want to see all ships' systems as well."

Four extra screens came up, each displaying a series of numbers and telltales that Ean couldn't understand.

The civilians started a mass exit—apparently this was the end of the session—while the military started analyzing what each ship had done and when. Captain Helmo stayed at the podium to answer questions, but Abram and Michelle disappeared. Ean stayed where he was until Radko touched his shoulder. He got up to follow.

This time, she led him through the reception room where the civilians were now helping themselves to refreshments—even though he'd only recently eaten, the smell of the food made his mouth water—down another corridor and into a small meeting room. The room had two guards outside.

He was the first one there. Was it a type of prison?

He had five minutes to wonder what he could have changed about last night before Michelle and Abram came in together.

"Governor Jade is like a limpet," Michelle said. "So hard to disentangle once she gets her suckers on." She sat down, rested her head on the table, and closed her eyes. "My bones hurt."

Abram clasped her shoulder in a quick gesture of encouragement.

Michelle looked tired and ill. The skin on the cheek facing Ean was white and waxy and very fine. She looked young and vulnerable and hardly old enough to leave home, let alone be running a ship full of VIPs on a mission where one misstep could turn into an interstellar war. Suddenly, Radko didn't seem as young anymore.

"Are you the youngest person on this ship?" Now that he thought about it, Ean could remember the princess's being proclaimed heir not long before he—Ean—had left to join Rigel's cartel. That proclamation would only have happened when she came of age.

Michelle opened her eyes and looked up at Ean. The dimple flashed out in a smile. "Not anymore," she said, and sat up properly as Rebekah swept into the room.

Rebekah nodded at Michelle and Abram and ignored Ean. Ean nodded at her, as if she had greeted him, too.

Two orderlies followed, bringing welcome tea and sandwiches. Ean poured because he could see that despite his seeming calm, even Abram's hands were shaking slightly. Ean seemed to be recovering better than the other two. Maybe that was because he had rested and eaten while they'd had to work. Or maybe because he'd had more exposure to the lines.

Rebekah looked down her nose at him. He didn't have to be a mind reader to know what she was thinking, that he didn't even know it was the host's job to pour. He didn't care. He was just sorry he'd put the others through such a terrifying experience.

He pushed sandwiches toward Abram. "Eat," he said, and made it an order. He held the plate almost up to Abram's face, so that he had to do something. Abram took a sandwich to avoid a scene.

Ean held the plate almost under Michelle's nose. "You, too."

Michelle went whiter if that was possible.

"I'm the expert here," Ean reminded them. "I know what to do." He didn't, but food had helped him.

Michelle reluctantly took a sandwich.

"Expert," said Rebekah. "You've spent your whole life mending second-rate lines and learning bad habits. I wouldn't call you an expert."

Ean placed the plate between Abram and Michelle and watched Abram take another sandwich without prompting. He smiled. In this, at least, he was the expert.

He didn't want the other linesman sniping at him all the time, demeaning him. Maybe he deserved it. After last night, the Alliance probably wouldn't let him anywhere near the ship, but he was at least along for the ride. He hoped.

"Rebekah, let's agree on one thing. You are the ten they hired. You are the expert. I'm here by accident." Two more sandwiches disappeared. "So let's now work together on it. Maybe I can help. This is too important to let anything get in the way."

"Help," said Rebekah. "You'll probably get us killed."

He wondered if that was her real fear.

"You started late. You're untrained."

He'd had ten years of training.

"You *sing* to the lines."

Did everyone know that? Or had she done some research of her own last night, too?

"So you don't hear music?" Abram asked, taking another sandwich.

"There is no music," Rebekah said. "He's crazy, untalented, and wild. If he'd been taught properly, he wouldn't hear any music. And those rumors you hear about the strength of his lines are just that. Rumors." She leaned forward, as if by getting closer, she could convince them. "I know you think you have brought along the two best tens, but you haven't. He's a dud."

Rumors? In the silence that followed, Ean realized the sandwich plate was empty. He stood up and went over to the door. He couldn't contribute to the conversation. It was about him, not at him, and Abram and Michelle would do what they would. But this was one thing he could do.

"Could we have some more sandwiches, please," he asked one of the guards outside the door.

He went quietly back to his seat.

No one else had moved although they all watched him.

"Look at him," Rebekah said. "He has no idea how to behave in real society; no idea what is proper."

He supposed she meant the sandwiches. It wasn't proper, but it was necessary. Was she really complaining about his linesmanship or about his coming from the slums?

Abram finally blinked and took a mouthful of tea. "You seem remarkably well informed," he said.

"I'm a linesman. I have to know what threatens us."

"Threatens?" Ean couldn't stop the word.

"A wild talent with no control." She spoke to the others, as if one of them had asked it. "He's not trained."

He didn't want to start defending himself, but she kept on about that. "I did ten years' training."

"With second-rate trainers who all said that you did your own thing, no matter what they taught you."

Sometimes the way the trainers did things twisted the lines into the wrong shape.

"By the time you came into the cartels, you had already learned so many bad habits, no one could fix them. They should have been trained out from childhood."

The sandwiches arrived then. Either they'd had them pre-made, or someone else's sandwiches had been diverted. He knew, subliminally through line one, it was the latter. This was a ship that looked after its boss first and everyone else second. It was also a ship that—collectively—knew the sandwiches were for Michelle and Abram even though Ean had asked for them. How did it know that?

"However I do what I do"—Ean wondered if he should just shut up—"I *am* a certified ten. If the Grand Master had been worried about my abilities, then surely he wouldn't have certified me."

"He is only certified because Rigel chose a public certification." She was still talking directly to Abram and Michelle, still acting as if they had made the comment. "He would never have passed a private ceremony."

Ean remembered the ceremony. He'd been embarrassed and ashamed. Other tens were certified in a private audience with the Grand Master, but Rigel had refused to pay the extra cost. "You can go in with the lower grades. They'll find your level there just as well, and we'll save on the cost of the special ceremony." Rigel could be funny about money. Sometimes he was lavish, sometimes miserly.

So Ean had endured the humiliation of being publicly tested for every level along with a hundred other linesmen. They'd had to send for special testers above level seven because they didn't have anyone suitable there.

"I'm beginning to think Rigel's cleverer than he acts," Michelle murmured to Abram. "Let's take another look at that contract later."

Abram grunted what might have been assent.

Ean thought it was time to get the conversation back on

track. "We're here to talk about the ship," he reminded Rebekah. Not about how unfit he was for the task. They'd found that out last night.

"I'm finding this conversation particularly interesting," Abram said. He poured them all more tea—except Rebekah, who hadn't touched hers. "It's important to know our tools."

So Ean sat back and sipped tea while Rebekah and Abram discussed just how bad he was.

"The rumors about his strength. How do you think they started?"

"He's a con man and a charmer. Most of the tens are at the confluence."

All of them were. Except him, and now Rebekah. And who was going to repair the higher lines now?

"He's done basic repairs on every ship for the last six months. Naturally people are grateful to him. They feel a sense of loyalty."

"Surely that is the cartel's fault," Michelle said. "If you leave only one person doing maintenance, people are bound to be grateful to him. Particularly if he does a good job."

At least Michelle was defending him.

"But that's just it," Rebekah said. "He appears to do good work, but it—"

"Falls apart and needs repairing again immediately," Abram suggested.

"No," said Ean, because one thing he did know was that his lines were clean.

"No one knows," Rebekah said. "No one knows what damage he is doing, because no one can tell how he repairs the lines. He *sings* to them. As if that's going to do any good." She leaned forward again. "Suppose a line fails while it's passing through the void."

Abram nodded. "Can I get a list of ships he has repaired in the last six months? I might check what has happened to them."

She nodded back.

Ean sipped more tea.

"So why didn't Ean go out to the confluence?" Abram asked. "Surely, if you didn't want him repairing the lines, the smartest thing to do would be to send him out there and leave other tens doing the repairs."

"At the confluence?" Rebekah was shocked. "Think of the damage he could do."

Ean had pleaded and bargained to get out there. Rigel had always refused. "We make more money doing repairs," he'd said.

Ean realized he was biting his bottom lip and tried to stop. He took a sip of tea, but his breath caught at the wrong time, and he breathed in a mouthful of liquid. He missed the next bit they said while he was coughing tea everywhere and mopping it up, but he did hear Michelle say, "The cartels have to take some of the blame for what has happened. Leaving one person to make all the repairs, then blaming him for getting the kudos seems a little harsh."

Rebekah flushed an ugly brick red. "You are not a linesman," she told her. "The confluence, it's . . . You have no idea."

Abram coughed gently. She closed her mouth on an audible click of teeth.

Abram glanced at Ean and then at his comms. "It is time we talked about the ship," he said.

Ean carefully folded the cloth he'd used to mop up the tea and didn't look at anyone.

He continued to look at the cloth while they watched videos of the various linesmen discussing their experience. The highest was a six, the lowest a three. They all said the same thing. They could tell that the ship had lines, but they couldn't recognize which lines or what levels. All of them agreed it felt like higher-level lines. All of them sounded a little awed and overwhelmed.

"Not much to go on," Abram said, when they were done. "We're hoping you two will find out more."

"And we don't know what triggered the pulse?" Rebekah asked.

"No. Could be proximity. Could be detection of weapons. Could be someone on the ship who thought the Haladeans got too close."

"One hundred kilometers is too far out," Rebekah said. "We need to get closer. You have to be close to the lines to read them."

At least she was thinking, now that she had finished deconstructing Ean's character.

Abram raised an eyebrow at Ean, who nearly didn't see it except that Michelle nudged him with her knee. He hoped he understood the question. "I have always worked close to the lines, too." Even ten kilometers was too far away. "I don't see how we can get close enough to talk to them"—he caught Rebekah's scowl at his unfortunate use of words—"without getting ourselves blown up."

For the next fifteen minutes, they discussed the lines. Ean didn't contribute much. Compared to Rebekah's experience, he knew nothing, and if what Rebekah said was true, then anything he did say was likely suspect anyway. Was he really as bad as she claimed?

Michelle nudged his knee again. He looked up, and had absolutely no idea what the question had been. Abram and Michelle exchanged a quick glance. Michelle shrugged and lowered her eyelashes in what looked almost like a tiny nod.

Abram stood up abruptly. "We're all tired. Maybe we could think about this and reconvene later. After dinner. Back here at 21:00." He looked at Ean. "You should get some rest."

"Yes, sir." It was effectively an order, in a tone that demanded a military response. Ean stood up, nodded to them all, and left the room. Michelle came out with him. From the corner of his eye, Ean saw Abram turn to Rebekah once they had gone. More discussion about him? Or a serious talk about what they could do with the ship?

Once outside, reaction set in, and he had to tuck his hands under his arms to stop them from shaking. He was almost glad Michelle walked with him because it meant he had to keep himself together as they passed through the foyer, now teeming with military and civilian predinner drinkers, nodding to people he'd met last night. At least six of them tried to waylay Michelle, but she said, "Business," and kept walking alongside Ean.

The lift, mercifully, was empty, and Michelle used a code to take them straight to their floor.

Ean said, "You don't need to guard me all the time." And the one doing the guarding shouldn't be the Emperor's oldest daughter. "I'm not likely to damage your lines." Except that he already had if Rebekah was right. Line six. He leaned back against the wall and tried not to think about that.

Michelle's mouth twisted down in a half wince, half smile. "Is that what you think we're doing?" She followed Ean out of the lift, through the central room with the three couches at the end, and down to Ean's room. She even followed him inside.

Ean looked at her, then turned away. Michelle could do what she liked, but he was going to get clean. He felt soiled and dirty. He turned and walked through the bedroom toward the bathroom, pulling off his shirt as he did so.

"Not the fresher," Michelle said, and beat him to the door. "It was hard enough to get you out of it last night, and there were two of us then."

She blocked the whole door. The geneticists had built for height. Not too tall to be freakish but tall enough to give an imposing physical presence. Ean's eyes looked straight into hers. She smiled at him, showing dazzling white teeth. "Let's sit on the bed for a moment and talk."

That was probably an order, too. Ean turned and walked back to the bed and sat on the end of it. It was a big bed—probably the third largest bed in the whole ship. He deliberately didn't think about anything, and most especially didn't think about last night. Or today's meeting.

Michelle sat down beside him. "Is that what you do, make for the fresher when you're upset?"

Ean fell back onto the bed and covered his face with the shirt he still carried. "Is there some point to all this?" He didn't want to look at Michelle, didn't want to hear her answer.

Michelle was silent for so long that Ean thought she was waiting for him to look at her, so he finally lowered the shirt. Michelle was staring at the opposite wall—which suited Ean fine.

"Abram likes you," Michelle said, eventually.

And everyone sang to the lines, too. Ean covered his face again. He didn't want to hear lies.

"But his first job is to protect the people on this ship—me especially, but everyone else, too—and he's got a problem. How do you get someone close to that thing without getting them killed? And we need that ship."

"It's only a ship," Ean said. Yes it was new and unknown and exciting, but it was still just a piece of machinery.

"The Alliance is very fragile at the moment," Michelle said. "Gate Union is delaying jumps for Alliance ships. It may not seem much, but it's limiting our access to the void, and it's going to get worse. Plus, with the line factory at Shaolin gone, Redmond owns all the lines, and we know who they're affiliated with. They can stop us buying line ships."

"Would Redmond remain affiliated with Gate Union if they controlled supply of the lines?" Michelle might be being overly pessimistic. "After all, they'd drop half their potential market," Ean said.

"They don't need to do it forever. Just a few years. No ships, no jumps. We can all see what will happen then. It doesn't matter how much military power we have, without the void, without the ability to travel faster-than-light, we can see that we will become second-class citizens compared to those who can."

They could set up their own void gates, but even Ean could see the danger in that. It only took one ship to deliberately jump through to the wrong place, and you destroyed a planetary system.

"Plus, we've a dozen internal wars threatening to tear us apart. If we can't pull together, the Alliance won't exist in twenty years. You can imagine what will happen to a world like Lancia."

Ean couldn't. Lancia had been a major power broker in galactic politics for the whole four hundred years the Alliance had been in place. If he'd thought about it at all—and he hadn't—he would have assumed that Lancia would go on to become the same in Gate Union.

"We *need* this ship. We need a rallying point." Michelle's voice was bleak. "Not to mention that if Gate Union or Redmond get hold of it and work out what it does, then they have a weapon that can defeat us."

Ean really should have studied more politics.

"You've taken good care to make sure they don't." Three jumps in a row, and another one tonight if he was hearing the lines properly. He wasn't looking forward to that.

Michelle laughed a mirthless laugh. "They'll find us, and it will be much faster than we want them to. If the media can't do it, the linesmen will."

"Linesmen?" Surely she didn't mean him. Ean felt sick. "You think I—?"

Michelle pulled the shirt away from his face. Blue eyes gazed into his. "No. We don't. As you said earlier, you're an accident. No one knew you were coming. But we pulled a lot of strings to get Rebekah Grimes on board. And everyone knows the cartels are pro–Gate Union."

Even Rigel had been, and if Ean had thought about it, he would be, too.

"You think Rebekah is a spy?" She worked for a cartel. She would do the job she was paid to. "But she's a ten."

Michelle laughed. A genuine laugh this time, one that showed her dimple. "She's politically savvy. She wouldn't be where she is if she weren't. But we're not talking about politics."

They weren't?

"We're talking about you, and why Abram let Ms. Grimes pick you apart earlier."

He didn't want to talk about that. "It's not—"

Michelle put up a hand to silence him. "None of us want to get killed. It's Abram's job to know all about the weapons we use."

So he was a weapon now. A defective one.

Michelle could almost have read his mind. "Don't write yourself off yet. A wild talent like yours may be just what we need. We don't know. Right now, anything you say is just as valuable as anything Rebekah Grimes says."

So that's what this little pep talk had been about. Contribute, or else. It made Ean feel better even as he felt embarrassed about his earlier behavior. "Thank you."

"I don't think you're defective," Michelle said.

It was honest, at least. He was still staring at her when Abram arrived in the doorway. "How did you go?"

"We had our chat." Ean was glad to look away. "She pointed out that I needed to pull my weight." Withdrawing into himself was probably the stupidest thing he could have done.

"I didn't quite put it that way."

Abram smiled. "At least you got the message," he said to Ean. He sat down on the padded seat near the dresser. "I spoke to Admiral Katida. She's known about you for four years, at least. Although—in her words—that cartel master of yours kept you secreted away until the confluence."

Four years. Ean had been certified two years ago. He'd been ready at least three years before that, but Rigel had made him wait.

"Most apprentices take ten years before they try for certification," he'd said. "You should take your time, too."

Most linesmen were certified around the age Ean had *become* an apprentice. "I'm twenty-five," he'd said back then. "Ten years older than that new apprentice you just took on. I've been training for *five* years."

"And that new apprentice will probably train for ten," Rigel had said. "Wait until you are ready, Ean."

Ean had been certified in the same ceremony the new apprentice had failed certification. He'd wondered ever since if Rigel had deliberately pushed the apprentice through fast to fail.

Abram's voice was dry. "There was some debate, apparently, as to whether you really were a ten."

"I wonder if Katida sleeps with the ones she thinks are going to be tens," Michelle said. "Just in case, I mean."

"No." Ean thought of the twins. That he could answer with confidence. "She waits until they're certified." He started to pull on his shirt, then stopped, thinking. If Katida really did sleep with all the tens, shouldn't he have met her by now? She'd had two years.

He sighed. Thinking was counterproductive. Rigel had told him that, lots of times. "Your job is not to think, Ean. It's to do. I give you the jobs, you do them." To be honest, he hadn't thought much. He'd been happy. He'd been doing work he loved. Life really had centered around work, lessons—Rigel still made him learn—and the local hotel near the cartel house. Rigel had kept him too poor and too busy to afford the fancy restaurants and bars the other linesmen went to.

He finished pulling on his shirt and saw that the other two were watching him. They spent a lot of time watching him. As if he were some wild creature that might turn around and bite them at any moment. Ean shrugged.

After a moment, Abram resumed. "He did the lines for one of Katida's captains, who's quite impressed. Apparently, they always had problems with the lines on that ship but haven't had any since."

"And the rumors about how good he is?" Michelle asked.

"She's heard them. She thinks we deliberately chose him because of that."

How did you subtly ask a question like that? Excuse me, what do you think of the ten we brought along?

Abram stood up and gave Michelle's shoulder a quick squeeze. "You did well, Misha," and left them.

Ean stood up, too. "I really am going to use the fresher," he said, and left Michelle sitting on the bed. This time he waited until he was in the bathroom before he removed his shirt.

FIVE

EAN LAMBERT

DINNER THAT NIGHT was a buffet.

Admiral Katida and Tarkan Heyington swamped him as soon as he arrived.

The Tarkan was dressed equally skimpily today. This time it was a lace-up vest and tights that showed every bulge. He pressed in warm and clammy against Ean's side.

Katida took his arm on the other side. "How's the planning going?"

He wondered if he should lie, and did, a little. "Intense." There hadn't been much planning yet, not from where he was.

Rebekah Grimes swept by in a swarm of admirers. Her gaze glanced through and past him.

"She really doesn't like you," Katida said. "Not used to having competition." She pulled Ean toward the buffet. "The fish is exceptional." The Tarkan came, too. Ean helped himself to a plate of fish as an excuse to give himself some room. The three of them found a seat at one end—so both Katida and the Tarkan could watch the room, Ean realized—and settled down to eat. Admiral Varrn joined them not long after.

Katida was right. The fish was excellent.

They spent the meal discussing the ship. This time, Ean listened more carefully to what they weren't saying rather than to what they were. He'd always had a good ear for emotions in voice. Varrn was optimistic and excited, the Tarkan pessimistic, and Katida was worried. Very worried. He could hear it loud and clear coming through on line eight.

Impossible.

Ean closed his eyes and tuned out the background noise. Then he tried, with varying success, to tune out the lines of the ship. Lines two to five were easy to block out. Line six not so. It seemed to recognize him and want to be around. Ean couldn't block that one out. Line one—on this ship line one was always strong—he didn't have a hope. Lines seven and eight were normally quiet. No one knew what they did. No one knew how to use them. Seven was still quiet, but eight was definitely strong, and he knew it was coming from Katida, not from the ship. Line nine was quiet. Ship line ten was quiet, but there was another line ten. Rebekah. Strong and confident and right now showing overtones of impatience.

He opened his eyes and looked over to see who she was talking to. Governor Jade.

People didn't have lines. His trainers had drummed that into him. Ships had lines. Machinery had lines. Even comms had lines.

But never people. Lines didn't have personality, either. He was imaging that line six wanted to be around and that line one sounded like the ship.

"You need a nap. I can show you my bed," Katida said.

They were all silent, watching him.

Ean shrugged. "I was thinking."

"You always think with your eyes closed?"

"Sometimes," he admitted.

"Bizarre," Tarkan Heyington said.

AT 21:00, Ean was the last back to the small meeting room.

Michelle had showered. Her hair was still damp. It curled around her face. Ean breathed in deep. The fizzy smell was stronger, still pleasant and clean. If he'd thought about what

Lancastrian royalty smelled like at all, he'd have thought of heavy, overpowering scents, as oppressive as their owners.

They talked for an hour and got nowhere. If they didn't know what the lines were, they couldn't do much to prepare.

Finally, Ean asked, "Can we listen to the linesmen again?" It was an idea that had started to form after listening to Katida on line eight. Maybe he could pick the line level from their voices.

He could see that Rebekah thought it a bad idea, but she didn't argue. She'd been polite for the whole hour so far. Maybe while Michelle had been having her talk to Ean, Abram had had one of his own with Rebekah.

This time he closed his eyes while he listened.

The clean smell of Michelle, beside him, mingled in with the sound of the linesman's voice. He breathed deep and forced himself to concentrate on the sounds, but he still missed the first two totally. He'd have to listen to them again.

The level six was totally awed. "I can't describe it. It was—" And for a moment, Ean was back in the cart going up to Rigel's house, listening to Kaelea trying to describe the confluence.

"Replay the first two," he said, when the six was done. Yes, they had some of that awe, too. "Rebekah, tell us about the confluence." He didn't open his eyes.

"It is not—"

"Tell us," said Abram. "I don't think we have many other ideas at present."

They obviously didn't because Rebekah started telling them about the confluence. Or maybe Abram's talk had been harsher than Michelle's.

"It's . . . you have to be a linesman to truly appreciate it. It—" Her voice took on the same awe the others had, although her awe came across strong and loud and, in this room at least, totally swamped the other lines. It even swamped the clean smell of Michelle.

It was so strong, he gripped hard at the edge of the table, worried for a moment that they had jumped again without his knowing. Going through the void was changing the way he perceived the lines. Did it change all linesmen? It wasn't a question he could ask Rebekah.

When she had finished, Ean opened his eyes, just in time to catch the puzzled glance Abram and Michelle exchanged. Rebekah didn't notice. She was still lost in the glory of the confluence.

Michelle half shrugged. "I still don't know any more about the confluence than I did before."

"No one does," Ean said. "I've never heard a linesman even explain what it is, but they're all lost in the glory of it. Those who've been there, that is." He hesitated. Should he say this? But Michelle had implied any theories were welcome. "They talk about the ship the way linesmen talk about the confluence."

"That's ridiculous," Rebekah said.

Abram replayed the vids; this time, he closed his eyes. Afterward, he replayed the meeting-room security tape from where Rebekah had started talking about the confluence.

Even Rebekah agreed there were similarities in the way they sounded when they spoke about the ship and the way she sounded when she spoke about the confluence. "But I am a ten," she said, "talking about something unknown but incredibly powerful. These are sixes and threes. The things they respond to are unlikely to be as powerful as the confluence."

"Why not?" asked Ean. "I heard a seven talking about the confluence the other day, and she sounded like you only not as strong. Just because they can't control the lines doesn't mean they can't hear them."

"No one *hears* lines except you."

It didn't matter whether they heard them, felt them, or saw them. They responded to them.

"What makes the confluence different?" Abram asked, and Michelle said at the same time. "The Haladeans kept this quiet until Redmond attacked. We could probably find out when someone last saw those two warships. It might be earlier than we think."

Abram raised an eyebrow. "Six months, do you think?"

"Maybe." The confluence had appeared six months ago.

Even Rebekah looked intrigued. "So the ship came because the confluence was here?"

Or the ship came first and caused the confluence, but Ean didn't say that.

Radko tapped on the door and came in.

"Ma'am, sir." She nodded to Michelle and Abram. "The captain wants to jump in fifteen minutes. I'm to ensure nothing interrupts his schedule."

From the way her eyes sparkled as she said it, and the way the dimple half showed, Ean thought the captain's words might have been stronger than that.

"He needs permission to jump," Radko added.

Ean tried to stop the color rising in his face. He'd bet this was the first time the captain had ever had to ask permission to jump. He stood up, then hesitated. It was Abram's call.

"Go," Abram said. "We'll talk some more about the confluence, then finish up here." He followed them out into the passage. "Radko." It was quiet enough so that no one inside the room could hear him.

"Sir?"

"Tell the medic to be sure he doesn't touch him while we're jumping. That's important."

"Yes, sir."

"When the medic gives the okay, tell Captain Helmo he can jump."

"Yes, sir."

They left at Radko's usual long-legged stride. Ean was definitely going to be fitter by the end of the trip if he walked around with her much.

"Captain's not too happy with me I guess," Ean said.

"Spitting," Radko said cheerfully. "You touched his ship. Without his permission."

He didn't think Abram had heard about that yet, didn't know what he would do when he did. "But line six is okay." He could hear it clear and straight in his head.

"Tai—the chief engineer—says it's never been better." Radko stopped outside the hospital and looked serious. "Captain Helmo lives for the ship. It's like a violation."

He felt guilty about what he'd done but not sorry. "It's such a beautiful ship," he said. "We couldn't have line six out even by a little bit."

He was glad to see the medic, to change the conversation.

"Commodore Galenos said that you are not to touch him

while we jump," Radko said. "And you're to let me know when you're ready."

"Do you want to be knocked out?" the medic asked.

Ean shuddered. What if he was unconscious and couldn't get out of the forever in the void. "No. Please."

The medic nodded. "On the bed then, and I'll just keep an eye on you. There's not much else I can do."

"I don't need this," Ean said. "I can go to my own room."

"The commodore is law on this ship. If he says you come to the hospital for jumps, you come. And after what you did to those two, I definitely want you here. I want them here, too," he added. "But I'm not sure about the close proximity. Radko. Let the captain know he can jump."

"Yes, sir." Radko strode off rapidly.

Knowing the jump was coming made it worse. They had seven minutes. The minutes stretched. After what seemed hours, Ean suggested, "Maybe you should be with Abram and Michelle. They might have problems after last night." He didn't want to be near anyone when he made the jump, didn't want anyone—even the medic—to see him when line ten came in.

"Believe me, I will watch them," the medic said grimly.

One minute to go.

The medic pushed the comms. "Galenos. I need security where you are."

There was no answer, but one wall lit up as a screen and Ean could see into the meeting room, where the other three were still discussing the confluence. Rebekah still couldn't find words to describe it. He wondered if it was because it was something so far outside human perception that linesmen couldn't think of anything to compare it to, or whether it was just so awe-inspiring they didn't want to desecrate it by describing it with ordinary words.

The alert chimed, and line nine came in strong. Ean put his hands over his ears in an instinctive move to block out what was coming. Which was stupid, he knew, because it wasn't the sound that was the problem but the forever that came with it.

The high notes of line ten sounded, and Ean was lost in

the void again. The lines were so clear in here. It was almost as if they were talking to him.

A very, very long time later—seconds in real time—he came back to the present, to find he was curled up, whimpering. The sound of the lines vibrated deep in his bones.

He must have gone to sleep. He woke to an argument.

"Seen those symptoms before," the medic was saying. "*Strathcona. Davida.* Probably the *Balao*, too, if they hadn't all died. I want him off this ship before the next jump."

"But he hasn't done anything wrong," Michelle said.

"Can't you *see* him? Comatose. That's exactly how the crew of the *Davida* came out of their last jump. The man is a walking bomb. Jump with him again, and he's likely to send the ship crazy."

They were talking about him. Ean could feel the lines— straight, happy, and melodic. "The ship's fine," he said.

They didn't hear him.

"I read the report on the *Davida*," Abram said. "Didn't those symptoms happen after the jump?"

What symptoms?

"How do we know that?" the medic asked. "Someone had to trigger it. How do you know it wasn't someone already on the ship? Someone like him. He's already interfered with the ship once."

"Already interfered?" Abram asked sharply.

Fixing line six would haunt him forever. Ean sat up, surprised at how shaky he was. The room twirled in a mad kaleidoscope of color and sound. He didn't know which was up and which was down. He fell back onto the bed, only he fell farther than he expected and hit the floor hard. Fine, so now he'd just fallen out of bed in front of three people who thought he was crazy. "If the captain's worried about line six, why doesn't he get Rebekah to look at it?" He knew it was fine, and Rebekah would be lying if she found anything wrong.

A strong hand gripped the top of his right arm.

"Leave him there," the medic said. "He'll only fall out again."

"What about line six?" Abram's voice, close.

"It's fine," Ean said.

He heard the beep of the comms, the captain answering,

and Abram's crisp voice. "Captain Helmo. What did Linesman Lambert do to line six?"

"It's the doing it without permission that's the problem." Ean could still hear the anger.

Michelle cut in over Abram. "So what did he do?"

Ean heard the breath the captain drew in. "He fixed it." A grudging admission that he hadn't done any real damage.

"Fixed it?" Abram's voice could have cut glass. It sounded as if he thought Ean had also caused the problem to start with. "Do you want Linesman Grimes to look at it?"

The explosive "No," carried a strong subtext. No one touched his ship. What happened when the higher lines needed servicing? Did they never get serviced?

"The ship seems happy enough about it," the captain said, still grudging. "But linesmen can't go around changing the lines just because they feel like it."

Under different circumstances, Ean thought, he and Captain Helmo might get on fine. *The ship seems happy about it.* How many people put emotions to their ships?

Ean struggled to sit up. This time it was Michelle who helped him, he could tell by the clean fizz that got up his nose and made him sneeze. He managed to stay upright and even open his eyes. Abram was frowning at them both.

He didn't want Abram to think he had deliberately vandalized anything. "The ship." Ean had to clear his throat before he could speak properly. What had he done that had used his voice? "Line six had a problem," he said. "I fixed it. When I first came on board. I didn't ask the captain if I could." He struggled to his feet. "I'm going to my own room."

Michelle came with him. "Because otherwise you'll end up in the fresher again," she said.

Right now, Ean could do with a hot shower. He felt dirty and soiled, and nothing he could do would ever make Michelle and Abram look on him as a real person. He'd had too many chances, and he'd blown every one of them. Maybe they'd put him on the first shuttle to the ship and hope he'd be vaporized. Then he wouldn't be a problem anymore.

Without Michelle's guidance, he would have taken a dozen wrong turns. Who knew where he might have ended up.

"How many more jumps do we have?" he asked when he had enough voice to talk.

"That was the last." Michelle guided him into his cabin. Ean flopped onto the bed.

She sat down beside him, and said, "You can't keep making enemies like this."

Ean bit his lip and nodded. This was another pep talk he deserved. Maybe the medic was right. Maybe he really was crazy. Maybe that was why Rigel had kept him sequestered and busy at the cartel house; because when he stopped to think about it, that was what Rigel had done. Maybe he'd had good reason to.

Michelle said, "You scare some people." She patted Ean's cheek. "You don't scare me."

Yet. How much crazy behavior could a person take? Not that Ean felt crazy. He felt normal. All crazy people felt normal, he supposed.

Michelle sighed, and stood up. "We get to the ship tomorrow."

They might be dead tomorrow night. Ean raised himself on one elbow. "Michelle."

Michelle paused in the doorway.

"Thanks."

Michelle's genetically enhanced smile flashed suddenly, but she didn't say anything.

Ean flopped back onto the bed.

SIX

✦

JORDAN ROSSI

ON THE VID, Rossi watched the scientists swarm over the viewing center. They were like ants. You couldn't get rid of them once they'd arrived. Oh, you tried, but they always came back, hunting for the crumbs of truth that fitted their theories, twisting the little pieces of knowledge they gleaned about the lines to suit.

This much was fact. Line nine took a ship into the void. If you didn't have line nine, you never got anywhere. Your ship traveled at sublight speed. Subsublight speed really, because there were engines that could travel at .4c, while a Bose engine puttered along at a quarter of that speed. But only ships running a modified Bose engine controlled by line six ever made it out of the void. Scientists knew this. They had done experiments.

Rossi cynically wondered if any of those early pilots had known they were signing up for an instant death sentence.

Line nine could take you in and out of the void forever. Scientists had done experiments on that, too. To the onlooker, the ship disappeared momentarily. Less than a second, and it was only the machines that told them the ships had ever disappeared at all.

But line nine couldn't move you through the void. You needed line ten for that.

Not that anyone knew what the void was yet.

Oh, the scientists had lots of theories. Another dimension. Hyperspace. Even another state of matter. They had a dictionary of words to describe it, too. Havortian space, Havortian state, antispace. Jordan Rossi didn't care. He didn't have time for scientists. The void was the void. The lines were the lines. If the scientists wanted to know more about the lines, why didn't they use linesmen as scientists?

But, of course, no self-respecting linesman would want to be a scientist. Once you had the lines, that became your life.

At least, for Jordan Rossi it had, and he couldn't imagine anyone else's feeling any different. He'd felt the lines all his life, even before he knew they were lines. As a young boy, he'd spent every moment he could at the spaceport, where the majority of lines congregated. Much to the annoyance of his merchant mother, who held that the ports were dirty, filthy places inhabited by lowlifes.

He'd taken the line tests at age five and moved into the cartel house proper at age ten. He'd certified at seventeen, which was the earliest one could be tested.

Because he'd been so obvious a linesman at such an early age, the scientists had been particularly interested in him. Throughout his early years, life had been a series of tests along with his lessons, until twelve-year-old Rossi had issued his cartel master with an ultimatum. Get rid of the scientists, or Rossi found himself another house.

Rossi hadn't seen a scientist since. Not until now, when the cooperation between the houses and Gate Union dictated that they allowed Gate Union to send its soldiers and its scientists in, to share the discovery of the confluence.

As if any linesman would share line secrets.

It was an uneasy truce, the first in a long time, that threatened relations between the two groups. Gate Union didn't understand how important the confluence was to the linesmen. They didn't realize how sacred it was.

On the vid, Rossi watched Linesman Geraint Jones complain about the placement of a new experiment and smiled with satisfaction as Jones prevailed, and the tight-lipped scientists started to dismantle their equipment. The confluence belonged to the linesmen.

Today, however, Jordan Rossi had something more to worry about other than the effects of the confluence on his psyche.

He flipped to a news channel, where he watched Emperor Yu stride down the passageway, ignoring the reporters crowding around him. Yu's face wore its usual inscrutable expression.

The reporter's voice-over continued. "Still no sign of Emperor Yu's daughter, Lady Lyan, who was due to be married here tonight in a private ceremony on Lady Lyan's yacht."

Of course it would be on the yacht. No sense spending lots of money for a wedding that wasn't going to happen, was there. Except for the planetary representatives, there was no visible sign of a wedding. And Sattur Dow, striding along stone-faced behind his emperor, didn't look like a man whose bride had run off on their wedding night.

"As yet, there is still no information on the whereabouts of that yacht—the *Lancastrian Princess*—which departed two days ago, local time." The picture changed to the *Lancastrian Princess*. Rossi had been on real yachts. This was merely a sleek, fast freighter, totally unsuited to the heir of the richest group of worlds in the Alliance and Union combined.

The reporter signed off. "We'll bring you events as they happen. Until then, this is Coral Zabi from Galactic News, keeping you informed."

Rossi switched the vid off. "Sweetheart," he said to the screen, "if you really were keeping us informed, you would know where she is by now."

Two days, and still no sign of the Alliance ship here at the confluence. They could have been here in a quarter of that time.

Fergus looked up from his screen. "They didn't register a jump anywhere close."

It wasn't going into the void that was dangerous, it was the coming out. No one cared where you started from, all they cared was that you didn't jump out in the same time and place as another ship. Most ships registered with the gate world closest to their starting point, but you didn't have to.

And while it was technically illegal, there were ways around using your own ship name.

Lyan's ship had jumped somewhere between 18:00 and 24:00 hours. Thousands of other ships had jumped during the same time. Fergus would have to check every record to find where Lady Lyan had gone.

But they knew where she was coming, so why wasn't she here yet? And why hadn't Rebekah sent them a message?

Fergus was back working on his screen. "The representative from Gate Union wants an update. And the Sandhurst seven has been hanging around, looking hopeful."

"Let her hang." For the first time in a long while, Rossi had something more to think about than the confluence and his body. This could be the opening salvo in the war everyone was expecting. "Organize a meeting with Gate Union in three hours," which would give bitch Rebekah three hours more to get a message to them. "I'm going out to see what the confluence has for us today."

SEVEN

EAN LAMBERT

ONE HUNDRED KILOMETERS, and they might have been a million miles away. The ship was a tiny speck on their radar.

The military and the civilians had gathered in the foyer to watch it on the screen. Ean had gone there, too. He'd made an effort this morning, dressing carefully, smart enough that even Rigel would have nodded approvingly. He'd even thought about depilating, but that was probably carrying it too far. If he was to die today, it wasn't worth the hour it would take.

"Doesn't look like much," Katida said.

Even as she spoke, the image zoomed in, larger and larger, until the sphere filled the whole screen. Why was it, Ean wondered, that as far back as humankind had existed, they had always imagined alien ships as spheres but had never been able to build their own that way. It wasn't even practical. All that wasted space inside the curve.

It looked dead. It felt dead. If there were lines on the ship, Ean couldn't feel them. The Haladean ship had been ten kilometers out, but Captain Helmo had said the Alliance linesmen sent in by the other five ships—which had all arrived days before Michelle's—had corroborated that. Surely they hadn't gone as close.

Spacer Radko coughed discreetly behind him and inclined her head. She seemed to have been designated his messenger. Or maybe she was Abram's personal assistant.

"Excuse me." Ean bowed to Katida and left. He held his head high as he followed Radko. If he was going to die or be dumped here, he would do it with dignity. Less than a third of the people he'd known as a boy had survived to adulthood. Many of their deaths had been ugly or messy. He wanted a cleaner end.

Rebekah was already in the small meeting room. Maybe he should have come here first. Abram arrived not long after. Michelle didn't, and from the way Abram started speaking immediately, Ean didn't think she was coming, either. He felt as if he'd lost his only support, then laughed at himself for the notion. He was dreaming if he thought the heir to Lancia would in any way support him. She was just friendlier than Ean had expected. It was probably part of her training. Make people comfortable, make people trust you.

"Anything?" Abram asked.

Both linesmen shook their head.

"Captain Helmo said his linesmen felt it, too," Ean said. "How close were they?"

"It wasn't this ship specifically," Abram said. "We sent two others in first." Of course they would have. No one would take this particular ship of dignitaries and militia without first ensuring they would be safe. "They're still here."

"A hundred kilometers out?"

Abram nodded and pulled up some data. "Linesman grade six," he said. "I believe they went in as close as fifty kilometers."

"Can she feel the lines now?" Ean knew it was a she although he didn't know how.

Abram keyed some more commands. "Captain Rab," he said to the face that came up on the wall screen. "Your linesman. Can she feel the lines now?"

"No, sir." A commodore must outrank a captain. "Hasn't been able to feel it since we got back."

"Is it distance, does she think?" Ean asked. "Or something else?"

The captain's gaze turned to him. "It's not clear, Linesman." Either he had good video pickup or he knew who Abram was with. "She didn't feel any lines at all initially, and never on the shuttle. Only after we sent a droid to see when it would trigger the defense mechanism. I couldn't give you an exact distance, but she started to feel it beforehand. We jumped out. When we jumped back, at one hundred kilometers, she couldn't feel it anymore.

"So," said Rebekah after he'd clicked off. "We can get in half as far again with no danger."

"We believe so," Abram said. "Obviously, we won't be doing it in this ship."

"I wonder what the admirals would say if they knew we could go closer," Ean said.

Abram's voice was dry. "Believe me, Linesman, they all know. They wouldn't be where they are if their information-gathering skills were that poor."

"But you—" Ean closed his mouth on what he'd been going to say. He thought Abram's security would be good enough to keep this a secret.

Abram sighed. "The Alliance is a lumbering beast, four hundred years old now. It's had plenty of time to develop holes."

Almost as if in agreement with that, a new note sounded on Abram's communicator, and Captain Helmo's face appeared on-screen.

"Incoming ships," he said tersely, and his face disappeared, replaced by two small ships.

"More holes than even I thought," Abram muttered as he zoomed in on the first ship. It was a small cruiser; fast, luxurious, and large enough to hold twenty people in comfort. The logo emblazoned full-length down the side was the familiar red and gold of Galactic News.

The second ship was media as well. It looked to be a similar model, except that the logo on this one was Blue Sky Media.

Michelle's face appeared in the bottom, right-hand corner of the screen. "I suppose we should be grateful the media's intelligence is still better than Gate Union and Redmond's combined," she said. She was sort of smiling, but the smile turned down, and her dimple didn't show. "What do you want me to do?"

"I'll get Helmo to talk to them first," Abram said. "We'll

bring you in later if we need you. At least they came in far-ther out, rather than closer. I can imagine what would hap-pen if they vaporized themselves. The whole galaxy would know." He keyed up Helmo again. "Captain, warn them that they are in the middle of a military zone and that they must abide by your commands." He keyed off, and muttered under his breath. "And tell them you'll shoot them if they get in the way."

He looked at Ean and Rebekah staring at him. "I mean it. If they do anything to trigger that ship—" He pressed his lips together.

The media didn't believe that rules for others applied to them. If they wanted to go close to the ship, they would. They'd go right up to it if they could. Ean was surprised at how annoyed he was about that. They had no right to meddle with things they didn't understand. Besides, the Alliance had gotten here first. It was their find, not the media's.

"So let's get in there," Rebekah said. "Before they do."

Abram nodded. He looked at them both, looked at Ean, then at his comms. He clicked the comm unit on again. "Captain. Tell them that if they stay where they are for the moment, Lady Lyan will come out to their ships personally to give them an interview and explain what is happening."

"Personally?" Captain Helmo said. "Is that—?" He cut off what he'd been going to say, but he didn't like it.

"Personally," agreed Abram. "But they must stay where they are."

"Understood. Sir." Captain Helmo clicked off this time. Line five vibrated with the snap of it.

Abram turned back to Ean and Rebekah. "I don't want both of you going out together. Not initially."

"As senior linesman, I should go then," Rebekah said. She was almost quivering with expectation.

Abram nodded.

"I thought—" Ean said. Wasn't he the expendable one? The crazy one who was supposed to kill himself.

Abram's quelling gaze told him he thought too much. "We have a shuttle prepared," he told Rebekah. "I'll take you down." He looked at Ean. "Wait here," and left, giving last-minute instructions to Rebekah as he went.

Ean flung himself into a chair with more force than necessary. So they didn't trust him even to be the guinea pig and get himself killed. He was useless here, and they wouldn't let him do a thing. He closed his eyes and lost himself in the music of the lines. Line six was still strong. Line one held an undercurrent of worry. It was the ship's job to protect Michelle. She could have done the interviews equally well through line five—the communications line—without having to leave the ship.

You couldn't sing something like that better. It wasn't a problem you could fix except have Michelle back safe. It showed that ships really did have soul although most linesmen would have said Ean imagined it. Maybe it was just Captain Helmo's worry leaking through.

A higher-than-average number of ship captains died of brain tumors that began in the right auditory cortex. Common theory was that because the lines were pure energy and ended on the bridge at the Captain's Chair, the line energy irradiated the brain. If the lines could leak into a captain's head, then why couldn't the captain's thoughts leak into the lines? Helmo was close to his ship.

If you took that further, could the lines have been trying to talk to him yesterday while he was in the void?

EAN felt—through line five again—when the shuttle left. Abram didn't come back immediately.

Radko arrived first, bearing the ubiquitous pot of tea and three glasses. After she left, Ean poured himself a glass and was halfway through it before Abram arrived back with Michelle. He tossed a uniform shirt to Ean. It was plain, with nothing on the pocket at all. The name stenciled above the pocket was WHITE.

"I want to see that contract again," Abram said to Michelle.

Michelle brought it up.

Ean silently poured them both tea—Rebekah wasn't here to sneer at his uncouthness—while Abram read the whole contract, frowning. "This contract says that you now work for us—the Empire of Lancia—and that you will carry out whatever work we ask you to do on the lines," he said.

It was a standard contract except for the length. And the agreement that extra training would be provided and that Ean paid some of those costs, but Ean wasn't going to bring that up now.

"What happens if we ask you to do something you don't want to do?" Abram asked abruptly.

What could you do to the lines except fix them?

"Something a regular linesman wouldn't do."

"Well," said Ean, not really sure what he meant. "There's the code of conduct. All the cartels abide by that."

"And if something is against the code of conduct?"

"The cartel master takes responsibility for disciplining any linesman who breaks the code." A heavy weight seemed to settle on Ean's stomach, bringing acid and bile. "What exactly is it you want me to do?"

"What happens to the linesman?"

"It depends how bad it is. The cartel master gets rid of him. If he's lucky, he goes to a lower cartel house. If he's unlucky." Ean shrugged. He ended up working for what scraps he could get or getting out of the lines altogether. Not that Ean planned to stop working with the lines. Ever. He'd find a way. Somehow.

He poured himself another tea with hands that shook. The tea was sour in his mouth. He forced himself to face the truth he should have faced a day ago. "It won't make any difference to me." His voice was steady if a little hoarse. "You heard Rebekah. Everyone thinks I'm crazy."

Whether he did or whether he didn't do what Abram asked, no one would ever buy his contract. Except perhaps Rigel, but even he couldn't buy it back if Ean had violated the code of conduct.

Two days ago, he'd been a ten, stupid enough to think that someone would buy his contract because of that. Maybe not the higher cartels, but definitely some of the secondary ones. Rebekah had proven what a dream that was. He gripped the glass hard. There was nowhere to go from here. Except back to the slums, and he wasn't going back there. "Just tell me what you want me to do."

"You seem to have an affinity for line six." Abram's gaze could have been compassionate if Ean wanted to interpret it that way. He didn't. "I want you to break line six on those two ships."

Out of the corner of his eye, he saw Michelle put up a hand to cover her mouth, but his end-of-line employer didn't say anything.

"I don't break lines. I fix them."

Abram pointed to the uniform shirt he'd tossed Ean earlier. "Do whatever you have to do to stop them coming any closer than they are now. Michelle will get you onto the ships."

Ean gripped the shirt so tight it creased. "And Lady Lyan will, presumably, explain why I have to sing while she's being interviewed."

"She will do whatever she needs to as well."

Ean stood up, clutching the shirt to him, and walked out without another word.

He'd liked Abram and Michelle, had even started to think that maybe not everything from Lancia was bad. He should have known better.

Yes, he went straight to the fresher and scrubbed until the water ran out. Michelle and Abram would no doubt think it typical of him, part of his general craziness. They hadn't cut off his water supply yet. Captain Helmo would do that soon, he was sure. He wiped his eyes, still wet long after the water had run out and tried to work out what to do now.

Technically, they owned the contract and could ask anything line-related of him. It was only the code of conduct that had stopped the sabotages of the Great War, and that was why the code was enforced so strictly in the cartels. But these people weren't cartel. The cartels couldn't touch them—except perhaps refuse to service their lines, and how likely was that, given that Lancia was one of the richest empires in the galaxy. Someone would do it, and it would soon be forgotten.

Except for the linesman who'd betrayed the code. He'd never be forgotten. Nor would he ever work as a linesman again. Ean closed his eyes and leaned against the side of the fresher. That was the point, wasn't it. He'd never work anyway. No one would buy his contract.

How was it that Lancia still screwed up his life, even ten years after he'd left it?

Even so, linesmen didn't betray the lines. Rebekah Grimes would have laughed at him for that and called him crazy again, but they didn't. Their job was to protect the lines and keep them safe and well.

WHEN he arrived back at the small meeting room, he found nine armed spacers waiting with Abram, plus Michelle, who had changed into what Ean was starting to recognize as formal attire. Charcoal trousers and a matching jacket today, with the crown of Lancia embroidered on the pocket.

"What if I don't do it?" he asked Abram.

"If you genuinely try, and fail," Abram said, "then that is fine. It was the best you could do."

"What if I don't try at all?"

"We have a jail. You are staff. You disobeyed orders." Lancian jails were always overcrowded.

"And if I refuse to go?"

Abram looked at the nine soldiers. "You won't refuse."

Ean looked at them, too. Radko was among them. "So are they here to protect Michelle or make sure I do what you want me to?"

"Both," said Abram. He handed Ean a blaster. "It's not loaded, but you need it to look the part."

Ean took the blaster and looked at the spacers. Nine serious faces stared back at him. Ten, if you counted Michelle's.

"The shuttle is ready," Abram said. "Blue Sky Media first." He put out a hand to stop Ean. "Do what you have to. Do what you can."

Four soldiers fell in front of Michelle, five behind. Radko, who was last, beckoned to Ean. "Try to march in time," she said softly.

He let his ear pick up the rhythm of their steps and walked to the same beat.

ON the shuttle Michelle said, "Don't blame Abram. His job is security, and he's doing what he has to do to ensure that."

Ean just looked at her.

"Both of us are doing what we have to do to ensure survival." Michelle sighed and looked as if she would have said more but didn't.

It was just a pity their survival was going to destroy his. No matter what, he was going to work with the lines. He'd find a way.

Radko spoke up from where she was seated. "Commodore Galenos has our full support," she told Ean. "We trust him. He makes hard decisions sometimes, but he has to." Other spacers nodded.

"I support him, too," Michelle said. "No matter what he does."

They didn't have to destroy the lines though, did they? Or their careers?

Ean got more nervous the closer they came. "I'm not sure I can do this," he told Michelle, as they docked.

Michelle just smiled. A tired smile, but at least her dimple showed. He was starting to think of that as her honest smile. "Just do what you can. That's all Abram asks."

If he didn't do it, the media would move close to the other ship and likely vaporize them all to dust. That was the only reason he was even considering this.

Ean stepped on board the media ship, heavy-hearted.

The reporter was Sean Watanabe. Ean knew his face from countless vids, once would even have been impressed to see him this close. Watanabe came to greet them in person. Genetically, he was a good match for Michelle although Ean was pleased to see that Michelle managed to win the subtle presence standoff between the two. Why did he care?

"Lady Lyan. So good of you to agree to meet us." The robo-cameras were already rolling.

Ean could hear the lines. Poor lines, not badly maintained but not well maintained, either. Line one was a mess of egos and jockeying for favors, line five was overworked and really needed attention. Line six was fine.

He felt sick thinking of what Abram had asked him to do. He had to talk to the lines. Privately, because he was sure neither Abram nor Michelle would appreciate the media's filming it.

Maybe he could use how he felt.

He gasped and clutched at his stomach. He caught the

attention of one of Watanabe's hangers-on, one who looked like an assistant but not too important to be missed.

"Do you have any—?" Ean gasped and clutched at his stomach again. "Toilets?"

The assistant looked at him, askance. Luckily, Radko came to his rescue. "Allergic to shellfish," she confided in a loud whisper. "Barfs it up."

"Oh," said the assistant.

"But does that get him out of work?" Radko asked. "Not on our ship." The whole ship was fiercely loyal to Michelle, but they were always ready to spoil her reputation.

"Toilet," Ean begged.

The assistant led the way.

If Michelle noticed them drop out, she didn't give any indication of it.

The toilets were tiny cubicles that Ean could hardly fit into. This wouldn't be what they offered Lady Lyan if she asked, he'd have bet. Ean locked the door and really did spend some time retching. He didn't want to do this.

The ship noticed his discomfort. His mind filled with the music of the ship lines—almost as if *they* were trying to fix *him*.

Before the void, he wouldn't have known what to do next. Suddenly he did. The lines had tried to talk to him in the void, hadn't they. Why didn't he talk back? He could explain what the problem was. The lines had a right to know what was happening. He had a duty to tell them.

Ean sat on the floor, head on the bowl, and started to sing. He sang of the strange ship one hundred kilometers away. He sang of the Haladeans and what had happened to them.

"Maybe we should check if he's all right," the assistant said.

"He's fine," Radko said. "He always sings when he's stressed. It's his way of coping. Leave him awhile."

He sang of the Alliance and what they were trying to do. He sang of the distance limits and how Abram needed the ship to stay at least one hundred kilometers out. Finally, he sang a bargain direct to line six. I will fix your other lines after this is done if only you heed the hundred-kilometer limit.

Line six sang back, deep and heavy. Agreement.

The agreement vibrated deep in his bones.

He couldn't move for a long time after he'd stopped singing.

"Are you okay?" the assistant asked eventually, anxiously.

He forced himself to answer. "I'm fine," and staggered out of the cubicle. "Everything's fine," he said to Radko, and weaved off down the corridor with no real idea of where to go.

Radko caught up with him, and said quietly, "Go back and wash your face and hands. Make it look as if you have been sick."

The assistant wrinkled her nose and pressed into the wall as he pushed past her back to the washbasins.

Reaction set in as the adrenaline left. By the time they reached the others, the back of his uniform was saturated with sweat. The assistant really had a right to wrinkle her nose then, but she had disappeared as soon as it was decent to do so.

MICHELLE had bought a change of clothes. Back on the shuttle, she stripped and wiped herself down with a towel. "Interviews are hard work," she said.

Ean could imagine.

"Did you do it?" she asked.

Ean nodded and tried not to look at her. Her legs were longer than he'd expected. Even when he looked away, he could still see an expanse of bare calf out of the corner of his eye.

He remembered once, years ago, when someone had tried to sell pictures of a naked princess and some foreign dignitary. Michelle appeared comfortable with her own body. The whole thing had probably been one of those manipulated media things that Tarkan Heyington loved so much.

"You should have brought a change as well," Radko said quietly from beside him.

Michelle handed him her towel when she was done. "I can relate to the perspiration bit," she said, as Ean wiped himself down. It was a bit late now, the sweat had dried into his clothes.

"Me, too," Radko admitted. "I sweated buckets down there in those toilets. Have you heard him sing?" She looked at the other soldiers as she asked, not just Michelle. They all shook their head.

"It's like space and deep and high and clear and people and—" She trailed off. "It's just—"

Michelle paused halfway through pulling on clean pants. "It sounds like the confluence."

Radko shrugged. "I've never heard the confluence."

Michelle finished getting dressed, watching Ean all the while she did so. Ean tried not to wriggle uncomfortably.

"I really wish you had experienced the confluence first-hand," she said to him.

Yes. Ean did, too. Then maybe he wouldn't have gone on and on about how everyone talked about the ship and the confluence in the same way when really they were just talking about the lines in general. Because that's what Radko was describing. His singing the music of the lines.

Except Radko wasn't a linesman. Why would Radko talk about his singing the way linesmen talked about the confluence or the ship?

The bell chimed for their arrival at the Galactic News ship. Michelle strapped herself in, but took the time to give Ean a reassuring pat on the shoulder before she did.

THE second ship went much the same as the first one, only this time Ean didn't have any trouble convincing the assistant—young, male, full of his own importance—that he was unwell.

All the lines on this ship were bad. Ean took the time to strengthen some of them first—Abram wouldn't be happy, but he didn't have to know—before he sang them the song of the ship and how important it was to keep the distance.

Then he sang the bargain song. Stay far away and I'll come back and fix you when we're done.

The lines didn't believe him.

"How do we know?" Deep and heavy. Line six.

"How can we trust you?" Deeper still, and it got into his bones. Line nine.

Even line ten came in, high and clear, and the other lines let it speak alone.

"Can't you hear it through the lines? It's my promise." He would make good on that promise unless he was dead, and even then Abram would have to get someone else to do it for him.

"It's a deal." Rich and warm and pleasing to the ear, and not something Ean heard often. Line eight. He nearly stopped singing at the unexpectedness of it. Lines seven and eight never got involved. No one even knew what they did.

"Deal," he agreed, trying to match the tone.

The assistant banged on the door.

"Leave him," Radko said. A struggle started up outside.

"He's crazy. You're both crazy, and I'm calling security."

Ean stood up, flushed the toilet for effect, and staggered out as two security guards with Tasers rushed in. He walked straight into a Taser zap. Radko felled both security by rolling at them and kicked out at the assistant at the same time. When she stood up she had a Taser in each hand.

"I don't want to use these," she said. "But I will if you won't listen." Her voice was uneven, and she was panting. It had looked effortless.

The two guards twitched.

"They're crazy," the assistant said. He started to stand up.

Radko's aim didn't waver. "Tell him to lie down, or I'll fire on one of you."

The guard didn't even bother to speak. He just lifted a leg and hooked it between the young assistant's legs. He went sprawling again.

Ean staggered to his feet. Now he really did want to be sick.

"What do you want?" asked the second security guard.

"Nothing," Radko said. "My friend here was unwell. Okay, he stayed a long time in the toilet but—" She half shrugged. "This—" She waved a hand at the sprawled assistant. "He started banging on the door and—" She waved her hand again. "And then he called you."

"He was hiding something," the assistant said. "He played music to hide the sound of what he was doing."

Radko ignored that. "When you burst in, you had Tasers. We're Lady Lyan's bodyguard. We're trained to react to things like that. I'm sorry."

She turned the Tasers off and offered them, handle first, to the two guards. Ean held his breath.

The first guard sat up and took his with a chuckle. "You're fast enough, but I doubt this one will stay long in Lady Lyan's bodyguard."

"He's not well."

The second guard wasn't so forgiving or so believing. "And the music?"

"He's young. It's what he does when he's not feeling well." Radko glanced at Ean, then turned and confided to the guards. "He's the youngest on the ship. We baby him a bit."

"Doesn't look that young," one of the guards muttered.

Radko shrugged. "Yeah," she said, and her look implied it wasn't just that he was *young*. She was either a brilliant actress, or she really did believe there was something a little strange about him. "Not to mention he's popular with a certain VIP who travels on our ship. She *likes* having him around."

From the sudden knowing smile on the guard's face and the way he looked Ean up and down, he had gotten totally the wrong idea. Ean was mortified. "It's not—"

"You must have tapes," Radko interrupted. "Why don't you look at them and see what he was doing."

Tapes. Inside the cubicles. Ean felt sicker than he had a moment ago. Who would put tapes there?

"Let's do that," said the second guard. He hauled the assistant up. "Let's go back to the security office, shall we."

Radko looked unconcerned, but Ean could see that her shirt clung to her back with perspiration.

They called Radko's boss. Until now, Ean hadn't even realized that one of Michelle's security detail outranked the others. It was the woman called Bhaksir. She leaned back against the wall with her arms crossed and listened in grim silence to the tale. Then they looked at the tapes. There wasn't much to see. Ean, on his knees, leaning on the bowl to start with—he was glad he'd done that. It would have looked stupid if he'd just started singing—then humming to himself, and finally straightening up and starting to sing.

The lines reacted to the sound, and Ean started a counter-melody under his breath. "Don't worry about it. It's just your security replaying the tape."

They didn't like it. Line eight offered to destroy the tape.

"You can do that?" Ean asked, amazed.

The line replied an affirmation that wasn't really words, just assent.

"Not yet, and make it natural if you do," Ean sang. "Please."

"He's doing it again," the assistant cried. "Make him stop."

Thankfully, that was when they got to the end of the tape, where Ean staggered out of the cubicle.

"Doesn't look so bad," the first guard said to the second, who just shook his head.

"Radko," Bhaksir said, her voice as cutting as a razor. "Your job is to keep Spacer White in check." It took Ean a moment to remember the name on his pocket was White. She turned to the guards. "Our apologies. It won't happen again," and she looked forbiddingly at them both.

"Yes, ma'am." Radko sounded subdued.

Bhaksir glanced at her wrist comm. "Lady Lyan's interview has finished. We are holding her up," and she swept them out of the office in an icy wave.

Radko had to help Ean out. He was still unbalanced from the effects of the Taser.

Behind them, through the partially repaired line one, Ean heard Guard One say to Guard Two, "It takes all sorts."

Guard Two replied, "I bet someone pulled major strings to get him on that ship. Wonder who he is?"

"Don't know, but I want to listen to that tape again. Man can sing if nothing else."

There was a pause. Ean felt the wave of frustration that swept out after that, and they all heard the thump on the desk. "Damned electronics. They spend millions on the latest interview cameras but they're too mean to fix up our security computers. This whole place will fall apart one day, and serve them right." It sounded like a regular complaint. No music followed them.

RADKO started shaking once they were on the shuttle. "That was too close."

Bhaksir clapped her on the shoulder. "Nice job."

Ean was beyond shaking and suddenly so exhausted, he couldn't sit up straight. He didn't like espionage. He slumped into his seat. "I am never going to work for Galactic News."

"Because of their security? Or because of the assistants they employ?" Radko asked.

"Because they mistreat their lines."

BACK on ship, Ean showered again and wondered what to do with his clothes. Espionage was dirty work. Interesting that Michelle had come prepared with a second set and that she needed to use it. What else had Abram asked Michelle to do?

He made his way down to the workroom.

Abram had just finished interviewing Radko and Bhaksir. "Good job," he said to Radko, and she straightened at the praise. Not that Ean could see how she straightened because she'd always walked tall and upright.

Ean wondered if he should wait, but Michelle came down the passage behind him, so he couldn't go back. He went into the room.

Abram nodded to the two guards, who left.

"Linesman Lambert."

He should probably stand to attention like Radko and Bhaksir had. Instead, Ean helped himself to a glass of tea. It gave him something warm to hold. Michelle came over for one, too. Ean gave her the glass and poured another for himself. He looked at Abram queryingly. Abram nodded—was he ever likely to say no to tea—and Ean poured a third glass.

Despite everything, when he was around them, Ean still liked Abram and Michelle.

"So did we get the result we needed?" Abram asked.

How did he answer this without sounding even crazier?

Abram waited until Ean had settled himself on one of the couches—the couch he was coming to think of as his—then raised an eyebrow. "Linesman?"

"I made a deal with the ships," Ean said finally.

"You made a deal." On anyone else, the tone would have been icy disapproval. Abram just kept his voice neutral, with a slight uptilt at the end that denoted a question. "With whom?"

"With the ships."

He could see them both thinking that one over. Abram asked finally, "Was any human on either ship involved? Apart from yourself?"

At least he didn't flat-out discount it. "No." Ean warmed his hands around the glass. "I explained the problem. No ship wants to be vaporized. Then I made a bargain. I would fix their lines if they cooperated."

"And the ships agreed?" He couldn't read the expression on Abram's face, and the tone was still neutral.

"Those ships . . ." Ean was indignant just thinking about it. "Have you heard their lines? They're a mess. Neither company should be allowed to run a ship. Especially not Galactic News."

Abram finished his glass of tea while he thought. "So these ships want to be fixed, and that's why they entered into an agreement with you."

That wasn't all of it. "They don't want to be vaporized either."

"Who does?" Abram's voice was dry. "Are they likely to honor this agreement?"

"Yes." The lines didn't lie.

"What about shuttles?" Michelle asked. "I get that the ships will somehow stop themselves going closer, but won't they launch shuttles when they find the ship won't do it?"

"They'll stop the shuttles, too." Ean was confident about that. He trusted the lines. He looked straight at Abram. "We have to honor our side of the bargain as well. I promised we would fix them. We must do that. If I'm dead, we still have to do it." If Abram wouldn't, he'd do it on his own.

Abram nodded and made a note on his comms. "Understood, and it will be done."

Ean breathed out in relief. He might not like what Abram asked him to do, but he trusted the man. If Abram said it would happen, it would.

Abram stared at the comms a moment longer, then stood up abruptly. "Excuse me a moment," and left.

Ean knew where he was going. Who would believe such a crazy story? Who did Abram even have to corroborate it? "He's gone to see Captain Helmo," he said.

Michelle half shrugged, but didn't say anything. She'd showered, too, and damp hair curled around her face. Ean breathed in the clean smell of her and wondered what she used to wash with. Whatever it was would probably cost him a month's pay.

"If he wants a doubter, he should wait until Rebekah gets back."

"You and Helmo don't get along," Michelle pointed out. "He's likely to be anti anything you say."

Ean leaned back against the couch and closed his eyes. "Captain Helmo talks to his ship. He'd make a bargain with it." Rebekah wouldn't. How was she getting on, anyway? If they'd had time to visit two ships, then Rebekah'd had time to get as close as they would let her. Come to think of it, Abram had taken a risk, letting Michelle travel on a shuttle while someone could have triggered an attack. Either he wasn't worried she'd trigger it, or he was more desperate than he let on.

Michelle went to sit on her couch. Ean breathed in deep as the movement wafted more clean smell across. "Rebekah?"

"Hasn't found anything yet," Michelle said.

They wouldn't just be relying on the linesmen; of that Ean was sure. Who would be doing the other work? The observers or people on the other ships? Abram had implied that the other ships had been there longer.

"Why didn't you just do this whole thing quietly? Your other ships have been here—how long? Days? Weeks?"

"We didn't get a chance to do that," Michelle said. "Redmond has been planning to attack Haladea for months. The lines alone know why. There's nothing on Haladea except farms. Their only real export is the drug, starfruit."

Starfruit hadn't been popular in Lancia's Oldcity. Too expensive, and there were synthetic aphrodisiacs available. Although Ean had heard that the natural drug gave sex a totally different experience.

"What do you mean, planning? Couldn't they just attack?"

Michelle winced. "Taking over a world, or in this case three worlds, isn't quite as simple as sending in a warship. There is planning involved. Logistics, politics. Anyway, we all knew it was going to happen."

"And you didn't do anything about it?" Wasn't that the whole point of an Alliance of worlds? To support each other when they were threatened. If Ean remembered Rigel's lessons correctly—and how could he not, for Rigel had loved history—the Alliance had become an alliance to protect each other.

"We told them about it, naturally."

He was sure that would have been helpful.

"But none of us could do anything about it. We thought it was a back way into starting the war, you see. Because Redmond was now allied with Gate Union, so protecting Haladea could be construed as an act of war."

So they'd left Haladea to be gobbled up by the enemy. A bit like Ean was going to be gobbled up by the Linesmen's Guild once this was over. Or would have been if he'd destroyed the lines. Ean felt some fellow sympathy for the tiny nation.

"The Haladeans knew the Alliance wouldn't help them. So they did something smart, from their point of view anyway. They used their right as a member of the Alliance to call a security council."

Security councils were private meetings, Alliance representatives only. Every member of the Alliance had a right to call one, and other members were obligated to attend. Ean remembered that much from Rigel's training. Come to think of it, that particular piece of information had probably come out when the recent meeting had been called. Ean hadn't paid much attention at the time. He'd been busy mending lines, and he'd thought that Rigel had a cheek, drumming politics into him when he was so tired.

"At the meeting, they told everyone about the alien ship. They forced our hand."

Ean looked at her.

"Politics," said Michelle, and didn't even look apologetic. "We all knew the Haladeans would lose against Redmond although we didn't know at the time they were down two warships, and the Haladeans knew that if they brokered a deal with just one world, they had no hope. When whoever they made the deal with got the ship, they would still leave the Haladeans to their fate. So they made a deal with all of us. We get the ship in return for protecting them." She shrugged. "It precipitated a fight we all knew was coming but no one wanted just yet."

If Redmond took Haladea, they'd have gotten the ship anyway.

"I still don't see why it's so important to have the alien ship," Ean said. "Why not let Redmond have it?"

"A weapon like that can win a war. It's not something you want your enemy to get hold of."

"The media are here now. They'll send the information back to their networks. Redmond and Gate Union will know soon enough."

"You can't communicate through the void. Those ships will have to find a relay point to report in. They need a more populous sector to do that. Abram would have preferred you to have simply broken the lines." Michelle sighed. "We never expected much lead time. Not when every member of the Alliance insisted on sending a representative to watch what we're doing. We don't trust each other."

He couldn't have broken the lines. So he might have prevented them all from being vaporized, but he'd still brought the enemy.

Abram came back then, looking bemused.

Michelle smiled her dimple smile. "Captain Helmo says that making a bargain with one's ship is perfectly acceptable?"

Abram nodded. "Although," he said to Ean, "I'm to tell you that if you try to bargain with this ship, you'll be taking a spacewalk, sans suit."

Ean doubted this ship would accept a bargain without communicating it to its captain first.

Abram turned to Michelle. "You'll need to calm some people. Tarkan Heyington, in particular, is upset because you didn't take him along to the media ships."

Michelle sighed and put down her glass. "Back to work."

REBEKAH didn't get back for another four hours. She had nothing to report.

Abram switched crews on the shuttle and sent Ean out immediately to see if he could glean anything by getting closer to the alien ship.

They still thought he was of some use, at least. It was strange to think he wanted to be of some use to Lancia, to the Alliance, but even after they had tried to make him break line six, he couldn't blame Abram or Michelle for it. They were doing their best.

Bhaksir and Radko were two of the spacers who traveled with him.

"Don't you ever get a break?" Ean asked Radko.

"You get used to it," Radko said cheerfully. "You take your breaks when the ship's in port."

Ean wasn't likely to be on the ship long enough to have a break in port.

EIGHT

JORDAN ROSSI

THE FIRST GATE Union official Rossi had met with to discuss Lady Lyan's impending arrival had been a middle-level bureaucrat from the nearest world. He'd gotten the impression then that Gate Union thought Lady Lyan was the cartel's problem and wasn't interested.

This time, there were two Gate Union representatives, and they weren't happy at being kept waiting. One was Ahmed Gann of Nova Tahiti, the most important backroom manipulator in the union, the man who made or broke presidents. Rossi didn't know the woman—Jita Orsaya—but she wore her corporate clothes with an upright precision that screamed military.

Something had changed.

"Lady Lyan isn't coming here," Rossi said. She'd have been here by now if she were.

"She never planned to," Orsaya said, and Gann didn't look happy at that revelation.

If Gate Union knew, then Rebekah certainly did as well, but she hadn't bothered to tell him or Naidan even though she must have told her own cartel master. Gate Union could only have gotten that information from Sandhurst.

Sometimes Rossi hated politics.

He made a mental note to pass that bit of news on to Fergus to pass on to the Rickenback cartel master and to Naidan to pass on to her cartel master at Laito. Let them take it to the other cartels. Maybe Sandhurst was starting to move.

"Has Linesman Grimes contacted you yet?" Orsaya asked.

"No."

Orsaya chewed at her bottom lip. "We've three people on that ship," she said. "And not one of them has contacted us. Galenos's security is too tight."

Even Rossi had heard of Commodore Abram Galenos. "So you don't know where it is?" He was fishing. He hoped it didn't sound like he was.

"No." Orsaya chewed her lip again.

The bureaucrat and the soldier exchanged glances. Orsaya nodded.

Gann said abruptly, "We are aware of the political machinations among the linesmen. That Sandhurst will soon take over the Linesmen's Guild."

Not if Rossi could help it.

"Not all Union worlds agree with putting the power into one cartel."

But some obviously did because Sandhurst must have the backing of at least one or more Gate Union worlds. Interesting that he'd said it so bluntly and so early in the conversation.

But then, one didn't have to be a higher-level linesman to see that coming. Admiral Markan, of Roscracia, had been all over the vids lately, hinting at the need for stronger action against the Alliance, particularly line-related actions, like access to the void gates. Fergus, Rossi's ever-knowledgeable assistant, had pointed out that Iwo Hurst, cartel master of Sandhurst, had dined five times with Markan in the last two months.

Gann looked directly at Rossi. "We are concerned that she is passing on her information simply to her home cartel and that Sandhurst will use that information to ally with a certain Gate Union faction in the hope that both will rise to power."

So was he. Rossi kept his face impassive.

"If she is contacting anyone, I would like to know about it." Gann paused a moment. "It will be to both our and to your guild's mutual benefit."

Yes!

There was never any doubt in Rossi's mind that he would become guild master after Paretsky died, but it would be handy to have help taking Sandhurst down. He hid his smile under a tight frown. La Dame Grimes would finally get the ending her manipulations deserved.

Rossi inclined his head. He understood. Clearly.

HE considered, momentarily, keeping it between himself and Rickenback, but House of Rickenback couldn't take on Sandhurst on its own.

"Book me a meeting with Naidan," he ordered Fergus when he was back in his rooms. "A private meeting. And I want you to come." If anyone could find out what Sandhurst was doing, it would be Fergus.

He should have stipulated no food, but by the time he realized it was in the same private dining room as their initial meeting, they were there. Let Fergus sit near the wine spray then.

"You're becoming as bad as Grimes," Naidan accused when she saw Fergus. "Bringing members of your own house to every meeting."

"Hardly." Rossi felt better than he had in months. Maybe this was all he'd needed—something to take his mind off the confluence. "He has no lines, remember. Besides, I want him to do something for us, and I see no point repeating everything." He smiled, and raised his glass of Lancastrian wine in salute. "Why don't you invite Eda? Save you repeating everything later, and she might be of use to us as well."

So they waited while Naidan's assistant was called and came in from what looked to be a formal function. Rossi ordered another glass of wine while they waited and had nearly finished that by the time she arrived. He raised his glass to her. "Sweetheart."

She scowled at him.

"You finally made it."

"This had better be important, Jordan." Eda was like her boss, not one to suffer fools.

"We shall see," Rossi said, the wine making him mellow. "We shall see."

He summarized for them what he'd learned. "We're not the only ones worried about Sandhurst's trying to take over the cartels. Gate Union is worried, too, because there is a faction inside Gate Union helping them."

He could see that the news had rocked them, except Fergus, who always knew things weeks before anyone else did and had already pointed out Hurst's new friendship with Roscracia.

"Gate Union doesn't get involved in cartel business," Naidan said frostily and almost sounded as if she believed it.

Rossi didn't even bother to deny it. "They are also very interested in Rebekah Grimes's whereabouts."

"Half the galaxy is looking for the ship she's on," Naidan said. "The media will find her, and soon."

"Plus they knew she wasn't coming here even though she omitted to tell us where she was going."

"Do you think she knew she wasn't coming here?" Eda asked.

She'd known. Part of it at least. Otherwise, she would have met Lady Lyan at the confluence itself, and why would Gate Union have seeded Lady Lyan's ship with three spies? Which must have been quite a feat in itself, given Commodore Galenos's reputation.

Rossi ordered himself another glass of wine. "The union offered us a deal. We provide information about the whereabouts of la Dame Grimes as soon as we know it, plus any extra information about what she is doing, and it will help us defeat Sandhurst."

"How?" Eda demanded, and Naidan asked at the same time, "So what did you tell them?"

The wine arrived. Green Lancian wine. It was the only wine that would do given their conversation. He raised his glass.

"I accepted the deal, of course."

NINE

EAN LAMBERT

EAN HAD AS much luck with the ship as Rebekah, which was absolutely none.

"Maybe you should put me in a lifeboat and send me closer," he suggested.

Bhaksir, who turned out to be in charge again, vetoed his suggestion. "Not unless Commodore Galenos okays it first."

Maybe he would, but not while the media was here. For the moment, the media knew it was a ship, but they didn't know what it could do. Seeing a ship fried—no matter how small the ship—would change that.

HE was quiet on the trip back. He'd wanted to prove himself, to show that he could be useful. If he was honest, he'd wanted to prove he was better than Rebekah, that he could do things she couldn't. That wasn't going to happen.

And why should it? If he was even more honest, he had no real right here. Rebekah was the one they had chosen. He was just lucky to be alive. Michelle had gone in intending to kill him. Let him not forget that. Michelle might appear kind and personable, but she had deliberately set out to kill a man in cold blood for revenge.

Yet Ean still wanted to impress her. Impress Abram, too. Even though they were Lancastrian, and he had never expected to ever want to impress someone from his home world.

Stupid, stupid, stupid. The medic wanted him off the ship before the next jump. The captain wanted him gone, too. Both his employers—Abram and Michelle—were hard enough and realistic enough to do it. And they were prepared to destroy him as a linesman in pursuit of their goals. Even if he did come up with something, would anyone believe him anyway? Rebekah thought he was crazy. Even his stupid thoughts about the way the ship sounded like the confluence had turned out to be wild fantasy. Radko had proven that when she talked the same way about the normal lines Ean had sung.

Bhaksir came over to sit beside him. "No one expects the linesmen to work this far out."

Ean managed a smile. Was he that transparent? "Thanks."

ABRAM gave them an hour. "Eat first, then we'll discuss what's happened so far before we send Rebekah out again."

It turned out to be a major mealtime. Breakfast, Ean realized. He'd been up all night. No wonder he was so depressed. He should wash, he supposed, or at least shave—or depilate—but he went in to get something to eat instead.

Rebekah, of course, ignored him. He only looked for her the once. It would have been nice to know what she thought of her trip. He'd find out in an hour, he supposed. Sometimes it would be nice to talk to someone who was experiencing the same things he was.

Because he was feeling lonely, he joined Katida and Heyington again. They were watching the vids, two big screens on at the same time, one showing Galactic News, the other showing Blue Sky.

"Are they back already?"

Line communication within a sector was instantaneous, but if you wanted to transmit between sectors, you either had to wait for regular communications jump ship—which out here would probably be every ten days, at best—or jump into a more populous sector. For a story like this, the media ships would jump and come back afterward.

"They haven't been yet," Katida said. "Which is somewhat worrying. They should be back by now with more reporters in tow." She frowned at the screen. "I wish we knew what was keeping them here."

Ean had a horrible feeling he might know, and it had to do with the deal he'd made with the ships. Both ships had agreed not to move past the boundary. Maybe they took that as "don't move at all."

"The ships are broadcasting," he said. "Maybe they have a comms ship elsewhere in the sector."

"Their news is not going out of this sector," Katida said.

How did she know that?

"They're preaching to the converted. Us and any space tramps this far off the usual routes."

"Space tramps?"

"Free traders. We are so far off the regular lanes here, I'm surprised anyone found the ship to start with."

He'd never heard them called space tramps, but it suited. Free traders lived on the edge of civilization, digging through out-of-the-way places, always hoping for the next big find. They had their ships—mostly old and patched together—but they couldn't get regular work. Ean had heard that some of them didn't even have lines above six on their ships.

A free trader would probably have found the ship and sold that information to Haladea. Was he rich now? More likely dead. It wasn't information anyone wanted spread around.

Katida put an arm around his shoulders. "I haven't seen you all night," she said. "And you and I are both going off duty soon." How did she know that? "Why don't we use some of that recreational time profitably?"

He wasn't sure she even wanted to. There was none of the spark of the first night. Tarkan Heyington, ever faithful by her side, was exhibiting more sexual tension. And he was dressed for it, too, in a tubular top that came around under his arms and laced up at the front, leaving his arms and shoulders bare. It would have looked good on someone like Michelle, but on the Tarkan it just bulged. Why did some people dress for fashion even when it never looked good? One of the twos at House of Rigel had dressed the same way when she went out. On her it had been because she genuinely didn't know what looked good or bad. But then, who was Ean to talk? He didn't know much better although he did know what looked bad on Tarkan Heyington. Maybe Heyington still saw himself as thin.

Katida smiled at him. A curve of her lips; the warmth didn't reach her eyes.

Ean thought about calling her bluff but knew she would go through with it whether she wanted to or not. She was that sort of woman.

"Why do you do it, even when you don't want to?"

She didn't pretend to misunderstand him. "You're a ten."

She was an eight even though she didn't wear eight bars on her pocket. He could hear the lines vibrating in her now. She was more nervous than she had been last time he'd spoken to her. More worried.

"So why not nines?" If she slept with them because they were higher lines than her, then why didn't she sleep with nines as well? One of the threes at Rigel's house slept only with fours and above. Ean had never slept with her although he'd heard tales of others who had. Wild tales.

Katida's eyes narrowed.

Ean bit into eggs and toast, so he wouldn't have to answer if she asked anything.

"Because they *are* tens," Heyington said. "Because they're the ultimate line." He put a soft hand onto Ean's knee.

Ean moved it off.

Katida pretended to watch the news after that, but Ean knew she wasn't paying any attention to it because the tea in her glass didn't go down at all.

Or maybe, he thought, as he helped himself to another glass to go, it was simply that the tea tasted bad. It was the first bad food he'd had on the whole ship. It was so bad it made him queasy. He placed the glass on one of the clearing trays as he left the room.

THE meeting didn't turn up anything new.

Ean found it hard to concentrate. The night, and the day

before, were catching up with a vengeance. All he wanted to do was sleep.

The tea had left a bitter taste in his mouth. He ran his tongue around his teeth to try to clean them. It didn't work. Finally, he had to excuse himself to go to the bathroom so that he could wash the taste out of his mouth. That didn't work either. He leaned his forehead against the basin. Maybe he could go to sleep here, and when he woke up, the awful taste would be gone.

He took so long Michelle came to find him.

"Sorry." Ean straightened up. "Just tired," he said, and wished there was some way to stop making a fool of himself in front of Michelle and Abram. "Everything's catching up." He followed her back to the meeting room and knew he was walking like a drunkard.

After the meeting, he made straight for his room and was asleep before he even fell onto the bed.

EAN dreamed that a monster of noise came out of nowhere and swamped the ship. It was aimed at the lines, at line six in particular, but was indiscriminate and sliced all the other lines from one to seven as well.

He dreamed that he couldn't wake up to stop it.

Line six was destroyed, and in his dream all Ean could do was sing the fragments of noise together and place them somewhere safe, for later. *"I'll fix you when I can,"* he promised. They came, because they trusted him, because he had fixed them before, and waited where he told them to wait.

He dreamed—distorted through the badly damaged line one—that Captain Helmo was coming for him, rage and grief making their own song as he strode purposefully through the ship. "I am going to kill him."

He couldn't wake up.

Through the distorted line one dream he saw the captain come into his cabin. He really was going to kill him. It took Abram and Michelle and two more guards together to pull him off.

"What has he done?" Abram asked.

He still couldn't wake up.

They called the medic.

Captain Helmo tried to kill him again while they waited, and even with four people holding him off, he nearly succeeded. Ean's dreaming self pondered that there might be some truth about the story that captains went mad when their ships did. He couldn't move, even as the captain's fingers closed around his throat.

This was one horrible dream.

Then he did wake up, with the medic's scowling face above him. "Triphene," the medic said. "Probably administered it to himself after he did it to give himself an alibi. Although why anyone would use triphene is beyond me. It tastes foul."

Ean hardly heard him. The clamor of the damaged lines got into his head. His put his hands over his ears, but it didn't shut the noise out.

Line six was silent. It could have been dead, except that Ean could still hear the fragments in that special place he'd put them to keep them safe.

He wasn't sure if he was awake or if this was still the dream.

"I have to fix the lines." His throat was sore, and he had no voice. Was that from being strangled or from singing line six?

"You're not touching the lines." Captain Helmo's voice was as raw as his.

They took him back to the central office Michelle and Abram shared. This time he was definitely under arrest. There were at least ten guards, plus Abram, Michelle, Captain Helmo, and the medic. It was a squeeze. Why didn't they just take him to the jail?

Michelle was the only one who sat down. Ean couldn't tell what she was thinking.

"Did you do it?" Abram asked.

The broken lines of the ship reverberated in Ean's head, so he could hardly concentrate. He shook his head.

Captain Helmo seemed to have lost his murderous rage, at least. "Of course he did it. He's the only person on the ship capable of it."

"There is one other," Abram said.

"Two," Ean said. Katida could have done it.

They didn't seem to have heard him, and he was glad about that. He didn't want to get Katida into trouble.

"She was off ship at the time."

"Not that far off ship," Abram said.

She was fifty kilometers away from an alien spaceship right now. Then Ean glanced at the time and realized that less than forty-five minutes had passed since their meeting had finished. She had probably just arrived.

"And since the lines are gone, we cannot ask what Linesman Grimes was doing at the exact time of the impending problem."

Rebekah Grimes would never destroy the lines. Not like this. It was against the cartels' code of conduct. She had a reputation to uphold. Which only left Admiral Katida, Ean supposed, and if Katida had slipped the triphene into his tea, then the medic was right. It tasted foul.

"It's hard to believe that someone who refused to break the lines on another ship would do so on his own," Abram said. He looked tired. "Let's see the security from his room."

Communications was line five. Ean winced at the noise as the damaged line came on. So, too, did Captain Helmo. He wasn't a linesman, Ean could tell that, but he was definitely sensitive to his lines. Abram and Michelle winced, too.

"I could fix that," Ean said. "So it didn't hurt, I mean."

If looks could kill. "Engineer Tai is giving it his highest priority," Captain Helmo said stiffly.

Abram just shook his head.

They watched the video. From the time Ean had staggered into his room and dropped onto his bed—he'd almost missed—to where the captain had first burst in with Abram and Michelle behind him.

Ean didn't need Abram's soft, "Attack starts now," to see when the attack started. He could tell by the way his body suddenly convulsed. He started to shake, knowing what was coming, knowing that he couldn't stop it.

The figure on the bed struggled, and Ean hugged his arms close at the helplessness of it. Couldn't the idiot even move?

Then—still prone on the bed—he started to sing.

Ean looked down at the floor. No one would believe what the song was for. Not while they believed he'd destroyed the lines.

"I've never seen anyone do that under triphene," the medic said. "Maybe he wasn't under at the time."

Abram turned to look at him. "How long does the drug take to kick in?"

"Why, depending on the dosage up to an hour if he takes it alone. Ten, fifteen minutes if he takes a stimulant."

From their point of view, he'd had ample opportunity. He'd even spent such a long time in the bathroom that Michelle had come looking for him. Ean didn't look at anyone. He didn't say anything. Anything he said would incriminate him further.

The whole thing—from Ean's flopping onto the bed to Captain Helmo bursting in—was over in less than twenty minutes. It had taken longer to get the medic to come and dedrug him to wake him up.

After it was over, Abram turned to Ean. "And your version?"

He nearly asked what was the use. Who else could possibly have done it? But that was being stupid, and the longer they delayed, the harder it would be to fix the ship.

"I drank some tea at breakfast. It tasted foul, so I only had one mouthful. After that, I went to the meeting. The tea left a bad taste, so I went to the bathroom." He might as well mention that, because they would. "Then, when the meeting was over, I went to bed."

"And the singing while you were in an apparently drugged state."

He remembered the dream and his inability to do anything. "Line six." He had to put a hand over his mouth for a moment. "They would have destroyed line six."

"They did destroy it," Captain Helmo said, his voice raw.

"I can get line six back for you if you let me do it now," Ean said. He was going to do something as soon as they locked him up anyway. He just hoped they didn't gag him.

He was shocked to see Captain Helmo consider it before he discarded the idea. "No."

"You say your engineers can't get it back?" Abram said.

"Why not let him try then. He can't do any more damage than he has already."

Captain Helmo opened his mouth to argue.

"That's an order, Captain."

Did anyone give a captain orders on their own ship?

Helmo closed his mouth to a thin white line, but he didn't argue.

Abram turned to Ean. "And you, Linesman, had best make good on your promise. Go with the captain now. You are still under guard and under his orders. Understand?"

Ean nodded. Clearly.

"Is that wise?" the medic asked as the guards and a tight-lipped captain gathered themselves to leave. "He's clearly on the edge of insanity."

Ean wished he hadn't said that while the captain could still hear him.

Abram just beckoned to one of the guards. "I want you to go through the security tapes and find out exactly what both linesmen have done in the last ten hours. I want to know everything they did."

For at least half of those hours, Ean had been on the shuttle with Radko and Bhaksir and the others. That was some comfort, at least.

"Yes, sir."

Abram turned back to Ean. "You mentioned a third linesman. Who is it?"

So he had heard. Ean thought about denying it, then answered reluctantly. "Katida." And if she was innocent, he was sorry, but who else could it be?

For once he actually managed to shock some expression into Abram's reaction. "Admiral Katida's a linesman! A ten."

"She's an eight," Ean said. "But nothing above seven was harmed." Lines eight, nine, and ten were still there, still clear, although obviously agitated at present about the other lines.

"So we could still jump if we wanted to."

"If we had the engines," Captain Helmo said. Ean could see him testing the air, finally realizing that the higher lines were okay.

Abram said to the soldier he'd asked to check the security

tapes, "Check Admiral Katida as well," then said, "Dismissed," and Ean was carried out with the mass of them exiting the room.

THE engineers, all linesmen—mostly threes and fours, but there were two sixes—were already working on the lines. They worked with the shell-shocked expressions of people who'd been through a major natural disaster.

Chief Engineer Tai was one of the sixes. "You're letting *him* work here?"

They obviously thought he'd done it.

"He says he can fix line six." Then Captain Helmo surprised Ean by adding, "He was, supposedly, doped on triphene at the time."

"Convenient," Tai grunted. "Line six is gone," he said to Ean. "Totally."

Ean just nodded and looked around the crowded workshop. "I need somewhere to do this." He tried not to flush. "I can be . . . noisy."

"You'll do it here," Captain Helmo said. "Where we can all watch you."

The engineers and the guards. He'd never had a real audience before. To settle his nerves, Ean asked, "Can I get a glass of water then?"

One of the guards got the water.

Ean took a deep breath. There was nothing for it then.

His first notes started off-key. He never sang off-key. He nearly scattered the shards of line six, which made him pay attention and forget his audience. He couldn't afford to do that.

He hummed softly to get his voice back, then started to sing, soft at first, then louder and deeper, until he got down to the level of line six.

The shattered shards of sound started to knit back together. Gently, gently, for the line was fragile, coaxing them into position, careful not to pull too hard.

You didn't break lines on a ship, not lines that had been together and happy like this. If they had to put in a new line six, they might as well replace all the lines. The other lines would never accept the new one. They would never have been the same harmonious ship they had been.

He lost track of time, he lost track of his audience. This was his job. This was what he could do.

He only stopped when his voice finally gave out.

Ean gulped a glass of water—someone had placed a jug beside the glass—and gulped another one immediately after that.

He looked around at the silent engineers and guards, all of them just staring at him, and wondered how long they'd been silent for. His guard had changed, and Radko and Admiral Katida were there. Radko leaned against the wall, foot up against it, her usual pose. She was watching the guards and engineers. Katida was like the others, staring at him.

"Are you under arrest, too?" His voice came out as a husk of sound.

He was embarrassed about the question as soon as he'd asked it. One didn't, and if she was, he'd put her there, hadn't he. She probably hated him.

"I'd heard about you," Katida said. "But one has to really experience it to understand." She sounded like Kaelea talking about the confluence, or Radko talking about his singing. He had been so wrong about the confluence and the ship being the same because of the way people talked about them. Maybe if he'd been around higher-level linesmen more, he might have realized it was normal.

Then she smiled at him, just a baring of teeth. "I'm here because someone outed me as a linesman, and right now only you and I can fix line seven."

"And Rebekah." He was glad they had another higher-level linesman. This ship needed all the help it could get. It still didn't answer if she was under arrest or not.

"Commodore Galenos wants to see you," Radko told Ean.

He nodded. "I'll just finish line six," took another gulp of water, and turned back to the lines, preparing to sing.

Radko punched him in the stomach. Not hard, just enough to knock the breath out of him. He gulped in air the wrong way and doubled over, coughing.

It was the only sound in the workshop. Even the noise of the lines stopped momentarily.

"When the commodore calls, you come."

He nodded and followed her out, still gasping for breath. Two guards followed.

Admiral Katida's admiring voice followed them. "Who is that soldier?"

When Ean could finally breathe properly, he sang an apology to line six as he walked. He'd be back to finish later. Line six sang back. It understood. This was a military ship. There were other priorities.

He was bemused at that. He'd expected the line to take his side, not Radko's.

The lighting was dim. It must be ship-night. He'd been working all day. He was suddenly aware how hungry he was and how tired. He hadn't slept in what felt like days.

Radko led the way back to the central workroom. No one was there—except him and the guards. Then she left, presumably to find Abram.

Ean dropped onto a couch and lay back with a sigh. He closed his eyes for a moment; even the dim lighting hurt them. In seconds, he was asleep.

TEN

JORDAN ROSSI

"YOU KNOW THAT Rebekah Grimes left her assistant behind," Fergus told Rossi. "He's not happy. Not happy at all."

Rebekah Grimes went through assistants like other tens went through lovers. "He probably did something to annoy her," Rossi said. He knew Rebekah's temper.

"Apparently not. The Alliance refused to take him. He's not happy."

"With the Alliance or with la Dame?"

"With Rebekah."

Typical. Rebekah's assistants were usually chosen for their looks, not for their administrative talents. Rossi had always wondered if somewhere in the background lurked an ugly admin person who did all Rebekah's real work. She wouldn't have gotten where she was without someone trustworthy to do her dirty work.

Three days, and still no information on Rebekah's whereabouts. Rossi was starting to wonder if they'd ever find out.

"He and I had a long chat last night. He's looking to work for one of the other cartels."

It wouldn't be beyond Fergus to hint that might be possible.

Many of the nonlinesmen who worked for the cartels—
like Fergus—were halfway to being linesmen themselves.
They had tested for line ability, apprenticed to a house, and
done the training, but had failed the final certification test,
the one that determined what level linesman you were. Others were groupies, hanging around for the prestige it gave
them. Rebekah always chose the groupies.

"I've pretty much promised him a job if he lets us know
when Rebekah calls him."

Sometimes Fergus overreached himself. But not this
time.

"Maybe we can palm him off to House of Rigel."

"You wish," Rossi said. "Rigel is too tight to take anyone
who isn't a true linesman." He'd find a lower house to take
him even though the man would be expecting Rickenback.
"You didn't promise which house?"

"Am I stupid?"

That was one thing Fergus was not.

ROSSI found he was going to have to make good on the job
offer sooner than he expected. Fergus called him two hours
later. "Rebekah wants her assistant to meet her at Eco in the
Pleiades Sector."

"Well done," Rossi said, and called Ahmed Gann first,
then Janni Naidan. "We've promised Rebekah Grimes's assistant a new job," he told her. "At another house. Can you organize it?"

"Don't know why you can't do your own dirty work," she
said. "If Rebekah's not where he says she is, I'm not ruining
my reputation just to place him." For Naidan, that was a mild
grumble, so Rossi knew she didn't mind too much.

Jita Orsaya and Ahmed Gann were in his office before he'd
even gotten off the comms to Naidan. Orsaya was wearing a
uniform this time, and no surprise, it displayed the five stars of
an admiral. Her uniform was beige, which was such a neutral
color that Rossi could think of at least four Gate Union worlds
who wore the color. Carina, Yaolin, Garam, and Greater Be.
He'd have to ask Fergus later which one she was from.

Fergus just shrugged. He could stop most people. He hadn't even tried with these two.

Orsaya paced impatiently. "Let's go," she said.

Go where? But it didn't take long to realize that she meant Rossi was to come with them. To Eco?

He was engulfed in sudden panic. "I can't. I have too much to do here."

"What he means," Fergus said from behind them, "is that nines and tens don't leave. They can't."

Traitorous, traitorous Fergus who'd wanted to leave for months and didn't understand how the confluence dragged at you and filled your life so that you didn't need to leave.

They stared at him. He could almost see their thoughts as they worked through it, realizing that what Fergus had said was true. Nines and tens came here, but they didn't leave. Except Rebekah Grimes, who would do anything if the price was high enough.

"It's like a drug," Fergus said.

"It's not. It's—"

"The only way you'll get him out of here is if you drag him out."

"That's not the reason I have to stay. I have work to do."

The soldier and the bureaucrat glanced at each other. Orsaya nodded once, then took out her blaster and changed the setting. "Very well."

Rossi didn't believe she'd do it. "You don't have to threaten me. We can send someone else." Naidan maybe.

She fired.

ELEVEN

EAN LAMBERT

EAN WOKE AT a rough shake from Abram. It seemed only seconds later, but someone had brought in tea and sandwiches while he'd been asleep. Suddenly, getting some of those sandwiches was the most important thing in the world.

He only noticed that the guards were gone—Radko excepted—when he had the sandwich in his hand. The sandwich tasted like sandpaper. Radko could handle him on his own, he supposed. She had proven that already.

Michelle, whom he hadn't even noticed until now, silently handed him a glass of tea.

He wasn't sure he wanted to drink tea ever again.

"It's not drugged," Michelle said, and poured herself and Abram a glass as well. They didn't offer Radko one. She was obviously on duty. She even stood away from the wall, with both feet on the floor.

"Drink it," Abram said, and it was an order.

"Yes, sir," and he did, and even though he knew it didn't contain triphene, his mouth still remembered the bitterness, and he imagined he could taste it.

"Rebekah's shuttle hasn't returned," Abram said. "And two Gate Union ships appeared some hours ago."

"So she's been captured." His voice was scratchy.

Michelle made a sound that could have been a humph of disbelief. Radko looked openly skeptical.

Abram's face showed no real expression, but his voice was exceedingly dry, as he said, "We think it more likely she has joined them as a collaborator."

"But the shuttle is yours." They were trained soldiers, and loyal. He would have heard it in line one if they hadn't been. How could they be beaten by a single linesman?

This time Abram's face did show expression—raw, naked grief—but only for a moment. "Yes," he said. "The shuttle is ours, and the people on it were combat soldiers. At least whatever she did had to be fast; otherwise, she could never have taken them." He took a deep breath and drank two mouthfuls of tea before he spoke again. "The Gate Union ships are each exactly one hundred kilometers out. It seems they are well informed."

Ean chewed another sandwich slowly. Rebekah Grimes was a linesman. Under contract to Abram and this ship. She wouldn't break the contract.

Abram's dry, factual accounting went on. "Both ships sent shuttles. Both shuttles stopped fifty kilometers out from the alien ship. They've now returned to their parent ships, but we believe they will move closer next time."

"She wouldn't break contract," Ean said. "It means that no one would trust the cartels. Are you *sure* she—"

"You bastard." Radko launched herself at him, her elbow connecting with his chin, knocking his head back so that he—literally—saw stars. His teeth snapped together so hard he was glad his tongue wasn't in the way. He would have bitten it off. Hot tea went everywhere; the glass flew up and came back down to bounce on his head.

"Ten people are dead, and all you care about is a stupid contract." She punched him in the stomach, in the face, in the chest. Hard, heavy thumps that made him double over in agony and made his head ring. "And instead of chasing after them, we have to stand around while you sing songs."

Michelle pulled her off while Abram stood empty-eyed and watched.

Ean was just glad the future empress of Lancia was strong

enough to hold her own. He wiped away a trickle of blood, not sure if it was from his nose or his mouth. "You've already tried and convicted Rebekah, but you tell me how she can overwhelm ten trained guards." Or break lines. Linesmen fixed lines.

Radko stepped back to attention. Silent tears streamed down her face. She was shaking, but she stood tall and proud.

"Rebekah made two calls to Gate Union after our offer of a job but before she left the confluence to join our ship," Michelle said.

They were crazy. "You knew she was a spy, but you still let her come."

Michelle had found a cloth from Ean didn't know where. She wiped the blood off his face. "We needed a ten. At the time, we didn't know I'd find you."

He wasn't much use.

"We always knew the ten would work with Gate Union," Abram said, his voice back to the usual neutral tone he used when talking business. His work voice. "I thought I could manage that. I was wrong." He looked at Radko. "Dismissed," he said.

"Yes, sir." She marched out, head high.

"Apologies for letting my emotions get the better of me, Linesman." Ean heard the subtext underneath, Abram didn't need to say it aloud. Apologies for letting my staff hit something when I wanted to hit out. He held out his hand. "I'll get your comms fixed."

Ean handed it over silently. Somewhere in the fighting, Radko had smashed it. He hadn't noticed when. He picked up the sandwich he'd dropped, plus the now-empty glass. He went over to get himself another glass of tea and tried to stop his hands shaking. He couldn't afford to make a fool of himself in front of Michelle and Abram again. He took a deep breath and tried to concentrate.

Now that he was listening for it, he could hear the distress in line one. If he'd thought about it before, he would have put it down to the destruction of the lines.

He saw, out of the corner of his eye, Michelle give Abram's shoulder a quick squeeze.

"Are you sure everyone on the shuttle is dead?" Ean asked.

Abram's voice was bleak again. "I can think of a dozen ways a single person can disable a combat-trained team. None of them involve keeping the team alive." He shrugged. "We don't know. There's us and five other ships out there searching for that shuttle. It has disappeared."

Shuttles didn't disappear. Not without a trace.

"Can't you track it?"

Abram compressed his lips into a thin, tight line. For a moment, Ean thought he wouldn't answer. "It takes military know-how to hide a shuttle," he said eventually. "We're fairly certain it's on one of the Gate Union ships by now."

"We can't just march in and accuse them," Michelle said. "Not without proof. Not without provoking a showdown we can't afford to have."

Abram visibly shook himself, as if trying to force himself to forget the shuttle. "At present, we don't have void capability. We're moving everyone but crew and essential personnel off this ship onto the other ships, so they can jump if anything happens."

What did he expect to happen?

"Collect your bag and make your way down to shuttle bay four."

He hadn't finished fixing line six. And they hadn't found out anything about the alien ship yet.

"But I'm crew."

Ean looked down at his uniform. It had been an instinctive protest, but it was also starting to feel true. On a Lancastrian ship? Who was he kidding? He took another sandwich and chewed it, even though his mouth was almost too sore. It tasted of metal and blood. He was so busy trying to chew he almost missed the glittering approval of Michelle's smile.

Abram opened his mouth to argue. An alarm cut him off. Captain Helmo's image appeared on-screen, the star map behind them.

"A third ship has arrived. From the fifth quadrant." Ean could see it on-screen. It had come in directly behind the alien ship. It was already much closer than the ones within the hundred-kilometer limit and was still moving closer.

The alarm was continual now, a steady wee-wah that got into the bones and made Ean shiver. Loud enough to hear but not so loud that you couldn't talk over it. Captain Helmo and Abram seemed calm, almost slow in the face of it.

"Pilot would have to be Yannikay," Captain Helmo said. "No one else could get that close and still be going that fast."

"How close can she get?"

"I've seen Yannikay couple two freighters together."

It looked like she was planning to do that here.

They watched the screen as the ship got closer. Abram touched some controls, and distance figures showed up on the starfield. Thirty kilometers. Twenty kilometers. Ten. A green field started to spread out from the alien ship.

The alert changed to a wee-wah-wong, and got louder.

"That's our limit," Abram muttered.

Yannikay's ship flickered out. She'd jumped.

The Gate Union ships disappeared almost in unison.

Abram shook his head admiringly. "The woman can fly." He pressed more buttons. "All ships, jump when you can." He turned to Ean. "Line six, can it jump?"

"I—"

Line six sounded an affirmative in Ean's mind.

"It says it can." Ean wasn't so sure. "Jumping will probably destroy it."

"For the good of the ship," line six insisted, and line one as well. Ean just shrugged. "It says it can." The engineers had done good work. Ten hours ago, neither of these lines would have had a hope.

Abram nodded. "Do what you can." He pressed the comms again. "Bhaksir, stand down." She must have been at the shuttles. "We're going to jump instead."

It was one way to get out of going on the shuttle, Ean supposed. He wasn't sure which was worse. A shuttle where you would almost certainly get vaporized or jumping in a ship whose lines weren't strong enough. At least the saboteur hadn't destroyed lines nine and ten. But surely, if it had been Rebekah Grimes, she would have done all the lines. Although breaking one line would take less effort than breaking them all, and line six powered the engines that took you through the void. It was sensible, Ean supposed, and pretty much what Abram had planned for the media ships.

The green field kept coming.

"First shuttle gone," an emotionless voice said from the comms.

For a moment Ean thought they meant the Gate Union shuttles, then he realized the Alliance must have shuttles out there as well.

The green field moved inexorably out and engulfed a second shuttle.

"All shuttles gone," the emotionless voice said.

The green field kept moving outward.

The bell chimed for the jump. The deep, sonorous voice of line nine started in his head.

Ean readied his voice. All he could do was sing the pieces of line six together for as long as he could.

He suddenly remembered. "The media ships. They'll be destroyed." He changed his song to include a frantic warning on line five, and projected with everything he had. "Jump. Jump now or you will die." It was too late. He knew that a ship couldn't jump without preparation. The two ships were doomed.

Line ten cut in.

Another line came on as well. A line Ean had never heard before.

TWELVE

EAN LAMBERT

IN THE ETERNITY that was the jump, Ean had forever to hear the new line. A heavy, irregular thump-kerthump heartbeat that was out of sync with his own. His own heart tried to match the rhythm.

Line six was disintegrating. He tried to sing it back, but it had no reserve.

Yes he did. Three other line sixes were in the void with him. All were in bad shape, but one was stronger than the others. Ean called some of that line to him, to shore up his own six.

The other-level lines gave what they could, too.

Then eternity ended, and Ean was back on the ship.

Michelle sounded shaken as she said, "I wonder how far you have to be away from him to not feel it."

Ean's heart tried to get back his own rhythm. He couldn't breathe.

"We're still alive at least," Abram said, and from the sound of his voice, he hadn't really expected it.

"Maybe I should pay Rigel some more money."

The comms pinged. Captain Helmo.

Ean gasped and still couldn't get any air into his lungs.

Abram thumbed the comms first. "Medic. Here. Now. We've what looks like a heart attack."

The medic would probably say it was a good thing.

"Captain," Abram said to the main screen, while Michelle started pressing down on Ean's chest. Quick hard blows on top of the damage Radko had inflicted earlier.

All Ean wanted to do was breathe.

"Oxygen," Michelle demanded of Abram, and Abram dragged out an emergency kit from under the counter.

"Put it over his face."

Even with the oxygen mask on, he still couldn't breathe.

The medic arrived then, at a run. He already had paddles out.

Michelle stepped aside.

The shock jerked Ean up. Again and again, until he thought he'd die from it.

Finally, his heart found his own rhythm, and he could breathe again. He gasped in air.

"Commodore, Your Royal Highness." Ean had the feeling Captain Helmo had been watching, waiting for the attention to turn back to the comms."

"Yes." Even Abram's voice was hoarse.

"Three other ships came through with us. The two media ships and the alien spaceship."

Ships never traveled the void together. That way led to ships' disappearing, or both of them exploding when they came out.

Four ships together would have caused an explosion almost equivalent to the strength of a sun.

"Not only that," Captain Helmo said. He flicked up a star chart behind him.

Ean looked at it while he greedily breathed in oxygen. It looked like the same star chart, except that the stars were different, and there was no green field coming out to meet them.

"They all came through in the same relative positions," Helmo said.

"That's impossible." Abram stepped up to the screen, as if he could see it better up close.

Ean didn't care what was impossible. He lay back and listened to the lines. Line six was weak, but it was there.

"You did good," he said, but no sound came out of his mouth.

All the lines were there. All the lines were whole. And there was another line. The slow thump-kerthump of the new line. It permeated the other lines, changing their tone ever so slightly.

An alert cut into the comms. Engineer Tai. "Engineering to Medic. Engineering to Medic."

"Here," the medic said tersely.

"Admiral Katida has collapsed. Looks like a heart attack." He was gasping himself. "A couple of us are having problems here."

The medic left at a run. Ean breathed in oxygen and listened to the sounds. Abram and Captain Helmo checked statuses. Helmo of the ship, Abram of the people.

Abram made an early public announcement. "This is Commodore Galenos speaking. As you may be aware, the weapon on the ship we were studying was triggered by a Union ship. We have jumped out of danger. Her Royal Highness, Lady Lyan, will address you in the large meeting room in half an hour. Until then, please allow us time to ascertain the status of the ship."

He cut off the sound, and the comms squawked again immediately. Abram ignored it, but he didn't ignore Helmo when he signaled five seconds later. They must have multiple channels.

"Lines are fine," Captain Helmo reported. "Not good, but they're all there."

They weren't unchanged, though. Ean knew he should tell them about the new line, and he would. In a minute.

"Crew are mostly sound," the captain continued. "The engineering department is worst affected. Admiral Katida, too."

"Linesmen," Ean tried to say, but they didn't hear him.

"All of the affected are linesmen," Captain Helmo said.

"I see." Abram glanced back to where Ean was still lying on the floor. "The higher levels the worst affected?"

"Yes."

Abram grunted at that.

Soon after that, two paramedics came in. Ean hadn't heard anyone call them.

"Put him on a couch," Abram ordered them.

"We could take him to the hospital," one of them offered.

Abram and Michelle looked at each other.

"No," Abram said, and Ean was glad about that.

They put him on Michelle's couch. He tried to protest, but he still didn't have any voice and he was too weak to struggle. Faint, fizzy overtones drifted up and tickled his nose. It helped him to center and take back control.

Abram, Michelle, and Helmo were still talking.

"Fiendishly clever," Abram said. "And deliberate. Take out our engines—after incapacitating the only person on this ship who could prevent that from happening—then trigger the ship. We'd be helpless."

"But they didn't trigger it straightaway," Michelle said. "That's what I would do."

"Because they had people on this ship. They had to get them off. They knew that when this ship was damaged, we would send as many people as we could to the other five ships. They gave those ships time to get away."

"Or maybe just to give Linesman Grimes time to get to her ship."

"No," Abram said. "She had plenty of time. Ean had hours after the Gate Union ships arrived to work on line six. She would have had time to get wherever she wanted to." He looked to the screen. "What time did the last shuttle of evacuees reach our other ships?"

Captain Helmo checked figures offscreen. "Forty-five minutes prior."

"Enough time for the traitor to send a message to Yannikay, who must have been waiting. I wonder how they're getting messages through the void?"

"Katida will be disappointed," Michelle murmured. "That's another thing she doesn't know."

All three of them laughed suddenly. Stupid laughter, totally out of proportion to the joke. They laughed till tears came out of their eyes. What the spacers around Captain Helmo must have thought Ean had no idea. Even he smiled. The laughter was infectious. On line one, the whole mood of the ship lifted with it.

"Oh, and the media want to interview Lady Lyan," Captain Helmo said, which set them off again.

Abram eventually wiped his eyes. "It's good to be alive."

Michelle stood up. "I'd best go tell everyone what's happened."

Abram went with her. Ean was left alone. Abram was right. It was good to be alive.

THEY came back, still in good humor.

Michelle dropped onto Ean's couch. "So anyone left on this ship is loyal to us."

"It's not quite that simple," Abram said. He looked at Ean. "Do you think you could eat or drink something now?"

Ean wasn't sure. He ached all over, but that was probably Radko rather than the lines, and he needed a drink so he could talk about the new line. He nodded.

Abram called for food, then turned back to Michelle. "Neither Ean nor Katida were given a choice to stay. And although we believe our own people are loyal, we always have to consider they might not be."

Ean shook his head. Line one wouldn't be so strong if the ship had traitors.

Michelle patted his leg. "We know you're not. At least, if you are, you hide it damn well. We've talked about the possibility a lot."

Abram blew out between his teeth. "And I really hope Katida isn't either, but you can never tell." He looked apologetically at Ean. "You understand that we can never be 100 percent sure. We will always consider you a potential risk."

Food arrived then, along with tea. Ean was too weak to sit up, so Michelle sat beside him and supported him. He was conscious of the warmth of her body. Another time, another place, he would even have enjoyed it. He found time to be glad Michelle didn't know what he was thinking.

She held the glass to Ean's lips.

The tea still tasted like triphene.

It hurt to swallow—all the way down, even into his stomach, where it felt like someone had kicked him.

"What about—?" He still couldn't make any sound.

"Although," and Abram gazed quizzically at him, "I'm not sure how much of a threat you are without your voice."

Or how much of a help he'd be either. He was useless baggage if he couldn't sing the lines.

"Right now you're the only one who can possibly explain what's going on out there. Why those ships came with us. Why all the linesmen had heart attacks."

His heart still wanted to keep the beat of the other line.

"The lines." It was no use. He couldn't make a sound. He gestured impatiently for Abram's comms and stylus.

It was hard to even make his hands work. The words were shaky, and practically unreadable. *The line. From the other ship. A different rhythm.*

They looked at his words for so long that he thought they couldn't read the writing.

"Which line?" Abram finally asked.

Ean shrugged.

"You mean to say that you, of all people, can't tell which line it is."

"It's not." He took the stylus again. *A new line. A different line.*

They stared at that one a long time, too.

"Are you saying," Michelle asked finally, "that there's a line eleven?"

Ean shrugged, then nodded. Line eleven was as good a description as any for the moment.

Abram got up to pour them all some more tea. Ean thought he might have needed time to think. "And it's on that ship and somehow reaching across to cause heart attacks here. Is it a weapon?"

Ean shook his head. *All four ships.* He twined his fingers together. *Came through the void, and now they're . . .* He twined his fingers again. *Line eleven very strong. Like a heartbeat.*

"All four ships," Abram said. "It can't just be coincidental that, not counting the alien ship, the two ships that came through are the ones you made an agreement with."

Ean tried, unsuccessfully, not to flush.

"So it wasn't coincidence?"

Talking to them. His writing was becoming more legible,

at least. And faster, but it was still a slow way to communicate. *Telling them to jump. Line eleven heard and jumped, too.* It happened sort of like that, anyway. He didn't know why the other ship had jumped with them.

"So now we're linked to two media ships as well as the other one. Do you know how to unlink?"

He shook his head.

Michelle sighed. "I suppose I'd better give those interviews. They look like they'll be around awhile." She started to laugh. This laughter wasn't catching like the other.

"Sorry," she apologized, and wiped away tears of what could have been mirth or could just have been tears. "It's just so . . . Here we are on one grand, last-ditch attempt to save the Alliance, which none of us really believed would succeed. We came out here to collect a prize that may just prevent a war. We should be dead. Instead, we have the prize. And now we have our own tame media as well."

She wiped her eyes again. "I might set up that interview."

THE couches also served as an interview area. Ean's couch was the interview chair.

Michelle changed into a deep blue jacket with a lighter blue shirt underneath. The color brought out the blue in her eyes; the soft lights around her added sparkle. She looked good. She always looked good, Ean thought, but she looked really good today. Even the shadows under her eyes were gone, hidden with powder.

She faced the reporters' screen looking honest and trustworthy and every inch a future ruler.

Ean and Abram watched it in the large meeting room, along with the remaining dignitaries. There weren't many left. Twenty at most. Neither of the Tarkans were there. Captain Helmo joined them.

Sean Watanabe, from Blue Sky Media, had the first question. "Lady Lyan, has the Alliance claimed this ship then?"

Michelle's eyes opened wide, innocent. "The Alliance has always claimed this ship, Sean. After all, we found it."

Coral Zabi, from Galactic News, demanded, "Why force our ships to travel with you?"

Michelle's ready smile flashed out. "Primarily to save your lives," she said. "You saw what happened to the shuttles."

Both reporters nodded.

"That field wasn't going to stop. If we hadn't saved you, then your ships would have been vaporized, too."

"But why fire in the first place?" Watanabe asked. "If you control the ship, then surely you could have prevented what happened?"

Michelle's face hardened, and her expression became grave. "We are still investigating the properties of the ship. We knew—and Gate Union knew—that the automatic-defense system was still on. We knew—and Gate Union knew—that it could be triggered by any ship going closer than a specific distance. That is why our ships were so far out."

"So you're saying that the Gate Union ship accidentally breached that boundary." Coral Zabi.

"Accidentally, Coral? If you watch the vids, you will see the ship deliberately went close enough to trigger the defense mechanism. It jumped as soon as it triggered it, which meant it knew what would happen."

"And that," said Admiral Katida from behind Ean, "is as close as you get to a declaration of war without actually stating it as a fact."

She looked unwell, and a lot older than she had yesterday. Ean pulled out a chair for her. She dropped into it with thanks. "Heart problems. At my age."

Abram smiled. "If you didn't listen to the lines, Katida, it wouldn't be a problem."

She raised an eyebrow at that.

On-screen, Michelle was fielding questions from two suddenly animated reporters who scented a news story bigger than they had expected.

"And why is Lady Lyan declaring war on Gate Union? I thought we were preventing one."

"We are," Abram said. "But we cannot ignore a deliberate attack. Particularly not when the media were there to film it for us."

This part of space was less isolated. Abram estimated this broadcast would reach fifty billion people at least, and go on from there.

Katida raised her eyebrow again. "That's not Gate Union's style."

Abram smiled a hard smile. "Oh, I'm sure they didn't plan it." According to Abram and Michelle, what they had planned was that the media ships would be destroyed along with Michelle's ship. "The best-laid plans, Katida."

Katida rubbed her forehead. Her skin was parchment yellow. "Being in the hospital, you don't hear anything."

The medic had implied all gossip came to the hospital. Maybe it just didn't reach the patients.

"I don't like not knowing what's going on."

Ean thought she wouldn't have complained if she had been feeling well.

"And I don't like luck playing such a big part. I like to be in control."

"There's really only one piece of luck we've had," Abram said. "Lady Lyan's bringing Linesman Lambert on."

"That's not luck," Katida said. "That's just common sense. Pick the two top linesmen to do a job like this even if one of them does turn out to be a traitor."

No one had proven definitively yet that Rebekah was a traitor. She might simply have died along with the other shuttle crew. Abram had said they lost contact with the shuttle in the attack on the lines. Tai and his engineers had taken four hours to repair line five enough to call them. By then, it wasn't answering, and it wasn't on the grid.

Katida turned to Ean. "And how are you, Linesman? I see line six survived the void, which no one expected."

Ean smiled at her. It was nice to have someone interested in the same things he was—the lines. How had Katida lived without it?

"Speechless," Abram said for him. "Literally," he told Katida. "And that's where our luck may run out. A singing linesman who can't sing isn't a lot of use."

Katida studied Ean. "You've more problems than your voice." She looked at Captain Helmo. "Did you have to be so rough?"

They had no idea what she meant.

"Didn't he attack you?"

All three of them gaped at her.

"That's not . . ." But, of course, she couldn't hear him. Ean just looked at the two Lancastrians and shrugged.

Captain Helmo looked ashamed. "I didn't realize I was so rough," he said. "I apologize."

Ean shook his head and held out a hand for Abram's stylus.

"You were just one of a whole series of things that happened," Abram said. "Don't worry about it, Helmo. I'm more to blame than you." He glanced at the screen. "Looks like they're winding up." Ean wasn't sure if it was deliberate, but he didn't hand over his comms.

Michelle joined them two minutes later. Damp tendrils of hair curled around her face. Did she always sweat at interviews?

She dropped into the chair next to Ean and gulped the glass of tea Abram had ready. "Strong enough?"

"Admirably," Abram said.

On-screen, Sean Watanabe was still talking, but Galactic News had switched to the attack.

Katida stared at it. "That's Yannikay's ship."

She probably hadn't seen it before. She would have been working on the lines when the attack happened and had the heart attack afterward.

Katida watched in silence. "I cannot believe they let the media film an attack like that."

"I'm sure they weren't meant to survive it," Michelle said.

Ean borrowed Michelle's comms. *How does everyone know Yannikay is part of Gate Union?* The ship wasn't a military ship. *Couldn't they just say we did it?*

Katida smiled. "Here's some of that luck Abram was talking about earlier. Yannikay is the only one who could have flown that close to another ship. She's definitely the only one who could jump from there. And she works for Gate Union."

Michelle smiled at Ean, the dimpled smile. Ean couldn't help smiling back. "Unlike you, Yannikay doesn't hide her abilities. When she sees that video, she will let everyone know it was her. It was superb piloting."

Ean could see Katida watching them and wondered what she was thinking. Whatever she thought, it was probably wrong, but line eleven came in particularly strong just then, and neither linesman had time to think of much for a while except to concentrate on breathing and staying alive.

Afterward, Abram's smile was almost malicious. "Line eleven a little much for you, Admiral?" He ignored Ean's gasping.

Line eleven. You didn't have to be a mind reader to interpret Katida's thoughts. She pulled herself up with dignity. "I can see a lot has happened in my absence."

"Let me tell you about it," Abram said, and the two soldiers walked off together.

Captain Helmo stood up, too. He bowed to Michelle, nodded at Ean. "I'll be getting back to work as well."

With Michelle effectively on her own, dignitaries started to swarm. Ean recognized none of them. The ones he knew—Tarkans Heyington and Reynes, Governor Jade, Admiral Varrn—must all have been moved over to the other ships when the lines went down.

He wandered off. First down to Engineering, where everyone stopped work and looked at him, making him feel like a freak in a sideshow.

"You want to work on line six?" Engineer Tai asked.

Ean shook his head. *Can't talk,* he mouthed, and finally borrowed Tai's comms to write it down. *Just came down to see how the lines were.* They should give him a comms of his own, but he didn't think Abram trusted him enough for that.

The lines were doing well. They all needed more work, but they had good engineers here. Line eleven ticked an impatient beat behind them all. Was it his imagination, or was it stronger?

Ean handed the comms back to Tai, nodded at the other engineers, and left. An excited babble of talk started up behind him. He'd bet Rebekah Grimes didn't get that freak reaction when she walked into a room. Or maybe she did. He rubbed suddenly cold hands down the side of his trousers. He didn't fit in here even if he wanted to.

After that, he went in search of the one person on the ship who wanted to see him least.

He ran Radko down in the cafeteria.

It was crowded and noisy, and she was laughing with Bhaksir and some of the crew who had traveled with them on the shuttle. Ean would have left, but by then someone had seen him. The silence spread out in a ripple of jabs, and whispered, "*Linesman's*," until everyone was looking at him.

What had he done?

Radko didn't move.

He wandered up to her table. Might as well do what he'd come for.

She studied him, then flushed all over. He could see it on her hands as well as her neck and face.

"I didn't—"

He held up a hand to silence her and borrowed her comms. By the time he could talk again, he'd probably have borrowed every single comms on the ship.

"Well done, Linesman," Bhaksir said quietly from beside Radko. "I hear you saved the ship. And us. And our mission."

He shook his head.

"Hear, hear," said everyone around her. Except Radko. Someone started clapping, and everyone in the cafeteria took it up. Someone cheered. Soon everyone was cheering. Ean put his head in his hands. He didn't deserve this.

He remembered the comms, and wrote, quickly, *Later, can you show me the laundry please*, and passed it under the noise to Radko, who looked at it and burst out laughing.

"I'll do your laundry for you."

He shook his head. If she did that, he would still have to ask next time.

Still laughing, she got to her feet. "I'll show you now." It wasn't a real laugh. No one seemed to be laughing properly at the moment.

Ean followed her out, still holding her comms.

"I'm sorry about—"

Katida thinks Captain Helmo did it.

"No." Radko was horrified. "I can't, I mean. He shouldn't take the blame."

She'd really been a proxy for Abram, who couldn't do it himself, so if anyone should take the blame, Abram should.

It's done. And I've no clean clothes.

She laughed a more genuine laugh this time. "If you didn't keep sweating so much, you would still have a day's supply, at least."

He shrugged.

They went to his room first, and she helped him gather the laundry into a cloth bag with his name on that he didn't even know he had. "Always bag it. No one wants to find your smalls floating around the corridors." Then they went through a maze of corridors to the laundry room tucked away near some sleeping quarters.

"There's probably one on your floor, but I don't know where it is. There's probably even someone to do the laundry for you."

Abram had once implied that Michelle had a servant to do things for her, but Ean had never seen one.

He tossed his clothes into the machine, and Radko showed him the button to press to start it. "You don't have to stay around. Come back in an hour."

Thanks. He gave her back her comms.

"Why don't you come back to the cafeteria?"

He shook his head. Away from people was good. She left him after he assured her—via sign language—there was nothing more she could do.

"You know where to find me."

He didn't really; he was lucky she'd been eating, but he nodded.

Left alone, he sank to the floor—the laundry didn't encourage loiterers by providing seats—and leaned against a machine that wasn't currently in use. It was peaceful in here with no one to stare at him and no one wondering if he was a traitor or not. Just him and the lines. Badly formed lines right now, for sure, but when he got his voice back, he would fix that. And even now he could hear Engineer Tai and his people working on them.

It was funny that only lines seven and below were damaged. Surely that meant that whoever had done it had been a level seven. Or had they simply been targeting line six, which was the worst, and the damage had spread out? Who could do that to a line? Not Ean.

Line eleven was unhappy. Agitated almost. It was a pity they didn't have a higher-level linesman to calm it. And that was a thought. How would you test for line eleven anyway? That would shake the cartels.

He would have dozed, but the beat on line eleven kept trying to interfere, so all he could do was try to breathe evenly and not let it take over.

No one would know if he had a heart attack here. He'd be dead before they found him. Maybe he should go, but by then it was all he could do to control his breathing. He didn't think he'd be able to walk as well.

Line five became busy. They called the medic for Admiral Katida. She was either a very strong eight, she was a lot older than she appeared, or she had a weak heart. Abram, demanding to know where Ean was. Radko telling him she'd left Ean in the laundry. And finally, Captain Helmo's angry, irritated voice. "I don't care if it wants to talk to him. Tell it that he was damaged and that we are repairing him. When he can communicate again, he will. Meantime, it will have to wait." That went from line one to line five, then through the other lines, all the way up.

Line eleven quieted after that.

The emergency team found Ean then and dragged him off to the hospital. *Wait,* he tried to say, *my clothes.* But they didn't understand him, and no one offered him a comms.

He found himself in the bed next to Katida's.

"We're a fine pair," she said when she could finally sit up. "If I'm in proximity with that for too long, I might get a pacemaker."

Ean wasn't sure it would help.

They lay in silence for a while. He half dozed, aware of the music of the lines in a way he'd never been before. Aware of all four ships spread out in the emptiness of space. All four sets of lines were damaged, he realized. Even the alien ship's. They were a limping bunch of invalids.

Line one on the alien ship, in particular, was a tiny whisper of sound. If there was anyone left on that ship, they were in a bad way.

"Ean." He realized, subliminally, it wasn't the first time Katida had said it. He looked over.

Her fingers pleated the sheet that covered her. "Lady Lyan is—"

What did Michelle have to do with anything?

"She has a reputation. Her body is a weapon she uses in

much the same way as Galenos would use a blaster. Don't think that because she—"

Ean just stared at her.

"Damn." Katida breathed deeply. "You're a nice enough lad. She's a shark, that's all."

She could talk about sharks.

"Just be careful. And don't get too attached."

Ean could have told her that the first time he had met her, Michelle had tried to kill him, that Michelle owned his contract, and that was all. Instead, he just smiled his thanks and they lay there again in silence.

THIRTEEN

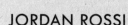

JORDAN ROSSI

WHEN ROSSI CAME around, the emptiness that had been the confluence ached inside him, making him lethargic and unable to move. Everything was dull and muted, even the normal ship sounds.

He stared around the cabin and wondered if he would die.

He didn't notice Fergus seated near the bed until he said, "You'll thank me one day."

"I'm going to sack you."

Fergus ignored him. "We're not going to Eco anymore, we're going to Barossa, along with every other sightseer in the galaxy. You should probably watch the vids before you get there." He turned the vid on and went back to his own comms.

Rossi was seriously going to sack Fergus as soon as he could get enough energy to call Rickenback.

On-screen, Coral Zabi was interviewing Lady Lyan. At first Rossi didn't even bother listening. He wanted to die, and failing that, he wanted to get back to the confluence as soon as he could. Maybe he could kill Fergus now and escape.

Finally, some words seeped through, and he realized he was hearing them for a third time. The vid was set to continual replay. Another reason to sack Fergus as soon as he could.

Lady Lyan. "The Alliance has always claimed this ship."

Coral Zabi. "Why force our ships to travel with you?"

Lady Lyan. "To save your lives. You saw what happened to the shuttles. That field wasn't going to stop. If we hadn't saved you then you, too, would have been vaporized."

Coral Zabi, looking at the screen. "According to Lady Lyan, Gate Union deliberately triggered the defense mechanism on the alien ship."

The video cut to the ship in question, and Rossi forgot his misery enough to sit up. "What is that thing?" It was a perfect sphere.

"An alien ship," Fergus said. "Watch this. It can only be Yannikay. Superb piloting."

On-screen, a ship appeared out of the void, dangerously close to the alien ship, and moved in closer. Way too close. Rossi clutched at his sheet. Every spacer's nightmare. Lady Lyan's well-spoken accents continued in the background. "That ship deliberately went close enough to trigger the defense mechanism. That it jumped as soon as it had meant the pilot knew she had triggered it."

They watched a green pulse travel out from the alien sphere. They watched two shuttles destroyed and the pulse travel inexorably closer. Rossi hoped the media camera was unmanned because it was going soon.

Then, suddenly, the green field was gone, and the star field behind changed.

"They jumped." He was stupidly relieved. "They cut it close."

Fergus sighed. "You weren't listening. They didn't jump. *Lady Lyan* jumped and took the media ships with her."

It was impossible, and Fergus should have known better than to even listen to such far-fetched rumors. "The media make up their own stories."

"Not this one they don't." Fergus picked up the remote. "This one is so far-fetched they don't have to." He flipped three channels in quick succession.

On the first, a serious-looking scientist was explaining just how impossible it was for three ships to travel the void and retain the same spatial ratio. "The explosion would take out a solar system."

"Technically, there were four ships if you count the alien ship," Fergus said.

On the second channel, two political commentators agreed it was a declaration of war. "The preemptive strike definitely came from Gate Union," one said.

On the third, a broadly grinning Yannikay was being interviewed about the split-second timing required for such a jump. The interviewer was obviously a pilot himself, caught up in the technicalities of it.

"Go back to the second channel," Rossi ordered. If he concentrated hard, he didn't notice the emptiness as much. Why would Gate Union strike now? Did they want the ship so badly they were prepared to risk a whole war on it? Or were they more ready to declare war than even their allies realized. "But why, for the lines' sake, let the media film them making a preemptive strike?"

He didn't realize he'd spoken the last aloud until Fergus said, "Current gossip on this ship is that the media weren't supposed to survive the attack."

"Then Gate Union should have made sure of it." He looked up as Jita Orsaya entered the room. Traitor Fergus had to have called her. She wouldn't have known he was awake otherwise.

"It did," Orsaya said. "But you can't hit something that isn't there, Linesman Rossi."

"So they had to know what you were planning and were ready to jump."

"Lady Lyan jumped," Fergus said. "She took the other ships with her."

"We both know that's impossible." Four ships together in the void like that—it would be like a sun going nova.

"Obviously not," Orsaya said, and looked around as Ahmed Gann hurried in.

He was out of breath, probably called by the same call that had brought Orsaya but farther away. Or maybe Orsaya was just fitter.

At least Gann had the decency to allude to how they had brought him here. "We regret what happened, Linesman, and if what you say is true, then we understand we have a problem with the confluence to deal with later." What *he* said. He hadn't said, Fergus had, and Fergus was a liar. "But you understand we didn't have time to discuss the issue."

"Maybe we should have discussed it," Rossi said. "Maybe you should learn not to take everything at face value." He deliberately ignored Fergus.

Orsaya seemed to lose patience with the small talk. "We have long suspected the confluence acts like a drug on linesmen," she said. "Particularly the higher levels. Can we get to our immediate problem now?"

"Go ahead," Rossi said, but only because he knew that once they stopped talking, he could do something about his immediate problem, which was getting back to the confluence. Some crazy part of his brain imagined he could still feel it waiting for him, ready to fill him with exultation if only he'd let go.

"We are working together on this," Orsaya said.

"Of course we are."

Her look told him not to compound his earlier stupidity with further ignorance. "The Gate Union factions are working together," she said. "We're meeting Rebekah Grimes at Barossa."

"Sweetheart, you don't—"

If she'd had a good reason, he'd be dead right now. "We expect you to work together. We want that ship. We want its secrets."

And they thought a linesman could give it to them.

"We'll be at Barossa in twenty minutes," Orsaya said. "Have your questions ready for Linesman Grimes."

Rossi nodded. When he finally managed to contact the House of Rickenback, he would demand they did something about Fergus and Orsaya both. He was a linesman level ten. They had no right to treat him like this.

FOURTEEN

EAN LAMBERT

SHIPS ARRIVED HOURLY to gape at the alien ship. Within twenty-four hours, space was so crowded the gate controllers refused to let anyone jump closer than five thousand kilometers. They still came, even though they weren't close enough to see anything.

Abram invoked martial law to force them to stay at least four hundred kilometers out and to have a jump registered. Lucky, Admiral Katida said, they had jumped to Alliance territory.

Ean didn't think it was luck at all. Captain Helmo would have prepared the jump. Of course he would jump to somewhere he considered safe. For a Lancian ship, safe would be somewhere near Lancia, he supposed, but he didn't ask. He didn't want to know.

His memories of Lancia were of always being hungry and cold. And of the lines. The music had been with him all his life. He'd grown up with the big line five at the exchange near the junction, the tiny two at the liquor house on the corner near where Old Kairo lived in his box. He hadn't known what it was back then, but the music had been as real to him as anything else.

Even people had music sometimes.

One day, when he'd been around five years old, the Cann siblings—Joshua, Marieke, Trini, and Wen—had taken him down to the spaceport with them.

"Because you're small, you see," Wen had explained. "There's advantages to being small. You can fit in spaces we can't."

His father said the Cann family was psychotic, but he said that about everyone in the block, and Ean didn't know what psychotic was then. He liked the Canns because they all had the music. So he'd trotted off down to the spaceport with them, more than a little pleased with his elevated role. These were important people. Joshua Cann had gouged out a policeman's eye with his bare fingers, Trini Cann carried two big knives she used to slice people with.

"Will I be in your gang?"

Trini had turned on him with one of her knives. "Why would you think that?"

"Trini." Wen put out a hand to stop her. "He's only a kid. Don't scare him." He'd turned to Ean. "It's a family gang. You're not family. But you can work for us."

"Okay." Ean had liked Wen best. Wen's music was kinder than the others. Deep and strong.

They'd skirted the spaceport, keeping close to the electrified fence that crackled and snapped with every step and towered so high, Ean couldn't see the top of it. They walked so long, Ean had wanted to stop, but he'd known even then it would be a foolish thing to do. He could hear from the grim determination of their music that nothing would stop them. Nothing.

The roar of shuttles taking off and landing got louder as they got farther around. So loud that eventually he put his hands over his ears to stop it hurting.

"Here," Joshua said finally, stopping at a spot where the fence didn't crackle or snap as it did in other places. He pulled Ean's hands away from his ears, forcing him to listen. "There's a gate down there." He pointed farther along. "When you get inside, go to the gate and press the green button. Got that. The *green* button."

At the time, Ean hadn't known his colors at all, but he'd nodded anyway. He knew buttons.

Marieke brought out a metal band and a pair of rubber tongs. "Make it fast," she said. "We'll have five minutes at most before someone comes to investigate." She'd shoved the band up against the weak spot in the fence, where it had flared brightly. Ean could feel the heat from where he stood. It hadn't been an adventure for a while now. He turned to run.

Trini and Joshua picked Ean up and pushed him through the hole they'd made. His ankle caught the side of the hoop. It burned, but he was too scared to scream. This was far worse than his father's beating him after the Juice man had been.

He fell onto the ground on the other side, even as Marieke's band of metal flamed momentarily, then disappeared. The crackle and sizzle reappeared.

"The green button," Joshua reminded him.

Ean ran to the gate. There were two buttons. He pressed them both. Again and again.

The Canns piled in. Trini had her knives out.

"Make it fast," Joshua said to her.

She came straight for Ean.

Ean turned and ran. Out onto what he knew now was a landing pad. He hadn't known then. He'd been so focused on escaping, he didn't hear the scream of the engines as a shuttle dropped down onto the pad. All he'd noticed was that the Canns turned and ran the other way. Then he felt the heat above him and ran faster. He put his hands to his ears to stop the noise, tripped and rolled, but by then he was past the danger.

Years later he realized just how lucky he'd been. It was a small one-man shuttle, he'd cleared it in time, and by then spaceport security had swooped down on the Cann siblings.

Ean lay in the shadow of the ship as the pilot turned the engines off and jumped out. He didn't dare breathe while the pilot walked away, and a security team carried off the Canns.

Gradually, he became aware of the music. Sad music. Hurting music. He lay, hands over his ears, listening to the song while he tried to work out what to do, crooning quietly under his breath, trying to make the music better. Because it was wrong to be so crooked, and he knew that.

Half an hour later the pilot returned. He had another man with him.

"I'd be grateful for anything you can do, Linesman," the pilot said. "Life support keeps failing."

"Payment up front," his new companion had said. "I wouldn't put it past you to not have the money." This man had music, too. Stronger music than anything Ean had heard before.

He heard the chink of comms against comms as the transaction was made. That was a familiar sound. His father paid for Juice the same way.

Then the man's music joined the sick music, and the music fought for a long time, but when he was done, the music was straighter, clearer, although it was still a bit crooked.

"That should do it," the linesman said, eventually.

Ean wanted to tell him the music wasn't straight yet, but he didn't move.

"Thank you," the pilot said. "I'm eternally grateful, Linesman." They'd both walked away again.

Ean didn't move till nightfall. Once it was dark, he made his way across to the gate, where he pressed both buttons and let himself out.

He hid every time he saw the Canns after that. When he was seven, they were part of a robbery-gone-bad in one of the upmarket shops in the Royal sector. In the fight that followed, a security guard was killed. Marieke Cann died in the shoot-out. Joshua Cann died not long after from complications to an untreated eye injury sustained in the same fight. A fitting end for him, Ean's father had said. Wen and Trini spent ten years in jail.

Ean had other priorities. He had a name for the music now. Linesman. And once he asked, it wasn't hard to find out more about lines and linesmen. He determined to become one.

He spent a lot of his time near the spaceport, trying to get close to the lines on the shuttles. When he couldn't do that, he stayed near the big line five at the exchange. Or outside the liquor shop, begging with Old Kairo.

He practiced straightening every line he came across, for the lines seemed to prefer to be straight. The liquor store two was the straightest line on Lancia when Ean left.

It was Kairo who had explained that Ean was unlikely to ever get a line apprenticeship.

"That's not for the poor like us," he'd said one day,

three-quarters of the way through the bottle of Yaolin whiskey Ean had shoplifted for him. Ean thought he might not
have said it if he wasn't so drunk. "That's for the rich, with
their money, who can afford to recognize talent when they
see it." He spat on the ground, or tried to. "And good citizens." Another spit, this one more successful. He waved the
bottle at Ean. "Keep stealing like this, you'll get a record,
and that will be the end of your line dreams."

Everyone in the slums knew about criminal records.
Everyone had them. It was almost a badge of honor. "What
do you mean?"

Kairo fell flat on his back and started to snore.

Ean asked him about it again once the old man had gotten
over the grouchiness of the alcohol-induced headache. "Why
do you say a record will mean the end of my line dreams?"

"Who told you that?"

"You did."

Maybe Kairo hadn't fully recovered, for he'd scowled as if
he wanted to deny it, then shrugged and said, "It's the truth,
boy. The line guilds don't take criminals. Don't take slum kids,
either. You might as well get the idea out of your head right
now."

"I *will* be a linesman," Ean said.

"Look at you, Ean. You're filthy. You can't read. You can't
write. You can't do your sums. You steal." And Kairo had
looked hopefully at the empty bottle beside him. "A criminal
record's an easy way to say no to someone they don't want
anyway."

"But I didn't get caught."

"I don't know how you've survived so long as it is. You're
too naïve for this place, God knows how. You should be dead
already. You'll get caught one day. And that'll be the end of
it. You've no hope, kid. Give up now."

The only thing Ean had given up was stealing. He didn't
want a record if they could use that to prevent his becoming
a linesman.

CARTEL masters occasionally came to Lancia to recruit prom-
ising youngsters. Ean approached them all. It took years of

humiliation and knockdowns to realize that while he was on Lancia, he would never become a linesman. More years of scrimping and saving—and yes, sometimes stealing—to get enough credits for the trip to Ashery, where even though there were four cartel houses, he knew already that Rigel's was the only house that would suit him. Or even take him.

When he stepped onto the ship to Ashery, he had promised himself he would never return to Lancia. He still had no intention of doing so.

Not even if the *Lancastrian Princess* was orbiting the planet right now.

Which, in fact, it wasn't. It was halfway across the galaxy, near a world called Barossa, an almost-forgotten Alliance world which most of the galaxy hadn't even heard of until now.

Preparations for war went on around them.

Initially, they were fighting over a ship, so the battle cruisers that arrived to cluster around them were primarily here to protect the alien ship and the *Lancastrian Princess*.

Abram was preparing for a larger battle. "If they move on us and that ship, it will be the start of an all-out attack on the Alliance."

He'd called a full war alert on Lancia, overriding one of the Lancastrian admirals who had protested at the need—at the cost—of a warm-start mode for the surface-to-space missile stations. Ean, seated quietly on his couch, hadn't commented on the fact that a commodore could override an admiral.

Even Katida was busy making war preparations of her own for Balian, the world she came from.

Michelle didn't think Gate Union would attack. "They're not ready for it. They'll pull back."

"They've been preparing for this a long time," Abram said grimly. "Starting early might not be much of a setback."

"But we have the ship."

"Which is just sitting there," Abram said. "If it continues to sit, people will assume it's not a threat," and they had both glanced at Ean and glanced away again.

Line eleven stressed occasionally, but Captain Helmo seemed to have that in hand. He'd tell the ship to tell line eleven that Ean was still being repaired. The information flowed up through the lines, and the new line quieted.

It was interesting that the ship listened to Captain Helmo, who wasn't a linesman. Current theory said that only linesmen could control the lines.

I feel like a line myself, he wrote on Katida's slate. Abram still hadn't returned his own comms.

She was amused. "Maybe you should keep thinking of yourself like that. Just another tool in the arsenal."

Katida always thought in military terms. Maybe he should think that way, too. If tools were useful, they'd be used, not discarded. If he made himself part of the toolkit, then they'd use him, and he'd get to work with the lines. No one threw away a useful tool.

FIFTEEN

JORDAN ROSSI

REBEKAH GRIMES GREETED Rossi as coolly as he greeted her. "I'm surprised you could tear yourself away from the confluence, Jordan. You seemed especially taken with it."

Orsaya, who'd accompanied him to the meeting room, promptly sat down and turned on her comms. Another admiral—this one four stars—had accompanied Rebekah, and he sat down and checked his comms, too. Rossi wasn't sure if they both had news or if they were pretending to give them privacy. The presence of the extra people made the meeting less awkward, at least.

He smiled an artificial smile at the other ten. "They must have paid you a lot of money, Rebekah." Even the confluence couldn't keep Rebekah away when high sums were involved. She had her own drug—money.

"Of course, but Janni must have told you."

It took a moment to realize she was talking about Janni Naidan. Sometimes he forgot she had a first name.

"But the Alliance didn't hire just me," Rebekah said. "They hired another ten as well."

That was impossible. All the tens were at the confluence.

"Ean Lambert."

Crazy Ean Lambert, who sang to the lines and did the lines-alone-knew what damage. "He's not really a ten." He'd thought she meant a real one.

"As he himself pointed out, he is certified."

"That's rubbish, and everyone knows it." If the people who'd been running the ceremony that day had more experience, or even if they had been able to think faster and call in someone who did, the whole certification farce would never have happened.

"He's certified, and he's servicing lines," Orsaya said, without looking up from her screen. "If you hadn't been so wrapped up in the confluence, you would have noticed that he's building himself a reputation. He's been doing all the higher lines for the past six months."

Rossi felt sick. The damage he could do.

"The Alliance thinks he's so good, they've taken him on." Even though they had come to the confluence specifically to hire Rebekah, and had their choice of every other certified ten while there, they had gone to crazy Ean Lambert. He wondered if they'd tried to hire someone else and hadn't been able to.

Rossi sighed. "So you want us to pressure Rigel to pull him."

Orsaya did look up then. "That won't do any good."

"Sweetheart, Rigel is easy to manage." You could bully Rigel or you could bribe him. Either worked.

Orsaya smiled a thin smile that showed just how much she disliked him. Rossi knew he had to pull himself together. The confluence was turning his brain into mush. He didn't normally make enemies of allies. He had the charm, and his was usually the voice of reason, which was why, unless House of Sandhurst succeeded in taking total control, he would be the new Grand Master and not Rebekah.

He wished Paretsky would hurry up and die and that the black hole inside that used to be the confluence didn't call so strongly.

"It's not Rigel you have to manage," Orsaya said. "Lancia owns his contract now," and she said, with some wistfulness, "I wish we had thought to do it."

Both linesmen stared at her.

"That's impossible," Rebekah said eventually. "He's a ten."

It didn't happen. The lower lines contracted out to non-cartel houses, but nothing over a six.

"Sweetheart," and Rossi knew it was a deliberate take on his mode of speech. "Didn't you notice the uniform he was wearing?"

"But that's—" Rebekah stopped. "He's useless."

"Lancia doesn't seem to think so," Admiral Orsaya said. "And after you left, he somehow connected with this alien ship and managed to lock the *Lancastrian Princess* and two media ships to it so that they all jumped together. Not bad for someone who's 'not really a ten.'"

"It was definitely the ship's doing?" It was a question Rossi had to ask. Imagine what they could do if they could bring multiple ships through the void together. He could see, suddenly, why the two factions of Gate Union were working together on this and why the linesmen needed to as well. If the Alliance grabbed this technology, they could take a whole phalanx of warships through to the same spot instantly. It would change the face of warfare and give an almost unlosable position to the side that had it.

"I want to feel the lines of that ship," Rossi said.

"We all do," Rebekah said.

"We are in Alliance territory," Orsaya said. "Commodore Galenos has set a four-hundred-kilometer no-go zone. The only level-ten linesman who is likely to get close enough to those lines to feel them is the man you denigrated just now."

Abram Galenos hadn't yet made admiral although it was popularly agreed it should have happened years ago. According to which media you listened to, that was either because Emperor Yu refused to let the man who was guarding his daughter be given his proper due, or that Galenos had turned down at least three offers of promotion because he felt it his duty to guard the Crown Princess. Rossi thought the former more likely. The Emperor could be demanding when it came to family—or so the rumors went.

Either way, Galenos in charge made it harder.

SIXTEEN

EAN LAMBERT

ON THE THIRD day after their move to the new space, Abram called Ean to the small meeting room. A barrel-chested stranger stood proud to one side. He looked up with a fawning half smile that faded as soon as he saw Ean.

There was only one person he could be expecting with a smile like that.

"Ean. This is Messire Gospetto." Messire was an old-fashioned honorific, used for artists and masters. One hundred years ago, Rigel would have been Messire Rigel. Rigel would have loved it. "He'll be working on your voice. Gospetto, this is the man you will be working with."

Ean smiled and held out his hand. He wasn't surprised when Gospetto stepped back.

"But I am working with Lady Lyan," Gospetto said.

Abram's gaze went hard.

"I am coach to the greatest singers and speakers in the galaxy. I am famed for my ability to bring out the best in them. I came here to work with Lady Lyan. The pinnacle of my career. Final recognition of everything I have done."

Abram said, "Lady Lyan has her own voice coach. Whom, naturally, we would have called had she been available.

Unfortunately"—and the bite in his voice was clear—"we had to settle with what was available."

Gospetto drew himself up, affronted. "I do not stand here to be insulted."

Ean had worked before with trainers who didn't think much of him. He held out his hand for Abram's slate. *I'll work with him.* If he was as good as he claimed, there had to be something he could learn. Besides, he was genuinely starting to worry that he might not get his voice back.

Abram blew out a long breath. "We couldn't get anyone else," he admitted, which was bound to endear him to Gospetto. "Do what you can. If he's no good, I'll send him away." He turned to Gospetto. "We want breathing exercises and voice control, so he doesn't keep straining his voice."

He left them then.

Alone, Gospetto stared at Ean in a leisurely way. Ean recognized the gaze. He'd been subjected to similar ones all his life—since he'd become a linesman, anyway, because no one really looked at slum kids. He hadn't even realized, until he'd left Lancia, that people like him were invisible to most people. It was the look that took in the plain uniform—with no decorations that Gospetto recognized—and the lack of expensive adornments, and said "you are nobody; why are you wasting my time?"

Ean knew how to deal with those looks. He stared back openly, taking in the other man's high-heeled boots, the bulge of fat around his stomach, which reminded him of Tarkan Heyington—did this man own one of those close-fitting shirts, too—and the fashionably plaited hair. For the last six months, Rigel had also plaited his hair.

"So," Gospetto said eventually. "Let's hear your voice."

Ean just shrugged.

Radko slipped into the room and took up her customary stance against the wall. They hadn't spoken to each other since she'd showed him where the laundry was, but when he'd come out of the hospital, the clothes were neatly folded on his bed.

"Well, come on."

Maybe this wasn't going to work. Ean tried to borrow Gospetto's slate, but the other man moved away as if he thought Ean was stealing it.

"He can't talk," Radko said. "His voice is strained."

Gospetto raised his arms and looked heavenward, like the character in a rock opera Ean had sneaked into once when he was small. "And they expect me to do something about that."

Everything about him was theatrical. As if he was playing a part. Ean wondered what the real Gospetto was like underneath all that acting.

Radko rolled her eyes and didn't care that he saw it. "You teach him how to manage his voice, how not to strain it again." It sounded like an order from Abram. "Breathing exercises and voice control." Her own voice dripped sarcasm. "Surely, even you can do that."

What had Abram told her?

"And that's really going to help when I can't hear how you use it," Gospetto muttered, but he set Ean to breathing and wasn't happy with the results. "You have the lung capacity of a Nend," and made Ean breathe deep and hold his breath.

"That's a myth," Radko said. They both looked at her. "Nends with no lung capacity. They just can't take as much oxygen as most humans can, so they breathe very shallowly off their home world."

"Suddenly a simple spacer is an expert on alien beings," Gospetto said.

He should be careful with his insults. There was nothing simple about the spacers on this ship.

"I used to work with one," Radko said. "And they're not alien. They're modified Terran stock. Like the Aquacaelum. The only aliens anyone knows about are on that ship out there."

Ean didn't think there were many of them. Line one was much too quiet. He borrowed Radko's comms. *Then they're probably all dead.* Or so alien he couldn't even recognize the line as people.

She read it, frowning, and didn't comment. But she did tap something onto her screen—sending it on, he suspected—after which she put her comms away.

Gospetto sniffed. "That ship is a myth," he said. "Something trumped up by the Alliance to start a war because they're scared Gate Union is getting too strong."

Did he realize what ship he was on? Ean borrowed Radko's comms again. *We didn't start it.* He didn't know when it had become "we" rather than "the Alliance." He was a linesman, logically allied to Gate Union. And he hated Lancia. Didn't he?

Gospetto pushed the air out of Ean's stomach and made him stand taller. "You can be sure there were machinations behind the scenes that made it look like that, but I guarantee you something the Alliance did triggered the whole thing."

DINNER that night was one of the interminable buffets. Katida joined Ean as he moved his way down the line. "This will probably be the last night we have the ship to ourselves. The evacuated hordes will start returning soon. Galenos can't keep them away forever. Unless you can pull a miracle out of the lines." And she paused expectantly.

Ean shook his head, suddenly not hungry. Gate Union and Redmond wouldn't wait forever either.

Nor would line eleven.

Katida patted his hand. "You can only do what you do," she said. Which would have been comforting except that another admiral came up then, and they started discussing exactly how long it would take before one of the idiot sightseers ventured too close and fried themselves and every other ship in the vicinity.

Gospetto was talking to two dignitaries—he obviously considered the military lesser beings—near the salad bar. The dignitaries hung on every word. He saw Ean and didn't, quite, move away. He was as bad as Rebekah. Ean just smiled and reached past him for some salad he didn't really want.

"Fresh greens," Michelle said from behind him. "You can't believe how much I want some."

Gospetto homed in faster even than Governor Jade. "Lady Lyan."

"Messire Gospetto," Michelle said. "I hear you're not happy with your present task."

Gospetto drew himself up to his full height. "I don't know where you got that idea," he said, and the way he deliberately didn't look at Ean showed exactly where he knew the idea had come from. "I am sure you are mistaken."

Michelle leaned in close and pitched her voice low enough

so that only Ean and Gospetto could hear. "Don't ever call my head of security a liar again." Then she straightened and smiled at a dignitary standing across from them. "Senator Yee, and how is your government taking these latest events?"

"Not well at all," the senator admitted. "I just wish something would happen."

"Don't we all," Michelle said, and wandered off with the senator. She hadn't gotten any greens.

Ean was left alone with Gospetto.

"I suppose I deserved that," Gospetto said. "But it doesn't make me like you any better."

Ean just shrugged and piled a clean plate with salad, then didn't know what to do with it. One of the soldiers clearing plates took it out of his hands and whisked it over to the table where Michelle and Senator Yee were now sitting. Ean nodded his thanks. This ship looked after their princess. They always had.

Line one hummed suddenly with pleasure.

It was funny that Captain Helmo talked to the ship and managed the lines, but the happiness of line one depended more on the happiness of Michelle—and the whole crew, really—than just on Helmo. It was funny, too, that none of them were linesmen. If you listened to the guild, the only people who had any influence on the lines were linesmen, which obviously wasn't true. Maybe the lines communicated with everyone, not just a select few. Yet only that select few communicated back.

Ean stared at Michelle's table, not really seeing the guests around it. Linesmen were so convinced the lines needed them. But did they, really? Did they simply need people?

THE next morning Ean had a thread of voice back. He doubted it was anything Gospetto had done but was sure he would claim it, and he did.

"But you mustn't speak," Gospetto said. "You should rest it for another week, at least."

As if that was likely to happen. "There's a war on."

Gospetto waved an airy hand. "Don't believe everything you hear on the media." He leaned close. "This is a plot, set up by the Alliance because they are scared that in the future, Gate Union will come to rival their power. That's how incumbent governments work. Cut them down before they become a threat."

The future he was talking about was now. Should he remind Gospetto he was on an Alliance ship?

"If they were serious about war," Gospetto said, "they'd be using that ship out there to threaten Gate Union. Instead, it just sits there. It's empty threats, my boy, empty threats."

The only reason they weren't using the ship was because *Ean* didn't have any control right now. Ean thought his grasp of politics was subtly better than his voice coach's.

"Now, let's see you breathe."

They did breathing exercises for an hour, then Gospetto told him to come back in the afternoon.

Ean took sanctuary on the couch in Abram and Michelle's workroom. He was dozing on his couch—Michelle's interview couch—listening to the lines, when Abram and Michelle came in.

"We can't fob the dignitaries off with broken lines forever." Abram was blackly pessimistic. "They're building all these paranoid theories about what we're doing and why we're not bringing them back now the danger is over. We'll have to let them return."

"I could go out to them," Michelle suggested. "Shuttle between the three ships."

Abram shuddered. "No Misha. That's a security nightmare."

Ean stood up.

"Stay," Abram said. "We know where you are all the time. It's easier to watch you in person than watch the vids."

Everywhere he went? Ean sat down again. It was almost as bad as being on the media ships.

"No," Abram said to Michelle. "I'd rather bring the traitors back on ship. We'll have a better chance."

"I thought Rebekah was the traitor," Ean said, husky-voiced, then wished he'd kept silent. "She's gone."

Abram poured them all glasses of the requisite tea. "Rebekah wasn't working on her own."

Michelle brought Ean's tea over for him. "We have

representatives from every Alliance nation here. Nations always look after themselves first, the Alliance second. Even Lancia does. If I thought Lancia was better off without the Alliance, I'd be ditching them, too."

Once Ean would have believed that. Emperor Yu would desert his allies if it would benefit him, but his daughter wouldn't. She was honorable.

"I would." Michelle went back to pace around the center console, while Ean pondered the unreality of using the word "honorable" to describe a member of the Lancastrian royal family. But it fit.

Michelle said, "Even those left here ask why we aren't doing anything. I'm running out of excuses."

"Why don't you tell them the truth?" Ean asked. That they were stuck here because he, Ean, couldn't help them.

Michelle came back to drop gracefully onto her own couch. "Would you tell anyone—enemy or friend—that your only weapon is helpless right now?"

At least they thought of him as a weapon. Or more likely they thought of the ship as the weapon and him a faulty tool that might or might not be able to make it useful.

"Don't fret it," Abram said. "Our public stance is good for a few days yet. We didn't start this thing. They did. Of course we're not taking preemptive action."

Abram tapped, unthinking, on the console. Ean wondered if he realized the beat matched that of line eleven. "And our original argument still holds. Line six is weak. If—when— the alien ship fires, we cannot guarantee their safety."

"And that's another issue altogether," Michelle said, and Abram nodded. "The best military in the world can't keep everyone out forever. Someone will slip through the exclusion zone eventually. Probably the media. And when that ship triggers, it will be a PR nightmare."

Abram seemed to have come to a decision. Ean wasn't sure if the talking had helped or he'd planned on doing it anyway. "I'll warn the diplomats and military on the other ships that we cannot guarantee their safety but that they are welcome to come back if they wish." He looked frowningly over them both. "And full protective gear, Misha. All the time. Even when you're alone."

Michelle made a face.

Abram turned his full frown onto Ean. "I'll order a suit for you, too. It will take around a week. Meantime, be careful."

THE first shuttleload of diplomats arrived midafternoon. Ean got into the lift to go to his afternoon session with Gospetto and found himself pressed up against Tarkan Heyington and Admiral Varrn. Radko squeezed in as well.

"Linesman," and the Tarkan pressed closer. "It is good to see you."

Ean smiled and nodded at them both.

Radko got out at the same floor Ean did and followed him to the meeting room.

"Am I under guard again?" His voice was improving slowly.

She rolled her eyes. "I'm supposed to be protecting you," and leaned against the wall while Gospetto ran through the breathing exercises.

At dinner that night, Katida said, "Good to see you have some voice back. You'll need it soon. Galenos and Lady Lyan are under increasing pressure to do something."

He glanced around. For the moment, they were alone. "Do you think there are traitors on board?"

Katida rubbed her forehead as if a headache was starting. "Why don't you come back with me when this is over? Some time in my military would do your paranoia a lot of good."

"So you think I am paranoid?"

"Ean"—and she leaned close because they could see Tarkan Heyington making for their table—"you should treat everyone as a potential traitor. Even me."

"But you—" By then, the Tarkan was slipping into the seat on the other side of Ean.

NEXT day the small meeting room was in use. Radko found a quiet passage where the three of them could stand.

"This is outrageous," Gospetto said. "I demand to see the commodore. I cannot work like this."

"Just do it." Ean had more voice back today. He actually had some volume.

"You should not be talking yet."

Gospetto crossed his arms and raised himself to his full height—in heels—and glared at them both. "Commodore Galenos. Now."

"He's busy," Radko said flatly. She crossed her arms and stared him down.

There was no question who would win the staring contest. Ean stood, breathing in fully as Gospetto had taught him, and waited for his voice tutor to accept it.

Finally, Gospetto muttered, "I *will* talk to him about this, whether you like it or not," and started Ean on breathing exercises.

Half an hour later, Gospetto said, "So, let's hear you hum."

This was it. There was no way he could hum without the lines hearing him, and Katida had hinted last night that he had to talk to them soon. Ean took a deep breath and hummed direct to the lines.

Line eleven came in, loud and powerful, and sent Ean to his knees.

"Not like that," Gospetto said, but Ean ignored him.

"Not so strong," he begged, giving up the humming for real voice with the little breath he had left. "I can't . . . I am very weak," and thankfully the line calmed to something that allowed him to breathe.

Every other line on all four of the ships was listening, and Ean could feel each of them pouring in support, shoring up the line—his line—as best they could. He realized, bemusedly, that they were mending him. Lines didn't mend humans. Humans mended lines.

"No." They were all weak. "You can't afford to waste your own strength."

"I said stop," Gospetto screamed, and grabbed Ean and shook him. A detached part of Ean noted that he wasn't using any voice control at all.

Radko reached out to stop Gospetto, but four line eights reacted simultaneously—before Radko had even moved away from her wall—to repel him in a sonic boom. He hit the other side of the tiny corridor with a thump that made Ean's teeth rattle.

Gospetto turned a funny green color and started to choke.

Ean's bones ached with the lines.

Gospetto's comms had fallen into the middle of the corridor. The front was shattered, but the speaker still worked. "Messire Gospetto." Abram's crisp voice. "You said he couldn't sing for another four days. What is going on?"

Abram couldn't possibly have heard Ean sing. Unless he was still getting the residue from their first trip through the void. Or maybe he was watching through the comms.

Radko picked up the comms. "He looks like he's having a heart attack, sir."

"Lambert?"

"Gospetto."

"Line eleven is giving *Gospetto* a heart attack?" Even Ean could hear the skepticism in Abram's voice.

Radko glanced over at Ean. "More like line twelve, sir."

"Line—"

"You should watch the security tapes, sir. And I need to do something about Gospetto before he dies on us." Radko clicked off.

Paramedics arrived then and made straight for Ean. He knelt in the corridor and rested his forehead on the rubber floor. "I'm good. Look after him," but they insisted on checking Ean first, leaving Radko to deal with Gospetto.

"I'm fine." He just wanted to sit for a minute, but the lines were insistent. One of the paramedics helped him to his feet while the other moved across to help Radko. "I'm fine," he sang again to the lines, and they finally quieted. Ean slid to the floor, where he sat with his back against the wall.

Radko came over to crouch beside him while the paramedics—both of them now—worked on Gospetto. "You okay?"

He felt like a giant tuning fork.

"I don't— I haven't got any control." His voice came out louder and with more power than he'd expected, so strong that it echoed in the passageway. Gospetto moaned at the sound, or maybe he just moaned. Ean stopped, and said softly, "I can talk." He could talk. "I can talk," more loudly. It wasn't full strength yet, but whatever the lines had done as support had definitely improved his vocal cords.

"What do you think the lines are, Radko?"

"Had you asked me that ten days ago, I would have spouted something about lines of energy, Havortian fields, and other rubbish." The classic textbook answer. She dropped from her crouch to sit beside him and lean against the wall, too, as they watched the paramedics. "Now, I have absolutely no idea."

"Neither do I."

One of the paramedics said, "He's stable." They loaded Gospetto onto the stretcher. Strange to realize they had come prepared already with a stretcher. They disappeared down the corridor with their load. Ean and Radko remained sitting.

Eventually, Ean said, "It wasn't funny. That joke about line twelve."

"It wasn't a joke."

"Oh."

They sat in silence for a time. Ean was just about to get up when Radko said, "Are you human, Ean?"

What was human? To a Lancastrian noble, a boy from the slums was less than human, but a linesman wasn't. Yet he was still the same person. At the moment Ean didn't feel very human. He had more affinity with the lines than he did with other people. Going through the void had changed him, and kept changing him every time he did. Surely it affected other linesmen the same way. Or maybe Rebekah Grimes was right. Maybe he was crazy.

No one knew how the lines worked, even now, five hundred years after their discovery. Lines were energy. And certain humans had an affinity with that energy.

Most people didn't even believe lines were sentient. Ean did. Today, they had even tried to mend him. Ean, a human, who wasn't a line. If that wasn't sentience, what was it?

As to what made a linesman, no one knew that either. There was no particular gene that said, "this person has an affinity for that particular energy." Or not that they had discovered. You either had it, or you didn't.

There were tests you could do to show if you had the potential to become a linesman. Basic tests like perfect pitch and a tendency to left-handedness. Or more advanced ones like how your right auditory cortex responded to the Havortian line tests. But it didn't always show true. Some people did well on the tests, went into the cartels, and studied for years but couldn't pass certification.

Of course there were lots of theories, but until Ean had contracted to Rigel, all he'd had access to were the rumors and wild stories. One popular theory in the slums had been that it was caused by radiation and that the linesmen were irradiated in secret by their government before birth. Another theory was that the linesmen were aliens, planted among the humans by the line owners.

Ean thought he was human, but Radko's question was reasonable under the circumstances. "You could ask the medic," although he thought Ean was crazy. "Maybe there is something wrong with me."

Radko stood up, a long unfolding of legs. "That sort of wrong I wouldn't mind having," she said.

Even if he was crazy, Ean would die rather than lose the lines. "The music—" was indescribable. He followed her down the corridor. "I'd better go see if Captain Helmo will let me talk to the lines."

"Let's see Commodore Galenos first."

They were halfway to the workroom when line one sounded a distress note.

SEVENTEEN

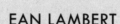

EAN LAMBERT

"SOMETHING'S WRONG," EAN said. He started running. "Where?" he asked, but line one couldn't tell him.

He could be running away from the problem.

"Call Abram," he ordered Radko.

She loped after him, touching her comms as she went. "Linesman says there's a problem, sir."

"Ask him—" Ask him what? Ean stopped. Line one was people. "Ask him where Michelle is." Start with the thing most important to the ship and work down. Michelle was the logical place to start because the lives of everyone on the ship revolved around her.

"He wants to know where Princess Michelle is, sir."

Abram's voice came strong out of the comms. "Shuttle bay. She went down with Tarkan Heyington and Admiral Varrn to meet the latest shuttle."

Radko took the lead this time, at a fast run. Ean just managed to keep her in sight.

The air lock to the shuttle bay was locked. That usually meant a ship coming in—but wouldn't that mean Michelle was this side of the triple doors, not the other?

"Shit." Radko pounded on the wall in frustration.

Ean checked the lines. Line three controlled the doors and line two the oxygen. "The outer bay isn't open," he said. He hoped he was hearing them right. "There's air in there."

Radko called Helmo. "Captain. We need to get into the shuttle bay. Now. Override please."

Captain Helmo's grim voice came back seconds later. "Override's not working," and the Klaxon blare of an emergency siren started. A group of soldiers rounded the corridor behind them—too soon for the emergency signal. Abram must have sent them.

They didn't even know if this was where the problem was yet. When things quieted down, Ean was going to learn how to communicate properly with the ship.

Ean pressed the door button. "Open the door. Please," he sang, and felt line eight through his bones as it connected through him to the ship and reached in and unlocked it for him.

Radko, who was still touching the wall, vibrated in time. Her hair stood out from her head.

They both fell—literally—through the door.

It saved their lives.

Weapons fired over their heads, chest high.

Two of the soldiers behind them went down. Line one keened a long, high note.

In a frozen moment, Ean saw Admiral Varrn standing beside Michelle, a weapon pointed at her back. Ean wouldn't have seen it if he had been standing. There were bodies everywhere, all of them in gray uniforms with black piping.

Then two spacers on the shuttle fired on him and Radko.

"No." Michelle jumped to protect Ean.

The force of the firearms spun her around, so that she fell on her back as she dropped to the floor.

"Hold your fire," Admiral Varrn called in the frozen second that followed. "Hold your fire," with Tarkan Heyington a panicked echo behind him.

It was a standoff. Abram's half dozen against what had to be thirty armed soldiers on the shuttle. What had happened to the shuttle pilot and crew?

Varrn used his blaster to usher Abram's people into the shuttle bay proper. "Close the door," and one of the enemy came across and did so.

"Throw down your weapons," and Abram's people, unwillingly, did so. Even Radko.

"Kill them all?" the man who'd closed the door asked.

"Load them," Varrn ordered. "We'll kill them later. Ship won't open the doors with warm bodies in the bay, even dead ones. It will take too long." He gestured to Abram's people. "You carry Lady Lyan's body."

Ean lay, numb, while four white-faced soldiers reached down to pick up Michelle.

"The others as well. Even the dead ones," Varrn ordered, pointing to the two who had been shot at the doorway. "They're still warm."

They all picked up a body to drag. Varrn's soldiers collected the others. Radko, who'd picked up one of the bodies that had already been on the floor, muttered to Ean, "This one's still alive."

Ean's wasn't. His was definitely dead. A huge burn had blown half his face and chest away. He looked toward Michelle. Both weapons had landed on her chest and torso— they had fired down—so her face was unmarked.

Line one kept up a keening note of distress throughout. It made it hard to think.

Ean and Radko—slower than the others—had just pulled their bodies on board when the shuttle doors slammed, and the emergency override opened the bay doors. They exited in a cloud of instantly frozen oxygen.

In the sudden release from gravity, they floated into each other, live and dead bodies.

Ean watched the screen. Surely a ship should be able to control its own doors. But that was the whole point of emergency overrides, he supposed. For the times when the ship couldn't help you, and you still had to do it.

Varrn had obviously spent a lot of time in free fall. He swung himself over to where the four were tending Michelle and pushed them aside. "Let me see." With his shark teeth, he looked like he was going for a meal of dead meat.

He laughed suddenly, and made it look more so. "You're lucky, Tarkan. She's wearing a suit."

Every face on Ean's side brightened, even Radko's. What did that mean?

Varrn thumped Michelle's shoulder, sending her body spinning again. "To think that Lady Lyan didn't trust us. On her own ship."

"Kill the others now?" asked the guard who'd closed the door.

"Wait till we get to the other ship. We might need them as a bargaining tool if Galenos comes after us too quickly," Varrn said. "We'll toss them out an air lock later. Tie them together for now. They'll be round before we land."

Their captors fashioned makeshift chains by looping rope from the shuttle nets around each foot and locking the rope into place with the key locks usually reserved for locking the rope onto the cargo nets. When they were finished, each person's right leg was fastened to the person in front of them, while their left leg was fastened to the person behind them.

Radko managed to get locked just behind Ean.

"They might be good as hostages," Tarkan Heyington suggested. "Commodore Galenos has always valued his people."

"It's a lot of work," Varrn said. "I'm not doing it." He loosed a toothy smile in Ean's direction. "This one we keep. If Lady Lyan is prepared to die for him, we might be able to use him."

Every conscious Lancastrian soldier glanced at Ean.

Varrn moved close. "I never expected her to put herself in the front of a weapon for anyone." Another toothy smile. "You are one valuable bargaining tool."

"Tool" was the right word. Ean could have told him why Michelle had saved his life. No point destroying the tool you had worked so hard for. Not that anyone would thank Michelle for it. Not even him.

He backed away, clumsy in free fall, until the rope on his ankle stopped him.

"Galenos has launched a shuttle," one of the enemy soldiers said, and Varrn moved away. A moment later, he added, "And one out from the second ship. And the third."

Ean held on to a strap against the wall and wondered what to do.

Line one was fading. By his shortness of breath and the unsteady beating of his heart, he thought that maybe line eleven was still there. Or maybe it was just fear.

* * *

VARRN was right. The soldiers did come around before they reached the parent ship. None of Abram's shuttles was anywhere near them yet. The enemy soldiers strapped in, and they strapped Michelle down, but they left the Allied soldiers floating.

"You ever landed untethered?" Radko asked.

At least she was still speaking to him. He shook his head. He'd been in lots of shuttles—especially in the past six months—but he'd always been strapped into a seat.

"Take hold to whatever you can and hang on tight," Radko said. "When gravity kicks in, you'll hit hard."

She was right, and even though Ean was prepared for it, he hit the wall, then the floor, with a bone-jarring thud that winded him. He banged a knee and saw momentary black from the pain.

This time they got a stretcher for Michelle. Four enemy guards left at a trot to take her to the hospital, while the line of prisoners was marched to a holding cell. Ean soon got the hang of the short, fast steps and marched in rhythm with the others although line eleven still made him want to change the beat.

This was definitely a military ship. It had the look and feel of the less luxurious parts of Michelle's ship. And they were preparing to jump. Ean heard the deep sonorous notes of line nine kick in. The void alert sounded.

He put his hands to his ears. Maybe, if line eleven could hear him, he could get a message to Abram.

He opened his mouth and sang.

Line ten kicked in.

Line eleven heard him, along with every other line on five ships. They jumped together, in through the eternity that was the void, only this time the lines—four sets of them, anyway—surrounded him and protected him.

EIGHTEEN

JORDAN ROSSI

ORSAYA SWITCHED TO an unmarked ship to go to Barossa. The new ship looked like a freighter and was probably as much of a freighter as the *Lancastrian Princess*. It bristled with arms, and everyone on board—except Rossi, Fergus, and Rebekah—carried weapons.

Rossi spent the trip trying to drag information out of Rebekah Grimes, who showed considerable reluctance to tell him anything about the mysterious ship or its lines. He wasn't sure if she was keeping it from him or if she genuinely didn't know.

"We are working together on this," he pointed out.

"I'm not stupid, Jordan. I've told you as much as—" They both looked up as Orsaya entered the cabin.

"We're having problems getting a jump into the sector," she said. "Too many tourists apparently."

Her meaning was clear, but Rebekah didn't get it. Or chose not. Rossi took out his comms.

Orsaya nodded. The first polite interaction the two of them had exchanged.

"This is Linesman Rossi," he said to the gate controller. The controller would see from his ID, and from the bars on his shirt, that Rossi was a level-ten linesman. "I need to get to Barossa."

"Sir." He was gratifyingly apologetic. "Traffic around Barossa is *extremely* heavy right now."

Rossi waited.

"I can get you in to ten AUs out."

Eighty-five light-minutes.

"Or if you can wait, sir, I'll put you on the priority list for the next available slot."

They wouldn't get in much farther even if they did wait, and Rossi had no plans to end up part of a supernova of a thousand ships just to get a few thousand kilometers closer to their target.

"Ten AUs is fine," he said. "Send it through to the captain."

"Thank you," Orsaya said, when he clicked off. It seemed to him that the words came hard.

She arranged for a shuttle to take both linesmen to the four-hundred-kilometer limit.

"Observe that limit," she said. "The Alliance will happily blow you out of the sky if you don't."

Fergus hadn't been going to come, but when Rebekah said, just before they departed, "This ship was attracted by the confluence, you know. It arrived not long after," he changed his mind.

Rossi scowled. So Fergus didn't even trust him to reconnoiter on his own. He hadn't contacted Rickenback yet, but when he did, Fergus would be looking for another job.

At four hundred kilometers, there was a faint hint of something that might have been confluence-like that tugged at the empty spot inside him and made him want to cry.

"We have to get closer," Rossi said.

Fergus watched him the way a lynx eyed a rickenback it was planning to bring down for dinner.

Rebekah's eyes narrowed. "We couldn't feel it this far out before," she said. "Something has changed. Lambert was right, though. It *is* like the confluence."

Comparing this to the confluence was like comparing the model of an atom to an atom itself, but there were similarities.

"We have to get closer," Rossi said again.

"Can you hear music?" Fergus asked, just as the confluence likeness swelled and filled Rossi's mind with awe until he thought his heart would burst with the grandeur of it.

The alien ship they were watching on-screen blinked out.

Rossi cried out—he couldn't help himself—but he didn't think Fergus or Rebekah noticed.

An angry Admiral Orsaya met them in the briefing room. "How are they doing this?" She wasn't upset with them.

"It's definitely confluence-related," Rebekah said.

Rossi nodded.

An orderly buzzed Orsaya. "Captain Wendell reports he is exactly where he planned to be, Admiral. But he does have company."

Orsaya looked as if she'd like to throw the comms at him. "Two media ships, one alien ship, and one goddammed Alliance warship." The last was almost a shout.

"Yes, Admiral."

Technically, the *Lancastrian Princess* was a modified freighter. Rossi bet it was armed well enough to function as a warship.

"Exact same positions as before the jump," the orderly said. Rossi was surprised he remained so calm given that Orsaya was radiating an almost-physical anger. "Captain Wendell is going to compromised plan B."

"At least something is working to plan," Orsaya muttered. She clicked off and turned to the linesmen. "So, tell me what you discovered about the lines on that ship."

NINETEEN

EAN LAMBERT

WHEN THEY CAME out of the eternity of the void, Ean was on the floor. He couldn't breathe. Guards yelled at him, and the only reason they didn't touch him was because Radko stood over him and protected him. Abram must have warned her because she didn't touch him.

"Let him recover."

"What's he making that noise for? Shut him up."

He was still singing a single note.

"It's how he copes with the jumps."

The guard didn't believe her. "No one gets affected by the jumps."

Ean gasped for air and tried to stand up. He tripped over the rope that chained him.

"Just move," the guard ordered.

Finally, Radko loaded Ean onto the back of the guard in front of him—his name was Losan—and they resumed with a shuffling walk that had more to do with the timing of line eleven's beats than anything else.

"I can't breathe," Losan said, and they had to stop and let Ean down. Losan stood, hands on his knees, gasping for breath, and no matter what the guard said, neither he nor Ean could move for two minutes.

"Maybe if I just lean on you," Ean said, finally, and they resumed their eleven-beat shuffle.

Losan did it hard. By the time they reached the holding cell, he was gasping harder than Ean.

"Crazy," one of the guards who'd escorted them said. "Enjoy the loony—both of them—but don't kill him, or Admiral Varrn and Tarkan Heyington will have your blood. Oh, and Admiral Varrn wants their uniforms. He thinks they might be useful."

"Wonderful," the new guard in charge said. "Why do we always get the dreck jobs?" He surveyed the prisoners. "I'll unlock you one by one. Fold your shirt and pants and put them over here. Boots and belts there. If you try anything, I'll shoot."

He didn't mean *he* would shoot, exactly, because he took care to remove his weapon and place it on the desk at the other side of the room. There were four other guards with blasters, which they held ready.

He started at the front of the line and unlocked one leg at a time, so that even while removing their uniforms, they were still always fastened to at least one other person.

Ean just lay on the floor, glad to be stationary, and tried to get his breathing under control.

As he stabilized, the music of the lines crystallized. This ship had the strongest lines of the five. Line one was almost as strong as Captain Helmo's line one. Maybe, if he listened hard enough, he could hear what was going on through the ship, like he sometimes could on Michelle's ship.

The stronger the line, the better he could hear it. Which meant, he supposed, that he would always be able to listen in on line one on Michelle's ship—Abram wouldn't be happy. There was a knack to it. Each ship had its own signature sound, and each line had its own tune. Together, the two made a unique music for each line. All you had to do was concentrate on the right music and let the rest fade into background.

Finally, he mastered it.

Varrn, Heyington, and another man were arguing about the ships.

"Those five ships are the exact same positions as they were before the jump," the third man said. "That had to be planned."

Ean could tell they were talking face-to-face, not through the comms, so the line had to be picking up ambient sounds from the ship. How little of the lines did they really use? Imagine the things you could use it for. Like spying.

Maybe Ean wouldn't tell Abram about being able to do this.

"As was that attack on our linesmen."

What attack?

"She came prepared, gentlemen. Even down to wearing a suit on her own ship. She and Galenos probably planned this. They've been waiting days for this exact attack."

"She's got a trace," Varrn said.

The other man snorted. "Trace my eye. You can't take four—five—ships and place them exactly where they are just on a trace. Jumps like that take skill and time to prepare. And as for Helmo's even trying it. He's crazier than Yannikay and likely to get us all killed. Even his precious Lady Lyan."

Something in the line changed, Ean couldn't tell what it was.

"No, gentlemen. Lady Lyan had help on this. She knew in advance this would happen. Galenos knew in advance where we would go. And only two people could have told him that."

"Are you accusing us, Captain Wendell?" Tarkan Heyington asked.

"One of you," Captain Wendell said. "Yes."

There was silence. Ean was sure if he could manipulate the lines enough he could see what was happening as well, but he didn't have the strength, or the knowledge, to do it.

"And the other of you has to be thinking what I'm thinking," Captain Wendell said. "You said they didn't control the alien ship, that they hadn't been near it. Yet here it is, along with two tame media ships Lyan has been feeding propaganda to for days. In our territory. At the same time as every linesman on our ship succumbs to a heart attack.

"We are vulnerable, gentlemen. One of you has given away a strategic location and made us susceptible to the same sort of attack we used on them. Not to mention that the first attack should have destroyed their ship altogether but, how convenient, it didn't. They were expecting that attack and protected their lines somehow."

The guard shook Ean, jerking him out of his trance. Every line on the ship shuddered. The lights went down momentarily. He lost track of what was happening with the captain.

Ean stared at him.

"You. Out of your clothes. Now." The guard hit him. "Get undressed."

He and Radko were the only two still in uniform. Everyone else was in their underwear and socks. Ean hadn't even felt them undo the rope on the left leg. He started to undress with hands that shook. It took ages to pull off his boot. The guard hit him twice. "Hurry up."

The second time, Radko said, "Leave him be," and jumped on the guard.

Her reaction was totally out of proportion to what the guard had done. "I'm fine," Ean said, but she ignored him, belting into the guard with the same single-minded strength she'd used on Ean days earlier. Maybe she just liked to hit things when she was upset.

Three of the guards converged on Radko, which made the Alliance guards swarm around to protect her. Ean, under the melee of bodies, lost track of what happened then—except that Radko, who was still tied to him, nearly pulled his ankle off.

When it was over three still bodies lay on top of him, which was almost as bad as a line-eleven-induced heart attack.

"Nicely done, Radko," said the Alliance prisoner who'd been at the head of the line. The name on the pocket of the uniform she was putting on was SALE.

"I think he wrenched my ankle," Radko said.

What about his ankle?

Someone pulled the bodies off. Ean didn't know if they were dead or alive. They were certainly still. He looked away from the two remaining guards on the floor not far away, one of whose head was twisted at an impossible angle.

"Who's got the key?"

The guard had dropped the key. It was lying under Ean although how it got there, Ean didn't know because he hadn't moved.

They unlocked the rope between Radko and Ean first and Radko's ankle immediately swelled to three times its normal size. She used the dead guard's knife to slice off part of his shirt for a makeshift bandage, then said, "Damn. I suppose we should have kept their uniforms."

"Don't worry about it," said Sale. "Not sure any of us want to be sensible about something like that right now."

"Could mean the difference between us rescuing Princess Michelle or not," another guard said.

"Or the time between getting caught because we delayed to take their uniforms off."

As soon as Sale unlocked the Alliance ropes, two more guards set to clipping the same ropes back onto the unconscious—and dead—enemy guards. Two others picked up the weapons and checked them. Losan and a fifth guard went over to the door.

"They're key-coded," Losan said.

Radko used Ean's shoulder as support to get to her feet. "Ean can open it," she said, hopping over to the wall. "Just don't ask him to support me after you do it."

"He can't fight. If he supports you, he'll at least be useful."

Radko hopped over to the door. "He's like a live wire after he's done something with the lines. My hair's still standing up from last time."

She did have a lot of static in her hair.

"Or maybe he should help me," Radko said. "He'd throw me the length of the corridor much faster than I could move." She jerked her head at Ean. "Come and do your thing, Line Twelve."

"Line Twelve?" Sale asked.

"It's a joke." Ean stood up. It hadn't been funny the first time.

"No joke."

Ean put his hand on the keypad. He wasn't sure he could do this again.

Five line eights came in to answer him, and he nearly shook apart with the vibration that sent him to his knees. "All the way to Princess Michelle, please," he begged, because he couldn't do this for every door. Through the lines he heard Captain Wendell order someone to check on the prisoners. Wendell's affinity for his ship was as strong as Helmo's. "And lock all the other doors. Please," which might slow Wendell's crew down.

"Can you walk?" Radko asked.

He nodded, not sure he could. "We must hurry. The captain knows something is wrong."

She hauled him up, hissing at his touch. Her hair stood out straight from her head again.

"I'll follow."

"We all go together."

The other soldiers finished re-dressing. At least Ean still had his uniform on. It would be mortifying if he couldn't even get dressed.

They left at a run. Radko half leaning on him, half supporting him with Losan on the other side of Radko, his arm around her shoulders. Occasionally, Ean and Losan touched.

"Oh God," Losan would moan then, but he did it in the rich, deep tones of line eight. "Oh God."

"Shh," said everyone.

They came to a locked door.

"Ean."

"Wrong way," Ean said with certainty. All the doors to Michelle were unlocked.

So they turned to the other door even though it led to a tiny corridor they could barely run through. Radko had to support herself as she hopped through.

"This is a Greunig cruiser," Sale said. "The hospital will be aft. We're heading fore."

"This is the way." Ean could feel it in the way the walls tingled, in the urgency of the *Lancastrian Princess*'s own line eight. "We have to hurry."

They turned into an even narrower tunnel. Sale wanted to turn back, but it was too cramped. Ean didn't tell her that the door behind them was locked now. He didn't know how he knew that. He tried to listen in to line one but couldn't concentrate. He did hear line five, however.

"They know we're gone."

No one said it, but he could almost hear their emotions. He'd brought them into a trap. They all thought it, except Radko, who patted his shoulder. "Trust the lines."

It sounded like something he would say.

They came out into the shuttle bay via one of the access tunnels, behind the bulk of a shuttle preparing for takeoff, well clear of the guards waiting for them at the air lock.

Ean wondered for one sick moment if his desire to escape had overridden his original request, then the door opened, and twenty armed soldiers entered, running. In their midst, two more soldiers pushed a stretcher.

Radko pulled him back. The others had faded behind the shuttle. He hadn't noticed. Sale made a small move he hardly recognized as "come here."

She was standing under the shuttle. "Open that," she mouthed, pointing to an emergency hatch.

He hoped he understood what she was saying.

"I can't—" But someone—Radko again—was already hoisting him up so that he could reach.

Ean sang softly, under the noise of the engines, through the line of the main ship as a command to the shuttle. "Please, open. And please, no alarms."

The surge of the lines as they answered his request knocked them both to the ground. Losan caught them and swore softly. His hair stood out from his head. Ean could see the effort it took to let them go without making a sound.

Half of Sale's people were already through the hatch. Sale beckoned to Losan.

He and a woman called Craik helped Radko up first. They lifted her until she could grab the bottom of the emergency door and swing herself in. Then they hefted Ean up. His entry was more undignified. Two below lifted while two above grabbed his arms and pulled him in. They dragged him away from the door, teeth gritted, hair flying wild.

"The door," Sale whispered when everyone was in, and Ean crawled back to the emergency exit and sang to line eight again.

It felt like hours, but Sale led them out of the tiny passage— she obviously knew her way around this type of shuttle— and down into a storeroom. If they pressed their ear to the wall, they could hear the activity in the main cabin, where the guards were still strapping Michelle in.

"Treat her carefully, or Captain Wendell will bust you down two bars," one of the guards was saying.

Another time, another place, Ean thought he might like Captain Wendell.

Soon after that, the shuttle took off. Captain Wendell wasn't wasting any time separating Michelle from the ship.

TWENTY

JORDAN ROSSI

THEY JUMPED TWICE. The first jump was to pick up the Nova Tahitian councilor, Ahmed Gann, who came on board radiating almost as much anger as Orsaya.

"This is a farce," Gann raged. "We can't even manage a simple kidnapping."

"Maybe next time Markan will listen to us." Orsaya's eyes were flat and cold. "We told him it was a stupid idea."

Rossi agreed. Whoever had decided to kidnap Emperor Yu's eldest daughter deserved to be court-martialed, then sealed in a life capsule and sent into space with two oxygen cylinders and a very long time to contemplate the stupidity of what they had done as they waited to die. Still, it was almost as gutsy as something Lyan herself would have done, and if it had worked, would no doubt have cemented Markan as a power in Gate Union.

The only problem was, Admiral Markan of Roscracia dined frequently with Cartel Master Iwo Hurst of House of Sandhurst. On reflection, Rossi decided he was glad the kidnapping hadn't gone well.

"You know the worst thing," Gann said. "Roscracia is getting a lot of support right now. Divna Neumann had the cheek to call me up and tell me that if I didn't have the stomach for war, I should retire."

Rossi raised an eyebrow at Fergus.

"Councilor," Fergus murmured quietly. "Ahmed Gann's opposite for Roscracia. Believed to be easy to sway on a vote if you can make it persuasive enough."

One could always rely on Fergus to know things.

Rossi glanced over at Rebekah Grimes, standing tall beside Orsaya. She had a knowing smile on her face. He'd just bet he knew where some of that persuasion was coming from, too. Smooth-talking, ambitious Iwo Hurst.

He considered the two women together. No doubt la Dame Grimes thought she looked confident—almost regal—beside the soldier. He had news for her. Orsaya had a presence even Rebekah couldn't hope to emulate.

He smiled at the other linesman. Maybe one day he might tell her that, too.

The second jump was to rendezvous with the ship Lady Lyan was being taken to, the GU *Gruen*.

"The alien ship is nothing Wendell can control," Orsaya said. "We need to get Lady Lyan away from it."

"So we're sending her to another ship?" Gann asked.

"Exactly." She looked at Rossi and Fergus. "You two will take a shuttle with Administrator Gann to the *Gruen*. Linesman Grimes will come with me."

"Where are you going?" Rossi knew. She was going to the confluence. The confluence was his. Rebekah Grimes didn't appreciate what she'd had there. She'd left. And Orsaya was taking *her* instead of *him*.

He fought down the panic that engulfed him, already calculating how far it was to Orsaya's weapon. She had to let him come. It was his right to be at the confluence.

Orsaya nodded to an orderly behind them.

Rossi felt the familiar jolt of a blaster set to stun.

TWENTY-ONE

EAN LAMBERT

THE TRIP WAS a long one. The longest shuttle journey Ean had ever taken. By the end of it, he could only hear line eleven, and that only faintly. If he lost all of the lines, would Michelle's ship and the alien ship be able to come through together next time they jumped? Because he wanted them to. He needed them to.

Abram had to be doing everything he could to get Michelle back. If Ean could keep Abram's ship and the alien ship jumping when they did, then Abram would guess soon enough which ship Michelle was on.

What if he lost line eleven?

He needed to sing. That way the lines would hear him and help him to keep in touch with them. But they could hear the guards in the main shuttle compartment. If he sang, the lines wouldn't be the only thing to hear him.

He would have to sing soon.

Ean gripped his knees and tried to keep the tenuous thread alive.

They landed at last. The guards took Michelle off the shuttle.

"Door," Sale said, and Ean realized that without the

power of the other lines behind them, they were on a totally enemy ship.

"I think I might set off the alarms," he said.

"But you opened them before."

"Yes, but—" How did he explain it? "That was our ships helping. We came so far, they can't hear me. If I tap into line eight here, I'm tapping into their ship only."

"Line eight?"

"Line eight doesn't do anything," Losan said. No one knew what line seven or eight did.

"I think it does security." It seemed to take responsibility for the overall protection of the ship. Katida, who was a level eight, was going to like that if she could learn how to use it. But it didn't matter which line he meant or what it did. The lines belonged to this ship.

"So we're stuck here with no backup?" Sale said.

Ean nodded. "Sorry."

Sale smiled suddenly and patted his shoulder, even if it did make her hair stand out from her head, although not too much. "No, I'm sorry. You got us much further than we had any right to get. It's about time we did some of the work."

They did it the hard way, using small tools built into their belts to open an equipment locker, then using the equipment they found there to short-circuit the emergency door and push it open.

"Can't hide what we've done," Sale said softly. "But we're out, at least."

They exited the shuttle bay through an access panel similar to the one they had entered on the last ship.

The lines on this ship were well kept. Gate Union—or was it Redmond—kept their military ships in as good a condition as the Alliance did. If there was a war, Gate Union would be able to keep them better because they would have access to level-ten linesmen, which the Alliance didn't. Except him.

It wasn't long before line nine came in. "They're going to jump," Ean said softly. And he was going to sing. He had to. Otherwise, Abram would lose them. He put his hands to his ears, which didn't help at all, but it felt like it did, and started to sing.

There was no distance in the void. Line eleven heard him, and through line eleven, the other lines heard, too. They all came. They were clear as clear, and joyful around him. Ean greeted every single one of them. Every time he went into the void, the lines were clearer, and he knew that when he came out, the lines would retain some of that clarity. Something in the void seemed to be opening his mind to the lines.

When it was over, he heard Sale say to Radko, "He's not exactly a weapon you can keep hidden."

"Who'd want to?" Radko asked. "Half of what scares you is knowing what he can do." She turned to Ean, careful not to touch him. "Is Commodore Galenos still with us?"

He breathed deep and listened as he waited for his heart to settle—there were six sets of lines now, five of them were familiar, four very familiar—and nodded.

The others looked skeptical, and Ean had to remember that they didn't know what he got through the lines. "And line eleven. And the media. And Captain Wendell."

"Who in hell is Wendell?"

"The other ship. The one we were just on." Gate Union called their ships after the captain, so Captain Wendell's ship would be the GU *Wendell*.

On line five, calls for paramedics were the most common communication, particularly on the Gate Union ships. He breathed deep and listened while Sale's team absorbed what he had said. Underneath the emergency calls, he could hear another signal.

Radko just nodded as if she expected it. "Same formation as before we jumped?"

Not anymore. Captain Helmo had moved his ship almost as soon as they were out of the void. "Our ship—Michelle's ship—has moved. It's going—" He didn't know where it was going. In the void, he could hear where the ships were in relation to each other, but out here in real space, he had no idea.

"It'll be coming closer to one of the Gate Union ships," Radko said. "Galenos knows you have to be on one of these ships. He'll be hoping the princess is on the same one."

Ean finally realized what the other signal was. "He's trying to contact this ship." Trying to contact both Gate Union ships. The media were trying to contact them, too.

Captain Wendell was the first to answer.

Abram waited till they were both online.

"Captains," Abram said. "We can keep this up as long as you can. Or until all your linesmen are dead from heart attacks. Give us Lady Lyan, give us my crew who went with her, and call off this senseless war before it escalates into a bloodbath that affects civilians."

"What are you talking about?" the captain of the ship Ean was on demanded.

"Captain . . . Gruen, is it?"

She inclined her head. Ean heard it in the movement of line five rather than saw it.

"Please don't insult any of us by pretending to not know," Abram said.

Captain Wendell said. "You can't keep this up forever, Galenos. There has to be a physical limit."

"I am sure there is," Abram admitted. "We don't know what it is. We haven't reached it yet." Which wasn't a lie, and he sounded so sincere and honest that the other captains couldn't know that Abram was finding out along the way, too. "You can keep experimenting until we find it, if you like. Who knows how many of *your* ships we'll control before we reach it."

"Control?" Captain Wendell asked.

"We control your lines, Captain. Your ships do what we ask them to. Including telling us where you will jump through the void."

Now he really was bluffing.

"Think about it," Abram said. "And call me back when you are ready to free Lady Lyan and my crew. Meantime"—and Ean could feel the smile as a movement in the line—"the media want to interview Lady Lyan about being kidnapped. They are most upset that you have denied them access to her."

He clicked off.

Ean heard the lines move and felt line five damp down to a single thread. A secure line. He sang the same link open to Abram's ship.

"I don't think this line is as secure as you believe it is, Gruen." Captain Wendell's voice was hard.

That was true now, anyway. Provided Captain Helmo didn't answer.

"Can he control our ships?"

"What do you think? He has, just now, jumped six ships through the void in tandem. Last time he jumped, there were five. He's doing a damn good job of making it look like he controls them."

"So he could just destroy us."

"He won't destroy you while Lady Lyan is in your hospital. And he knows she's there, or otherwise he wouldn't be moving toward your ship right now." There was a pause before Wendell added, "And I have the other prisoners on my ship." Ean could imagine the *somewhere* that went with that, for Wendell must know by now that the prisoners had escaped. "He wants his crew back as well."

There was a deliberate message in there to Abram and Captain Helmo if they were listening. Ean could feel it. Captain Wendell really didn't trust the lines.

Crew were expendable. Michelle and Abram would, in the end, destroy Wendell's ship if the need arose. But Abram would never destroy Michelle.

"I never thought Lady Lyan would be of use to us anyway," Gruen grumbled. "I haven't seen much evidence of the Alliance fragmenting."

Wendell sighed. "Captain Gruen, this line is probably not secure."

"You're paranoid, Wendell."

One of them clicked the line off. Ean thought it was Wendell.

He became aware of the others, sitting watching him.

"He's not only loud, he's slow," Sale said.

Radko said, without heat, "He's not a stealth weapon, Sale. He's a line. He needs his own safe place on ship. Lines do."

Ean blinked at them. That joke truly wasn't funny third time around. Although sometimes he felt more empathy with the lines than he did with humans. "Abram and Captain Helmo are bringing the ship closer to this one."

Through line one he could hear Captain Gruen grumbling about the paranoia of a man who, given a job to do, started seeing monsters under the bed. "He's losing it."

Why could he hear the captains so clearly and not the rest of the ship? Because they were close to the lines, of course.

Captains spent most of their time on the bridge, and the lines—which started in Engineering—ended on the bridge. The brain—the chassis that housed them—was on the bridge.

"Where to?" one of the other guards asked.

"Princess Michelle first," Sale said. She seemed to be the team leader, like Bhaksir was in Radko's team.

"She's in the hospital," Ean said. "At least, Captain Wendell said she was."

Radko smiled triumphantly at Sale. "He may be slow, but he gets what we need." She held out her hand to help Ean up.

How long would it be before Radko had a team of her own? Not long, Ean thought. He shook his head at her offered hand, "I'm fine," and crawled up using his hands and knees. It was inelegant, but it worked. "What about you?"

"If you can move, I'll help her," Losan said.

"I don't suppose you know any access panels to the hospital," Sale asked.

Ean shook his head. "I could ask," but the other lines weren't close enough to do it for him. He would have to use the line eight on this ship. "I wish we were in the void. Our own ship could do it there."

They digested that in silence.

"So. Not safe?" Sale finally asked.

"Not safe," Ean agreed.

"Let's do it the hard way, then."

Sale was a complex mix of reasonable and irritated. Ean thought she might have been just a little bit scared of him. Was Radko scared of him, too?

He tried to drop behind Radko and Losan, but Radko waved him in front of her. "We can't protect you from the back."

He was useless. He couldn't fight. He slowed them down. He scared them.

"Drop behind me," Radko ordered Losan. "Ean, give him a rest. You can help me walk for a while."

"But what about—?"

"I'm getting used to my hair's standing out. I'm thinking of gelling it that way anyway if it's always going to do it." She leaned on Ean, and said through clenched teeth, "Not sure about the music yet."

"That is so weird, the way your voice changes," Losan said.

"Yours did, too."

She sounded like her ship, not like a specific line the way Losan had. Ean wondered if that meant Radko was more attuned to the whole ship than Losan was.

"Ean," Radko said softly, so that only he could hear.

He concentrated on helping her walk, didn't look at her.

"The void messes with your mind, somehow. You always come out of it depressed."

This time he did look at her.

Did he? "No," Ean said. "It's making me more attuned to the lines. Radko, there's this whole dimension out there that we don't comprehend."

"It still messes with your mind," Radko said. "Realize that and deal with it."

She was definitely going to be running her own team sometime soon. "And I think that's enough music for the moment," Radko said, and dropped back to Losan with a sigh of relief. Her voice still held ship music.

THEY used the maintenance tunnels where they could, and took some wrong turns and had to backtrack occasionally, but they managed to stay out of the public corridors.

"When we get back to ship, every single one of you is going to know the access tunnels for every ship larger than a shuttle," Sale said. "And have the tools to open them," as they struggled with a new lock.

Ean had no idea where they were. He tried to listen to line one but couldn't concentrate on moving stealthily and listening at the same time. Radko was right. He needed his own safe place to work and sing.

Eventually, Sale said, "If these numbers make sense, the hospital is up a level and down this next corridor. Go carefully now. There will be guards."

They turned into the corridor and found two maintenance workers in the shaft.

The workers hardly had time to realize someone was there before they were unconscious. Or dead. Ean wasn't sure which.

"Just what we need," Sale said. "When they're reported missing, they'll hunt for us."

At least they weren't on Wendell's ship. Captain Wendell would probably be making his crew report in every ten minutes, and if they missed, he'd send an armed team down to see why. It's what Abram and Captain Helmo would do.

"Let's hope we're off ship by then," Radko said.

All of them—Radko, Sale, and the other guards—stared down at the two spacers.

"Maybe," Sale said. "Provided the bastard doesn't regain consciousness."

Sometimes they took immense risks. "What are you going to do?" but Ean knew already.

"Losan," Sale said. "You're around the right size for the male."

"God," Losan said, as he started to strip. "The things I do for Her Royal Highness."

"And if you happen to address her by name while you're there—which you shouldn't—you'd better make sure it's Lady Lyan."

"As if," Losan said.

"Why wouldn't you call her by name?" Ean asked.

"Why? Only someone who calls her Michelle could ask a question like that."

She'd told Ean her name was Michelle. If she'd wanted to be addressed as Princess Michelle or Lady Lyan, then surely she would have introduced herself like that. Or maybe she just expected it. Ean shrugged. It was too late now.

"Shhh," said Sale. "Now, get in there and get back fast? If you're not back in fifteen we're moving anyway."

They moved up to the next level, with Losan and his unconscious prisoner.

"What's he doing?" Ean asked.

"Finding how many guards there are outside and inside the hospital," Radko said.

"But won't the guards know he's a stranger?"

"Clearly you've never worked on a military ship," Sale said. "He's a maintenance worker."

"Yes, but you'd know."

Radko said, "We are Princess Michelle's handpicked

guards. The Commodore would skin us alive if we didn't know the name and face of every person who came on ship—including you—the minute they came on board. On most ships, the active guards and the maintenance crew don't even eat in the same mess, let alone talk to each other."

"Shhh," Sale said.

Losan was back a nerve-wracking ten minutes later. "Four guards," he reported. "Two outside and two in. They're not expecting trouble." Which meant that Captain Gruen wasn't taking Captain Wendell's warnings seriously. She would soon. "They're wearing standard weapons. Blasters and knives at the least.

"There are five medical staff and three patients. Four now, sorry. Only one ward. Ten beds. Two rows of five. The princess is separated. At the far end, away from the door. She has one guard on each side of the bed."

They were speaking softly, but if Losan was right, the guards were just around the corner and down the corridor. Ean wiped damp hands on his trousers and hoped no one could hear them talking.

"Too many people for us to jump without tripping the alarm," Sale said. "We can surprise the two outer guards, but not the inner."

"Emergency hatch?" asked one of the other guards, and shook his head before she even answered.

"They'll hear us before we get in."

"Where do we go when we're done?"

"Shuttle bay," Sale said. "As fast as we can." Even Ean could see the chances of their reaching the shuttle bay without getting stopped were remote. "We kill everyone who gets in our way." She looked at Ean. "Since we will be seen, is there anything you can do, Linesman, to help us?"

She meant line eight. "I think—"

"What about an alarm somewhere else on the ship?" Radko suggested. "Hull breach alert will set people running and close off that part of the ship, and everyone else except emergency personnel have to stay put until the breach is fixed."

Thank goodness for Radko, who understood that Ean didn't understand what he could do.

"Of course," she added, "guards would be considered

emergency personnel in a situation like this. Half of them will make for the breach and the other half will make straight for the hospital."

"And if there were two breaches?" It would be better just to lock the guards in their quarters, to lock every door except for the ones in the corridor to the shuttle. Doors were line three, and they would work for him. At least, they had until now. Provided he didn't involve eight, which appeared to be the gatekeeper for security. The other lines seemed to accept that if a line like Ean asked something of another line, and line eight didn't stop it, then it was okay to do.

Wendell's line eight had protected its ship. This one probably would, too.

Ean could have done this before if he'd thought about it properly instead of being so fixated on line eight. He might tell Abram that when they got out, but he definitely wasn't telling Sale.

"I need to touch a lock." He didn't know how to describe a lock to the line.

"Hospital door okay?"

He nodded.

"Good," Sale said. "Let's go."

They took off at a run and started firing as soon as they got around the door. The guards didn't have a chance.

The dead men hit the floor together. The thump rattled the metal of the corridor.

"Linesman," Sale hissed, and Ean hurried over. Please let him be able to do it.

The staff inside the hospital were just starting to react to the external noise.

Ean put his hand on the lock and started to sing.

Line three heard him, and the locks clicked into place.

Someone on the other side came over to open the hospital door. Ean raised a hand to warn the others then, because he couldn't think of what else to do, dropped his hand to rest on the shoulder of the man who had opened the door.

"What the?" The orderly's voice took on the chattering tones of line three. His eyes rolled upward, and he fainted.

The guards by Michelle's bed hadn't moved. One of them pointed his weapon directly at Michelle's throat.

Radko waved her blaster at the stationary medical staff. "Touch any alarms, and I kill you. Stay still, and you'll stay alive." All the others' weapons pointed directly at the two guards.

"Stalemate," Sale said to the guard with the weapon aimed at Michelle. "You kill her, and you're dead. If I don't kill you, your own people will. I'm sure you have instructions to keep her alive no matter the cost."

She'd been wearing a suit, so why was she unconscious?

Ean felt line five come in. The signal originated from this room. It was instinctive to open his mouth and counter it before it could go anywhere. He held the line, and all the comms in the ship came to him, through him, and stopped.

They couldn't get a signal out, he realized. While he held the line, they couldn't call for reinforcements.

"Take them," he said through the guard's comms, because he couldn't stop the tune to tell them what to do.

Radko shot both guards in the head while everyone else—on both sides—was still reacting.

One of the orderlies pressed an alarm. It came out in Ean's song, but didn't get through to anyone else.

Sale snapped out of it quickly enough. "A trolley," she ordered, and Losan and another guard ran over to get the emergency trolley.

A patient moved her arm carefully, stealthily. Ean could see what she was trying for. The dead guard's blaster. Ean glared at her. "Don't try anything," he said through the now-dead guard's comms.

Craik collected the discarded weapons.

Losan and another guard loaded Michelle onto the stretcher.

"You, too," Sale said to Radko. "Your ankle will slow us down, and we need speed." She looked at Ean. "What about you?"

"I can run," he said through the comms.

She picked up the comms. "Let's go then," and they ran back through the main corridors to the shuttle bay and picked off anyone who had been unlucky enough to get themselves locked in the main corridor. All the emergency calls and requests for maintenance to fix doors went in through line five and out through Ean.

"I can almost understand this," Sale said, as they ran.

Ean slowed them down. It was impossible to sing and run at the same time.

After two main corridors, Sale said, "Put him on the trolley."

"Is that wise?" asked Losan. "Princess Michelle—"

"Better to have her alive and her hair sticking out than dead because we couldn't run fast enough." She gestured to Ean with her blaster. "Get on."

Ean thought she might shoot him if he didn't. He got on.

Three people on the trolley made more work for the trolley-pushers, but they still made better time.

Ean tried to avoid people, but the moment he touched the trolley, Michelle moaned and opened her eyes. "Ean. I can hear you through my bones."

"So can we," Radko said, and the vibration in her voice wasn't just from the rattling of the trolley.

The shuttle-bay door was locked, and Ean didn't need the lines to read the huge warning signs around it. There was no oxygen, a ship was coming into the bay.

"Sorry." It still came out through the comms.

Sale didn't even hesitate. "Can you hold the outer door open for another ten minutes?"

"Without oxygen?"

She nodded, and started pulling space suits out of the emergency lockers. "You ever worn one of these?"

He shook his head.

"I'll suit him," Radko said. "You do the princess. You," to Ean. "Just keep singing."

He did, holding the doors on the ship locked, holding the outer bay open and calling all the comms through him. The resultant noise wasn't really song, it was a waterfall of sound.

"You can almost understand what they're saying," Michelle said as she moved as much as she could to help those suiting her. It must have hurt because Ean could see the perspiration on her face, but she didn't say anything, or even wince.

Line eight came in then because the shuttle-bay doors

should have closed. Ean and line eight tussled for control of the door. He'd never had to fight a line before.

Radko snapped his faceplate closed and checked the seals. "Linesman's ready," almost at the same time as the two people suiting Michelle said, "Princess is ready."

They linked together to form a human chain. Radko clipped Ean in.

Sale broke the inner emergency seals on the air lock.

The alarms went through Ean and out into the emptiness of the shuttle bay.

They crowded inside the air lock, squeezed together so tight that the song of the lines passed through them all. By the end of the long twenty seconds it took to cycle the air out, Ean was accompanied by a chorus of human voices who couldn't help but follow his song.

As soon as the air was gone, Sale—in front—broke the outer seal and used the jets on her suit to get them to the shuttle.

Losan triggered the emergency lock on the shuttle.

They piled into that air lock—Michelle half propelling herself, half supporting Ean, and Radko supporting them both.

Air returned.

All the while Ean sang control of the locks, control of the comms, control of security.

The inner door whooshed open.

Sale and her people turned their weapons on the occupants of the shuttle.

"You," she said to the man in the pilot seat. "Take off now, or I'll fry you."

Craik stepped past Sale and put a blaster to the pilot's head. "Now," she said.

The pilot started to press buttons.

Sale looked around at the other occupants of the shuttle, who were all in various stages of standing up. "The rest of you, on the floor."

They dropped to the floor.

The shuttle took off.

Ean was knocked off his feet with the force of the acceleration, then lost his footing altogether as they entered free fall.

All the time he tussled with line eight for control of the song.

Radko touched his arm and was thrown across the shuttle compartment. Ean wanted to stop, to see if she was all right, but he couldn't. Not without stopping the song.

Sale said something—Ean didn't hear what under all the noise. Radko shook her head.

Michelle, her torso bruised and burned, pushed herself over to stand in front of Ean. She put a hand over Ean's eyes—not touching—and said, gently, "It's over now. You can stop."

Ean covered his ears, but it didn't help.

Michelle took her hand away and held Ean's gaze with her own, deep and intense. There was nothing but the deep blue of her eyes, so dark he almost drowned in the color, so strong it damped the music. Ean blinked and could finally stop.

"Look at poor Radko," Michelle said.

Radko's left shoulder was twisted out of place. Even as Ean watched, she sat up, and winced. "Anyone know how to put a dislocated shoulder back?"

"Sorry," Ean muttered.

"It's your revenge," Radko said, trying to sound cheerful. "For what I did when the others—" Her voice closed up with pain.

It took a moment to understand what she meant. "Your jokes get worse."

Michelle fainted then, which saved either of them from replying.

"She was wearing a suit," Ean said. At least they were in free fall, so Michelle didn't fall.

"She took close-range hits from two blasters," Sale said, gesturing Losan over to look at her. "No, don't you touch her," to Ean. "It stopped her from being fried, but that's about all." She waved her blaster at one of the prisoners, who seemed to think "don't move" didn't apply to him. "Sit down, Linesman, or I'll kill you."

For a moment Ean thought she was talking to him, then he realized the prisoner wore a cartel uniform of deep midnight blue, with a jumping rickenback stitched in gold on the pocket and ten gold bars above it. House of Rickenback had two tens. Jordan Rossi and Geraint Jones.

Geraint Jones was as tall and as skinny as a whippet, with ash blond hair. This man was sitting down. Ean couldn't see how tall he was, but his shoulders were broad, his arms were muscled, and his head was shaved. Not Jones, so it had to be Jordan Rossi.

According to Rigel, Rossi was a wily political manipulator with a voice an orator would be proud of. Ean smiled to himself. Gospetto would probably be pleased to teach him. Funny that Rigel had never said Rebekah was a political manipulator, too.

Losan finished examining Michelle. "We should have brought the medic with us." He moved over to Radko. "Let's look at your shoulder."

"Is she—?" Sale asked.

"I don't know. Best thing we can do is get her back to the commodore as soon as we can."

"So let's see what we can do about that. Craik." Craik was standing over the pilot, her weapon at his head. "Get him to contact the commodore." Sale swung back to Jordan Rossi, who had moved again. "Linesman, you don't get many warnings." She waved the weapon at the other prostrate hostages. There were two of them. One wore Rickenback colors but no lines. An assistant. Rigel had refused to pay for assistants. Wasted money, he called them, and Ean secretly agreed with him. What could an assistant do that you couldn't do yourself? The other man could have been one of the bureaucrats dining at the buffet on Michelle's ship every night. He looked what he was. A government official.

"Ean," Sale said. "Make sure it's only our ship he calls."

He nodded, hoping he could, and looked at the crowded pilot's seat. "Do you still have the comms?"

Sale tossed it across.

Ean caught it. "Go," he said to Craik.

Something hit the shuttle side on, knocking them everywhere. Ean made a clumsy grab for the comms, which had been jerked out of his hands.

"Strap Princess Michelle in," Sale ordered, but Losan was

already doing that, dropping a stretcher from the specially marked berth along the wall, clipping it into place, and settling Michelle with care into the webbing. There were two stretcher bays and three stretcher logos at each, one near the floor, one toward the ceiling, and the other halfway between. Only a military shuttle would expect to have to carry six stretchers at once.

"Minor damage to the landing gear," Craik reported. "A warning shot."

Captain Gruen's voice came over the loudspeaker. "Attention, the shuttle. This is Captain Gruen of the GU ship *Gruen*. You have fifteen seconds to surrender."

The lines were still wide open to him, and Ean knew without knowing how he knew that they would do anything he asked of them. Even Gruen's ship. Except line eight, which he knew now would always protect its ship first. He was heady with the sudden power, nervous, too. Lines trusted each other, and he couldn't afford to break their trust.

He thumbed the speaker on the comms and started to sing, taking back control of line five on the ship, so Captain Gruen couldn't order the gunners to fire again. This time, instead of stopping it with him, he sent it on, out through the comms channel, so Abram's ship could hear it because he couldn't hold Gruen's comms closed and keep a line open for Abram at the same time.

"Attention the shuttle." He sent Gruen's message straight through to Abram's command center. Could almost see— hear—Captain Helmo and Abram standing together, identical frowns on their faces, listening. "We have given you warning. Surrender now or we will fire again."

The pilot was already preparing for evasive action.

"This is your last warning. If you do not surrender now, we will fire."

Then the command to the gunners, which didn't go through. "Fire preset one." And after she realized they hadn't heard her, "Fire preset one," again.

"Get down there and press that button," Captain Gruen ordered someone on the bridge.

Ean locked the doors. He couldn't think of anything else to do.

Abram's ship launched a weapon.

Captain Gruen tried to open another comms line. "Wendell. Get your sorry ass online now and tell me what it is we're dealing with."

"Ean. Ean. Listen to me." Even that came out through the comms.

Radko stood in front of him and clicked her fingers. Ean stopped fighting line eight and slowly came back to real space.

"Commodore Galenos is talking to you."

It was Abram's voice. "Ean. Listen to me."

"I don't believe it," Jordan Rossi's rich voice murmured. "It's crazy Ean Lambert. Singing to the lines."

Ean half heard Sale's sharp, "You have a problem with that?"

He concentrated on Abram. "Sir." It came out as song.

"I want to talk to the captains."

"Gruen?"

"And Wendell. Yes."

Ean clicked them through, fighting with line eight for supremacy of line five. Ean won, just.

"Captain Gruen," Abram's crisp voice said. "There is a missile headed toward you. I hope you see it. We will detonate it if you do not stop firing on the shuttle."

At first, all he got in answer was a wordless snarl, then, "What in hell have you got here, Galenos?"

"We are trying to prevent a war Gate Union started," Abram said, which didn't answer her question at all. "If you harm anyone on that shuttle, you will escalate this war. Are you prepared to accept the consequences?"

Ean got the feeling Abram wasn't talking to Captain Gruen but to Captain Wendell.

"Ean, a private line please. You to me," Abram said.

Sure enough, as soon as Ean flicked over, Captain Wendell was on the line to Gruen. "If Lady Lyan is on that shuttle, then for heaven's sake, stop firing on it."

"We wanted her out of the way to destabilize the Alliance," she said.

"But if you kill her, the Alliance will come after us. They

have to. Not to mention they have that ship out there that can cause God-alone-knows what damage."

Ean couldn't keep listening to two conversations at once, and Abram was insistent in his ear. "Ean. Talk to me."

"Talking," he said, and hoped Gruen listened to Wendell and stopped firing because by talking to Abram, he'd lost control of most of the lines. "Michelle's here," because that was what Abram wanted to know most. "She's not—" He stopped. If he told Abram the ship would know, then what would happen?

Radko pushed off on the wall and came to a gentle stop in front of Ean. She held out her hand for the comms. He passed it over.

"Sir. Spacer Radko. We have eight personnel here. Two of our people are injured. One badly." That would be Michelle, unless she wasn't considered as personnel. "Four prisoners. All Alliance personnel are accounted for. Sale's in charge."

"Thank you, Radko." Abram's voice was crisp, but Ean could feel through the lines the tired sigh that followed. "They will fire on our ship shortly. Do what you can to get the shuttle to safety."

"Yes, sir."

At first, Ean misunderstood. "They'll fire at us." They hadn't gotten anywhere, then. They would still have to surrender to avoid being hit.

"They'll fire on the *Lancastrian Princess*."

"Lambert isn't known to have much grasp of logic," Jordan Rossi said, "but this once he does have a point. They'll fire on us, sweetheart."

Radko just gave him a flat, disinterested stare. "Do all tens continually put other tens down? Not you." She patted Ean's shoulder. "But you're not really a ten, are you."

He didn't want to hear that joke about line twelve again.

"He just likes the sound of his own voice," Sale said. Ean hoped she was talking about Rossi, not him. "So the commodore has bought us some time. What shall we do with it?"

How had he bought them time?

Radko saw Ean's expression. "He reminded them Princess Michelle was on this shuttle," she said. "They don't want to kill her, so they will try to prevent Captain Helmo's reaching us."

"But that's—"

"And they're all coming to get us," Sale said. "So if we stay here, we end up stuck in the middle of a three-way fight. You"—she pointed her blaster at the pilot—"show us on-screen."

He brought up the star chart.

There were three green dots, one red dot, two yellow dots, and one blue. Two of the green dots were close together. The red, yellow, and green dots made up an arc—almost a quarter circle—all around the same distance away from the central blue dot. The red and green dots were all moving, most of them toward the innermost green dot.

"This is stupid," the pilot said. "You can't outrun them."

Even as they watched, a smaller orange dot started out from the green dot that was farthest away. It headed for the red dot.

"Which one are we?" Ean asked, suddenly anxious. It looked like someone had fired on the red.

"Red," Sale said, succinctly.

The pilot pounded on the panel. "This is us," he said, pointing to the innermost green dot, the one close to the other green. "Now let's move, or we'll get caught in the cross fire." He was already sliding bars up, despite Craik's blaster at his head.

Ean understood what Sale meant. Red was Captain Helmo's ship. The green that had fired on it had to be Gruen. Why had Abram told Captains Wendell and Gruen that he was firing on them? As a distraction, he supposed, so they turned their attention to protecting themselves, leaving the shuttle alone.

"Make for the alien ship." Michelle's voice was hoarse behind them. "The sooner we get somewhere we can use—" She coughed weakly and couldn't continue.

If Ean couldn't control the lines before the alien ship fired on them, they'd be dead, but right now that seemed less important than getting there before Abram and Captain Helmo were blasted beyond repair.

"Go," Ean and Radko said, together, to Craik, and she waved the blaster in the pilot's face. "Do it. Toward the alien ship. Now."

"You're insane."

Ean could smell the pilot's fear. He didn't need the lines to tell him what the pilot would do next. Craik didn't either. She brought her blaster down on his skull even as he jumped out of his chair. She was already in the chair before he'd properly fallen.

Ean and Losan dragged the pilot over to a seat and tied his hands and feet before strapping him in.

"Ninety kilometers," Craik said.

Everyone was quiet.

On-screen all three ships—red and green—were firing at each other. So far the red dot was still there. Ean wanted to hear what was happening but knew he couldn't afford the time.

Craik did something to the screen, so they could see the dots on one half and the reflective sphere on the other.

"Eighty."

"Strap in," Sale said. "You, too," to the other three prisoners. "Put them at the front, so we can see them." Ean didn't strap in. He needed to stand to sing.

"Seventy."

The bureaucrat went ballistic. "Get us back. Get us back now." He unclipped his restraints and launched himself at Craik. Sale and Losan launched after him. "We'll die."

They subdued him with a swift uppercut to the chin.

"Strap him back in," Sale said.

"Sixty." Craik's voice was calm.

Line eleven was getting stronger. Ean took a deep breath.

"Can you feel it?" Jordan Rossi asked, his voice full of wonder. "It's like—" He broke off, as if he couldn't describe it. "The confluence—"

Ean was going to be very disappointed if he got to the confluence and couldn't feel it. Maybe line eleven was blocking it. Or maybe the trainers were right. Maybe he was defective.

Don't be stupid, he told himself. Line eleven was remarkable enough.

"Fifty."

He started to sing.

TWENTY-TWO

EAN LAMBERT

LINE ELEVEN ANSWERED, a powerful surge of joy that knocked Ean off his feet.

He forced himself not to panic, and to breathe when he could.

Subliminally, he heard the linesman's assistant cry out— the first sound he'd made—"The linesman," and Sale's seemingly disinterested voice reply, "He's fine. He always does that." She didn't sound worried although she had to be.

"He's choking."

"Oh, that one. He's having a heart attack," then, more sharply, "Give him some oxygen, then get back into your seat. There's nothing anyone can do for him right now."

"You're coming home," line eleven said.

"Forty," Craik said.

"Oh God," Losan said, and gripped the seat.

"I'm coming home," Ean agreed. Line eleven was part of him now. He knew that suddenly. He had a place in the lines here. The lines of the other ships echoed his thoughts. A place. He belonged. "Provided you don't kill us on the way in."

"Kill?"

"That thing you do." Line eight probably did it. Ean

changed his song to include all the lines. "When another ship comes close." He sang, as best he could, a description of the green field that came out and vaporized anything it came in contact with.

For a moment he didn't think they understood.

"Thirty," Craik said. He could hear the start of nerves in her voice because it vibrated along the lines. He didn't think anyone else could tell.

The lines hummed and thought for an eternity almost as long as the void. Finally line eight said, "The automatic-defense system."

"Can't you turn it off?" Temporarily, at least. He didn't want the ship damaged.

"No one has ordered it yet."

"Twenty."

He could feel the perspiration spreading out under his arms, down his back. Another time, another place, Radko would tell him he stank. Right now, he wanted to be in that other time and place.

"Please."

"It needs to be an order," line eight said gently.

"Who can order it?" He spoke through the comms. "I hope you're stopping, Craik." He didn't hear her reply, but the backthrust knocked him off his feet again, so he hoped it was all right.

"Why, you can."

It couldn't be that simple. "That's an order then," Ean said. "Turn off the automatic-defense system." Did the other lines accept him because line eleven had, or did they just accept the orders of anyone who could talk to them?

The lines heard his thoughts.

"You're of our line," line one said.

The acceptance of the lines engulfed him completely, overwhelming him so that he couldn't breathe. It was almost as bad as a line-eleven-induced heart attack. Ean laughed shakily. "Thank you." They were of his line, too. He would protect them and nourish them. Even if Lancia sold his contract.

Craik whooped at the panel. "Yes."

Ean turned to see. It took effort to see through his eyes

and not through the lines. The ship on-screen was no longer a reflective sphere. Instead, it was a long, low cluster of linked hexagons.

The others were cheering, too.

"Can I go forward?" Craik asked.

Through the lines, Ean heard Captain Gruen change her missile targets.

Craik didn't see it for seconds, then, "Shit. The ship we were just on launched a weapon at the alien ship."

Which was now unprotected, at Ean's request. "Protect yourself," he ordered the lines. "But please don't kill us, or Captain Helmo's ship." The lines would never recognize it as Michelle's ship. To them, the owner would always be the man who controlled the lines.

"Captain Helmo?"

He sang the distinctive ship music. Even before he was done, line eight had fired an offense. All Ean could do was pray.

He couldn't see the screens anymore, his head was filled with the sound of the lines. Sounds were magnified. He could hear twelve hearts beating, all a little irregularly, two more irregularly than the rest. The whoosh of the oxygen being forced down Jordan Rossi's throat. He even heard Rossi murmur, "If I die now, it's worth it, for whatever this thing is."

He couldn't have spoken more truly although right now, Ean was more worried about going deaf than dying.

"Take us in, Craik," he said, and prayed again.

No one spoke as she moved the controls forward.

"Ten kilometers," Craik said. "And this ship has counter-fired against the Gate Union ship."

That had been forever ago.

The shuttle engines were loud, and Ean could hear the whoosh of the air as it circulated. He even imagined he could hear the flicker of the lights on the panel Craik was handling with such finesse. Sights, sounds, smells, and taste were all combining together. He couldn't differentiate between them anymore.

"Seven kilometers," Craik said.

He'd missed eight and nine totally.

The shuttle sounds were gradually overtaken by the deeper throb of the engines of the alien ship. Impossible, because there was no way they could hear that until they were on board.

Gruen's ship had stopped firing.

"Six."

"Where do we go?" Ean asked the ship.

"Turn your engines off at—" Ean didn't recognize the distance in real space, but he could understand it in line space. "We guide you in."

"Five." The numbers were farther apart now. Craik was going slowly.

They reached the line space limit. "Turn off your engines," Ean said.

Craik obeyed instantly. They drifted for half a minute before something grabbed their ship and moved them sideways. Gravity returned with the movement. Ean, the only one standing, was knocked to the floor again.

"You should strap in," Radko said, and Ean crawled to a seat.

"Gravity close to Earth norm," Craik said. "And we're 4.73 kilometers from the ship."

"Hell of a kick for something that far out," one of them said.

"Suit up," Sale ordered, and from the way everyone checked the seals on the suits they were still wearing after their trip through the shuttle bay, Ean realized she wanted them ready to switch to the suits if necessary. Losan checked Michelle's suit, and Radko checked Ean's. "Prisoners suit up, too, if you can." Guards had to help the unconscious bureaucrat and pilot into their suits, while Jordan Rossi pulled his own on. The pilot, who was half-suited anyway, came round while they were checking his suit and nearly knocked Losan out struggling.

At least it would be one less person to carry. Or would they leave them on the shuttle? They definitely wouldn't be leaving Michelle. Or Radko.

Craik's quiet countdown went on. "We have moved 2.3 kilometers from our original position. Still at 4.73 kilometers from the ship—2.4, 2.5. Still at 4.73."

Two and a half kilometers had to take them some way around the ship.

"Totally under the other ship's propulsion now. We are, effectively, stationary," Craik said, just as another force took them and jerked them closer. The guards suiting Rossi went flying. "One kilometer. Still 2.5 laterally; 2.8, 2.9, 3.0, 3.2."

They were moving smoothly now. "Only 0.8 kilometers out."

"Almost a complete circuit of the ship," someone said. "Counterclockwise."

"Strap in," Sale ordered, and the guards suiting up Rossi strapped in hastily as Craik counted down—"0.4, 0.2, 0.0."

Ean didn't even feel them stop.

"Suits on," Sale ordered, and Radko leaned over to clip Ean's helmet on and ensure oxygen was flowing, even as she did the same to her own.

Now what?

They just sat there for a time. Ean thought they were waiting for him to do something. He unbuckled his seat belt.

"Wait till the all clear," Sale said.

He buckled it back on again.

Rossi still had problems with his breathing, but he'd obviously decided no one was going to do anything about it. He stood up and pulled himself properly into his suit. The Allied soldiers watched him.

A strong man. They would probably prefer a ten like Jordan Rossi rather than the one they had. Well, they had what they had, Ean decided.

Michelle had regained consciousness. Ean could see her face behind the translucent Plexiglas helmet, looking around with interest—and no small amount of pain. Her deep blue gaze met Ean's, and she smiled, and half nodded.

Ean smiled back.

Craik finally said, "Air contains mix of oxygen, nitrogen, and xenon with lethal amounts of radon. If you take your suit off, you'll be dead in half an hour."

"Suggestions, anyone?" Sale said. "We're five able bodies, four prisoners, and two injured and one—"

"Liability," Ean suggested. It was the literal truth.

Sale sighed. "I wouldn't call you a liability, Ean. We

wouldn't be here without you, and Princess Michelle would still be on the Gate Union ship. But you need protecting as much as Princess Michelle does."

"Two go with Ean to the bridge," Losan suggested. "The rest of us stay here to guard the ship and mind the sick."

"Or take all of us," Radko said. "We can use the stretchers. If Ean can vouch for us, the lines will protect us."

"Lines protect us," Jordan Rossi murmured. "You have a strange idea of how the lines work, sweetheart."

Everyone ignored him.

"The lines will protect *me*," Ean said. He knew that for certain; he wasn't sure about the others.

Their highest priority was to stop the Gate Union ships shooting at the *Lancastrian Princess*. He could see only two ways to do that. Find superior firepower on this ship and blast the Gate Union ships out of space, or take control of their lines and forcibly stop their firing. He preferred the second option, but how could he do it?

Michelle said, her voice weak, "I'd like to see the ship."

"What about anything else on the ship?" Ean asked. "Aliens, for example."

"You said days ago you think there's no one alive here," Michelle reminded him.

"I did?" He was still certain of that, but to risk Michelle's life.

Michelle looked at Radko and Sale. "We can't come to the biggest find in centuries and not look around."

"Okay." And this time, Radko made the decision. "I'll go on the same stretcher as you. We strap Mr. Bureaucrat down on another, tie the pilot and them—she nodded at the two Rickenbackers—to it, and they push that stretcher. Do you need to sit, Ean?"

He hardly heard her. The only way he really controlled the other lines was when he was in the void with line eleven. Could he do something then? Or maybe he could somehow delink the two Gate Union ships. Then if Captain Helmo jumped—and he'd have a jump ready, surely—he'd lose the enemy. And if Gate Union started firing on the alien ship instead, this ship could take care of itself.

"Ean?" Radko touched his arm gently. She was never afraid to touch him even if it meant getting zapped. She should be.

"Um."

Jordan Rossi was watching him with something approaching contempt. What must the other linesman think? A bumbling fool who couldn't even walk by himself. Once he'd been proud to call himself a ten. Now he was acting like he was the idiot half brother they were all ashamed of. And a little scared of, too. Worried he'd go berserk.

"I can walk."

"Let's do it, people." Sale handed out oxygen from the shuttle store, while Losan and two others set up the second stretcher and tied the prisoners to it.

Michelle reached out to pull Ean close enough that their helmets touched. "He's only a ten," she said softly. "Not worth your worrying about."

Rossi obviously heard the comment. He stood tall, sure of himself and his place, and raised a cynical eyebrow. But the observation somehow diminished him and made him suddenly ordinary. Ean smiled and gently patted the side of Michelle's Plexiglas. "Thanks."

RADKO checked Ean's oxygen. "When we get back to ship, he does basic space survival," she told Michelle.

Michelle nodded.

"A linesman who works on ships regularly would already know that," Rossi said, and the inference was obvious. Tens worked on ships because they had the higher lines. If Ean didn't know basic ship survival, he wasn't a real ten.

Even that didn't diminish Ean's peace.

"Comms." Sale held out her hand with the comms Ean hadn't even realized he'd dropped.

"You could use the shuttle comms," Jordan Rossi said.

Ean knew what Sale wanted. He took the portable comms and sang to alien ship line five. A song of communication and contact: a song to Abram.

The reply was instant. "Galenos."

Ean handed the comms to Sale and kept singing.

"We've landed safely, sir. Atmosphere inside the ship is lethal within half an hour. We're 3.2 kilometers from our entry point, sunside. We're now off to find the ship controls."

"Good."

Michelle took the comms. "Abram. We're safe here. We have Ean. Look after yourselves now." Which was so much what Ean wanted to say he almost stopped singing. "Before any diplomats get wasted," Michelle added, which Ean was sure was a pointed reminder that she—Michelle—wasn't the only one he had to save.

Abram just laughed. "Thank you, Misha," and Ean knew, as clearly as every other Alliance member listening, that Abram wasn't going anywhere until Michelle was safely back on the *Lancastrian Princess*.

Radko seated herself at Michelle's feet. Losan had put her shoulder back in for her, but Ean could see she was still in pain. She flexed her shoulder carefully and switched the blaster to her left hand. Ean hoped she could fire with the other hand.

Then they were off.

THEY found their first body two corridors up. It was octopedal in shape, with eight limbs from a round torso and a large head above it. Even though the limbs all extended from the same circumference, two sets of two were obviously arms and two sets were legs. The arms ended in three fingers.

"Two fingers and an opposable thumb," Sale said, on closer investigation. "And hard, horny growth at the bottom of the feet—analogous to hooves."

"Four hands," Craik said. "This ship is going to be a bitch to pilot."

"No decomposition," the prisoner pilot said, in a heavy, foreboding voice. Now that he was conscious, he was taking an active interest in the ship. He and Sale looked at each other.

"We're on a ship," Ean said. "You need sun and warmth for that."

"You need bacteria," Sale said. "And there are always bacteria on a ship." She rubbed her visor, as if she'd meant to rub her eyes, and moved on.

The next body—two of them—were at the junction of the same corridor.

"Similar height," Sale noted. About 80 percent of normal

human height. Most of the humans had to stoop to get through the doors.

These bodies hadn't decomposed, either. The skin was gray with black streaks. Ean wondered if that was because they were dead or if it was their natural color. They wore no clothing, but some of them had designs that appeared to be tattooed onto the skin.

This time it wasn't just Sale and the pilot who looked at each other.

After that, they found bodies everywhere.

It was a big ship, and the shuttle bay was nowhere near the bridge. It made for a long walk. In one big common area there were over a hundred bodies. So many they had to clear some away to get the stretchers through.

"It's like the *Balao*," Jordan Rossi said, his rich tones full of horrified fascination.

Crazy ship.

They had videos of the *Balao*. A news team had gone in soon after she'd been found and filmed every single room. People everywhere, their dead faces contorted in some unknown terror, bodies still preserved even after the ten years it took to find her. You could visit the ship, a macabre museum, if you wanted. They'd taken the bodies out, of course, destroyed the lines, and replaced both with plastic models. Ean had never been to the museum and never watched the video either.

He didn't realize he was singing a song of comfort to the lines until Jordan Rossi said, with some irritation, "Does he do that all the time?" Underneath, Ean could smell the fear through Rossi's line ten—or hear it, really, because smells didn't come in through the suit; but it registered in Ean's brain as a smell. He wasn't sure if Rossi was scared of him or of the ship.

"Yes," said Radko, short, sharp, and conversation-stopping.

Crazy ship. No one knew what made a ship crazy. Everyone knew if you jumped in one, you died. This particular ship had jumped three times since without incident. But no one had been *on* the ship when it jumped, Ean reminded himself.

One thing was certain. Michelle was never going to be on

this ship when it jumped. Her people would destroy the ship—and Ean—before they let that happen. So the only option left was to find the weapons controls and defeat the Gate Union ships by force.

As they got closer to the lines, Ean could hear just how bad they were, hurting as badly as the *Lancastrian Princess* after the attack, as badly as the *Scion*, the ship Ean had finished mending the day before Rigel had sold his contract to Michelle.

Even line eleven, which had seemed so strong, was damaged.

"The lines are bad," he said, to no one in particular, and Jordan Rossi half nodded in agreement.

Maybe they had some common ground after all.

TWENTY-THREE

JORDAN ROSSI

EAN LAMBERT WAS as crazy as everyone said. Crazier. And the way he sang.

Crazy Ean Lambert on a crazy ship. It could only lead to disaster.

This ship *was* like the confluence, and Lambert's song soared and swelled in and around it, almost as if he was talking to it. It was a song of comfort and calm, a song that said, "We're here. We'll help," and the confluence likeness of the ship calmed at it.

How dare he presume to know what the confluence wanted? How dare he even sing in the presence of it?

Fergus was no help. He watched Lambert with an open-mouthed fascination that bordered on awe. Rossi really was going to have to sack him. He felt a momentary regret for twenty years' good service, but Fergus and the confluence just didn't mix.

He concentrated on breathing. The confluence always took his breath away.

The Alliance soldiers had the upper hand for now, but this ship—this confluence—was his. Rossi didn't care how, but when this was over, the confluence would be his.

A ripple of amusement ran through the lines and even trilled out in Lambert's song. A strong sense of negation followed.

"These lines are already claimed," Lambert said.

So he was a mind reader now. It gave Rossi the creeps.

"You're thinking at the lines," Lambert said gently.

The magnificence of the confluence-like song came in then and made it hard to breathe, which saved Rossi from having to think. Even crazy Lambert had to stop singing for a while.

They stopped their relentless run to let the two linesmen recover. Rossi thought that if he'd been the only one affected, they might have kept running.

"Anyone remember how to handle a heart attack in a space suit?" the soldier in charge asked.

"Oxygen, get them out of it as soon as you can and into a hospital."

"You're guessing, Craik. When we get back, that's another thing you're all going to learn. You okay, Ean?"

Lambert nodded.

Soon after that, they came out into a large space that was the operations room or bridge. The screens were still on although the colors were in the blue spectrum. Come to think of it, the whole ship had a bluish tinge.

The combination of lines and confluence brought Rossi to his knees.

It was generally believed that line strength was even. No matter where you were on a ship, the strength was the same. That wasn't the case on this particular ship. Here on the bridge, the lines were so strong, it was difficult to think.

Lambert made straight for the covered-in hood, where the lines were strongest. The padded stool beneath it was low enough, and about the right shape to hold the body sprawled in front of it. From the seat, one would have a good view of the whole room. The Captain's Chair, presumably, and they had probably just met the captain as well.

A body was a body. So far as Rossi was concerned, it was just another piece of debris to clear away.

Lambert's song rose in the space, and multiplied, until it resembled a choir.

"How does he do that?" Fergus asked.

Rossi didn't care except that the other linesman was taking the sound of his confluence. If he kept singing like that, it wouldn't matter anyway. He'd have no voice left.

"UV filters," the lead soldier said, and everyone except Lambert snapped the filters on. The injured soldier—Radko—had to limp over to do it for him. Judging by the electricity that crackled around her suit, there was a lot of static on the line chassis. Lambert just kept singing. Rossi knew he imagined it, but some of the lines were starting to feel stronger.

With the filters blocking out most of the blue, the screens were almost ordinary. A starfield—maybe not the way humans represented them but obviously a starfield nonetheless. The ships were flickering bars of light. When Rossi put his hand close to a screen, he could feel the vibration coming from it.

The lead soldier, whose name turned out to be Sale, put her hand up to feel it as well. "This whole room is talking to us, and we can't understand it. Ean."

He half turned to look at her.

"Which are the weapons? And how do we use them?"

"I need to fix—" still in song, then Lambert looked at the prone Lady Lyan—unconscious again—and said, "Sorry." His song changed, rich and warm. Rossi imagined that line eight got stronger. Line eight. He tried to ground himself.

Fergus was studying the flickering bars of light on the starfield screen. "They're lines," he said. "Look. Ten for each ship."

Most of them came over to see.

They *were* lines. Rossi could feel it in that part of him that normally reacted just to the lines. He put a hand up to one particular set, and his line sense got stronger. He took his hand away, put it back again. He put his hand to another set. These lines were weaker, poorly maintained.

Imagine what you could do if you could tell the strength of the lines without having to physically visit the ship. Then Rossi snorted to himself. As if. No human had even come up with a tool to show the presence of lines—that's what linesmen were for—let alone display the health of them.

The lines flickered and faded as if they had gotten strong, then weak, then strong again. Lines nine and ten didn't flicker.

Which made sense, Rossi decided. No one was jumping. Then, far off to the edge of the field, lines six, nine, and ten flared into being, then steadied, and the other seven lines came on. Line ten was very strong.

"A ship just arrived," Rossi murmured and didn't question how he knew. He could feel it in the lines.

The ship in the center of the screen had twelve lines.

Rossi stared at it, convinced at first that the confluence was affecting his eyes. He nudged Fergus, who would soon be unemployed, but he could make himself useful while he still had a job. "What's that center one?"

"That's probably us."

Fergus was normally quicker than that, but it was too late then anyway because the starfield was replaced by a screen of pulsing lights and sound.

"What the?"

"This is the weapons system," Lambert said.

"I told you this thing was going to be a bitch to drive," Craik said.

That wasn't Jordan Rossi's problem. His was much closer. How to get Ean Lambert away from *his* lines.

Sale didn't, quite, throw up her arms. "You'll have to guide us," she said to Lambert.

"No, look," Fergus said. "They do everything by the lines. Color and sound." He indicated a row of lights showing strong on line eight. "These must be the weapons."

Lambert nodded. "Line eight is security."

How did he know that? No one knew what line eight did.

"And these must be the targets." Fergus indicated the fluxes that were roughly in the same positions they'd been on the star chart.

Fergus had always had a knack for lines. He'd come to House of Rickenback to train as a linesman, but he'd never been certified. Rossi often wondered how resentful that made him. And why the confluence hadn't attracted him the way it did real linesmen. He'd been immune.

"And the strengths would be the strengths of the lines," Fergus said.

Lambert touched the two weak sets. "So they will be the media ships. And this one"—strong on line eight and above but weak on the lines below and especially weak on line six—"this will be Captain Helmo." He sang the last, rather than spoke it, a tune Rossi recognized from earlier. His voice dropped back to normal. "The strength of the lines includes the people."

Crazy as it was, Rossi could feel they were right.

Fergus nodded.

"Might I remind you," Rossi said pointedly to Fergus, "that this is the enemy."

Fergus looked at him, then fell silent.

Line eight was exceptionally strong on Helmo's ship. Did that mean his security was exceptionally strong, too? Rossi could well believe that of Galenos.

Lambert continued. "So these two will be the *Wendell* and the *Gruen*. And this ship over here"—the one that had just arrived—"it has a ten on it."

That would probably be Rebekah Grimes. Rossi gritted his teeth in a smile that was closer to a snarl. First, Admiral Orsaya refused to take him to the confluence, had the cheek to stun him, in fact. Now she had obviously decided that what was happening here was more important than the confluence. She had better not think she was going to send him away from this ship now.

"God," said Craik. "Doesn't it recognize anything except lines? What happens if there's an asteroid in the way? It doesn't see it?"

"I just want to shoot them," Sale said. "Tell me how to do it."

Lambert sang to the lines.

The confluence swelled, sending Rossi to his knees. Line eight strengthened and kept strengthening.

"I turned the shield back on," Lambert said, his voice hoarse. "And we're moving toward Captain Helmo's ship."

Then his eyes rolled up, and he fainted.

"Brilliant," Sale said. "Now what?" She stamped her foot hard against the deck. "This line of yours," she said to Radko. "Is about as reliable as—"

Radko said mildly, "Lines need a safe place."

What in the lines did she mean by that?

"There's a lot of ambient noise," Fergus said. "Even I can feel it, and I'm sure Jordan can. He was bound to be overcome eventually. Both of them are."

Fergus really did seem to forget what side he was on.

Sale looked at him for a full half minute. "Okay," she said finally. "You two line experts"—she indicated Fergus and Radko—"can look after line twelve here. While you"—she looked at Rossi—"get me a comms to Commodore Galenos."

"I should be looking at the higher lines," Rossi protested. "There are two extra lines here, on this ship."

Sale looked exasperated. "I know that. We're on this ship, too, so get me that comms."

Fergus looked up from where he crouched beside Lambert. "The lines don't work that way. He can't get you a comms."

She glared at Fergus this time. "If Ean can get me a comms, then he can get me one, too. He's got ten bars on his shirt, hasn't he."

"Yes, but—"

"The lines don't work that way, sweetheart," Rossi said.

Sale looked from him, to Lambert, and back to Rossi again. "It's not exactly line twelve, is it."

What did that mean?

"If they do it for him, you can make them do it for you, too." She stepped up close and thrust her blaster into his chest. "And as you pointed out to your friend there. You are prisoners. You are expendable. If you want to stay alive, make yourself useful."

How dare she?

"He's a level-ten linesman," Fergus said. "You should treat him with more respect."

"I treat people with the respect they earn. So far, he hasn't earned any."

Rossi tried to move the blaster. He worked out every day and had muscles other linesmen envied, but her arm was rock solid. She was stronger than she looked.

"I am itching to pull this trigger," Sale said. "Just give me an excuse. I don't like you, Linesman, and so far you have done nothing except put other people down, including your own. Our linesman may only function half the time, but when he does, he delivers. Start emulating him, or you are just a piece of baggage I don't want to carry." She picked up the comms and held it out to him. "Now get me that line."

Rossi took the comms. He wasn't afraid of her, but he had no intention of dying right now, not with the ship-confluence so close.

Now, what exactly did she want him to do?

"Explain it to him, Radko," Sale ordered, and the injured girl sat back on her good leg with a sigh, leaving Fergus to attend Lambert.

She stretched out her bad ankle while she thought about it.

"What line is the comms?"

"Five." Rossi saw Lady Lyan watching him from the stretcher. How long had she been conscious? What had she seen? Then he was annoyed at himself. He was a level-ten linesman, with no need to worry how other people saw him. Especially not Lady Lyan, enemy and currently incapacitated.

"Use line five to make a link between this ship and ours," Radko said.

She had to be kidding. Yet line five was waiting; he could feel it. One didn't interact with the lines like that. Except, obviously, crazy Ean Lambert, and he had to admit it would be a lot more useful than just fixing the lines. Rossi stared at the comms.

Fixing lines was a complex mix of being aware of them and responding to them, and somehow using one's thoughts to manipulate the flow of the lines. It took natural ability and years of training to get into the trancelike state required. That's why most linesmen started young and apprenticed, then journeyed for years before they became certified. You started with the lower lines and graduated upward as you became more proficient. Finally, when your master deemed you could go no further, you tried for certification.

Line five should be easy for someone like Rossi. But he didn't have the faintest idea what to do.

Everyone was watching. He was aware of it in a subliminal way, in the same way he was aware of the huge bridge they were on and the dead alien bodies slumped over various consoles and on the floor. Why would a ship like this take so many people to run it?

He breathed in deep. *Open the comms*, and pushed the thought at the line as if he was mending it.

Everyone shuddered at the discordant sound that came

from the comms—even he did—but the line opened, and a flood of noise came through.

"Subtle," Sale murmured to no one in particular. She took the comms. "I take it everyone will hear this message."

"May not be a bad thing," Lady Lyan said.

"Personally, I'd prefer they had to snoop it, like everyone else." She thumbed the switch. "This is Sale on the Alliance ship"—she hesitated—"*Eleven* calling Commodore Galenos of the *Lancastrian Princess*.

"Come in, *Eleven*." Galenos must have been hanging over the comms to have answered so quickly. The line was weak and filled with static.

"Status report, sir. We have secured"—she made a face that couldn't be seen on the comms—"the ship and have turned the security system back on. We are now heading toward you."

"Good."

"Instrumentation is—" She paused, and Rossi could see she was sweating. "We will need you to gauge distance and speed. We cannot as yet do that ourselves."

"Understood."

Why was that so important?

Sale was sweating badly now. "Line twelve is down, sir."

Line twelve? Surely they didn't mean Lambert.

There were a few seconds' silence at that. Not long, but Galenos was normally prompt. "Same problem as before?"

"No," and "No, sir," from Lady Lyan and Radko together.

"Estimated time to resolve?"

"No idea, sir," Sale said.

"Thank you. We'll see you when you get here. Well done, all of you. Galenos out."

He clicked off, and Sale wiped her palms on her shirt. "Let's hope he got the message."

The noise from the comms still came through. The line was still open. They heard Galenos's voice through the static. "This is Commodore Galenos from the *Lancastrian Princess* calling the GU ships *Wendell* and *Gruen* and media ships *Galactic News* and *Blue Sky Media*."

He didn't include the third Gate Union ship that had arrived.

"Wendell," said a crisp military voice, and three other ships identified themselves as well.

"I presume you heard that transmission."

"It was broadcast on every channel," Wendell said.

"Without line twelve, we do not have full control of the automatic defense system. You know the limits." They'd been plastered over the media for days. "Have a jump ready."

"He got that message, at least." Sale was relieved.

"Line eight controls security," Lambert said, from where he was prone on the floor. His voice was hoarse and shaky. "And that joke about line twelve wasn't funny the first time, or anytime after."

"He knows who we mean," Lady Lyan said, her voice as shaky as Lambert's, and Radko said at the same time, "It's not a joke."

"There is a line twelve," Rossi said. "Line eleven and twelve, on this ship."

They looked at him as if he'd suddenly turned into one of the dead aliens, every single one of them with the same expression on their faces—at least, the Alliance soldiers did. The other prisoners just looked confused, except Fergus, who nodded.

"You just worked that out?" Sale said finally.

"A real line twelve?" Lambert asked. "You can hear it?"

This wasn't the time or the place to talk about how you felt the lines, you didn't hear them. Sale and Radko, and probably Lady Lyan as well, would jump to the defense of their crazy linesman.

"What does it sound like?"

"One of the new lines is obviously the confluence." Rossi knew that with a sudden certainty.

Fergus looked worried.

"That must be line twelve." Lambert looked disappointed. "I am deaf to it."

Lady Lyan sighed. "Don't you think it might be line eleven, Ean?"

"But I don't get the awe and the magnificence and the—"

"I don't care what anyone gets," Sale said. "We have a ship, basically out of control, heading toward the *Lancastrian Princess*. Do something about it."

TWENTY-FOUR

✦

EAN LAMBERT

EAN CRAWLED TO his feet the way he'd done so often lately, by rolling onto his stomach, then using his hands and knees to push himself up. It wasn't the sort of move he'd dreamed of making in front of other tens; but then, the dreams he'd had about other tens were just that, dreams. Reality was radically different. He had changed a lot from the sheltered linesman he'd been ten days ago.

And even if his dreams of being accepted by the other linesmen were crushed, he wouldn't change what had happened. He wouldn't change line eleven. Or even Michelle and Abram—although he'd thought he hated everything to do with Lancia—even if he could live his life over.

He crooned a tune to quiet line five. The static was loud and hard on the ears and added to the almost overwhelming wash of noise.

Line five was indignant. *"So rough. It doesn't know how to target its line."*

Now the lines were conversing with him. And why not? They were obviously intelligent.

"He's not used to lines like you." It was half song, half thought. One day he'd like to sit down with some linesmen

and compare how they communicated with the lines. Maybe every one of them did it differently. One thing was certain, these alien lines were far more used to aural communication than human lines were.

He changed his song to include line eight, and the on-screen displays changed back to the star chart.

"I hope someone can read these." It came out as song. If he sang too much to the lines, he'd start singing whole conversations. Then people really would know he was crazy.

They were already crowding around.

"We're moving fast," Craik said. "Which one is the *Lancastrian Princess*?"

Ean pointed to the one showing strong on line eight. He was getting used to the noise—somewhat—and could hear the ship song when he focused on it. Ships had their own song, and the captains—and the crew—helped make up the tune.

"These two are the media ships." Very weak lines all the way up to ten. "*Wendell*." Strong lines. "*Gruen*." The ship that had arrived earlier was strong on line ten, and he recognized it suddenly. "Rebekah Grimes."

Linesman Rossi nodded, as if Ean had confirmed something Rossi already knew.

"Just wait till I get my hands on her," Sale muttered. Ean glanced sideways at Radko and saw from the tightness of her lips, she was probably thinking the same thing. Revenge was a very Lancastrian thing. Rebekah didn't know it, but by killing Abram's people on the other shuttle—if that was what had happened—she had signed her own death warrant.

"You'll make sure Captain Helmo's ship is safe?" he asked line eight.

"Of course."

Ean changed his tune to include the other lines of the alien ship and checked them off one by one to see if they were okay.

"One?" Still heavy and depressed but getting better with people around.

"Two?" Fine. Needing some repairs, but otherwise good.

"Three?" The same.

"Four?" Likewise.

"Soon," he promised them. *"Once we've gotten past this little problem."*

"Five?" Better now.

"Six?" Heavy and strong, and likewise needing some repair. But it could go on.

"Seven?" Ditto.

Ean realized suddenly, that if he could talk to the lines, he could find out what line seven did. *"We'll have a long talk later,"* he promised.

"Eight?" Busy right now trying to avoid fire.

"Nine?" Fine, and thank you for asking.

"Ten?" Likewise.

"Eleven?" Contented now that Ean was here.

"There's another line," Ean said. *"I can't hear it. I can't talk to it. Tell it I am sorry, and ask if it's okay."*

He was met with silence. *"No,"* said line one, eventually. *"Only us."*

"Are you sure?"

Of course they were sure.

Maybe they couldn't feel the confluence either.

"Ean." Sale clicked her fingers in front of his face, then jumped back as if she was afraid of what he might do.

He slowly focused on her.

"Spatially, we're this close." She brought her thumb and forefinger together, so they were almost touching. "Do something."

"At least no one's firing on the *Lancastrian Princess* anymore," Losan observed. "Or on us."

"That's because they're all too busy preparing to jump." Sale turned away. "I hate this. I want to be doing something, not just waiting for someone else to do it."

Ean looked at the screen. "Should we bring them in the same way we came?"

"No." It was a general explosive no, from allies and prisoners alike; and echoed, too in the lines.

"The ship is too big," line eight said.

"Can we bring it inside the protection?" Ean asked, and spent time and voice explaining what he meant. They finally agreed on that.

The ships grew closer.

Captain Helmo was probably having a heart attack of his own. Sale looked like she was, and even Craik clutched at the air and looked as if she would grab the controls at any moment. Losan kept saying, "Oh God," over and over.

Sale was speaking calmly into the comms. "Moving closer. Cannot read distances."

An equally calm voice from the *Lancastrian Princess* came back at intervals. "Twenty kilometers. Nineteen. Eighteen."

"How does one pilot this thing?" Craik pounded on the panel in frustration. "I can't—"

"Careful," Sale said. "You don't know what you're hitting."

Craik pounded on her knee instead.

"Seventeen."

"You control the ship through the lines," Fergus said suddenly. "You'll never pilot it if you're not a linesman."

"Wonderful," Craik said.

"Sixteen."

"How close do we have to go?"

"This close." Ean showed them the line distance by holding his arms a handsbreadth apart, but they had no way of correlating it back to distances they understood. All he knew for certain was that it wasn't linear. The distance had halved between sixteen and seventeen kilometers.

"I want Yannikay," Craik moaned.

"Are you sure of this, Ean?" Sale asked.

As sure as he could be of the lines. Which meant little because he'd really only just met them. Ean shrugged.

"And thank you for that inspiring answer, too."

She'd have hated it more if he'd lied.

"Fifteen."

"I can't look," Craik said. But her eyes kept flickering over the panels, watching, guessing, trying to make sense of what was happening.

"Fourteen."

Abram's voice came through. "Should we jump?"

Everyone looked at Ean.

"Should they jump?" Ean asked the lines, then, more anxiously, *"You won't damage Captain Helmo's ship? Or*

the people in it," but he was starting to realize that to the lines people were part of the ship, not something separate.

"You want them inside the field," line eight said.

He nodded, then realized how the others would interpret that. "No. No. Don't jump."

Sale gripped the comms so tightly her fingers were white. "Ean says not to jump, sir."

"Thirteen," said the calm voice from the comms.

"Fine," said Abram.

"One of the other ships has just fired a weapon," Fergus said, seconds before Losan, who was watching that board, said, "Movement from the *Gruen*."

"You don't need me to tell you what to do," Ean said to line eight. *"Protect your own."*

He heard the line respond.

"Twelve."

Even Ean was sweating.

On the panel, something flared bright—and loud—as line eight's counterattack met Gruen's.

"Eleven."

It was deathly quiet on the bridge. Ean readied himself to sing. He didn't know what, or how he could help, but he would do what he could.

"Ten."

"Oh God," Losan said.

It was the only sound.

"Automatic-defense system not yet triggered," Abram said.

"Nine," said the calm voice.

Lights changed on the boards, and there was a burst of sound. Ean had no idea what it meant.

"Stationary at nine kilometers," said the calm voice from the *Lancastrian Princess.*

No one spoke.

Michelle took the comms from Sale. "How do we look, Abram?"

Abram took his time answering. "No idea," he said eventually, honestly. "We're inside the trigger zone. We should have set off the automatic-defense system. Is it still on?"

They all looked at Ean, who checked with line eight, then nodded.

"Apparently," Michelle said.

"Good. Then if Ean can guarantee you a safe path, let's get you home."

Ean tuned out then. If they planned to move on, he had some lines to repair.

TWENTY-FIVE

JORDAN ROSSI

AS LAMBERT SANG, the confluence that was the ship got stronger, until Rossi thought that his heart would burst with it. Then he realized that his heart was bursting, in a different sort of way, and he couldn't breathe.

He heard Sale's dispassionate voice. "Linesman's down. Losan, that's your job," and Losan was there to turn up the oxygen and do what he could for him, which wasn't much.

"This ship's going to be a bitch for heart attacks," Craik said.

Lambert sang through it all.

He stopped singing, once, when they started back through the ship to the shuttle. "I could stay on this ship," he said.

"Commodore wants you where he can see you," Sale said.

Radko added, "He wants you on the same ship as Princess Michelle, so if we have any problems, you can fix them." Rossi interpreted that as problems of the Gate Union kind. "You're our security blanket."

"Oh," Lambert said. His song changed. It sounded like he was explaining the whole thing to the lines.

Rossi just wished he'd shut up. His song got in the way of the ship-confluence, making it wax and wane.

Lambert kept singing as they made their way back through the long interior of the ship.

Somewhere, he didn't realize when, Rossi stopped fighting the confluence and let the ecstasy take him.

Sale stopped their progress halfway through, putting out a hand to stop both stretchers. "He's faking it," she said. Lambert wasn't the only one who stared at her in a spaced-out way. Fergus did, too—Fergus!—and Rossi could feel himself watching in a dreamy haze.

"You. Bureaucrat," Sale said to Gann, who was still lying on the second stretcher. "Up. Walk."

He didn't move.

Rossi had forgotten about Gann.

"Sweetheart. He's tied down." He almost didn't recognize his own voice; it had taken on the wonder of the confluence.

Sale stood back and let Craik and Losan untie their prisoner. When they were done, she prodded him with her blaster. "Up."

Gann got up, scowling.

Lady Lyan watched from the other stretcher. "Ahmed Gann," she said wonderingly. She looked at the soldiers surrounding them and smiled. It must have hurt. "You do well in your prisoners, people."

They all smiled back, and the ship-confluence smiled with them.

TWENTY-SIX

EAN LAMBERT

THERE WAS A whole phalanx of people to greet them. They cheered as they came through the triple doors of the shuttle bay.

The paramedics took Michelle first, Radko second, and Ean third.

"I'm fine," he protested, but they pushed him onto a stretcher and took off after the others.

Behind him, armed soldiers moved in to surround the prisoners.

Gospetto lay, bruised and gray, on the farthest bed in the hospital. He watched with disinterest as they carefully checked Michelle—he obviously didn't recognize who it was—and turned his head away when he saw Ean. Ean thought that might be the end of his voice lessons.

He planned to go to his own room, to shower and go to bed, but the medic ordered him to stay put. "You're under observation."

"I'm fine."

"Galenos's orders."

The medic wouldn't like that. He'd like it even less when

he heard about the bodies on the other ship. He'd want Ean out of his hospital so fast, he'd probably kill him to do it. Ean wanted out before that happened.

Abram dropped by an hour later.

He looked down at Michelle. "You live a charmed life, Misha."

Gospetto sat up, suddenly more alert. Abram and Michelle both half glanced at him. Ean knew, and he knew Abram knew, too, that if Gospetto hassled Michelle too much, the medic would probably slip the voice coach some triphene to knock him out.

"Truly charmed?" Michelle asked, raising a brow.

Abram just laughed. "Some of the fate has to go back the other way, Misha. Consider yourself grateful."

"But seriously," Abram said. "That's about as close as you've come to getting yourself killed since you were fifteen, and you stepped in front of that crazy free trader who planned to blow your father away. If you ever do that again I'll—" He didn't say what, but Ean thought it was more the audience that stopped him than want of a drastic enough punishment.

"It worked," Michelle said softly.

"You were lucky," Ean said, staring up at the ceiling. "Because if they had killed you, then your people would have killed me not long after, so it would have been a pointless sacrifice." Even now, the horror of what might have happened made him numb.

Michelle raised herself on an elbow to look at him.

"Linesman has a point," Abram said. "And you should be resting, incidentally. You've an interview in ten minutes."

Michelle grimaced.

It was Ean's turn to raise himself on his elbow. "She's sick," he pointed out to Abram.

"I know. It won't take long."

"It's called manipulating the media, Ean," Michelle said. "Using what you have to your advantage." She sat up. "You'll have to help me to the couch."

It was called cold-blooded and heartless, and for a moment Ean didn't like Abram much.

"You can do it here," Abram said. "More appropriate." He

bared his teeth in a parody of a smile at Ean. "More picturesque."

"Don't tease him," Michelle said.

THEY brought a portable video comms and set it up at Michelle's bed.

Abram didn't even let Michelle make up.

"She's bruised," Ean pointed out. The bruising had spread, and was visible at the base of her neck, across her shoulders, and down her arms.

"That's the whole point, Ean," Michelle said. "To show how badly I was treated." She was white and didn't look as if she'd last an interview.

Someone had knocked Gospetto out. Ean didn't know who'd done it—the medic hadn't gone anywhere near him—but he was unconscious, and that was a good thing. Otherwise, he would have tried to get into the interview. Even Ean knew that, and Abram must as well.

Abram moved Ean to another bed.

"You think I'll hog the interview, too?"

Abram's eyes were bloodshot, and he looked almost as bad as Michelle did, ready to drop although not as bruised. "If you have a secret weapon, Ean, it's best not to show everyone what it looks like."

"It's hardly a secret," Michelle murmured. "Not anymore."

MICHELLE lasted exactly four minutes into the interview. Long enough to assure the twin shocked faces of Sean Watanabe and Coral Zabi that she was fine, and long enough to start giving shaky answers to their questions of how she had been kidnapped and who had done it. Then she fainted.

Abram stepped in smoothly to cancel the rest of the interview.

Ean could imagine the mad scramble that must be happening on both ships to put that on air. In fact, he couldn't just imagine it, he could hear it through the lines.

"Isn't it bad to show weakness?" he asked Abram.

Abram watched the medic check Michelle. "Emperor Yu is sending a message." He said it absently, not really paying attention.

"The Emperor?" When had he come into the picture, and how could Abram know what message Emperor Yu wanted to send?

Abram turned to look at him properly. His mouth was a thin white line. "Don't mess with my daughter."

Ean didn't see how one could get that out of an interview that showed how weak Michelle was.

"For Aquacaelum and the Gaian worlds. Retribution will be swift. People will expect it after that."

Lancastrians knew revenge.

Abram sighed. "It's just a pity she collapsed before she named names. Now she has to do another interview later."

Couldn't they just do a media release?

Abram saw his look. "It's not quite the same."

The medic finished. Abram moved up to sit beside Michelle's bed.

"What happens now?" Ean started to ask, then realized the futility of it. Abram was asleep.

AS soon as Ean could escape, he did.

As he left the hospital, they brought Jordan Rossi in, pale and gasping and under guard. Losan was one of the guards.

"Lines a bit much for him," Losan said, unsympathetically. "He keeps going on and on about the glory of the confluence. We're sick of it. Then he keeps having heart attacks."

Line eleven still floored Ean on occasion, but nowhere near as often as Rossi succumbed. Was that because Rossi had spent less time with the line while Ean had gone through the void with it and was becoming used to it? And why did Rossi insist on mentioning the confluence every time he talked about line eleven?

Ean wandered down to Engineering. The lines, at least, were pleased to hear from him. They were better than they had been when he left, and today, Captain Helmo and Engineer Tai were happy to let him sing to them. Or maybe not happy, but Captain Helmo gave his permission anyway.

As he sang, line eleven came in strong. Ean wasn't sure how it joined in but suddenly he was singing to all six sets of lines, strengthening them. The *Lancastrian Princess*'s lines were strongest, because they were closer. The media ships' weakest. He still had to make good on that promise. He'd have time to do so now. He hoped.

To really fix them, he'd still have to go to each ship. He reiterated the promise he'd made to them those short days ago although it felt a long time now.

Line communication was two-way. As he sang, Ean could see the empty bridge of the *Eleven*, he could hear Coral Zabi's producers discussing a special angle to the Michelle story, he could smell the food Sean Watanabe was eating while his producers did likewise.

He was going crazy. Once, all he'd had to worry about was the noise, but more and more, the lines were spilling over into the other senses, so that he couldn't differentiate what was real and what was just a feedback loop. Watanabe's meal smelled damned good. It made his stomach growl with hunger.

Captain Wendell and someone who reminded Ean of Sale were going over a lunatic last attempt to try to break free from the Alliance. It wouldn't work, Ean realized suddenly, because line eleven considered the *Wendell* one of its ships now.

Ean changed his tune to include a comms to Wendell's ship. "It's a suicide mission, and it won't work. All you'll do is kill people."

He hoped it only went to the *Wendell*.

Ean couldn't see Wendell, but he could see the *Wendell* ship line surge in power, and he thought that might have come from the captain.

He sang until Radko risked life and limb to touch him and stop him. "Commodore Galenos said no more than two hours at a time until you can control your voice."

Ean blinked at her.

"A singing linesman who can't sing is useless. Know your strengths, Ean. And your weaknesses. And deal with them."

He blinked again, not quite in human space yet. Line one was clear as clear. He could hear Abram and Michelle talking quietly over a tray of food in the hospital. The sound was so clear it made a picture he could see. Michelle leaning back, exhausted, picking her way through her thoughts. Abram, equally exhausted, picking at the food on his plate. Neither of them ready for this. He could even hear Michelle's pain and Abram's exhaustion. It vibrated through him as if he were a string.

He was mixing the lines so badly, he could smell their food, too.

"Offer them their ships as a gesture of goodwill," Abram was saying. "We don't want prisoners from two warships."

He was talking about the *Gruen* and the *Wendell*. Ean could feel that through line one as well.

"No," Ean said. "They can't do that."

"We don't want you to lose your voice," Radko said, and he had no idea what she meant.

"I have to tell them." He made off down the passage. His voice was raw, his legs unsteady. Maybe Radko was right. Maybe he should stop for a while.

Radko sighed and followed.

He burst into the hospital. "You can't give the ships back," he told Abram and Michelle.

"We can't?" Neither of them looked surprised that he knew what they were discussing. "Why not?"

"Because they're part of the fleet now."

"They're Gate Union warships," Abram said. "The Alliance would fight over them."

"Not the Alliance," Ean said. "The fleet. Line eleven's fleet. It's not going to let you take two of its ships back. Not without a fight."

THUS ended what the media were calling the Seven Day War.

Michelle used the filmed attack on the *Eleven* to demand—and get—agreements from both Gate Union and Redmond. Emperor Yu used the kidnap of Michelle to demand—and get—Aquacaelum and the Gaian worlds kicked out of the Alliance.

The kidnap plan turned out to be deeper than anyone expected. They took seventeen Alliance worlds with them.

Michelle called it a pyrrhic victory.

"Seventeen of the strongest worlds," Katida said, and Ean could hear the sense of betrayal through her line.

"At least we've only got loyal ones left," Ean said.

At its peak, there had been 277 worlds in the Alliance. Time and wars and natural attrition had whittled this down, until in Ean's day there were 112. Now there were 95.

Katida snorted. "They'll be like rats deserting a ship until all that are left are the weak worlds who have no better option and those your charismatic Lady Lyan can convince to stay. She's going to be busy."

Back on Lancia, when Ean's whole world had been his little neighborhood and the lines, the fact that Her Royal Highness was holding together a wobbly alliance seemingly by charisma alone would have seemed laughably unimportant. There was probably no one Ean had grown up with who would appreciate what she was doing. And why should they, when their immediate worries were whether they had enough to eat that day or somewhere to live.

If Katida and Michelle were correct, if Gate Union won the war, then Lancia would become a third-rate world like Dante. Ean himself would rather go back to Lancia than live on the hell that was Dante. The people of Lancia wouldn't appreciate that Michelle had worked herself nearly to death for them, had been prepared to die for them, in fact. No, all they would see was the failure at the end.

That's all Emperor Yu would see, too, for he didn't accept failure.

"You're quiet this morning," Katida said. "Are you worried about today?" For today was the day the two powers signed the peace treaty, although no one thought that would last long.

Ean shook his head.

He and Katida had gotten into the habit of breakfasting together even if they never saw each other during the day otherwise. Ean thought Katida might deliberately be doing it to keep an eye on him. Not because she didn't trust him—he could feel through the lines that she did—but because she wanted to make sure he was all right.

Sometimes they talked lines. Sometimes they talked politics. Katida thought Ean needed schooling in politics. Today, it was politics.

"An alliance of weak worlds makes for a weak alliance," Katida said.

Ean was still unsettled by the realization that all the work Michelle and Abram had put in would still come to nothing if Gate Union ultimately defeated them. "Isn't that why you have an alliance? Because you are weak on your own."

"Sometimes," Katida agreed. "Sometimes you do it because it makes good business sense. Look at Gate Union and Redmond, allying even though they hate each other because together they are strong enough to take on the Alliance and beat it."

Ean wasn't sure if that meant she agreed with him or not.

Katida stared broodingly down at her plate. "I knew the Alliance was falling apart. I just hoped it wouldn't happen in my lifetime. Lady Lyan had better produce another miracle soon, or even Balian will pull out." Balian was Katida's home world.

Katida looked up into Ean's shocked face. She looked tired. "I'm only one person," she said gently. "I'll do what I can, but politics tends to get in the way. Ultimately, I have to support my government or be tried for treason."

Ean tried to remember who the Balian ambassador was and couldn't.

"We're just lucky we have the *Eleven*." Katida stabbed at the food on her plate as if she'd like to kill something. They ate in a morose silence for a time.

"Everyone's worried about Gate Union," Ean said eventually. "But Redmond's the only one with line factories now. Hasn't anyone thought about that?" He had. Gate Union might control the void entries, but right now, Redmond controlled the supply of lines.

"Oh yes," Katida said. "You can be sure we have. The one saving grace in all this is that Redmond did destroy the lines at Shaolin. I hear tell some factions in Gate Union aren't happy about that. Especially given Shaolin is unofficially Gate Union territory. Redmond says it was coincidence, of course, but no one believes it."

Ean remembered the dinner party of the first night and the deals being struck. "So do you think Varrn truly didn't know how the earthquake worked?"

"Who knows with a two-timing shark like Varrn. Even if he did, he would have tried to make us think he didn't."

Katida sat back to look up at one of the screens on the wall. The screens in the dining room were perpetually on now. "Redmond's not the only problem Gate Union has. Or us. This could be the start of the end for the Alliance."

Ean turned to look at her. "We just won a war." Sometimes Katida was too paranoid for her position as an admiral, but in this case, Michelle and Abram were as pessimistic as she was, and Ean still didn't understand why.

She waved it away. "The fact that they tried what they did shows who really is in command over there. And it's not good. You see, Ean." She moved her plate aside to draw on the tabletop with her finger. "There are factions in Gate Union. Over here we have Yaolin and Nova Tahiti and their supporters. They've been ascendant for the last few years, and it's mostly because of the people they have in power."

Individual people were more important in politics than Ean had ever thought. If Michelle and Abram weren't Lancastrian, then Lancia wouldn't be as powerful as it was in the Alliance. Emperor Yu was feared, often hated, and even Ean could see that no one supported Lancia for Yu. He certainly didn't. They were supporting it for the combination of Yu's daughter—who would inherit the throne—and for the steady military presence of Abram Galenos.

Katida jabbed at one of the spots she'd drawn. "Ahmed Gann, from Nova Tahiti, is the most powerful backroom manipulator in Gate Union. When he makes a deal, it can make or break worlds."

Why had such a powerful man been on the shuttle with Rossi then?

One might as well ask why Michelle was out here with the *Eleven*, Ean supposed.

Another jab, another spot. "And Yaolin has Admiral Jita Orsaya, who practically runs the Yaolin fleet."

Ean didn't have to ask what Katida thought of Orsaya, he could hear the approval through her line.

Katida circled the ring of worlds she'd made. "These are what we call the moderate worlds. The ones who don't want all-out war."

It was nice to know some people didn't want to fight. Ean heartily approved of that.

"Every single one of their economies is heavily tied up in trade with Alliance worlds, you see. If Gate Union takes this war to the next logical step, it will stop the Alliance using the void gates."

"I don't see why that's a problem," Ean said. "We'd just start up our own gates."

"If I were Gate Union, and that happened," Katida said, "my first thought would be to hack into the new void gate and send two suicide ships in together to blow it and whatever world was close by—probably Lancia—into a supernova."

Ean stared at her, the breakfast he'd eaten roiling queasily in his stomach.

"We're thinking of doing it to them, too," Katida said.

Her line told Ean they weren't serious but that they had considered it. He picked up his glass of tea and drank while he considered what to say. He had to hold it in two hands because his hands were shaking. Could the aliens have found a way around two ships appearing together in space? Once he knew the ship better, maybe he could ask the lines.

"Even if we don't blow each other's gates and surrounding worlds to pieces," Katida said, "the Alliance access to gates will be heavily restricted. Our economies will suffer." She tapped the tabletop where she'd drawn her map. "And so will theirs. That's why they don't want war. That's why they wouldn't have tried to blow us out of space to get the *Eleven*. And it's definitely why they would never have tried to kidnap Lady Lyan. For fear of the exact reprisals they got."

She drew another dot on the table, away from the other two. "That's why it means that Roscracia and their faction are in the ascendant. They want war. They have a lot of support and—if rumor is correct—they have the Linesmen's Guild behind them as well."

Ean hadn't heard that rumor. "Why do they want war anyway?"

"Power. They can see the Alliance falling apart. They see it as a chance to become the only political group in the galaxy." Katida snorted. "I don't know why they bother because if they wait long enough, the Alliance will fall apart naturally."

That could take fifty to one hundred years, Michelle had said.

"But they don't want to wait, and Admiral Markan, of Roscracia, is determined it's going to happen now. He's almost as charismatic as Lady Lyan, and he talks a lot of sense. The longer the war drags on, the more it costs each world. A single political unity will enable better trade and more affluence."

There was one flaw in Katida's argument. "If that's so, then why was Gann involved in the kidnap?"

"That." Katida shook her head admiringly. "Fiendishly clever of Markan. Gann is his biggest threat inside Gate Union, so Markan sets him up. And Orsaya, too, for she was in charge of trying to get the alien ship. Markan needs Gann out of the way because Gann alone can sway the council. So I hear, and this is rumor, mind."

Where did she get her information, sitting on the ship like this?

"Markan called in a lot of favors to get the council—and the military—to agree first to Yannikay's little exercise, then to kidnapping Lady Lyan. But since Orsaya is in charge of the operation, if anything goes wrong, she gets the blame. No doubt that's why she called Wendell in to do the actual kidnapping. He's the best."

It seemed unfair to Ean. "So they know Markan organized it, and he still wins."

"Not exactly wins in this case, for we've still got that ship out there. I imagine Markan thought he'd be head of the Gate Union fleet by now. Instead, he has to finagle a new council meeting and ensure that everyone knows where the blame lies. He's up against Ahmed Gann, who is most unhappy."

She hadn't gotten that information from Ahmed Gann because, through the lines, Ean had heard Abram interrogate Gann. Spoken with, Ean corrected himself, because at that level of politics one didn't interrogate one's enemies, one "spoke with" them. The whole thing had been very civilized.

He hadn't told Abram he could hear through the lines yet although he suspected Abram already knew.

He turned to the screens himself.

The news today was all about the signing of the peace treaty. Coral Zabi and Sean Watanabe were both on-screen—different screens—talking about it.

The sound was up on the Watanabe screen. "This is Sean Watanabe from the special convoy traveling with the Alliance ship *Eleven*, reporting to you on the historic treaty that is to be signed in just minutes."

Abram hadn't told the media their ships had been effectively confiscated. Instead, he'd brokered a deal with both groups, allowing them to tag along and report on what happened with the alien ship. Whoever had made the actual deal had done a brilliant job. The ships had been named, specifically, and it was generally thought in media circles that if they changed ships, the Alliance would use that to back out of the deal.

It was the media who had pointed out that the *Eleven*—everyone had picked up Sale's broadcast and was using the name—was a long way from the nearest servicing depot and that if they couldn't take their ships away for servicing, they'd have problems. So the Alliance had "reluctantly" included servicing in the agreement and gotten themselves more concessions out of it because the media really wanted to stick around.

Ean was going to service the first ship soon.

He had asked Katida who'd made the deal, and she'd just said, "Watch any contract you sign with Abram Galenos or Lady Lyan. They always get what they want."

His own contract had another ten years to run.

On-screen, Michelle and Ahmed Gann appeared together in the doorway.

A rustle of expectation swept through the dining room.

"Convenient that one of our prisoners turns out to be Gann," Michelle had said. "I really worry that our luck will turn soon. It's been too good for too long."

"Luck has nothing to do with it," Katida said. "They kidnap Lady Lyan, naturally they will send someone of equivalent stature to bargain for her release. Don't forget everyone expected us to be making concessions to get her back."

Privately, she'd said to Ean, "What was lucky was your being kidnapped along with her."

"I wouldn't say that was luck," Ean had said. They were lucky they hadn't been killed. "And we weren't exactly kidnapped. Only Michelle was. The rest of us were collateral damage."

However it had happened, Ahmed Gann apparently had authority to deal on Gate Union's behalf, and now they were here to broker a peace settlement that Ean didn't really understand; but it involved Gate Union's giving up some pretty hefty concessions in order to placate the Alliance, not to mention getting its prisoners back.

The Linesmen's Guild had also given up some concessions to get Jordan Rossi, with a lot more reluctance and—so rumor had it—only after Gate Union had interceded. One of the things they had given up was Rebekah Grimes. That particular bargaining point had been nonnegotiable. Everyone on the *Lancastrian Princess* knew what would happen to Rebekah Grimes. Ean felt sick when he thought about it. He wondered if Rebekah knew yet.

Another thing they had given up was Fergus Burns, at Sale's and Radko's insistence. They'd thought he might be able to help with the *Eleven* because he'd been able to read some of the instruments. Jordan Rossi wasn't happy about it, even though Ean had heard—at least three times through the lines—Rossi tell Fergus he was fired as soon as they got back to Rickenback.

He didn't know what Fergus thought.

On-screen, an admiral in a beige uniform with the formal Gate Union rainbow sash over her left shoulder, and the blue-striped sash of her home world over her right stepped next through the door, followed by Abram.

"Jita Orsaya," Katida said, watching her. "I'll bet she's spitting."

Like Katida, she looked ageless. Her face and figure looked young, but something about the way she held herself made Ean think she was quite old. He tried to see her hands but couldn't.

Orsaya was an admiral, Abram only a commodore, but no one questioned his right to be the military representative for the Alliance.

The meeting was held on planet, on the supposedly neutral world of Iris.

"It's not," Katida had confided to Ean. "It's loyal to Gate Union."

"So why go there?" Ean asked. What could be more stupid than walking into an obvious trap?

"Jita Orsaya has given her word we will be protected through the signing of the treaty." Then Katida did the baring-of-teeth smile whose meaning Ean still hadn't worked out. "The Alliance has promised that if any one of the ambassadors so much as gets threatened, then we—that means you and line eleven—will start taking out cities."

Ean hoped it wouldn't come to that. He had dutifully moved line eleven's fleet close to the planet on request, but only after a dozen Alliance warships had descended on and disarmed the *Wendell* and the *Gruen*.

The prisoners came next. Two ships' worth, guarded by Abram's people. Captain Gruen was a petite woman with gray hair and permanent frown lines. She looked exactly as Ean expected.

Captain Wendell was a shock. Ean had expected someone like Abram, or a male Katida. The reality was a tall, skinny stick of a man with white skin and dyed maroon hair and a uniform that just made regulation.

"What do Wendell's crew think of him?" he asked Katida. The crew were impeccably dressed, as well turned out as Abram's guards, almost as if they were trying to make up for their captain's undress.

"Follow him to the ends of the universe," she said. "Don't be fooled by appearances, Ean. He's Gate Union's rising star. Youngest captain. Brightest mind. Although," she added, "this kidnap fiasco might set his career back a little."

Then came the linesmen. Jordan Rossi, big-chested and confident, smart in his midnight blue with the leaping gold rickenback on the pocket. The blue was almost the same color as Michelle's skirt and jacket had been that first night. Fergus Burns, same blue outfit but looking washed-out beside Rossi.

Ean couldn't tell what he was thinking, but as the camera closed in on the linesmen, he could see the black shadows under Fergus's eyes and white lines around his mouth. As for Rebekah Grimes, he couldn't tell what she was thinking either. A cynical half smile turned down one corner of her mouth, but that could have meant anything.

The ceremony didn't take long. The agreements had been made days before, the contracts checked and triple-checked by the lawyers and everyone else. All they had to do was sign them.

The only exciting bit was when Gruen refused to go when the prisoners were being handed over. "I'm staying with my ship," she said. Her own people had to drag her out, and she went screaming all the way.

"One crazy ship in the making," Katida said.

Captain Helmo would have stayed with his ship. "Wendell didn't want to stay with his." Ean was disappointed.

"Don't underestimate Wendell, Ean. He's not stupid enough to fight a fight he'll lose. He'll be back—with a crew—to collect if he wants it. When we're not expecting it."

"Maybe we should have kept the captains," Ean said. No one understood the bond between captain and ship, and it was definitely stronger on some ships than others. Being asked to choose between your allegiance to your world and your allegiance to your ship would be hard. He wondered what Captain Helmo would do. Steal the ship back if he could, probably, and take a dive into the void with it if he couldn't, with the lines in full agreement.

Ean shivered at the thought.

TWENTY-SEVEN

JORDAN ROSSI

JORDAN ROSSI FELT like doing some screaming of his own.

He watched, stone-faced, as they sedated Hilda Gruen and carted her off on a stretcher to the hospital.

"What about you?" the orderly asked Captain Wendell.

"I'm fine," Wendell said.

He wasn't fine. Rossi could see the anger that radiated out from him, could even feel it in the lines—and if that bastard Lambert had tainted his linesmanship, Rossi was going to strangle him with his bare hands even if he had to listen to the lines singing while he did it.

Rossi remained stone-faced as he watched on-screen the wrap-up of the short ceremony. He continued to watch as the Alliance representatives—including their tame media—left. It was dusk when they did, and the six ships hung as low, artificial stars in the northern sky. Not long after their shuttles reached ship, they blinked out.

He didn't think at all, because if he did, he'd think about the ship-confluence and how it had been taken away from him.

He and Wendell made a silent circle of two inside a relieved, chattering crew, who hadn't expected to get out alive.

The silence of the ship-confluence was like an empty hole in Rossi's soul. He mocked himself for it. *You hated the confluence.* But it didn't ease the pain.

FINALLY, he and Wendell were summoned to a meeting.

It was held in the largest senate hall on Iris. Ahmed Gann was there with another man. Tall and thin, with the classically handsome features of a politician. Both of them were dressed in the long black ceremonial robes of the Gate Union Council. The rainbow sash of Gate Union crossed the left shoulder while the sash on the other shoulder denoted their home world. The green nebula for Nova Tahiti on Gann's, the blue-striped sash similar to the one on Orsaya's uniform on the other man's.

Rossi still hadn't worked out which world she came from. Once Fergus would have told him immediately, but there had been more important things to know these last few days.

"Council has convened a meeting for this evening," Gann said to Orsaya. "They're looking for someone to blame. Markan has called in every favor he has. The odds are stacked against us."

It seemed to Rossi that Gann was a lot more comfortable around Orsaya than her own councilor was.

Orsaya's face was grim. "I hear you." She and Gann looked at each other and sighed in unison. "So this is it?" Orsaya looked at her own councilor. "You are aware of the consequences from here?"

He had a politician's voice, clear and ringing. "If we lose or do nothing, we drop down to a second-class world. If we win, things will remain as they are. We are aware that Roscracia and its allies will try to crush us. Our worlds have voted. We say try this one last thing. It is worth the risk."

Orsaya nodded at Gann. "You know what to do if you need to."

"I know what to do." He half bowed to her, and he and the other councilor left.

Orsaya stared after them. "Once in the void," she muttered, and turned and left the room herself.

"You realize there's a third option," Wendell said, as he

and Rossi followed her out. "You win, and Markan decides to destroy you anyway."

Rossi had no idea what they were talking about.

"Roscracia was always going to destroy Nova Tahiti and us with it," Orsaya said. "The trick is to win so powerfully that they can't. If we win, it will take a coup to oust us."

Wendell raised an eyebrow.

All Rossi had been worried about was Sandhurst's taking control of the line guild. He'd spent too long at the confluence. He was out of touch with important happenings.

The large senate hall where the hearing was to be held was awash with uniforms, full of top-level military from the Gate Union worlds. Prominent among those on the first row of curved seats that faced the dais was a dark-haired man in the distinctive purple-brown camouflage uniform of Roscracia. The name on his pocket said MARKAN. He was laughing with an admiral dressed in scarlet. So this was the infamous Admiral Markan who wanted so badly to go to war that he had talked Gate Union into what had to have been the stupidest kidnap plan in a long time.

Not that it looked to have destroyed his standing any, from the way he and the other admiral were laughing together, but that could have been for show. Rossi knew as well as anyone how important it was to always look as if you were winning even when you weren't. Although based on what Rossi had just witnessed, Markan wasn't going to be laughing for long.

Sometimes politics even turned his stomach.

There were two lonely empty seats on the raised dais. So, it was to be an interrogation.

Orsaya took a seat in the bottommost tier facing the dais, close to the far left. She exchanged a cold nod with Markan, seated in the middle of the same row. Given how they obviously felt about each other, it was probably a good thing everyone had been asked to leave their weapons at the door.

Rossi tried to work out who in the crowd were pro-Markan, pro-Sandhurst, and who were on the Gann/Orsaya side. He couldn't tell.

The only other civilian in the room was Iwo Hurst, the Sandhurst cartel master. He was seated in the second row, behind Markan.

Hurst looked at Rossi, then away.

Admiral Orsaya frowned at Hurst. "What is he doing here?"

Markan said, "The line cartels feel a linesman should be involved in the questioning."

Oh yes, there was no doubt Roscracia fully supported House of Sandhurst's bid for line supremacy.

"Surely, then, Leo Rickenback should be here."

Surely Janni Naidan should, given that Gate Union knew well who the cartel power brokers were, and that Morton Paretsky and Rebekah Grimes were both unavailable. Although Rossi would have settled for Rickenback. Leo was his cartel master, after all. The only communication he'd had from Leo so far was a cryptic apology, which didn't make any sense at all. Maybe it was for not being able to get here.

Iwo Hurst said smoothly into the tense silence, "As you can imagine, Rickenback is somewhat busy right now. I am here in his place."

Rossi knew he was missing something important. It was a pity Fergus wasn't here. He could work out the nuances faster than anyone.

"This is military business, not line business," Orsaya said.

"Lines are involved," Markan said. "It is appropriate to have a linesman here."

There were a lot of nods in the crowd. Rossi wondered if Orsaya was overconfident of her ability to take Markan down. He had a lot of support here.

The two admirals matched stares.

Another committee member stirred. This one wasn't an admiral. He was only four seats away from Orsaya. "I concur with Markan. It is appropriate to have a linesman present when we are discussing lines."

Rossi revised his imaginary pro-Markan count up. So many people so obviously supporting the Markan faction meant those worlds would support Sandhurst, too. It hadn't been this bad when Orsaya had dragged him off on this crazy escapade. What had changed since then?

He laughed to himself. What had changed was that in between, there had been a botched attempt to first murder, then kidnap the Crown Princess of Lancia. It should have made the Orsaya/Gann faction ascendant. He suspected it had done the opposite.

Orsaya looked at the committee member who had spoken. Her expression was eloquent. Didn't they already have a linesman present?

"An unbiased one," the committee member said.

He would keep, but Rossi would remember him. He could have pointed out that Hurst technically wasn't a linesman, just a cartel master, but he didn't. He wanted to know what Hurst planned.

"Very well," Orsaya finally agreed after another long, cold pause. She turned back to Markan. "I know what you are doing. Remember, this is my operation. If you—or your linesman—obstruct us, I will put in a formal complaint."

Orsaya might have said she was in charge, but she let others do the questioning, only intervening when the questions went off track.

What had happened? How had it happened? What was the ship like? How had they gotten onto the other ship? How did the alien ship control the Gate Union ships?

Wendell's answers were as clipped as Rossi's own.

"Listen," Rossi said finally, angrily, when they started on about the new lines. "I had experience on that ship. I had experience with those lines. You took me off. You exchanged me for that—" He couldn't say bitch here, linesmen had to show some solidarity. "Rebekah Grimes." And for Fergus. "What sort of stupidity is that?"

Orsaya fixed him with an icy glare. "The stupidity is entirely your own, Linesman."

How dare she call him stupid?

"Linesman Grimes engineered the death of a shuttle crew. If you fail to realize the implications of that, you are stupider than even I thought."

Twice.

Iwo Hurst opened his mouth as if to argue, then thought better of it.

"Lancia's terms of exchange of linesmen were nonnegotiable." Orsaya's lips straightened into the thin line Rossi was coming to know so well. "Maybe, Linesman, if you want us to believe we are working on the same side, you might start cooperating, and telling us what we want to know."

The military gentleman sitting beside Orsaya—another admiral—leaned close to her and said under his breath, "Maybe we should just kidnap Lambert."

"Believe me," she said, equally quietly back, "if I could, I would."

Rossi heard it, clear as clear, through the lines.

TWENTY-EIGHT

✦

EAN LAMBERT

REBEKAH GRIMES WAS tried for war crimes two hours after the ships moved to Alliance space.

Ean was the only one who didn't attend the trial. It didn't make any difference. He could feel it through the lines, heard it on line one more clearly than if he'd been there. And on Rebekah's line ten.

It was a somber ceremony. The only sounds were the voices of the witnesses called to trial—there weren't many of them—the questioners—Abram, Michelle, and Captain Helmo—and Rebekah Grimes's clear, succinct answers.

What had happened after the shuttle had left the *Lancastrian Princess*? She didn't know. Why didn't she know? She just didn't know. How had she killed the crew on the shuttle? No comment. Why did she destroy the lines? She had no idea what they were talking about. How had she ended up on a Gate Union ship? She was a linesman, trying to get home. Naturally, she would hail the closest ship.

All the way through, Ean could hear the satisfaction that emanated from her line. They couldn't prove anything.

At the end, Abram said, "Linesman Rebekah Grimes. We accuse you of the deliberate murder of at least ten Lancastrian soldiers, along with the destruction of a shuttle belonging to the Empire of Lancia. We accuse you of conspiring in the attempted murder of Crown Princess Michelle of Lancia, and of all occupants of the *Lancastrian Princess*.

"You can accuse all you like," she said. "You cannot prove any of it."

"Circumstantial evidence points to your being involved." The lines vibrated with the emotion in Abram's voice. "As such, you have been tried and found guilty."

"I'm a linesman," Rebekah said. "Outside the jurisdiction of the Alliance or Gate Union. The cartels will try me and find me guilty or not."

The cartels would never find her guilty. Ean understood that now. She'd been working with Gate Union and the cartels. Not to mention, she was a level-ten linesman.

Abram was the one who executed her.

The execution was followed by a wash of satisfaction from the lines. It was done. Their coworkers had been avenged.

Afterward, Ean stayed in the fresher long after the water ran out.

TWENTY-NINE

JORDAN ROSSI

THE GRILLING WENT on for hours.

The investigative committee wanted to know everything. The ship?

"Massive," Rossi said, remembering the big common room where they'd found over a hundred bodies. "It will crew at least a thousand, probably more."

The aliens?

"Dead." Then he amended it to, "It's a crazy ship. Like the *Balao*. Bodies everywhere."

That started a hum of excited conversation that didn't stop until Markan demanded silence.

The new line?

Rossi stared out across the room. The new line was his. These people could never comprehend the magnificence of line eleven. His gaze moved down to Iwo Hurst, in the second row, as intent as anyone else on his answer. Give them the lines, and he was giving it to Sandhurst, too.

The scarlet-uniformed Centauran admiral laughed, half-hopeful. "There is just the one new line, isn't there? I mean, is it likely that we'll see a whole new set of lines one day?"

Rossi refused to think about the twelve lines displayed on

the ship. Of the inane joke Sale had dared to make. "Isn't one line enough?"

"Didn't someone mention line twelve?"

He stared the admiral down. "Only as a joke."

The weapons?

"I have no idea, but a linesman turned them on and off."

"Linesman?" Iwo Hurst sat up, but he was drowned out by the scarlet admiral asking, "What sort of weapon caused the heart attacks?"

The truth about a linesman's weakness was for linesmen alone. "They used line eleven," Rossi said. "I'm not clear how."

"How did they know enough about the ship in order to make that happen?" Markan demanded. "You said they hadn't been on it before."

"It was as new to them as it was to us. I think." Rossi paused to consider his answer. They'd think he was trying to remember how it had worked rather than just working out what to avoid saying. "Some form of human-line interaction," he said eventually. "Much like the way linesmen interact with lines now, I suppose."

Like Linesman Lambert did, anyway.

No one had invited the shuttle pilot to this session. He would probably have talked about the singing, which Rossi didn't want to do. The pilot had worn the same beige uniform as Orsaya, so no doubt he'd reported everything to her, but from the looks of this room, Orsaya would try to keep some facts close to her chest. She might need them soon.

Rossi chose his words carefully again. He had to tell the truth, but he also wanted to misdirect Sandhurst. If House of Sandhurst became the de facto line guild, he'd lose any chance at obtaining line eleven, for Sandhurst would keep it for their own tens. "They had a linesman with them. Ean Lambert," and the glance he exchanged with Iwo Hurst showed how much use that would have been. At least, he hoped that was the way Hurst interpreted it. Now, he needed to misdirect everyone as to how much of the work Lambert had done. "But they made me work, too. For example, I was the one who worked with line five so they could contact the *Lancastrian Princess*."

Let Hurst know how invaluable he'd be. There was grim

satisfaction in the knowledge that he *had* linked the lines, but he wasn't going to mention just how he'd done it.

Luckily for him, he'd mentioned the magic word—Lambert—that could be guaranteed to distract Orsaya.

"What sort of things did Lambert do that you couldn't?" Orsaya asked. It was the first question she'd asked in hours.

Here he could redirect with equanimity, given that Orsaya had implied that la Dame Grimes would be imprisoned until the Linesmen's Guild could get her out and therefore wasn't around to call him a liar. Long enough for him to go back to his line, at least. "I'm not clear. Lambert and Grimes both spent time going close to the ship, apparently. They're linesmen, so I imagine they learned something from those trips."

"How do you think Lambert did it?" the admiral beside Orsaya asked.

Rossi could feel their excitement through the lines. He was tired, that was all. He was imagining things, and whatever Sale had made him do to the comms had done something to his nerves—not that he normally had nerves—and he still hadn't settled. That was all. And if Lambert had done anything to his ability to read the lines, he was going to kill him.

He'd had enough.

"It's a crazy ship," he said. "Another *Balao*, with dead bodies everywhere. Lambert is as crazy as the ship. Not only that, he taints every linesman he comes in contact with."

Through the lines, their excitement reached another level although you couldn't tell from their faces.

"You came in contact with him," Orsaya said. "Are you tainted?"

He'd walked into that one. He could see the other questioners drawing away. Iwo Hurst, too. He could imagine how Iwo would use this later.

"Of course not," Rossi said, ignoring the whisper of the lines that told him he lied.

Orsaya leaned closer. She was as crazy as Lambert was.

"Crazy or not," Admiral Markan said, and he obviously wasn't doing it to save Rossi's reputation, "we need that ship. If we attack now, we—"

"Lose another ship," Wendell said.

"We are prepared now. We won't lose—"

Orsaya cut across them both. "We don't need the ship. We need Lambert, and if you haven't worked out why yet, Markan, maybe you could leave me to do my job because I have."

This was taking Lambert worship too far, but she seemed to have acquired another devotee because Wendell gave her a sharp glance, then nodded.

She might even be right because there was no denying that Lambert did control the *Eleven*.

"We need the ship, and we need linesmen," Iwo Hurst said. "Sane ones," and he deliberately looked away from Rossi as he said the last.

If Rossi let him get away with that, then Hurst would be Grand Master within a month.

"Like those from the House of Sandhurst?" Rossi said. "They're going to be a *lot* of use, given that everyone except Rebekah Grimes has spent the last six months at the confluence doing absolutely nothing." It didn't matter that he'd done the same. He was here now, and he had to break their confidence in Sandhurst.

He could see he'd scored. Orsaya was right. The last six months had left people worried about the higher-level linesmen.

Orsaya supported her chin on her clasped hands, elbows on the desk, and visibly relaxed. Rossi thought she had never looked so dangerous. "How do you plan to get the ship, Markan? March into Alliance territory and take it from them? Right under the vids of two of the largest media organizations in the galaxy."

"If you ask me, the Alliance is a little too fond of manipulating the media," one of the other interrogators muttered. "*I* wouldn't like them that close all the time. Too worried it would backfire on me."

"I hear their tame media cost them a fortune," the admiral from Centaurus said. "Galenos had to agree to maintain their ships for them."

There were chuckles around the room. "That's the media. Out for anything they can get."

Wendell sat up straight. "What do you mean?" Rossi

didn't need the lines to feel the sudden energy crackling from him.

Markan shot the original speaker a poisonous glance. "We can handle the media."

Orsaya laughed. "Isn't that what you said just before Yannikay so publicly declared war on our behalf by deliberately attacking three Alliance ships and leaving the media to film it?"

"That was hardly—"

"They're calling it the Seven Day War, and they blame Gate Union for starting it."

"And who botched that particular piece of action?"

Wendell jumped to his feet. "Objection." He stalked to the edge of the dais. Rossi thought he was about to jump down and throttle Markan. By the way half a dozen people around Markan jumped up, hands to weapons they didn't have, they did, too.

Wendell settled for a clenched fist and remained on the dais although he did look as if he'd like to hit someone. "The brief was to kidnap Lady Lyan. That was done. We carried out our part of the operation. Despite all the problems."

"That was nothing—"

"Nothing to do with you? Markan, you gave me the order. I was there when Orsaya tried to argue you out of it. We both did."

Rossi looked around to see where the dark green uniform of Wallacia—Wendell's home world— was. There, a man and a woman in almost the highest tier, in the center.

"We all have operations that go bad, Markan. Be big enough to accept that and don't start blaming other people for it. Particularly not when those other people did their job. Despite everything."

It should have gotten Wendell a reprimand from his own boss, but the woman just looked at the man beside her and shrugged.

Orsaya's cold voice cut across the tension. "And despite all your plans for takeover, Admiral Markan, you forget one important thing." Her gaze swept the whole room. "You all forget it." She let the silence grow until Markan looked as if he was about to speak. "We don't even know if we can beat the Alliance yet, especially not while they have that ship."

Markan subsided.

Iwo Hurst said into the silence that followed, "Assuming you get the ship, you will need a linesman."

Rossi could see what he was doing. He would have done it himself. Pull the attention back to the things that were important to you, and all Hurst wanted was the *Eleven*.

In his dreams.

"Allowing Ean Lambert near a ship with lines is tantamount to inviting disaster," Hurst said. "Who knows what damage he might do."

"Maybe you should have thought of that six months ago," Orsaya said. "When you sent all your linesmen off to the confluence and left Lambert as the only one available to fix the higher-level lines. Think of the damage he might have done to *those* ships."

At least half the people in the room moved uneasily at that. Even Rossi would have done so except he'd heard it all before.

The Centauran admiral said, "We've had ships repaired by Lambert. Our captains are more than happy with the results. So much so that they're demanding Lambert now. More people should sing to the lines, I say."

Iwo Hurst didn't, quite, move away. "Anything Lambert did would have been accidental. I'm sure he had no idea what he was doing or how."

From where Rossi had been, it had looked as if Lambert knew exactly what he was doing.

The awkward silence that followed that was broken by Wendell. "You said Galenos made a deal with the media ships. What was the deal?"

Markan gave him a sharp look. "How is that relevant to what we are discussing here?"

"Maybe we're all getting tired," the admiral who'd first mentioned the media said. "I know I am. I'm sure we'll get back on track after some food, maybe a drink."

Orsaya and Markan looked as if they could go for hours more, but half the room was already standing. "Excellent idea," the Centauran admiral agreed.

Rossi followed Orsaya and Wendell into the restrooms. He was more exhausted than if he'd spent a day fixing particularly bad lines.

"You said they made you use the comms," Orsaya said to him, as she washed her hands. "That you managed to do part of what Lambert can do."

"Sweetheart, don't think I want to do what Lambert does." But a traitorous part of him did. The ability to use the lines rather than just repair them. It made his heart beat as fast as the confluence did. "Lambert has no idea what he is doing, and the whole thing is likely to fall on top of him and whoever travels with him. One day, your enemy, Lady Lyan, will be just another corpse in stasis, people visiting her in a museum just like they do to the *Balao*."

"The people aren't in the museum," Orsaya said repressively. "They're in labs being carved up. Or rather"—she finished drying her hands—"trying to be carved up, because no one has yet managed to circumvent whatever stasis field surrounds them enough to do it. No one knows if they're even dead yet."

Wendell made a sound like he wanted to be sick, and to be honest, the thought turned Rossi's stomach, too, but he wasn't squeamish.

He looked at Wendell. He was young for a captain, and that reaction—along with the white skin under the bad dye job—didn't fit what Rossi had heard about Gate Union's up-and-coming finest. "No stomach for it, Captain?" he asked, maliciously. It was nice to be able to put someone down. It made him feel more normal.

"No stomach," Wendell agreed, which effectively stopped any further baiting. He blocked the door as Orsaya started to move out.

It occurred to Rossi then that they were the only three in this washroom. Surely that was unusual, given how long they'd been interrogated and how close these particular facilities were to the meeting rooms.

"You help me get my ship, and I'll get you Lambert," Wendell said.

Who cared? If Rossi never saw Lambert again, it would be too soon. But Orsaya was listening.

"How?"

"Through the media ships," Wendell said. "Did Galenos really agree to service them?"

"Yes." She showed him something on her comms. Presumably the Alliance–media contract that dealt with servicing. Rossi started to push past, but Wendell was about as immovable as Sale. He didn't want an undignified fight, so he moved back to lean against the wall. It would be nice to get back home, where he was treated as befitted his rank.

But he didn't want to go home. He wanted to go back to the *Eleven*.

The tiled wall was cold behind him as he finally accepted the truth. His whole life, everything he'd known about the lines, was nothing compared to the lines on the alien ship. He *had* to return to it.

Wendell scanned the contract. "Maybe this time they have been too clever. If anything goes wrong, they'll have to fix them quickly, or they'll be in breach of their contract. Galenos must have hated whoever's idea this was."

"The Alliance has always manipulated the media," Orsaya said. "It's been effective to date. They wouldn't change it now, not even for Galenos."

"He wouldn't have wanted this, and he usually gets what he wants." Wendell frowned at the screen. "What are we missing?"

"What has this to do with Lambert?"

"Could you get my people onto a media ship?"

Orsaya nodded. "But how is that—"

"Galenos is legally contracted to take those ships with him, so he'll want them ready to jump. Always. Suppose one of the higher lines is damaged. What will he do?" And before Orsaya could even speculate on what he would or wouldn't, "He'll send a linesman to fix it. And how many linesmen has he got who can do the job?"

One.

Wendell started pacing. The excess movement made his long and ungainly body oddly graceful. "Get me and my crew onto a media ship, and I'll get you Lambert."

"How? You take him back to the *Wendell*, I suppose. What if they manage to control your ship like they did before?"

"I control my ship. No one else."

Orsaya nodded.

Rossi couldn't move. His heart started to pound. Wendell could take him back to the *Eleven*. He would go with Wendell to the media ship, and Rossi could make his own way from there.

"Take me with you," he said.

"No," said Orsaya.

"Yes," from Wendell at the same time.

"I need him at the confluence," Orsaya said. "If we can't get Lambert, he's the only one who has any experience with line eleven."

Two short weeks ago, he'd have given anything to get back there.

"I am a linesman," Rossi said. "I can do whatever I want." He didn't need to wait for Wendell; it would just be convenient. As soon as this damned interrogation was over, he was going back to the *Eleven* any way he could.

Orsaya's smile was cold. "Linesman, you *don't* have any choice. Have you checked your contract lately?"

He stared her in the eyes and refused to give in to her bluff.

"Sometimes we learn from our enemies," Orsaya said. "Although I'm sure you cost us a lot more than Lambert cost Lancia." She pulled up another contract on her screen. This one had Jordan Rossi's name at the top.

Rickenback had sold him? Rossi felt dizzy, had to put a hand to the wall because the floor threatened to rise up to meet him. He hated that the weakness showed.

"Impossible." You didn't sell contracts over line six. The cartels controlled the sevens and above.

"Sold," Orsaya said. "For a lot of money and a chance for Rickenback to be Grand Master of the new body that is overseeing all the cartels."

Rickenback would never agree to it.

"Otherwise, that honor would have gone to Sandhurst," Orsaya said.

She was talking nonsense. "You yourself said you didn't want Sandhurst." The military had no business poking into line business. The cartels wouldn't allow it.

"You knew that," Orsaya said. "I knew that. Maybe Cartel Master Rickenback knew that. What a pity someone forgot to tell the other cartels. One can be too devious in politics sometimes, Rossi. I believe Rickenback was under a lot of pressure to take the position." She added, mock-consolingly, "Not to mention that you were effectively a prisoner of the Alliance and not expected to make it back to the cartels."

"The cartels don't work that way," Rossi said. "They're outside regular politics." He would have been returned.

Wendell snorted. He sounded like a horned rickenback. "You're all playing politics."

Not where the individual linesmen were concerned. That was what the cartels were for.

Orsaya flicked her fingers dismissively. "Not that it matters," she said. "The new body won't have any real power. We—the military—will handpick every linesman we want. Now that we've seen how well it works."

"In your dreams, Orsaya." The linesmen would complain, but in a contract system where contracts were bought and sold, he could see how it would work. Especially in wartime, where Gate Union would apply pressure to ensure the linesmen worked only for their side. Some of the cartel houses would even do it willingly.

What would the military do once the war was over? Sell the contracts back to the cartel masters? That was unlikely. Rossi could see a future with two castes of higher-level linesmen. Those who stayed with the cartel houses, those who contracted out to the military.

"Once in the void, you can't change the path." It was an old proverb from the Yaolin worlds. Come to think of it, her accent had the tightness of Yaolin vowels as well. "Blame the Alliance for starting this. The linesmen will go to the military. The cartels will lose power."

Not if Rossi could stop it.

"Check your contract, Linesman," Orsaya said. "And be ready to move out tomorrow with me. Work with us, and I'll work with you to get you back where you want to be."

She wasn't taking him where he wanted to go.

Rossi said, his voice choked with the need of having to say it aloud, choked with the need for having to beg. "The real confluence is with the *Eleven.* I need to go back to the ship."

Orsaya stared at him for what seemed forever. He tried to keep his expression neutral although he could feel a muscle in his jaw twitch and knew she saw it.

Her voice was gentle, as she said, "Don't you understand? There's another ship—another *Eleven*—out at the confluence."

She was certifiably crazy.

Although . . . there were some similarities. As similar as someone talking about the pleasure of a good Lancian wine compared to the actual pleasure of drinking it.

"We've had all our nines and tens out at the confluence for six months," Rossi said. "Why haven't we worked this out ourselves by now?"

"You haven't had *all* of them," Orsaya said.

He didn't dignify that with an answer.

IN the end, Rossi got to go with Wendell anyway because, as Wendell pointed out, they needed a linesman to damage the lines.

"Use a disruptor," Orsaya said.

"What would that achieve except to tell Galenos he's under attack?" Wendell demanded. "Destroy all the lines, and he knows we're there. He'll send in half an army. Destroy one line, and he won't be expecting trouble."

"Galenos always expects trouble."

Linesmen didn't damage lines, they fixed them, but Rossi didn't point that out. He was going back to the *Eleven*, and that was all that mattered.

If Orsaya was right about the confluence—and maybe she was—then it was a weak ship compared to the *Eleven*. Even if she got her crazy linesman to help her. That was fine by Rossi. Lambert could have the confluence; he'd take the *Eleven*.

Wendell was one of the few people who could stand up to Orsaya. Even Markan would have backed down by now. This time, it was Orsaya who conceded. "But only for the first part. I want him out of there before the fighting starts."

THIRTY

EAN LAMBERT

THE FIRST VISITORS Ean accompanied over to the *Eleven* were a select company comprised of Abram, Katida, Captain Helmo, Governor Jade from Aratoga, and Governor Shimson of Xanto. Ean didn't know Shimson—or Xanto—at all. He was an older man. Governor Jade didn't know him well, either, for they were making the kind of small talk that two strangers might make.

Ean smiled at them both impartially, then looked uneasily at Katida. "Do you think you should come? Line eleven can be strong." He didn't want her to succumb to a heart attack.

Katida inclined her head toward the guards who escorted them. Sale and her team, and four other guards Ean knew by sight but not by name. The four new guards all carried medical cases and had paramedic badges on their pockets.

"Galenos assures me your people have training in emergencies like this."

In the shuttle on the way over, two of the new guards seated themselves either side of Ean, the others either side of Katida.

Radko wasn't there. Ean felt uneasy without her. He

hoped nothing went wrong. "Keep these people safe," he sang in a soft undertone to the lines.

The lines seemed amused at his protectiveness. "Of course we will. They are of our line," and he got distinct sounds of Helmo and Abram.

Ean looked thoughtfully at Abram. Helmo was part of the fleet for he was the captain, and the ship recognized him as such. Did the lines recognize Abram because he was from Helmo's ship? After all, hadn't the *Lancastrian Princess* lines considered the guards Rebekah had murdered as their own?

Abram and Governor Jade were talking to Sale.

Sale shuddered. "It's like walking in blind and deaf. You know things are interacting around you, but you can't see them and you can't hear them. Until he does something"— she indicated Ean—"and the displays change."

"So you don't see anything at all?" Governor Jade asked.

"Once you block out some of the blue, the screens look almost like a starfield. But as to how to use the boards." Sale shrugged. "I have no idea."

In the background, Craik counted off the distance.

"Engines off," Ean said, when the *Eleven* ordered it.

"Exact same distance as before," Craik said to Helmo, who nodded.

The ship grabbed the shuttle and jerked. "Forgot to warn you about that," Sale said.

Craik did the same countdown she'd done the first time they'd come in. "Stationary," she said finally, and Ean could feel it was so.

Ean sang a greeting to each of the lines on the *Eleven* as he waited for the all clear. The lines sang a welcoming chorus back. Katida clutched at her chest and looked as if she was going to choke. One of the crew members beside her reached for the oxygen tank and administered it.

"Gentle, gentle," Ean sang. "Weak lines."

"Fix," the lines offered.

Ean knew instinctively that their fix would be too strong for Katida. "No, please. Human. Fragile containers."

He wasn't sure they comprehended, but they didn't "fix" either.

They waited until Katida had recovered enough to stand. "Should we leave her here?" Abram asked.

"I am not coming out here just to stay on the shuttle," Katida said.

"I'd recommend she stay, sir," one of the paramedics said.

Abram turned to Ean. "Will it make any difference, here or on the ship?"

The shuttle was already on the ship. Ean shook his head.

They suited up. Ean was pleased to see that both governors required assistance, while he could suit himself now, for Radko had made him practice putting a space suit on. Lots of times. He was nowhere near as fast as Radko wanted him to be yet, but Craik checked his suit and didn't have to adjust anything.

They took two stretchers. The paramedics clipped their cases underneath them. Governor Jade looked dubiously at them. "Are we expecting trouble?"

Two stretchers for two linesmen. Ean wondered if Governor Jade knew that Katida was a linesman.

"It's best to be prepared," Abram said.

"UV filters on," Sale said. "We found last time that we missed a lot until we cut some of the blue spectrum."

Radko had taught Ean how to do that, too.

"This ship needs repair," Captain Helmo said.

How did he know that just by stepping onto the ship if he wasn't getting the information through the lines?

They stopped at the corridor where the first bodies were to let the visitors examine them—albeit at a distance.

Ean moved away and found he was singing the comfort song again. Sorry to the lines for their loss.

"But you're bringing more lines in," line one said.

For a moment, Ean thought it meant dead bodies. From where? Then he realized the line song had a note of hope in it and thought he detected a hint of Katida there as well.

"Not yet," he said hastily, and glanced over to where Katida, Abram, and Helmo were gathered over the aliens. Abram was not going to give Katida this ship. He wasn't either, actually. "But I'll get you lines, I promise."

He kept making promises he hoped he could deliver on.

Every line song, from one to eleven, soared hopefully.

Lines needed lines, although by the way they said "lines," Ean knew they didn't mean lines like them, they meant lines like him. People.

Katida leaned against the wall. "What was that for?"

Should he admit to it? He'd promised, hadn't he. "I think I just told them we'd get them a crew."

Governor Jade looked over at Abram. She looked as if she was glad to look away from the bodies on the floor. "It would have to be an Alliance crew, not a Lancastrian crew. After all, this ship belongs to the whole of the Alliance."

Shimson looked up, too, although he wasn't as squeamish. "Crewed from every world in the Alliance," he suggested, as if the idea had just occurred to him. Ean could tell through the lines that it hadn't, that he'd been waiting for a chance to say it.

Abram considered it.

"The Alliance is so full of holes, we might as well give the ship to Gate Union now," Katida muttered.

Yet she had suggested a combined Alliance crew to Ean yesterday morning at breakfast. Politics was strange.

"We'll need to move on," Sale said. "We've limited time, and I'm sure you'd like to see the bridge."

By the time they reached the huge common room, with its hundreds of dead, even Governor Jade had stopped shuddering at the bodies they passed. "We had to move some of these to get Lady Lyan's stretcher through," Sale said, indicating the makeshift path.

The UV goggles made the markings much clearer. On one wall, a massive mural swirled and seemed to jut out. It reminded Ean of the starfields on the bridge, but when they moved closer, he could see it was something else altogether. "No lines," he said.

"I haven't seen any lines yet," Katida muttered.

There were lines everywhere, but Ean knew which ones she meant. "You will, Katida. Wait until we get to the bridge."

Governor Jade stopped to study the mural. "It's impressive," she said. "I wonder if it's supposed to represent something."

Sale moved them on. "We've still a way to the bridge."

The bridge itself was just as Ean remembered it.

Captain Helmo avoided the Captain's Chair—walked quite far around it, in fact—and made his way across to one of the screens. If you could call them screens. Displays, maybe.

Abram leaned over for a closer look at the flickering bars of light. "I can't understand a thing."

Governor Shimson put out a hand, almost as if he wanted to touch one of the lights. "Amazing," he said. "You can hear and feel it, too."

Ean glanced at him sharply. "Are you a linesman, Governor?" Only a linesman should be able to recognize that.

"Me." Shimson laughed. "I'm afraid not. I had dreams of it once. When I was a lad. I tested high on the Havortian tests, you see."

"But you failed certification." It was more of a statement than a question. It was obvious now why he had been invited on this trip. Fergus Burns had been a failed linesman, too. The Alliance wanted to know if it was just Fergus who'd been able to see and feel the lines or other failed linesmen.

That could be interesting. It would mean that it wasn't just linesmen who could work on the *Eleven* but people who'd failed line certification as well.

Shimson laughed again. "At the time, I was devastated, of course, so I decided to kill myself. It was the best thing that ever happened to me."

"Killing yourself?" He obviously hadn't succeeded, for he looked alive to Ean. Even the lines counted him as a warm body in that part of himself that recognized the lines recognizing warm bodies.

"On Xanto, we have a suicide bridge," Shimson said. He stopped, looked at Ean. "Have you ever been to Xanto?"

Ean shook his head. Until recently, his whole life experience had been Lancia, then Ashery.

"You should go. It's a beautiful place. It's a wild world, with natural stone arches—imagine stone bridges, if you like—only they're a thousand meters high. There's one they call End-It-All. It's four thousand meters. It's a popular suicide spot. There's this perfect launching platform at the top. It takes a week to climb, so you have to be serious about ending it. And thirty seconds to get down. Some people say that's the best part. Going down."

Who would know? If you fell four thousand meters, you wouldn't live to say whether it was fun or not. Ean thought it might be a long thirty seconds. Rather like when he went into the void, but at least he knew he'd come out of the void eventually.

"Most people start off alone, but sometimes you meet up with others on the track. That's where I met Minerva."

"Your wife?" Governor Jade asked, and Ean thought from the way she said it that Shimson's wife was more famous than he was.

"Yes." Shimson's smile showed he was still fond of his wife. "We had a stand-up fight the day we met, and we've been fighting ever since."

"When did you decide to turn back?" Ean asked.

"Oh, we got to the top. It's the most beautiful place you can imagine." He smiled again. "We argued about whether we were going to jump or not, then we turned around and came down again."

"I'm glad you came down again," Ean said.

"So am I, Linesman, so am I." Shimson looked at the panels again. "Anyway, that was my brush with the lines."

Maybe. Maybe not. Ean looked at Abram and Katida but didn't say anything. They must have known; otherwise, they wouldn't have invited him. He took a deep breath and started to explain some of the line functionality as he knew it.

"Everything's based on the lines. See, here, the strength of the lines denote the strength of the ship. That's the *Lancastrian Princess*," waxing strong. "The media ships," not quite as weak as they had been in the lower lines, for Helmo had sent his engineers out to them. "And the *Gruen* and the *Wendell*." Both of them sad, lonely sets of lines right now. Ean looked away, feeling guilty. The lines were still strong, especially the *Wendell*, but there was no mistaking they were missing something. Their crew.

There were other ships on the display. The hundreds of sightseers, getting as close as Abram would allow them. He pointed out the *Gruen* and a nonfleet ship to Abram. "Can you see any difference between those two?"

"Not at all," Abram said. "Can you?"

"That's the *Gruen*." Ean could tell from the way line

eleven claimed it as its own. As for the other one, he didn't even know how to find out. He could identify its song—tired and old and wanting to retire—which he thought came from the captain rather than the ship itself. The lines were in reasonable condition although maybe someone should look at the higher-level lines. The higher-level lines on a lot of ships needed work.

Radko would have been handy, to tell him how he might have identified it. She always knew how to point him the right way.

He looked at the points on the display and had no idea how to identify any of the non-*Eleven* ships.

"It looks like a regular starfield," Abram said. "Sort of." He took out his comms and brought up his own miniversion of it. "Depth is not displayed as we understand it, I think." He showed his comms to Katida and Helmo. "I wonder if they're displaying their third dimension another way."

"Or if they're displaying it in more than three dimensions," Helmo said.

There were five dimensions. Length, width, depth, time, and the void. "Like in the void?" Ean asked.

Katida put out a hand to the display. "You can hear it. You can feel it. Maybe they're displaying depth through another sense. Like sound."

"But the strength of their lines is the sound," Ean said.

"Maybe." Katida consulted Abram's comms and compared it to the starfield displayed. She checked the comms again, then pointed to a strong line close to the one Ean hadn't been able to identify. "Which one is farther out?" Tired, old, ready-to-retire or the new ship, she meant.

Ean pointed to the new ship. It wasn't something he could have explained. The lines told him it was farther out.

"Exactly." She showed Abram and Helmo, who nodded. "Strong lines, for that is almost certainly Qarro's ship." Her eyes gleamed suddenly. "I wonder if you could find out for us."

"Let's not try it now," Abram said hastily. "Ean would probably sing it into the *Eleven*'s fleet. Try explaining that to Qarro."

"Try explaining that to the Alliance," Helmo said. "It would be taken as an act of war."

"Pity," Katida said.

"I might not even have been able to contact it," Ean said. "It has to be close enough for me to talk to it."

"Not even through line five?"

"I still need the other lines. All of them." At least, he thought he did.

"Hmm," Katida said.

Abram's comms beeped discreetly. "We've fifteen minutes before we need to start back," he said. "Can you show us the weapons, Ean?"

Ean wasn't sure if it really was fifteen minutes or if he'd done it to divert Katida. He sang the request, and the screen displays changed to the pulsing bars of light. "This is the weapons system."

"Beautiful," said Katida.

"And we think these are the targets. Other ships." Ean pointed to the fluxes that were roughly where the ships had been on the star chart.

The *Lancastrian Princess* was strong again, the media ships weak. The *Gruen* looked like it had on their earlier visit to the *Eleven*, but the *Wendell* looked almost dead.

Ean looked at it. "I don't think it should be like that."

"Is that the *Wendell*?" Katida asked.

"You can recognize it?"

She shook her head. "Weapons system, you said, and I know Galenos stripped the weapons on that ship."

Ean looked at Abram, talking softly over one of the boards with Helmo. "Why?" And if he did it for one ship, why didn't he do it for the other? The *Gruen* was still strong.

"Piers Wendell will come back one day to collect," Katida said. She looked at the lines on display. "How does it know there are no weapons there? Can it tell any ship's arsenal?"

It took a while to translate the question into line terms. By the time he was done, everyone was watching him expectantly, waiting for the answer.

"I think," because he wasn't sure he understood fully, "it's because they're part of the *Eleven*'s fleet." The lines were a persistent chorus of "our lines." "They share information." That seemed to fit in with what he knew of how line eleven kept the fleet together. "I don't think they can tell what other ships have."

"It's interesting they don't seem to have a "big picture" view like we do," Abram said. "When Gruen fired on the *Eleven* the last time you were on this ship, what happened? How did you know she had fired?"

He'd heard her through the lines. "She gave an order."

"So you heard Captain Gruen," Katida said. "But you don't know how the *Eleven* identified it as a threat. Or even if it did identify it as a threat."

"No."

"Hmm." She blew out her breath, Abram-style. "I think we have a little further to go before we can use this as a warship."

"That will come," Governor Jade said. "Once we have a crew on board, they'll work it out."

Shimson nodded.

Abram glanced at his comms. "We need to head back," he said.

Ean noticed he didn't comment on the multiworld crew.

THIRTY-ONE

JORDAN ROSSI

THEY DIDN'T GET to leave immediately, for the council meeting Ahmed Gann had warned them about started while Wendell was making preparations. Orsaya was called to the council.

"Wait here," Orsaya ordered Rossi.

For a change, he was happy to wait. Soon, Wendell would take him where he needed to be. When Wendell came into the apartments they'd been allocated, Rossi was sitting, sipping Lancian wine.

"Where's Orsaya?"

"Council chambers."

The blood drained from Wendell's face, leaving it white and stark. "The meeting they were talking about this morning?"

"That's the one." How in the lines did Wendell do any commanding when his emotions were displayed so obviously on his face?

Wendell went whiter, if that was possible. "How long since she left?"

"An hour, maybe less." Maybe Rossi should order some food to go with the wine. It was making him light-headed.

Wendell snatched the glass out of his hand. "We need to get there. Now."

"What the?"

"Hurry."

"Do you mind?"

"You don't understand," Wendell said. "I heard about that meeting. She's going to lose. No matter what she thinks she can do to beat Markan, she can't. The council will vote to remove Orsaya from her position. They'll put Markan in charge."

Wendell was as insane as the rest of them. "We can all see that coming."

"You still don't understand." Wendell pushed Rossi out the door. He was like Sale, deceptively strong for his build. "Once Markan is in charge, he'll cancel the order to get Lambert. He'll use House of Sandhurst to get the ship."

If Markan even realized there was a ship yet. Even Rossi still wasn't convinced there was.

"And if he cancels the order to get Lambert, I lose my chance to get my ship back." And Rossi lost his chance to get back to the *Eleven*. "We need her to sign those orders before she goes into that council meeting."

Rossi put on a spurt of his own. "Why didn't you say that?"

THERE were guards on the doors of the council building, barring everyone from entering. It was a big crowd, and there was a barrage of press drones. Obviously, someone scented news inside. Wendell walked straight past them. Half a block farther down, he swerved into a building with a big aircab sign, where he took a lift up to the rank and chose one of the smallest vehicles.

After he'd paid for a night's hire, he sat and did something on his comms.

"I thought we were in a hurry," Rossi said.

"We are, but this is delicate work. Don't talk."

Rossi didn't ask. He didn't want to know.

Ten minutes later, the aircab rose, out of the ranks, up into the sky, where it circled the city, then seemed to drop down again into exactly the same place.

"Didn't work?" Rossi asked.

"Of course it worked," Wendell said, as the aircar came down gently in the rank at the top of the council building.

There were guards up here, too, but they were expecting the cab, and the two of them. They checked their comms and waved them through. Wendell even made small talk with one of them. Rossi didn't think they'd ever finish.

"She'll be in the visitor's chamber at the back," Wendell said in the lift down. "Which is lucky for us because we don't want to have to walk through the councilors to get to her."

"You've obviously done this before," Rossi said. "How many times?" He hoped Wendell knew what he was doing.

"Never," said Wendell cheerfully, and they stepped out into the corridor with more guards. "Message for the councilor," he said to one of the guards. Rossi noticed he didn't say which councilor. "I have to deliver it personally."

He showed his comms.

Rossi wanted to know what the comms said. The captain had to be lying about never having done this before because he was too smooth not to have.

"You know the drill," the guard said. "Stay at the back until one of the stewards lets you through."

"Of course."

The guard let them in and closed the door behind them.

They were too late.

Orsaya was at the front of the chamber at the first speaker's desk, with Markan looking daggers across at her from the other speaker's desk. For a moment, Rossi thought Wendell would launch himself down onto the stage. He edged away slightly.

Markan was speaking. "We know what that ship can do. We know what power it gives to the Alliance, and we can only guess what secrets they might learn from it. We already know it has a weapon more powerful than our worlds can build. We want that weapon. We *need* that weapon. And who knows what else is on that ship that could be used against us."

He looked around, making eye contact with every councilor. Rossi looked, too, and noted there were admirals up the back, in some of the visitor's seats. They were familiar, like the scarlet-uniformed Centauran. These were the people who had been seated around Markan earlier in the day.

"You heard Linesman Rossi earlier. Right now, they don't know any more about the ship than we do."

Markan was preaching to the converted. Everyone in this room wanted that ship. Rossi could see already that they would do anything to get it. He crossed his arms over his chest, suddenly cold.

Beside him, Wendell twitched as if he wanted to jump into the middle of the conversation. As for Orsaya, she didn't even look as if she was going to interrupt. In fact, even though she wasn't smiling, Rossi could tell she was pleased with the way things were going.

"We *have* to take that ship from the New Alliance before they work out how to use it properly."

At least half the chamber nodded in agreement.

"We know it requires linesmen to work it." Markan made eye contact with the councilors again. "Ladies and gentlemen of the council, we all know that the only high-level linesman the Alliance has on call is faulty, whereas I, we—"

"I wouldn't say he's faulty," the scarlet-uniformed Centauran said. "He's damned good, in fact. At least our people think so."

If looks could impale, the Centauran would have been speared, particularly as some of the other people in the room were nodding.

Markan took a moment to recover, and when he spoke, his voice was slightly more clipped, but he managed to smile. "Nevertheless, Lambert is only one linesman, while we, with the support of House of Sandhurst, have a third of the top-level linesmen."

"Most of whom are nonfunctioning right now," interjected Orsaya. "The only—"

Markan overrode her. "The linesmen recover once they are removed from the confluence. Jordan Rossi proved that today."

How dare Markan drag him into this when he had so obviously snubbed him earlier.

Markan's voice firmed and echoed around the chamber. "Members of the council, I say to you. We *need* that ship. We need it *before* our enemy learns how to control it. We must attack now to acquire it, for without it, we sit waiting to be annihilated at the Alliance's whim."

He got a standing ovation for that.

"We cannot afford to wait, as Admiral Orsaya here is asking us to do. We cannot afford to give the Alliance a weapon that will allow them to win this war."

"It's only a weapon," Wendell muttered to Rossi. "Wars are won by people, and by the decisions they make."

The comment was lost under the cheers from the council.

A councilor wearing a sash with the same purple markings as Admiral Markan's stood up. "I would like to put a motion to the council. I would like to propose that the council stops mucking around and finally takes control of this war. I would like to propose that we place Admiral Markan in charge of retrieving this ship and that we ask that he does it immediately."

Ahmed Gann's clear voice rang across the chamber. "Even if it means that we are declaring war on the Alliance?"

"We are at war in all but name now," the Centauran admiral said.

"Councilor Gann," the Roscracian councilor said, "everyone knows your reluctance to bring this thing to outright war, but war is inevitable. If we don't act now, the Alliance will control the timing with that ship of theirs. One might almost say that you are helping them by holding us off."

"Because of the ship?" Gann asked. "You say"—and he held up his hands to silence the councilors. It was a measure of the respect they accorded him that they quieted and let him speak—"that what you want right now is the ship. You are prepared to initiate hostilities to get it. Why?"

"Why—" The word practically burst out of Markan's mouth. "We've just spent the last hour debating—"

Gann held up his hand for silence again. "I am not denying the logic of your argument, Admiral Markan. I am not denying I want an alien ship as much as you do. What I am asking is why precipitate a war we don't know we can win for a ship that's in enemy territory when we have another alien ship here, in our own territory, that we can collect without firing a shot."

The silence was absolute. Someone coughed and smothered the sound hastily.

"Admiral Markan, I have known about this second ship for days, and I am not even on the war panel. You are."

Rossi imagined he heard the swallow of the water as the

cougher took a mouthful. He definitely heard the soft thunk as the glass went back onto the table.

"If you knew this already, Admiral Markan—and you must, for after all, are you not part of the war panel—then why are you still pushing us toward fighting the Alliance right now? I ask myself what could you gain? Destabilization of the Alliance? Or destabilization of Gate Union?"

Fergus Burns had once said, "Never cross Ahmed Gann. He has a way of turning defeat into victory." Maybe he'd been right.

"That's absolute nonsense," Markan said, but he was drowned out by one of the councilors at the back calling out, "If you're so certain there is a ship here, Gann, produce it."

"That is what we were trying to do." Gann looked at Markan. "Is that why you insisted on this council being called so hastily, Markan? Because once everyone knew about this ship, your arguments would be useless."

He was clever all right, for Rossi knew as well as Gann and Orsaya did that Markan had not known about the ship. But anything Markan said now would sound like a lie. Rossi didn't plan on being alone in a room with Markan and Gann in the near future. Markan would likely kill them both and place the weapon he'd used to do it in Rossi's hand to make it look like Rossi had murdered Gann.

"But where is this ship?" the councilor insisted.

Gann turned to look at him. "It's at the confluence, of course. It has been here for six months."

Rossi didn't plan on being around when Orsaya failed to get her ship either.

When the noise had died down enough to hear, Orsaya took the microphone. "When Rebekah Grimes returned from working with the Alliance, she told us the alien ship was like the confluence."

She hadn't told them in as many words, and she definitely hadn't said the confluence was a ship. She had remarked on the similarities.

"Linesman Rossi confirmed it after he'd been on the *Eleven*."

He wanted to say it was a lie. He hadn't confirmed anything. But while Markan might have *thought* about killing

Ahmed Gann, Admiral Orsaya wouldn't have any scruples. If Rossi got in her way, she *would* kill him.

"You forget one thing." Until now, Rossi hadn't even realized Iwo Hurst was in the chamber, but here he was, large as life and sitting only two seats away from the Centauran admiral. "Our linesmen have been at the confluence for six months. Six months. And none of them have managed to produce this ship for you."

Orsaya gave a slow smile, and it was obvious to Rossi that Hurst had said exactly what she'd wanted him to say. "But Cartel Master Hurst, not *all* the linesmen have been at the confluence. And the only linesman who wasn't, managed to produce—and control—the *Eleven* for the Alliance."

"Linesman Lambert," the Centauran admiral said.

Orsaya nodded at him. "Admiral Ravenstone is correct. We have interviewed Linesmen Rossi and Grimes and everyone who was returned in the recent treaty. All of them say that Lambert was instrumental in retrieving the ship and in controlling it."

No one had ever said Lambert had retrieved the ship. According to Rebekah, they'd found it floating in space. Orsaya was as good with her lies as Gann was.

"I, too, would like to make a motion to the council," Ahmed Gann said. "I would like to propose that as an alternative to attacking the Alliance right now, we allow Admiral Orsaya the freedom to continue retrieving the second alien ship unhindered." The "unhindered" was emphasized, and he glanced at Markan as he said it.

"I second that motion," the Yaolin councilor said.

"I second Roscracia's motion," a councilor in a white sash countered.

The Roscracian motion failed. The Nova Tahitian motion was passed.

Beside Rossi, Wendell relaxed. "I'm going back to the ship. Be ready to leave at a moment's notice," and he strode out of the council chamber.

THEY departed as soon as Orsaya came out of the council session and signed the orders.

Wendell, his hair cropped close to his head and now sprayed an appalling green with the red still showing through on the roots, was dressed as the captain of a supply ship. "You know what to do?"

"Damage a line." It made his heart flutter a little because linesmen didn't damage lines.

"Line nine or line ten. Nothing less. It has to be a line they need to get through the void, and it has to be one they'll send Lambert to fix."

"Understood." He wasn't an imbecile.

"You have half an hour to do it. That's how long it will take to unload supplies. You must be back on the supply ship by then. Galenos will suspect something if it takes longer."

Rossi had no intention of returning to the supply ship. "Understood."

"Right." Wendell turned to his crew. Six of them wore casual clothes similar to that of Wendell's although they looked much better turned out in theirs. Presumably the rest of the fake supply crew.

Even Rossi was dressed in casual clothes, the first time he'd been out of Rickenback colors since he was five years old. He told himself it didn't matter because he was never going to wear Rickenback colors again, but every time he caught a glimpse of his sleeve, or the leg of his trousers, it made him feel uneasy, off-balance.

Everything would be fine when he got back to line eleven.

Wendell frowned at his crew. "Can't you look like workers?"

"Yes, sir." They obediently ruffled up, but they still looked as if they'd stepped off a modeling vid. There was something about soldiers, Rossi mused, the way they stood, the way they held themselves.

Wendell waved an arm half in defeat, half mock disgust.

"It's a media ship, sweetheart," Rossi said to him. "They probably expect their supply crew to come dressed for auditions."

"Maybe we should see if we can get one," one of the uniformed women said. She pushed one cheek forward and held the pose. "How do you think I'd go?"

"You won't get an interview, Korta," one of the casually

dressed soldiers said. "You're arriving in a supply box, re-member."

"Enough," Wendell said. He looked at the man standing to his left. By his pips and the logos on his pocket, he was the second-in-command and the navigator. "Have you gotten everything you need, Grayson?"

Grayson nodded. "Just be ready to come and pick us up when we have our package."

Rossi didn't ask what that meant. It didn't concern him.

EVEN if he hadn't felt the lines as they jumped, he would have known they had arrived by the way the *Eleven* filled his soul and made it hard to breathe. A distant eleven right now, but as the supply ship drew closer, the glory increased.

He was home.

He lay back and tried to breathe.

Grayson and Korta hovered over him. "Oxygen, maybe," Grayson said, while Wendell's blotched white face receded and came forward behind them.

"He'd better do his job. We're at the media ship," Wendell said. "Are you capable of moving?" to Rossi.

Rossi didn't reply, just stood up and followed them onto the shuttle.

Grayson and the rest of the uniformed crew packed themselves into two container-sized supply boxes.

"Unload us gently," Korta admonished one of the casually dressed women.

"You wish."

Korta made a rude sign and pulled the door closed behind her. Rossi heard the snick of a bolt locking into place from inside the container.

The six casually dressed crew started to unload, taking extreme care with the two containers, despite what they had said.

Wendell steered Rossi along the corridor.

"Where are we going?" Rossi asked. How soon could he break away?

"Engineering." Wendell led the way with sure steps that

said he'd either been on a ship like this before or he'd memorized the specs. "You had better be able to do this."

He paused at the door. Rossi thought Wendell was giving him time to recover, for the uneven beat of the *Eleven* was taking his breath away. Instead, he crowded close into Rossi's space—the rudest thing a spacer could do—and said quietly, "Other people can be as obsessed as you are, Jordan Rossi. I want my ship back. This is how I get it." He stepped back. "Not to mention, the lives of my crew depend on your doing this properly."

Rossi straightened his clothes though they didn't need straightening. Message understood. To Wendell, he was dispensable if he didn't deliver, and Orsaya wasn't here to override that. He straightened his shoulders, too, as he followed the other man into the Engineering area.

Inside, the lines of the ship were overwhelming. Rossi staggered, inadvertently falling against his new archenemy, Wendell. This was a simple thirty-people cruiser. The lines shouldn't be this strong. What had Lambert done to him while they'd been on the *Eleven* that made him feel the lines this way?

Lines one to six were fine, but lines seven and up were terrible. Wendell could have waited, and the lines would break themselves within six months.

Wendell gave Rossi a sharp glance but didn't say anything. "Are you Bonna?" he asked the sole engineer in the room.

"Who's asking?" He was just a kid, fresh-faced, with grease under his fingernails and smeared over his coveralls, which fit about as well as Wendell's did.

Rossi straightened his own clothes again. It was like an itch you couldn't scratch.

"We hear you buy things."

Bonna looked wary. "Who told you that?" He glanced from Wendell to Rossi and back to Wendell again.

Wendell scratched his head. Some of the green powder flaked off onto his shoulders. Rossi tried not to shudder.

"A mutual friend." Wendell glanced sharply at Rossi. His message couldn't have been clearer. Get to work.

Rossi didn't advertise to the world what he was doing, not

like Lambert did, so he watched while Wendell brought something out from under his jacket, concentrating carefully on separating the lines.

His concentration faltered when he saw what Wendell placed on the bench.

A disruptor.

Bonna leaned forward to look at it. "Where's the power pack?"

It didn't look to be missing anything so far as Rossi could see.

"I'm not stupid," Wendell said. He glanced again at Rossi. "He's got the power pack. After you give us the money."

Wendell had better not pull him into this.

Rossi gently teased the lines apart. Whoever had left the higher lines on this ship in such a mess should face a disruptor themselves. Still, the lower lines were clean. Someone had mended them recently. Galenos had probably sent one of his own engineers in. It wasn't this engineer, for sure, because he didn't have a solitary bar on his coveralls.

Bonna rubbed his nose and pursed his lips. "Weapon like this," he said. "Easy to trace."

"Extra easy," Wendell agreed, and pointed to something on the holster. "Note the markings. This is a new model. First of its kind."

Bonna nodded. "How much?"

"It's 350K."

"Daylight robbery."

"A new one would cost twice that."

More like ten times that, but if Wendell truly had been selling stolen goods, he couldn't ask anywhere near the real value.

"I'm not paying half price for something that's so easily traceable. Especially when I can't sell it for any more than that."

Rossi closed his eyes and let them haggle.

Fixing lines took a combination of native talent and mental skills, all honed with thousands of hours of practice. A good linesman could feel the energy exuded by a line, could sense whether it was damaged, and could use all those hours he'd spent training to push the line back into place. Beginners often accidentally pushed the lines out of shape. If they weren't stopped in time, they even broke the line. Rossi had never broken a line, and the last time he'd pushed one the wrong way, he'd been ten years old.

Sweat beaded his forehead. He slowly pushed line ten away from what it should be. The very act brought acid to his stomach and gave him heartburn.

He couldn't do it.

Bonna touched his arm. "Are you okay?"

In his exposed state, the touch was like a jolt of electricity. Rossi pushed him away. "Don't touch me," and realized that he'd pushed the line away, too.

Alarms went off on every board.

Rossi scrambled to push the lines back into place.

"Shit. Shit. Shit." Bonna pressed ACKNOWLEDGE buttons, and pressed them again when the alarms came straight back on.

Wendell pressed the disruptor against Bonna's chest. "What did you do?"

He looked as if the alarms had given him a fright, and he had automatically grabbed the closest weapon. He should have known better. If Rossi had succeeded in damaging a line, the alarms would have gone off anyway.

"Shit." Then Bonna realized what he was holding. He pushed it away. "No power pack, remember." He frantically pressed acknowledgments across the board again.

"Is this how you get out of paying us?"

"What?"

Wendell was line-raving crazy.

"Of course it's not."

"Give me 50K."

"Geez," Bonna said. "You must want that money bad."

"I want it now."

"Okay. Here's 50K." Bonna slammed his card down on the reader. "You are one crazy sumbitch."

Wendell checked the credits. Nodded. "Give him the power pack," he ordered Rossi.

Rossi had no idea what Wendell wanted him to do. "If you—"

Bonna cleared the alarms again.

"It's in your right pocket," Wendell said, and it was.

It hadn't been there when Rossi had boarded the supply shuttle. He handed it over.

Bonna snatched it out of his hands. By the time they exited, the disruptor had disappeared from the bench top.

Rossi stopped halfway down the hallway. "You are insane. You knew the alarms would go off. Why panic now?"

"So he didn't realize it was us." Wendell smiled and ran his hands through his hair. More green powder flaked off. He looked extraordinarily pleased with himself. "That went well. He won't even mention we were there. Would you?"

Well, no, not if he'd just bought a disruptor from them. An obviously illegal disruptor.

"And giving him a weapon of that magnitude—"

"Relax," Wendell said. "The power pack doesn't work."

"He's an engineer. He can get another power pack."

"The weapon is tagged." Wendell smiled again. "We want to catch who he sells this stuff to."

Certifiably crazy.

"Does Orsaya know you have little side projects like this?"

"Relax." Wendell started moving again. "It's all part of the preparation. We needed an excuse if we got caught. Keep moving, the others will have almost finished unloading by now."

Rossi stayed where he was and shook his head. He was right where he needed to be.

Wendell sighed. "Orsaya warned me about this." He took out a blaster and fired.

Rossi felt the familiar sting of a blaster set to stun.

THIRTY-TWO

EAN LAMBERT

EAN WAS ENJOYING the fresher when the line on the Galactic News ship went. In his father's apartment on Lancia, the fresher had been on a one-minute cycle, and the water had been almost cold and rationed, so that if his father chose to use the fresher that day, then Ean couldn't. One of the best things about becoming a linesman was his discovery of real freshers, where the water was hot, and you could stay until you were clean and warm, and longer if no one complained. Where you could cleanse five times a day if you wished.

He scrambled out and just remembered to pull on some clothes before he went running down to the central office. Michelle was the only one there, going over figures on one of the screens.

Ean wiped away a trickle of water that chose that moment to drip down his face. "I need to get to the Galactic News ship."

Abram had sent Engineer Tai over to mend the lower lines as soon as the contract had been signed, but Ean still hadn't been across to fix the higher lines. It was planned—in Ean's suddenly seemingly full schedule—for three days hence.

"Lines?" Michelle was already reaching for the comms as Ean nodded.

It beeped before she could get to it. Abram.

"Is Ean there?"

It was Michelle's turn to nod.

"Engineer Bonna from the Galactic News ship called. They've a problem with their lines. He's blaming the work we did the other day."

Michelle raised an eyebrow at Ean.

"It's not the lower lines," Ean said. "They're fine."

He sang softly to line eleven, and through that to the lines on the media ship. Line ten was worst, but all the higher lines were bad.

"Line ten mostly."

"Of course it would be." Abram sighed. "You can't fix it from here?"

"I—" He didn't know. He tried, but he wasn't close enough. "I think I could if I were in the void." There wasn't any distance in the void.

Abram tapped eleven-time on the console where he was. Ean heard it through the lines and through the comms. "It would be an interesting experiment, but for the moment I think we'll do it the old-fashioned way."

He clicked off, and, through the lines, Ean heard him call, "Sale. I want your team to take Ean over to the Galactic News ship. He needs to fix the lines. Take Radko with you."

Michelle made them all tea. "Sit with me." She patted the seat beside her. "It takes time to organize a shuttle."

Ean couldn't sit. He prowled restlessly. "I should have fixed the lines like I promised I would. Then this wouldn't have happened."

"You can't be everything to everyone, Ean. You have to accept that all you can do is what you can do."

It sounded like something she told herself. Ean looked at her and saw sadness in her face. "But what if you know you should have done something and didn't?"

"You don't live in what might have happened, Ean, you live with what you can control. Always look forward, not back."

It sounded like the Yu house motto. Always look forward. When Abram arrived, he blew on his tea, even though it was probably already cold by now, and said, "I want you to take Fergus Burns with you. I want you to assess his lines."

Ean choked. No one had ever asked him to assess lines before. "I'm not sure I'd know how," he said.

"How did you know Katida was a line eight?"

"I . . . You could feel it."

He'd heard about people like Fergus. They showed enough promise to contract to the cartels but they couldn't pass certification. The contract was automatically canceled on failure to certify, but some of the failed stayed on as personal assistants or other workers. For a while there, when Rigel had taken so long to get him certified, Ean had thought he'd end up as one of the failed as well.

Rigel never took the failed linesmen on, but Ean knew of at least three of Rigel's people who had ended up in other houses.

Yet even when he'd worried that he would fail certification, Ean had known he knew the lines. Was Fergus like that, too?

"Find out what he is," Abram said. "Find out what he can do. Teach him what you can."

Teach him. Ean could imagine his old trainers fainting with horror at the thought. Fergus probably would, too, if he knew about Abram's plan. Ean suspected he didn't.

"Gospetto checked his voice," Abram said. "Says he can sing." He grimaced. It could have been halfway to a smile. "Says he has better voice control than you."

Ean could imagine.

The lessons with Gospetto had continued twice a day over the last week. Every day, Ean could smell the rancid fear-sweat that grew stronger as the hour progressed. Gospetto had fainted twice.

Ean didn't blame him. The voice tutor's bruises were still fading.

Abram took a long sip of tea. "We don't know yet if Fergus is spying for the cartels," he said. "He's under guard until we can be certain that he is not."

"But you want me to teach him." The thought still gave Ean disquiet. No one had ever wanted him to teach the lines.

"I've been talking to the engineers," Abram said. "They believe that if you can make a linesman of him, he'll come over to our side automatically. Just for that."

Imagine if Ean had failed certification. What would he do to work with the lines? What wouldn't he do?

FERGUS was under guard at the shuttle when Ean arrived. He still wore his Rickenback uniform. Was he still a Rickenback employee then? Or did they just not want to give him a Lancastrian uniform?

His face was gray. He looked tired.

Sale's people waited for Ean. Radko was there, too, her ankle strapped, supporting herself on a pair of crutches.

Ean looked dubiously at her ankle. "What happened?" Last time he had seen her, she'd been fine.

"Hairline fracture," she said, and made a face. "They think. After all this time."

"Shouldn't you be on sick leave then?"

"What's the point? We're not in port. I can't do anything. I might as well work."

"She's here to keep you in line," Sale said. "To make sure you do what the commodore says."

Ean strapped in beside Fergus, who flinched away. Ean noticed. Everyone noticed. Not a good start although Ean wasn't sure if the start was bad for him or for Fergus. Lancastrians were loyal.

He sat back and closed his eyes. He'd been able to feel that Katida was a line eight. Maybe if he relaxed, he could feel what line Fergus was. If he was a line at all. Maybe he was a line eleven or twelve. How would he tell then?

The lines were strong in his mind. He sang softly to each of them. He didn't need the comms anymore, or the void— although it helped—to be aware of each of them. The last few jumps had increased his line senses. The lines were part of him now.

He had a special message for the Galactic News ship. *"We're coming. We'll fix you."*

Six ships, sixty-one lines. There was no signal from the

elusive line twelve that Rossi had spoken of. He was deaf and blind to it.

No indication what line Fergus was, either.

Fergus twitched beside him, and Ean opened his eyes. "Sing with me," he said to Fergus.

Fergus looked horrified.

"I'll tell you what to sing, and when."

He sang an explanation to the lines. *"Introducing Fergus, one line at a time. He's inexperienced. Be kind to him."*

"Line one, Helmo's ship," he said to Fergus, and sang a greeting to that specific line. "You sing it now."

Fergus stared at him wordlessly.

"That's an order," Sale said from where she was strapped in.

He stared at her, opened his mouth then closed it, and shook his head.

"An order, Linesman."

Ean thought it was the "linesman" that did it. Fergus shook his head again, opened his mouth, and started to sing.

Gospetto was right. He had a good voice. Clear, pure, and note-perfect even though he'd only heard the tune once.

Line one didn't even hear him.

What if they were wrong? Ean led him through greeting each of the other ones, then the twos, then the threes.

Nothing.

The only reason he didn't stop was because the lines were enjoying their time, each waiting patiently for its turn. They were starting to get personalities. If anyone ever said again that the lines weren't intelligent he'd . . . he didn't know what he'd do. It was an outright lie.

Nothing for lines four, five, and six, but line seven surged strong in reply.

Fergus stopped singing.

"It's okay," Ean said, soft and soothing, the way one would to a skittish animal. "It's the lines."

The only sound in the cabin was the machinery circulating the air.

"Let's sing it again. Okay?"

They sang it again.

Fergus got a reaction from every line seven.

"What do you hear?" Ean asked softly.

"I—" Fergus swallowed. "I . . . think they're saying hello." He blinked, and swallowed again. "I—"

"Let's try the next line," because it was unfair to the other lines waiting so patiently. Ean sang the greeting for the first line eight.

Fergus heard nothing from line eight up.

"Well done," Ean said when they were done.

The predominant feeling among the line sevens right now was a baritone eddy of hope. It hadn't been there before, and it sounded a lot like Fergus. Exactly how strong was Fergus if he could dominate the other sevens like that?

Did that mean Governor Shimson was a linesman, too?

That was another one for the cartels to reconsider. It was generally believed that the lines had an order of strength. That line one was lowest, and—until now—that line ten was the highest. That a linesman's ability went up the list and stopped when he, or she, could go no further. Fergus would never have gotten past line one.

They didn't even know what line seven did yet.

"Ready to dock," Craik said, and Ean put off his pondering and prepared himself for the security on the Galactic News ship. After their last encounter, what would they say when he started singing to the lines?

Radko was watching him. That seemed to be her job. He glanced at Fergus, then raised seven fingers to her. Radko nodded and noted something on her comms.

AS they moved in to dock, another call came over the comms.

"This is the *Argent*, carrying Executive Tenzig d'Abo of Galactic News. Shuttle, please stand down and make way for the executive."

"What the—?" Sale snatched the comms.

Abram was there before her. "*Argent*, you are in violation of the no-go zone. All ships need permission to enter this zone."

"Captain." Ean wasn't sure if it was an intended insult or if the person who was speaking didn't realize who he was speaking to. "We have *Executive* Tenzig d'Abo of Galactic News on board. We do not require permission to visit our own ship."

Sale checked the comms. "D'Abo's CEO of Galactic News," she said.

Her team was more tense than they had been a moment ago. Ean could almost feel the air crackle with static. Sale looked at Radko's bandaged foot with a hiss of annoyance. "Maybe you should stay on the shuttle," she said.

"If I need to run on it, I can," Radko said.

"Shuttle, please stand down to allow the executive to dock first," the person on the *Argent* said.

Sale frowned at Ean. What had he done? "We should come back another time."

"I'm not sure line ten could survive another jump."

Unbidden, Jordan Rossi's rich tones percolated into his mind. He imagined him saying, "Lines don't *survive*. They're bands of energy."

Why would he be thinking of Rossi right now? The less he thought about other tens, the better.

Even the lines had a taste of Rossi about them.

Sale's frown grew deeper, but she nodded. "Continuing on course," she told Abram.

"Thank you, Sale. *Argent*, you have entered restricted space without permission and are in violation of laws 874.2.3.1 and 874.2.3.2 and 27.2."

"Executive d'Abo has every right to visit his own staff."

"Why don't we let them dock first?" Ean suggested.

Sale's withering look told him he'd asked something stupid.

"We don't know who's on that ship," Radko said. Thank the lines for Radko, who at least explained. "Could be anyone. Including Gate Union people."

Maybe he needed more of that paranoia Katida wanted him to get. Except that the world wasn't always out to get them. Sometimes a ship *was* just a ship.

"Going in now," Craik said, while Abram and the person on the *Argent* argued about the rights the executive had to visit his own staff.

By the time Craik docked the shuttle, Abram had prevailed,

and the *Argent* had moved away to await a boarding party. It was now, according to the screen, placed midway between the media ship and the *Wendell*. D'Abo was threatening legal action, Abram was pointing out that Galactic News had signed an agreement to abide by the Alliance's conditions in order to have the media ship remain.

Ean tuned them out. He had work to do.

He sang softly under his breath to the ship lines while Sale dealt with the crew member who greeted them. By his coveralls he was an engineer although he didn't introduce himself. The name on the pocket said BONNA.

"If you'd sent a higher-level linesman in the first place, we wouldn't have this problem."

The lines told Ean he was hiding something. He wondered if they could tell him what Bonna's secret was.

The lines felt different today. The lower lines were much stronger. Especially line one. Engineer Tai and his crew had done good work.

Bonna looked nervous, and who could blame him with his secret and all, and a team of soldiers crowding him, hustling him along as if they wanted the whole thing finished before they even started. "This way." He led them toward Engineering.

As they walked, Ean sang line ten, strengthening it so that if they had to jump, ten would survive it. At least he wasn't the one slowing them down this time. Radko was. Ean stopped to help her. "You shouldn't be walking."

"I have a stick. I'm not an invalid."

She did have a stick, and he probably couldn't help much.

"Besides, I just got my hair to sit down from last time."

Her jokes got worse.

Sale said, across any further attempt at humor, or maybe she was making her own jokes, "I hope you all know the layout of this ship by heart."

"Yes, ma'am," they chorused obediently.

Except Ean—and Fergus, who shrugged and gave a slight shake of his head. Ean smiled at him, and he smiled back. The first bit of camaraderie they had shared.

"Sing," Ean invited him. "Sing line seven," and after a

momentary hesitation, Fergus joined him in singing to that line.

Ean expanded his song to include the other lines—all of them this time, not just the higher lines. Line one was definitely different today. Stronger and more familiar. Maybe it was getting used to him. Maybe he was getting used to it.

It was also, he realized suddenly, because some of the crew had changed. Half the egos had gone, and in their place was something he knew. It reminded him of Captain Wendell.

Ean slowed outside the Engineering door. "What if it's a trap?" he asked. Katida's wished-for paranoia was well and truly kicking in.

Sale looked at him uneasily. "What do you mean?" But she and Radko had already grabbed an arm each and started to bundle him back the other way.

"What if—"

What if he was wrong?

The door to Engineering opened, and ten dark-green-uniformed soldiers streamed out. Twenty. Gate Union people. Wendell's crew.

Sale swore. "Too many," she said. "Craik, Losan, cover us. The rest of you." She indicated a side corridor.

Ean hoped *she* knew the layout of the ship and wasn't leading them into a dead end. He stopped to help Radko.

"Go," Radko said. "Don't wait for me."

He ignored her. Fergus came around to the other side, and the two of them ran for the corridor, supporting her between them.

"Ean. Save yourself, or I'll kill you personally later."

A beam of light melted the bulkhead above him. The corridor was full of the acrid smell of melted plastic. An alarm started wailing.

At breakfast one morning, Katida had said they didn't use blasters on ships because they did too much damage. They used Tasers instead. Why would Wendell's people use blasters? Surely, they knew how dangerous it was.

The passage forked.

"Left," Sale called to the two soldiers in front, turning to blast one of the dark-green-uniformed people behind her. A blue light arced out, felled him. He rolled and kept coming although his face was contorted with pain.

Maybe that was why they didn't use Tasers. The people didn't stop.

The two soldiers who'd veered into the left passage came running back. "Half a dozen down there," one of them reported.

How many intruders could a ship this size hold?

They turned down the right passage. "There's a cargo compartment three doorways down," Sale said. "If we get in there, we should have some cover, and we'll be able to fight back. Ean, get ready to open the door if it's locked."

She really had looked up the specs of the ship.

Ean ducked as another blaster bolt crackled above his head. Radko let Ean and Fergus support her fully momentarily. Next moment a blaster bolt crackled past his ear, so close he felt the burn of it. A green-uniformed soldier went down. He stayed down.

The smell of charred meat followed them.

Ean gagged, then was too busy running and trying to work out how he could sing to unlock the door.

"They're switching weapons," one of Wendell's people called into his comms.

"Damn," Sale said. "They counted on us using Tasers."

They didn't make it to the third corridor. Four soldiers jumped out of the second, firing. Sale's people turned into the first.

"They're herding us," Sale said. "Forget this. We're not going where they want us to." She fired back around the corridor, both ways.

"Enemy ahead," Craik reported.

"Damn. How many soldiers does he have?"

Ean's breath burned in his chest. He should exercise more. Maybe he would after this although you would have thought that Gospetto's training would have doubled his lung capacity by now.

They ran down the only corridor that was empty. Sale was right. They were being herded. Ean felt like they'd run halfway around the ship.

Another blocked corridor. Four soldiers this time. By now

more of Sale's people had armed themselves with blasters. The soldiers went down. Sale's people jumped over them.

Radko turned to fire behind them. Ean stumbled over a body, and only just missed being fired on because the *Wendell* soldier firing his way pulled her weapon up at the last second. The wall above Ean's head melted in a line of molten plastic and sparking wires.

The moment stretched.

Another soldier pointed his own blaster at Ean, then pulled up and away, too, and turned to fire on Radko, who had already ducked and rolled.

"Move," she yelled at Ean.

They hadn't fired on him.

Fergus hauled Ean up.

"Thanks." Either soldier could have killed him, but they hadn't.

Radko was already standing, more agile on her one good foot than Ean was on two. Ean and Fergus each wrapped an arm around her waist and ran.

THEIR way was clear now.

The next door led to a large control room with monitors everywhere. And desks.

"Not perfect," Sale said, "but good enough." She raised her voice, and her weapon. "Everybody out." It started a mad scramble the way they had come. "Ean, can you open that door?"

"That door" had a red, flashing light beside it. Ean had already sung it open before he realized what the sign under the light said. RECORDING.

Craik and Losan were through—armed and threatening—before he could tell them they were about to make the galactic news.

Radko shoved Ean behind a desk. "Keep your head down and don't move until we say you can."

"But they're not shooting at me," Ean said. Maybe it was because he didn't have a weapon. "I can—"

What could he do?

Radko ducked behind the desk herself and dragged Fergus down, too, firing one-handedly over her shoulder as she did so. "Both of you stay down."

The programmers' exodus from the control room had bought them time. Outside the door, someone screamed, and someone else shouted, "No firing on the civilians."

"Unbolt those desks," Sale ordered, and two of her people did so, using lasers to slice through the metal struts that bolted them to the floor.

Craik leaned back out of the studio. "There's an emergency exit in here."

"Good," Sale said. "I have a feeling we're going to need it. Get down, Ean."

Ean realized he'd raised his head to see what was happening.

Radko pulled him down as a dozen *Wendell* soldiers entered running. Sale's people got the first two, but the next two kept firing continuously. Sale ducked behind an upturned desk that glowed hot to start with, then suddenly collapsed into a molten puddle. Exposed plastic-coated wiring in the wall combusted.

All Ean could smell was burned humans and acrid plastic fumes that made his eyes water.

Radko leaned out across Ean, snatched the fire extinguisher off the wall, and tossed it to him. "Put the fire out," she ordered.

One of Wendell's crew snatched up the room's other fire extinguisher at the same time. He sprayed the fire with foam while Ean was still struggling with the nozzle on his. Ean added his meager help and put out another fire starting in the same wall.

They looked at each other. In the long pause, which was probably only a second, Ean had time to notice that the name on the man's pocket was GRAYSON, and that he had a long scorch mark down the left side of his uniform. Then Grayson gestured to Ean with his fire extinguisher. His meaning was clear. Move. Thataway. Out the door.

"Ready to move, people," Sale said. "They'll lock this section down any minute."

Ean tossed the fire extinguisher at Grayson, who ducked.

The extinguisher bounced off the shoulder of the man behind him, who turned to fire at Ean. Grayson knocked the weapon away. "Watch who you're firing on."

That was at least three times they could have killed Ean but hadn't.

Grayson gestured with his fire extinguisher again.

Fergus stood up from behind the desk and lobbed a broken vid-screen toward Grayson. "Ean, back here."

"Move. Now. All of you," Sale ordered.

The edge of the screen caught Grayson on the arm.

"Now, people."

Sale's guards started running toward the recording studio. Radko grabbed Ean as she hop-stepped past.

They made it to the emergency exit in the inner room, only to find Wendell's people in the corridor outside.

"Shit," Sale said.

There was nowhere to run. Ean pressed against the wall and tried to work out how he could help. Singing to the lines wouldn't do anything because the lines couldn't control blasters. If they had disruptors, now. Then he could do something. But even Wendell wouldn't be crazy enough to use a disruptor on a ship. Locking the doors wouldn't help. Half of them were already damaged too badly to even close.

Their little group was only six people now, and two of them were unarmed baggage. Him and Fergus, and Fergus, at least right now, was moving carefully sideways toward a downed *Wendell* guard and the blaster at his side.

They were outnumbered three to one.

Radko and Sale and the others would be dead very soon if Ean didn't do something.

Perhaps he could make the fight more even. For some reason, they weren't shooting at him. Would they continue to spare him? More importantly, if he separated from the main party, would any of Wendell's people follow him, leaving fewer for the Lancastrians to fight?

If it didn't work, at least he would have tried.

Radko was busy exchanging fire with Grayson. He couldn't interrupt her. "I'm going to try and divert some of them," he told Fergus, who'd finally gotten his blaster and was lining it up on one of the enemy.

Fergus missed his target. "I don't think—"

Ean took off before he could think any more about what would happen if he was wrong.

In the corridor outside, three people raised their blasters.

"Don't shoot," Grayson roared from inside.

Ean paused, they paused. The tableau held for a heart-beat, then Ean bolted past them. They pounded after him.

He turned into the nearest passage, which split ten meters along, saw a green uniform down the end of the left one and veered right. He should have studied the ship plans like Sale had demanded. Not that she'd included him in that demand. Or had she?

It sounded like a thousand people behind him.

He tried to sing to line five, but his lungs and voice wouldn't stay in sync. He gulped in a huge breath of air when he meant to breathe it out. It slowed him down, so he stopped singing and concentrated on running.

Another junction. He veered left.

A blaster bolt sizzled on the wall in front of him.

Right it was then, and he was all kinds of idiot because he was heading straight where they wanted him to go.

He hoped he'd at least drawn enough of them off to save Radko and the others.

He stopped in the middle of the corridor and turned to face the soldiers.

They stopped, too. One of them gestured with her blaster.

Ean rested his hands on his knees and watched them. His lungs burned.

There was a whuff of smoke in one of the corridors they'd come from. Someone yelled. Someone else—it sounded like Sale—swore.

"Move," said the woman with the blaster.

Ean charged back the way he had come.

Only to run full pelt into Grayson, who rounded the corridor coming the other way as Ean got there, and sidestepped smoothly into his path at the last second.

It was like running into a wall.

THIRTY-THREE

GRAYSON GRABBED EAN while he was still falling and ran back the way Ean had just come.

"Who are we waiting on?" he demanded of the woman with the blaster.

"You're the last, sir."

"Good. Seal the door. I've delayed the Lancastrians, but that won't hold them long."

She didn't just seal the door, she sprayed something into each air-conditioning vent as well. It foamed into the vent, solidified in seconds.

The other soldiers were suiting up.

"You'll kill everyone on the ship." Ean sang a warning to line two. *"Watch your lines."* How did you tell a line the enemy had put something in the air-conditioning?

"The idea is not to kill anyone at all," Grayson said.

So why had they used blasters then? And what about the people they had already killed?

Grayson started pulling on a space suit. "We've stopped the air coming into this room. Suit up, or you'll die."

Someone thrust a space suit at him.

Every day since they'd returned on board after Michelle's

kidnapping, Radko had made Ean practice suiting up. The first three days, she had made him do it every four hours. He could do it in fifteen seconds now, which still wasn't fast enough according to Radko. Ean thought it was better than not being able to do it at all.

He pulled his suit on.

It wasn't fast enough for these people, either, judging by the way most of them twitched. He checked the essentials. Oxygen, thermals, radio. All okay. What would they have done if he still didn't know how to put his suit on?

Just assumed that he knew, he supposed.

Radko hadn't taken him out into space in his suit yet.

Grayson twitched more than the rest. He looked at the door. "It won't hold them for long," he said. "They'd better not blow that door while we're blowing out the other side. Ready?" he demanded of Ean.

Ean nodded, and hoped he was.

Grayson clipped a line to Ean's suit. They were all clipped together, Ean noted. "Blow it," he told his team.

The door they'd locked started to glow red. Sale and her people, presumably. Ean prayed they'd be on time.

One of the spacers in front pressed something against a bulkhead. Hot white light traced out the seam, and suddenly that section of the wall wasn't there anymore. Alarms sounded.

Wendell's people joined the rush of air out into space. At first Ean thought they were simply carried with the airflow, but they used their suit jets to pause outside—like a single choreographed creature—while the woman on the end turned and sprayed foam into the opening. It looked as if she was sealing the hole.

The hull of the ship they'd just blown out of was an enormous wall that stretched away to one side of him. He couldn't tell if it was above him or below him or beside him. On the other side was nothing.

He wanted to cling tight to the ship wall, but he couldn't get to it, and Radko hadn't yet shown him how to use the jets on his suit.

She had taught him the importance of not being sick in your space suit, but for a moment it was touch and go.

It was so empty out here.

The only thing between him and being lost in space forever was the thin line Grayson had clipped to himself and to another spacer.

He hoped the line wouldn't break.

The only sound he could hear was the others breathing through the helmet speakers.

He couldn't hear the lines.

For a frozen moment, Ean couldn't even think.

Then the reassuring alien beat of line eleven settled in his mind, and he realized he'd been hearing it all along.

He wanted to sing to it, but he couldn't open his mouth out here in the massive emptiness. He clung to eleven like the lifeline it was, and through it, gradually tuned in to the other lines.

Funnily enough, the lines on the Galactic News ship were fine, or as good as they had been before. What did the lines consider damage?

On an open channel on the *Lancastrian Princess*'s line five Sale was saying, "Sims, Helo, Tanaka, and Rajsan dead. Craik and Radko require surgery. The rest of us are injured but still functioning although Losan will require regen."

All those dead and injured. Because Ean had refused to turn back when Sale had wanted to. He took a deep breath— like Gospetto had taught him—then wondered if that was wise, given he was in space, with only the two oxygen tanks on his back for life support.

He followed the sounds and felt a moment of triumph when the combined lines five and one allowed him to see Abram standing, hands clasped behind his back, at the central console. Michelle was standing, too, pacing, scowling at the vid. Ean tweaked the line to see what she was seeing.

A row of space-suited figures, one of them bobbing up and down out of line, jets spurting at intervals on the others. He swallowed, watching it, and kept his mouth closed, just in case.

The voice-over accompanying the vid was dramatic. "Twenty fighters escaped the shoot-out on the Galactic News ship." A schematic diagram overlaid the screen. Ean had seen enough overlays now to recognize what it was. The ships in space. The *Argent* and the Galactic News ship in the center, with the *Wendell* completing a triangle below them, and the *Eleven* at the top center, the *Lancastrian Princess* on the top left. "As you can see, they are coming here, to the *Argent*." More dots joined the diagram, coming from the top left of the screen. "Lancia has dispatched three shuttles. They will arrive here at almost exactly the same time as the rebels." D'Abo's voice rose dramatically. "People, we are right in the middle of the battle zone."

Michelle groaned softly.

"Our vid team is standing by ready to record their entry." There was a dramatic pause before, "This is Tenzig d'Abo of Galactic News, bringing you the action as it happens."

D'Abo might be the chief executive of the company now, but he'd definitely done a stint in front of the camera. His smooth voice knew exactly how to milk every bit of drama out of the action.

"*Argent*," Ean heard Captain Helmo say to the *Argent* captain. "You have assisted in an act of war in Alliance territory. Prepare to be boarded."

Ean heard Michelle say wryly to Abram, "If we shoot them out of space, we'll do it on every channel. It will be a PR nightmare."

"No doubt that's what they're counting on." Abram tapped the counter, eleven-beat, and his voice took on more strength. "Still, they are in our territory, breaking our laws, killing our people."

"And they have Ean."

"And they have Ean," Abram agreed. He frowned at the screen. "Our shuttles will be lucky to get to them before they jump."

"Ean's resourceful," Michelle said, then rubbed at her temples the way Katida did, as if she had a headache or didn't really believe Ean was as resourceful as she claimed.

"Yes, Misha," Abram said softly, putting a gentle hand on her shoulder. "He is."

"Two hundred twenty-five degrees," Grayson's voice said in Ean's ear. It was the first time anyone had used the suit-to-suit communication.

Radko had at least taught him about that. Intersuit comms

had no lines, so Ean had only paid cursory attention to it. He did know you couldn't turn it off.

The space suits reoriented themselves. They were still facing the *Argent*, but more toward the rear of the ship.

"Maximum," Grayson said, and every suit except Ean's fired their jets in a long, sustained blast.

Through *Lancastrian Princess*'s line five, Ean heard someone say, "*Argent* has started to move."

Ean could see it. It was coming straight toward them, and it wasn't stopping.

By the time Ean remembered where the jet controls were on the suit they were up close against the side of the *Argent* and it was too late to use them, even if he could work out how to.

Luckily for him, he didn't have to. Other people in the line were firing jets. They slowed, but Ean wasn't sure it would be enough.

Up close, the ship was huge. Suddenly, the emptiness of space didn't seem so threatening anymore. Ean closed his eyes, opened them again, not sure which was better. Seeing when you went splat or waiting for it to happen.

A dark hole opened in the side. The shuttle bay.

Jets fired. Ean was jerked along as they snaked into the hole and veered to the left, steering well clear of the shuttle already in the bay. One by one, they clunked against the metal bay wall, even Ean. It wasn't something he controlled, but whatever it was held him fast.

The noise of the ship lines settled around Ean. It was like coming home.

The shuttle exited.

The shuttle doors closed.

The ship accelerated away.

The *Lancastrian Princess* commentary continued through line five. "Shuttle launched from the *Argent*."

Abram diverted one of his shuttles to investigate.

"*Argent* is making for the *Wendell*. Our shuttles won't catch it now," and in the background someone—it sounded like Helmo—muttered, "Pilot is almost as good as Yanni-kay. They're going close."

He heard the *Argent* shuttle hail the *Lancastrian Princess* shuttle that had diverted. "Don't shoot. We're innocent," in the panicked tones of Tenzig d'Abo, who didn't sound quite so smooth right now.

So Wendell was adding shipjacking to his list of crimes.

They didn't leave the shuttle bay. Instead, they swarmed into the second *Argent* shuttle, which was already full of people. They were wedged in so close Ean could feel three blasters through his suit but wouldn't have been able to dislodge a single one of them.

They waited. One minute. Two. Then one more person joined them, this time from the ship. Ean didn't need to ask who it was, he could hear it through the lines. Captain Wendell.

"Let's go," Wendell said, and the shuttle exited the bay.

"*Argent* has launched another shuttle," came through the *Lancastrian Princess*'s lines. "Headed for the *Wendell*."

The *Wendell* would open for its own crew, and Ean couldn't stop that. He didn't plan to ask it of the lines, wasn't even sure if he could right now. The only way he could help was to keep the ships together so that Abram had time to do something.

Abram had left a skeleton crew on the *Wendell*? How many people was that? Twenty, and he didn't ask how the lines had supplied him with that answer.

Given the number of green uniforms squeezing him in, the Lancastrians would be outnumbered, and on a ship the enemy knew intimately. Worse, the ship would be on the enemy's side.

Two of Wendell's men waved blasters at Ean, although how they got their hands free in this crowd he didn't know.

What did they want him to do?

The spacer in front of him put her suited hands on the three-step clasp that held Ean's oxygen tanks on. The tanks fell away.

She unclipped Ean's helmet for him.

"Approaching ship," Wendell said. Ean heard it through the comms. "Prepare for boarding."

The *Wendell* lines surged strongly at his words. This was one happy ship suddenly. Ean was going to have to tell Abram they had to keep the captains. Abram wouldn't like that.

"This is Captain Wendell to the *Wendell*," Wendell continued. "Ship. Plan G."

The ship responded to that although Ean couldn't tell exactly what it responded to. A Lancastrian accent replied, "Captain Wendell, this is the *Wendell*. Please stand off."

It was too late. Whatever Wendell planned had been done.

Grayson's voice brought Ean back to his own surroundings. "Abi, Marrl, you're responsible for the prisoner."

Marrl was one of the men holding blasters. He smiled threateningly at Ean, showing incisors as sharp as an Aquacaelum's, distorted through the helmet. Abi was the woman who had removed his tanks.

She pushed her blaster into his side, and said quietly, "Don't think we won't shoot you if we have to."

He hadn't been thinking at all, to be honest.

As they docked, the lines of the ship surrounded Ean, enveloping him in sound. He didn't need Grayson's, "Docking now," to confirm it.

"Let's go, people," Grayson said.

Abi prodded Ean. "Prisoner first," she said, and everyone squeezed together and pushed him through.

After all this, they were sending him out to get killed by his own people. And they were his people even though once he would have denied it simply because they were Lancastrian.

Maybe death was what they had planned for him all along although Ean couldn't see the point of waiting till they got to the *Wendell* to carry it out. The bay door opened. Ean stepped out carefully, hands high above his head.

Into a ship full of Lancastrian soldiers, comatose on the floor.

One—a woman with a bird tattooed on her face—it reminded him of Rebekah's butterfly makeup—had fallen awkwardly, a leg twisted underneath her. Another was propped up against the wall, as if they'd tried to hold on, then slid down.

ABI jabbed him with her blaster. "Move."

The smell that floated up and around him reminded him of the Juice his father used to smoke, and made his eyes water in the same way. His knees buckled as he realized. It *was* Juice. Or something from the halla plant, which was used to produce Juice. Probably the flower, which was reputedly used as a fast, knockout drug.

The reason for Wendell's people remaining in their space suits came clear.

The Lancastrians weren't dead. They were drugged.

And so was he now because he'd breathed the same drug in. He struggled to stay conscious, knew he was losing the fight.

He blacked out.

THE lines were calling him. Urgent. Frantic. Loud. *"Ready to jump."* The urgency reached fever pitch. *"Conscious. Conscious. Thinking."* The noise surrounded him.

Ean's heart was thumping in time to line eleven. He couldn't breathe. He couldn't think. He couldn't hear.

The lines clashed together in a discordant cacophony. The deep, stressed notes of line nine were strongest.

Somehow, through line one, he made out angry voices.

"Heart attack."

It wasn't a heart attack. It felt like the lines were trying to restart his heart, all of them doing it together, not quite at the same time.

"For God's sake bring him out of it now. He's obviously had a reaction to the gas."

Ean felt the hiss of something against his face, and a bitter cold washed through him even as the clear notes of line ten started.

It was the longest forever he'd been in. He was trapped here, unconscious, never going to get out. He screamed until his voice was gone, and he kept screaming long after.

AS consciousness returned, he could feel the lines fragmenting around him, breaking under the onslaught of his screams. His lines. Line eleven was there, strong but powerless against him. Him! Ean was the one fragmenting the lines.

He started to sing, but he had no voice. *"I need line*

voice," and, miraculously, line eleven heard him and gave him some line to use.

He started at line one, singing them together, stabilizing them. All six ships were there. Afterward, they joined their voices with his to help him with the line twos. Lines were communal, they helped each other.

Line three. By the time he reached line four, he had a veritable chorus of support. The singing got easier and faster, and the fragmented higher lines were knitting back together without his help.

He strengthened the bad lines. The higher lines on both media ships, particularly the Galactic News ship. He was right. You *could* mend the lines in the void. There was no distance.

He even sang line eleven, which had been there all the time and been very patient with him. He didn't realize how much the line needed it until he sang it, and line eleven surged back strong and relieved.

THEY were out of the void.

His heart tried to beat eleven-time. He found it hard to breathe.

THIRTY-FOUR

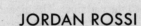

JORDAN ROSSI

ORSAYA DECLARED MARTIAL law on Confluence Station at 00:00 hours. At 00:01, the first Gate Union battleship arrived. Rossi heard it through his tainted lines. And the next, and the next. By 06:01, there were six battleships surrounding Confluence Station.

By 08:01, two massive passenger cruisers had appeared as well.

Rossi heard them all arrive.

He was back where it had all begun.

He could feel the confluence. It was like a poor man's version of the *Eleven*. A tantalizing glimpse of what he had lost. A hint of what it could have been.

He should have gone prepared, with a blaster of his own to use on Wendell. He should have used it.

He stood at the Plexiglas window of the viewing station. Three other linesmen were there. One of the twins from House of Laito, Nina Golf, the ten from Aquarius, and Geraint Jones from his own house.

Not his house anymore, he reminded himself. Did Jones know of Rossi's changed circumstances yet? Would he care?

To a linesman, the only important thing at the confluence *was* the confluence.

None of them so much as glanced at him. Why should they? He wasn't wearing house colors. They probably didn't even notice he was there.

He leaned against the Plexiglas and tried to lose himself in the glory of the confluence, but he had experienced a true eleven. He couldn't do it.

Orsaya believed the confluence was another *Eleven*, and based on what Rossi had experienced, it was probably true. And while Orsaya might have staked her career and her home world on finding it, the linesmen had tried for six months and not succeeded. Even Orsaya's pet crazy would have difficulty. Lambert could have it if he could find it, for the confluence was nothing compared to the *Eleven*. Rossi wanted the glory he was sure of.

Come to think of it, if Orsaya brought Lambert here to the confluence there would be no one to get in the way of Rossi's acquiring the *Eleven*. So instead of moping around here feeling sorry for himself, he should be planning how to return to the alien ship.

Rossi pushed himself away from the glass to go find himself a drink. He had plans to make.

Normally, he could have commandeered a shuttle easily simply because he was a ten, but the station was under martial law, and all the shuttles were on standby to ferry the inhabitants off the station onto the waiting passenger ships. He could see them now on-screen, station staff and linesmen alike, milling around the emergency evacuation points where they had been ordered to assemble, the first of them being shepherded on board.

The linesmen weren't going willingly. As soon as they realized they were being taken off station they staged a mass breakaway.

He was still trying to bully a shuttle out of the station commander when Orsaya arrived. The bastard had to have called her.

She was talking into her comms. "Leave the linesmen for the moment. We'll round them up later."

On-screen, the soldiers stopped trying to round up the linesmen and concentrated on shepherding the station staff onto shuttles. The linesmen disappeared quickly.

Rossi knew where they'd all be. At the viewing station. That's where he would have gone.

Orsaya watched with Rossi. "We should leave them all on station," she said. "It won't make one iota of difference right now."

He had no idea what she meant. "Worried they will interfere with what you are trying to do?"

Orsaya looked old and tired. "I'm trying to save their ungrateful lives. What we are doing is dangerous, Linesman. In case you forget, the *Eleven* has destroyed two ships to date, and the lines alone know how many shuttles. We are bringing a ship like that out here, into a populated area. I want everyone on a ship, ready to jump. Just in case."

"Us, too?" Sometimes he wondered if line eleven was addling his brain. All he'd needed to do was prove he was a linesman, and they would have shipped him off station.

"No. Not us. But we're going in with the only weapon that has any chance against it." Orsaya straightened and turned away. "And while it's nice to see you finally trying something, Rossi, don't. You're my backup plan. Lambert will be here in half an hour. We wait for him."

Wendell was half a galaxy away, surrounded by hostiles. Rossi judged his chances of success at less than 50 percent. Still, Orsaya put a lot of faith in Wendell's delivering.

"I can do this without Lambert." Orsaya would wait for the other linesman. If they let Rossi onto a shuttle now, he'd be away before they even realized he was gone.

"Have you seen what these ships can do?"

Of course he had. Firsthand, which was more than she had.

"Rebekah Grimes didn't know how to contain it. Go too close, and you will set off the automatic-defense system."

"And Lambert won't?" She put a lot of faith in her pet wonder boy. Rossi didn't care. He wasn't going anywhere near her imaginary ship, so that wouldn't be a problem. Even so, he was glad to hear another ship arrive then, something to distract her. "Markan has arrived," he said. Two more ships arrived in quick succession. Markan hadn't come alone.

Orsaya stopped and looked at him, and it was only then that he realized it wasn't something linesmen generally did, identify ships through their lines. Lambert's taint was stronger than he realized. Lines, but if such a short time near the crazy bastard could do that to someone, imagine how bad it would be if you were around him all the time.

Or how good it could be.

He pushed the traitorous thought away.

AHMED Gann came looking for Orsaya.

"I came in on one of Markan's ships," he said, at Orsaya's raised brow. "Markan doesn't know I'm here."

Orsaya's brow raised higher.

Gann looked around quickly, as if afraid Markan might interrupt them. He spoke rapidly. "We may have underestimated Markan and Hurst's ambition. And the strength of the Sandhurst faction."

Orsaya didn't look surprised. Rossi didn't think she was surprised. "Do you think it will amount to anything?"

"I'm more worried than I was a few hours ago," Gann admitted. "I thought everything was going to plan. Until Hurst started pushing the "crazy Ean Lambert" story, and "Lancia owns his contract, so we're letting the enemy in." It didn't help that the linesmen are complaining to anyone who will listen about being kicked off station."

Eleven of the tens complaining were from Sandhurst. And seven of the nines. Iwo Hurst would have manipulated the complaints. Rossi had seen him do it before.

"That's the thanks we get for trying to save their lives," Orsaya said. "Linesmen don't seem to have a brain among them."

She had better not be including Rossi in that damning statement, and he'd bet there was one other ten she wasn't including either.

Gann was always poker-faced on the vids. The expression he made then surprised Rossi, it was so readable. Disgust.

Resignation. "They're drugged out of their brains, and we're taking them away from their addiction." Gann made another face. "And Hurst is dangling the threat of linesmen walking away."

"We don't need to worry about their walking. We haven't had any top-level linesmen except Lambert for six months."

"I know that. They know that, too, but Hurst is a skilled manipulator, and they're genuinely worried about a lack of high-level linesmen."

Surely the Alliance had more to worry about that than Gate Union did. After all, the only high-level linesman they had available to them was Ean Lambert. Rossi pondered that as he watched the politician and the soldier talk. Gate Union—whether led by Roscracia or by Nova Tahiti—would still win against the Alliance. Even if the Alliance did have the *Eleven*.

"As soon as you bring that ship out, Markan and Hurst are done."

"I hear you."

Rossi didn't hear a thing except the words Gann was saying, but there seemed to be a hidden meaning, for Orsaya looked troubled. Maybe she wasn't sure she could bring the ship out.

"They've nothing to lose now, and they've still got a lot of followers."

"So it comes down to what we always worried about?"

"A coup," Gann said, softly. "And to work, it has to happen *before* you take the ship."

A coup. Rossi was half-inclined to believe Gann was hallucinating. Yet Orsaya believed him, and while Orsaya was gullible about one thing—Lambert—she had never been stupid about other things.

Rossi laughed. Or tried to, anyway.

Gann left as secretly as he had arrived. "I'll see what more I can find out."

Orsaya watched the door a long moment after he'd gone. Eventually, she sighed and looked away.

"It's hard to save people from their own stupidity," she said to Rossi, as she took out her comms and tapped a code into it.

Rossi had no idea what she meant.

"How does a war start, Rossi?"

He was glad she didn't seem to want him to answer that. She was the soldier, after all. Not him.

"Simple things. Stupid things. Greed or need. And some people can blind themselves to the long-term consequences for a short-term gain." She sighed again. "And some people can also blind themselves to facts. Have you ever hunted were-cats?"

She couldn't be asking a serious question. He was a linesman, not a hunter. Were-cats were massive game animals, as big as humans, and they considered humans their prey. They were native to the Wallacian worlds. A goodly portion of income from the smallest Wallacian world was derived from were-cat hunts.

"No. I thought not." It didn't surprise him that Orsaya had. "The thing about were-cats is you hunt them for weeks. You chase them halfway across the country. And just when you think you have them cornered, that's when they're most dangerous. That's when most people are killed in were-hunts. Right at the end, when they think they've won. But they haven't."

"And you consider yourself a were-cat."

Orsaya smiled a death's-head smile. "Not at all. No, the Alliance is the were-cat. Just when you think you have them beaten, they turn around and fight some more. And Roscracia and the people working with them are the deluded hunters who think they're moving in for the kill.

"We were able to hold Roscracia back until Iwo Hurst decided to take over the line cartels, and they realized they could help each other. The only thing that has stopped them so far is the fact that all the top-level linesmen were at the confluence."

Standing here, talking politics, wasn't going to get Rossi his line any faster, but politics were Rossi's bread and butter. "You act as if you don't want this war. As if you're scared the Alliance will win. Isn't that self-defeating in itself?"

"Oh, I don't think they'll win," Orsaya said. "But it will go much closer than the Sandhurst/Roscracia faction believes it will."

Orsaya's comms beeped. She checked the message, nodded to herself, and keyed in another code. She paused, finger ready to connect. "The problem is, Rossi, that the Sandhurst faction will destroy the Alliance. Utterly. And they'll do it by denying them access to the void because the cartels control the jumps and Redmond control the line supply. Imagine what not being able to move through the void will do to civilizations used to faster-than-light travel."

"Surely that could only be to your benefit." So a few worlds—like Lancia—would drop back to sublight speeds. Interplanetary trips that took months and years rather than hours. Never being able to move outside your own solar system because everything was too far. No one would miss them. Except Rossi would miss Lancian wine, and Grenache, and a few other things.

Yet there was something about the way Orsaya looked at him.

"Twenty worlds in Gate Union derive most of their income from Alliance worlds. Destroy the Alliance by restricting access to the void, and you have effectively destroyed twenty Gate Union worlds as well." She flicked on her comms before Rossi could answer. "Markan. What are you doing here? This is my operation, and you're not part of it."

"Changed orders," Markan said smoothly. "Surely you've received them by now."

"No. I haven't."

"I'll bring them to you, Admiral."

"Do so." Orsaya flicked off. "He's got more balls than Lady Lyan," she said to Rossi. She flicked on again, presumably to one of her own people. "Markan's coming here. Since he hasn't tried to take over the station yet, I'm guessing he's delaying."

The voice through the comms—Orsaya's second, Captain Auburn—said, "We haven't had any notification of a coup from Gate Union headquarters yet. He'll probably wait for that."

Rossi shivered at the casual way she said it. Ahmed Gann might not be expecting a coup, but Orsaya was.

Orsaya gave a mirthless smile. "Maybe they're having more trouble than they anticipated. Be ready."

"We are ready, ma'am."

"Good."

Rossi asked, "Are you just going to let him—"

Markan arrived then, with Iwo Hurst and a company of twenty soldiers. The atmosphere grew a lot more tense suddenly.

The glance Hurst gave Rossi was almost smug.

Rossi's gaze back was measured. It didn't take genius to realize Orsaya's home planet had to be one of those twenty worlds she spoke about. If he remained with her, and the Roscracians won, would Rossi get back to the *Eleven*?

"You are endangering my operation being here," Orsaya told the other admiral. "And endangering yourself and your crew. Get out now."

The *Eleven* arrived, in a burst of noise and an irregular heartbeat so loud it sent Rossi to his knees.

Didn't Orsaya realize what had just happened?

Rossi couldn't breathe. He opened his mouth to explain the miracle that had just occurred. The *Eleven*. Here. Lambert could have the confluence. The *Eleven* was Rossi's.

He couldn't speak.

Orsaya's comms beeped. Markan's did, too, but they both ignored them.

Orsaya glanced at Rossi. Her gaze sharpened, and she turned her attention momentarily from Markan to Rossi.

"Call the paramedics," she commanded one of her soldiers.

The loudspeaker crackled. Rossi knew who it was before the voice came through. Orsaya's second, Captain Auburn. Line eleven made the other lines clear as clear.

"Admiral Orsaya. Please pick up your comms."

Orsaya glared at the nearest speaker, then picked up the comms. "What?"

Markan was already answering his.

"Captain Wendell has arrived, ma'am. Along with the *Lancastrian Princess*, the *Gruen*, and the two media ships." Auburn paused for two full seconds. "And the *Eleven*, ma'am."

THIRTY-FIVE

EAN LAMBERT

LINE ELEVEN WAS stuck in the void. Ean could hear it. He tossed restlessly. It had been there forever. He had to get it out.

"I'm here," line eleven said, clear and strong in his head.

"No, no. Part of you is still in the void. I can feel it."

His own insistence was stressing the line. Ean forced himself awake, forced himself to ignore the echo in the void. "Sorry," and concentrated on pushing the double beat to the back of his mind so that what was left was the usual irregular beat of line eleven, which he could manage.

That allowed him to hear the other lines.

Gruen's ship, still mostly crewless and lost. Lines needed people, he realized, sentient creatures to interact with them and make them complete. *"I'll do what I can as soon as I can,"* he promised, and hoped he wasn't making too many promises he couldn't keep.

The two media ships, both in a flurry of communications and broadcasting.

There was absolute silence on the *Wendell*.

"Too many ships. Too close," Grayson said eventually. His voice shook.

Wendell's voice was calmer, but Ean could feel through the lines that he wasn't much better. "How did we come out of that alive?"

Ean could feel there were other—non-*Eleven* fleet—ships around. He wasn't sure if Wendell's comment was for arriving in the midst of them, or if, being the captain, Wendell had experienced part of that terrible trip through the void.

He never wanted to be unconscious going into the void again.

The *Eleven* was calming now that Ean had calmed.

The *Lancastrian Princess* was busy. Line eight was strong, and lines six, nine, and ten were poised ready to jump. Ean listened in to line five. At first it was a meaningless jumble of positions and strengths.

Burnley at 469. Four hundred crew. *Xavier* at 762.6. Two hundred crew. *MacIntyre* at 972. Four hundred crew.

The list went on.

They were enemy ships.

He'd brought his own ships to the enemy.

Ean pushed his oxygen mask off. An orderly pushed it back over his face.

Behind the count, he could hear another comms. "This is Gate Union ship *MacIntyre* calling the *Lancastrian Princess.* You have entered a Gate Union military area without permission. Please surrender and prepare for boarding."

That echoed, too, and at first Ean thought the echo was in his head, until he heard a woman's voice through *Wendell* line one. "What the hell is going on, Wendell?"

It was coming through the comms.

"I have your package, Admiral Orsaya," Wendell said, as if he hadn't brought five other ships along with Ean.

"Do you realize how dangerous that was?" Orsaya demanded. "Do you realize how close these ships are to ours?" while someone else on the station was yelling at him, "You are out of your mind, Captain, pulling a stunt like that. You'll be court-martialed for this."

Underneath, Abram's calm voice asked the *MacIntyre,* "Since when did the confluence constitute a military zone?"

Confluence? Ean must have misheard that. He struggled to push off the last of the lethargy caused by the double beat. He had called the *Lancastrian Princess* here. He had called it into a trap. He had to get it out.

"As of 0:00 hours Galactic Standard Time," the speaker on the *MacIntyre* said.

And underneath that Ean could hear other comms. From all the ships and the station. Frantic calls for medical assistance.

AFTER Michelle had returned from her kidnapping, Abram had moved the *Lancastrian Princess* back to two hundred kilometers away from the *Eleven*—against Ean's advice.

"If anything happens, the *Eleven* will protect you."

"If anything happens, I want the room to jump," Abram had replied.

If he had stayed inside the field, Ean could have sung to line eight to turn on the protective field and both ships would be safe now. But the *Lancastrian Princess* was well out of the protective zone. Not only that, Abram had been sending crews to the *Eleven* daily, so the field was turned off.

If he turned the field back on, he would protect the *Eleven*, and probably the *Eleven*'s fleet, but what if someone triggered it? The ships could jump, but if they really were at the confluence, everyone on the station would die.

Through line five, he could hear the comms on all ships. "I repeat," the captain of the *MacIntyre* said again. "Surrender now."

Ean remembered Captain MacIntyre, who'd been so proud of his ship, so convinced it couldn't be destroyed.

"Get up." That came through the *Wendell* line one, full of exasperation. It was only when Abi prodded Ean that he realized she was saying it, and she was in the room with him.

She prodded him again, a lot harder.

"Time to go."

It was time to do something although Ean wasn't sure what. Maybe he should just turn on the *Eleven*'s security system again, no matter what the consequences.

Why didn't Abram jump the ships away?

* * *

"IF you do not surrender, we will fire," Captain MacIntyre said.

Ean's first responsibility was to the *Lancastrian Princess*, no matter who else suffered. He started to sing to the *Eleven*'s line eight, to turn on the protective shield. At his first note, the lines came in so strongly it caught him unawares and tripped him up. He couldn't do anything for a moment. Even Abi's prodding couldn't make him move. He should be over unexpected heart-stoppers by now.

The lines were clear. Through them he could see Captain MacIntyre talking to Abram. Captain Helmo, half listening, half watching his crew, who were frantically busy right now, fingers flying over their boards. Captain Wendell, pacing impatiently at what looked to be a shuttle bay, talking through an open comms to the woman Katida had once identified as Admiral Jita Orsaya.

Orsaya herself was in some sort of large control room and looked to be in a tense standoff with a man who wore enough braid to be an admiral as well. The room was full of soldiers. Some of them wore beige, some of them wore purple camouflage colors. Orsaya wore beige, the other admiral wore purple.

Orsaya swept a hand across her comms. "Captain MacIntyre." The line went private. Private to anyone who couldn't hear the lines direct. "Do not fire on that ship. I repeat, do not fire on any of the Alliance ships unless I give an explicit order to do so. Understand?"

MacIntyre's emotions came strongly over lines one and five. Annoyance, exasperation, and a hint of anger. Ean heard the aside through the lines, to someone on the *MacIntyre* bridge. "Wish these people would bloody well talk to each other?" What MacIntyre said through the comms was, "Admiral Markan's orders, ma'am."

"I'll talk to Markan," Orsaya said, her voice cold, and she glared at the admiral in purple. "Meantime, do not fire on any Alliance ships."

MacIntyre clicked off with an almost assent.

Orsaya thumbed off the comms. "Galenos is just as likely

to call your bluff," she said to the man with her. Markan, presumably. "And you don't understand what that ship can do."

Then she called Abram. "Galenos. We have your linesman, and you are surrounded by enemy ships. We will not fire on you unless you fire on us."

As he listened to Abram's cautious agreement, a part of Ean marveled that he could hold so many threads in his mind at once. Was this how the lines did it? Still, he was only human, and he could only concentrate on one thing at a time. He sang under his breath to line eight. *Turn on the protective shield.*

He lost track of everything else for a moment, but he could tell by the increased activity of the lines everywhere that the shield had come on.

Orsaya opened her comms to all ships. "Nobody fire," she said. "You all know the consequences of setting that thing off. And have a jump ready in case you do."

Abi prodded Ean again.

He crawled to his feet, in the inelegant way he was getting so used to, and continued walking to the background of Orsaya's calling her assistant. "We've got people in transit. Get them onto the nearest ships. I don't care which ones, and don't take any complaints from the crews."

"Yes, ma'am."

Ean and Abi arrived at the shuttle bay, where Wendell was still pacing. Grayson, who'd changed his singed uniform and looked impeccably neat now, waited with him.

"I am never going to be so glad to get something off my ship," Wendell said, but held a hand out to stop Ean before Abi could push him toward the shuttle. "Why did the other ships come with my ship?"

It was time Wendell realized he'd never win this particular battle. "The ships are linked," Ean said. He hoped. They'd never jumped without him singing them all together, but this time they had entered the void before he'd started singing. And line eleven definitely thought of the Wendell lines as its lines.

Wendell stared at him as if trying to read Ean's lines; more probably trying to decide if he was telling the truth. He ran his hands through his hair, which was already sticking up. "How linked?"

What could you tell the enemy that would frighten them most?

"We have linked them to the *Eleven*, so that the *Eleven* is the master ship and controls the rest."

Wendell bit at his bottom lip, and his eyes blinked rapidly, as if he were thinking so fast his brain couldn't keep up. Then he stopped, totally still suddenly. "You can't unlink them, can you," and he nodded as if he finally understood something. "*That's* why Galenos is dragging the media ships around."

And two enemy warships, which Katida had once said would normally go back to the shipyard to be refitted. Ean thought it wasn't a good time to remind Wendell of that.

Wendell leaned on his comms, breaking into the argument Admiral Orsaya was having with Admiral Markan. "Your package is about to leave ship. He's singing some very interesting songs right now."

Ean hoped he meant the old-fashioned way—telling tales—and not literally talking about him singing to the lines. He didn't think Wendell had worked out yet how useful the singing was. He would, though.

He further hoped Abram and Michelle didn't intercept this message. It sounded like Ean was giving away secrets. Which he was, he supposed, only Wendell hadn't been meant to work out that they couldn't unlink the ships. Ean had been trying to scare him.

"Songs?" Orsaya was definitely thinking of the lines.

"I'll have Grayson tell you when he gets there."

"I'm thinking we should do this on your ship. If the *Eleven* goes off while he's shuttling between, then we're in trouble."

"No." Ean was sure it came out more explosively than Wendell intended. "We are linked to the Alliance ships. You might as well hand him back to Galenos now."

Abram and Michelle needed to hear this, but Ean couldn't open the lines right now because Wendell would hear him sing. It was his only advantage. He didn't want to give it away unnecessarily.

Not like he'd given away the information about the linked ships.

Wendell looked at Grayson. "You know what to tell her?"

"They can't unlink the ships."

Wendell nodded. "Don't take too long getting back. Orsaya is right. You don't want to be between ships when that thing goes off."

"It won't go off if people stop threatening my ships," Ean said.

Wendell waved him onto the shuttle, and Abi backed it up with a prodded blaster. "If they hadn't come along, there wouldn't be anything to threaten, would there."

THIRTY-SIX

JORDAN ROSSI

ROSSI BREATHED IN oxygen the paramedics had supplied and wanted to lie there forever, but Iwo Hurst was watching him as if he truly believed the ten had lost it, so he scrambled to his feet as soon as he could.

"Line eleven a little too subtle for you," he asked Hurst, making it sound like an insult.

Most of the cartel masters were lineless. Radeesha Devi, from House of Devi, was a one, and she was the only linesman running a cartel at present. The Grand Master was different. While he or she didn't have to be a high-level linesman—didn't have to be a linesman at all—he generally was, because high-level linesmen had more clout, and the position was voted in.

Hurst gave Rossi an unfriendly look.

Rossi smiled.

Orsaya was on the comms, talking to Captain Wendell.

Behind her, shielded by Hurst, Markan lifted his comms to his mouth. "Fire on the *Lancastrian Princess*," and the quiet way he said it meant that he didn't mean for Orsaya to hear.

He was crazier than Orsaya. Didn't he realize just how

dangerous that might be? Hadn't he noticed someone had switched the *Eleven*'s defense system back on?

MacIntyre's reply was loud enough for everyone in the room to hear. "I can't answer to two people giving alternating orders, Admiral. Right now, my orders say Admiral Orsaya is in charge."

Markan went a blotched purple. It matched the mottled color of his uniform.

Orsaya turned to look at Markan. She smiled, showing her teeth. "When you plan a coup, maybe you should be sure the stars are aligned favorably first."

It was another Yaolin proverb.

Markan pressed savagely on his comms.

Orsaya turned away. "Come. Let's finish our work here," and waited for Rossi to precede her out the door.

Rossi, for want of a better alternative, did so although his back itched until they were well away.

THIRTY-SEVEN

✦

EAN LAMBERT

EVER SINCE IT had been discovered, Ean had dreamed of coming to the confluence. He'd dreamed that he would be the one to discover its secrets, that he'd be lauded by the other tens as a result.

He'd never imagined creeping in this way. Not that they were sneaking, exactly. The Gate Union soldiers just marched along the corridors, ignoring everyone. If you didn't move, you got trampled.

Some of the people they passed were linesmen. Ean recognized Tomas Teng, a nine from Sandhurst, and the twins from Laito cartel. He would have liked to stop for the twins, to find out if they were really nines or tens. Katida would want to know. But the soldiers marched straight past, and when Ean paused, the guards behind pushed him on.

All the linesmen they saw were having problems breathing.

There were uniforms from every conceivable house, most of which he'd never seen in real life.

Behind it, he could hear the lines of the station, magnified somehow by the presence of the linesmen, crying out to be heard with no one listening. The higher lines hadn't been used since their initial use to transport the station and were atrophying in place.

He wanted to stop and talk to them, to tell them that someone understood, but the soldiers forced him on.

The factories grew lower lines ad hoc. Ean had seen them on the vids. Vast vats of chemicals that acted as the catalyst for the production of the lines. The ultrathin layer of native line—cloned from the Havortian—that started the reaction. Thousands of lines of light being drawn out of each vat, each one vibrating with the specific set of line energies. One in a hundred lines were pure enough to use.

But when you asked for the ability to move through the void, even once—as when transporting a station—you had to grow a full set of lines, and that process was slow, careful, and expensive. Ten tiny vats, side by side, made from the one batch of chemicals, because if the catalyst was different, the lines didn't meld. Each with the exact same amount of each line added because if that didn't match, you might as well destroy the lines before you wasted expensive catalyst growing them.

Once a full set of lines was grown, you didn't change them.

How many other lonely lines were there like this station?

Partway wherever Grayson and Abi were taking them, they were joined by a woman whose name on her pocket said AUBURN. Not much farther along, the woman he had recognized as Jita Orsaya joined them. She had Jordan Rossi in tow. Once Ean had wanted to meet other tens. Now the less he saw of them, the better, and from the look on Rossi's face, the feeling was mutual.

"What the hell was Wendell thinking?" Orsaya demanded of Grayson. "I gave him a slot and the room for one ship, not six."

Grayson said formally, "Captain Wendell asks me to tell you that the ships are linked, and that apparently even the Alliance doesn't know how to unlink them."

Orsaya stretched out her fingers hard, as if she had to do that or she might hit someone. "Understood," she said finally. "Wendell's just lucky he had enough room."

She turned to Auburn. "Are we ready?"

"The linesmen are gathering at the viewing center,"

Auburn said. Her uniform had the same number of pips as Helmo's. A captain, presumably. But not a ship captain because the lines didn't echo in her the way they did for Wendell or Helmo. "They're the liveliest anyone has seen them in months. Or they were until they all started having heart attacks."

"We have to ship them off," Orsaya said. She frowned at Ean. Why? He hadn't done anything yet. But he would, as soon as he could work out what would help Abram and Michelle the most. "Markan won't give us the time. I didn't even think he'd let me walk out like he did."

"We're ready for Markan," Auburn said.

Orsaya nodded, then frowned again. "Galenos doesn't want an escalation any more than we do. He'll hold off until the last moment." Which gave Ean some room to figure out what to do. He hoped. "If we can hold Markan off, we might all get out of this with nothing more than embarrassment on the Alliance's side."

Why should his side be the one to be embarrassed? "We haven't done anything," Ean said. Orsaya's side had kidnapped *him*. "Incidentally, you should know by now that kidnapping doesn't work."

Orsaya ignored the second part and attacked him on the first. "The confluence is ours. Your people jumped here."

"That wasn't their choice."

Orsaya looked at Ean. Her ageless eyes seemed to look right into his soul. She looked to Grayson. "It doesn't matter which ship initiates the jump?"

"No, ma'am."

Ean didn't need the lines to know what she was thinking. If Wendell could control his ship and keep jumping with it, then the *Lancastrian Princess* and the *Eleven* were virtual prisoners.

He froze, panicked, and felt Rossi's lines leaking amusement.

Should he tell her he had to sing to keep them together? It wasn't really the truth because they'd all been in the void when he'd started singing last time. But it would make her think she couldn't do it without him, and that would give him some time to work out what to do.

"You know that I have to—" But they'd stopped outside the viewing station. Ean recognized it from the vids.

His heart fluttered, and for once, it wasn't due to the lines. He was here. Soon he would experience the confluence in all its glory. He stepped forward.

Orsaya said, "Wait until we have it secured."

He waited.

The lines of the fleet made music in his head. All was well with the six ships. No one was shooting. No one was threatening anyone. He didn't realize he'd joined in the chorus—or that he'd extended it to include the lines on the station—until Rossi and Orsaya both turned to frown at him.

Not long after that, soldiers started herding linesmen out of the viewing station. An angry, fighting mob, because none of them wanted to leave—although many of them were hindered by breathing problems. Some of them attacked the soldiers. At least two linesmen went down stunned, and another bled from an open wound on his temple.

Ean recognized two tens. Nina Golf from House of Aquarius and Geraint Jones from House of Rickenback. Jones didn't even notice Rossi. Ean couldn't tell how Rossi felt about that. He sang under his breath to the lines he recognized as Rossi to find out.

"Get out of my lines, bastard," Rossi said, and would have lunged for him, but one of the soldiers guarding them restrained him.

Orsaya watched with interest.

"Sorry," Ean said, and he was sorry for his rudeness. Sometimes he forgot that human lines—like Rossi's—were different.

If any of the linesmen had noticed the ruckus, Ean didn't see. They were gone before it was over.

"All clear," one of the soldiers said, and Orsaya stepped aside to let Ean and Rossi go first.

Ean forgot about the others. This was it. He made his way across to the huge Plexiglas area that looked out over the confluence.

Nothing.

Disappointment dropped him to his knees. The back-beat of line eleven was stronger here. It was hard to breathe.

One of the soldiers hurried forward with an oxygen mask. Ean waved them away.

Rossi stared out at nothing, his face suffused with something that looked like hate.

Ean couldn't feel anything.

Failure tasted bitter.

Even the lower lines could feel the confluence. Yet Ean couldn't. Maybe Rebekah Grimes was right. Maybe he was defective.

Or maybe he was another Fergus. As blind to the confluence as Fergus was to everything but line seven.

He sat on the floor of the viewing deck and tried to pull himself together. Right now, he wanted a shower.

Michelle would understand that.

Michelle would understand his disappointment, too, but she wouldn't understand being pulled halfway across the galaxy when her ship was supposed to be in control. Michelle—and Abram—wouldn't be sitting around doing nothing.

Right now, Ean could have done with Michelle beside him, smiling her wry smile, cheek curving into that dimple. Or Radko, telling him the void was messing with his mind again.

Rossi blinked and came back from whatever private hell he'd been in. He stared at Ean. Ean kept his face impassive but couldn't stop his disappointment leaking into the lines.

Rossi's mouth curved upward in a malicious smile. "Confluence a little underwhelming, Linesman?" He emphasized the "Linesman" as if it left a dirty taste in his mouth.

Even dressed in casual clothes, he looked like a poster boy for the cartels. Tall and straight, the light gleaming off his bald head, the shirt emphasizing the muscular arms, the wide Plexiglas window with space and the confluence behind him. He could have been posing, but he wasn't. He fitted here. Ean didn't.

Ean looked out into space and didn't deny it.

Then, unexpectedly, Rossi got angry. "You have no idea what you have, and you are disappointed. *Disappointed*."

He stepped close, crowding Ean, so that Ean was forced back against the Plexiglas. "You make me sick with your tainted lines and your music and your crazy protectors and six ships following you around. Then you come here and have the cheek to say you are disappointed."

Two of Orsaya's guards pulled him away.

"I hope your precious line eleven is disappointed in you, too."

Line eleven probably was.

Even restrained and forcibly held back by the two soldiers, Rossi still looked far more a linesman than Ean ever would. Looks weren't everything, and Ean was making a place for himself, despite what the other linesmen thought of him. *He'd* discovered line eleven. He didn't need to explain himself to Rossi. So why did he say, "I didn't expect to be deaf to it."

"Deaf to it." Rossi lunged forward, and the guards lost their hold momentarily. If the glass had been any thinner, Ean would be breathing space by now.

They snatched Rossi back roughly, so that he banged his face against the window hard enough to cut his lip and draw blood.

But Rossi seemed to have lost any fight. He stared at Ean speculatively. "You really can't hear it?" and hope made his face brighten.

Ean shook his head.

Then the light died out of Rossi's face. "But you can hear line eleven?"

"Of course."

Rossi spat blood. "How many lines eleven?"

"Just the one, but there's something—" Wrong, Ean had been going to say. Part of line eleven was stuck in the void.

Rossi shook his head.

What if it wasn't his line eleven?

Ean started to sing. If they stopped him, he would fight them. He had to know.

Line eleven—his line eleven—surged in with its own song. Clear and strong enough to bring Rossi to his knees. Ean would have fallen, too, except he was already down.

The echo in the void didn't respond. Ean widened his song and finally received in reply the lost, lonely wail of a totally different line.

When he could breathe again, Ean said wonderingly, "There's another line eleven out there."

"Of course there is, sweetheart. Only out here we don't call it line eleven. We call it the confluence."

Line eleven was a beat. A metronomic thump-kerthump that had nothing to do with the glory and the ecstasy that everyone felt about the confluence. Line eleven *couldn't* be the confluence.

Rossi laughed at Ean's expression. "If you'd paid attention, you would have known that a while ago. It hasn't been the best-kept secret. Why do you think you are here?"

He'd assumed Orsaya wanted the *Eleven*.

Didn't she? But as he gazed at her, then at Rossi, Ean realized that wasn't what she wanted at all. She wanted the ship stuck in the void.

"Bright," Rossi said.

He was an imposing man, Jordan Rossi. Big in size, big in confidence. If Ean hadn't met Michelle first, Rossi would have overwhelmed him. If he hadn't heard Rebekah Grimes take on "crazy Ean Lambert," he would have been cowed by the brooding way Rossi glared at him. Two short weeks ago, he'd have been like the apprentices in the cart.

Ean laughed grimly to himself. Two weeks ago, he'd been a different person.

"What's so funny?" Rossi demanded.

He needed to clear his mind of what had happened today and work out what to do. He needed a shower.

He didn't realize he'd spoken aloud until Orsaya said frostily, "A shower?"

He didn't particularly mean a shower here, right now. "I think better in the fresher, and I have to work out how to rescue the line." And how to prevent Orsaya's getting it once he'd done it.

"Do your work here, and you can spend as long as you like in the fresher."

"Unbelievable," Rossi said.

THIRTY-EIGHT

JORDAN ROSSI

ORSAYA'S COMMS BEEPED. She flicked it on.

Rossi heard the tight vowels of a Yaolin accent. She switched her line to private and listened, frowning. Halfway through, she started moving her free hand in intricate patterns, twitching as if she couldn't keep still. The second time she did it, Rossi realized her soldiers were watching intently. If he were Ean Lambert, he could probably listen in and hear what secret message they were getting.

Lambert looked as if his world had fallen apart around him. And the lines—no, Rossi was imagining the lines reacting to that.

"I hear you," Orsaya said finally, and as she clicked off, beckoned to Lambert. "Get that ship for me. Now."

"I can't—"

Orsaya's comms buzzed again. She answered it on silent, nodded once. "I hear you," again.

This time she inclined her head toward Auburn. "Get Lambert away. I'll meet you at the shuttles. Take Rossi with you."

While they were busy pandering to Lambert, Rossi could work out how to take control of the line that was rightfully his. First, he had to get away.

Two soldiers came at him from behind, dragging him forward and toward Auburn, who'd grabbed Lambert. He struggled.

They made it to the door.

Only to be stopped by Markan and two teams of armed soldiers, weapons raised ready to fire.

Auburn stepped back. One step, two.

"Admiral Orsaya," Markan said. "Gate Union has had a change of government. Confluence Station is under my command."

Orsaya blew out her breath in a mannerism that reminded Rossi of Wendell. "You're a fool, Markan. You are dancing to strings pulled by Redmond and Sandhurst and ex-Alliance worlds like Aquacaelum. You start a war we don't even know we can win. In less than a year, worlds like Roscracia and Yaolin will be secondary citizens in a union we helped to start."

"Yaolin maybe," Markan said. "Not Roscracia. We will lead Gate Union, for we control the lines." He glanced out the Plexiglas of the viewing station, where the *Eleven* and its fleet of ships hung in the dark space. "And once we have that ship out there, along with our own alien ship, the Alliance is finished, too."

Orsaya's people were outnumbered two to one. Rossi hoped she would go quietly. He eased toward one side of the room, trying not to draw attention to himself. One of Markan's soldiers raised her weapon.

He stopped.

Orsaya's comms beeped. She raised her arm, then looked questioningly at Markan.

"Go ahead," Markan said.

It was Captain MacIntyre. "I have just heard from headquarters, ma'am. Admiral Markan is now in charge at Confluence Station." He sounded apologetic. "I will be following Markan's orders, ma'am."

"You're a fool," Orsaya said to Markan again.

Rossi refused to admit he agreed with her.

Gann burst into the room. "You need to get that ship now. They've had the coup at—" He stopped when he saw the guards.

"Ahmed Gann," Markan said. "Who would have guessed," but he didn't look surprised. He glanced away, across to Ean, then to Rossi. "Kill the linesmen," he told the soldier who had raised her weapon before. "Both of them."

For a moment, Rossi thought he'd misheard, but the soldier tightened her finger on the trigger.

And jerked back, spraying the beam across the ceiling as Orsaya's blaster hit her.

Orsaya's people picked off Markan's soldiers in a long, sustained sweep of fire. They had to have started firing almost before Markan spoke.

"Out, out," Auburn yelled, and the Yaolins raced toward the door, the two linesmen and Ahmed Gann shielded in the middle of them.

Beside him, Rossi heard Lambert's voice raised in song and felt it on every single one of his ten lines. Stupid bastard. What a time to try to talk to the lines.

Then he realized what Lambert was doing.

He was singing the alarms open.

Every alarm on station went off. Minor alarms, like servicing warnings, right up to the major ones—hull breach, asteroid proximity, life-support failure, and engine meltdown.

It was a clever move. On a ship or space station, there was only one thing to do when a major alarm went off. Get to the nearest emergency station and suit up.

Orsaya's guards were out the door while Markan's remaining people were still reacting.

THIRTY-NINE

EAN LAMBERT

THE STATION WAS full of noise, the lines were full of noise. Ean couldn't sing and run at the same time. He tripped once, and Jordan Rossi dragged him up.

"Don't stop," Rossi gasped, when Orsaya would have stopped at the nearest set of emergency suits. "Not a problem. Bastard's doing it."

Ean didn't need Rossi's rescuing him, and he didn't need Orsaya, either, but Rossi's grip was like steel. He kept running. At least Orsaya wanted him alive, and it was obvious the Roscracians didn't.

Ean was going to learn to sing while he ran. As it was, all he could do was listen.

Through line five he heard orders go out from six Gate Union ships.

"Weapons, armed."

"Prepare to fire."

A platoon of Roscracian soldiers rounded the corridor in front of them. Ean turned to run the other way, found himself grabbed by Orsaya and forced to continue the way they were going.

He heard Captain Wendell leaning on the lines, keeping them open. "For God's sake don't fire on the Alliance ships. You don't know what the *Eleven* can do. And if you do fire, have a jump ready."

At least Captain Wendell understood.

Two of Orsaya's people fired on the approaching Roscracians. Only two? A white, reflective sheet billowed out in front of them. The sheet heated, but none of the blasters came through. Orsaya's soldiers turned into a doorway under the cover of it. They sealed the door behind them.

Through the lines—from MacIntyre's ship—a single voice said, "Fire."

A burst of noise from the *Lancastrian Princess* knocked Ean against the wall. They had fired on the *Lancastrian Princess*.

Rossi hauled him upright. "I should leave you for Markan to kill."

They escaped out into another corridor and continued running.

Through line five, Captain Helmo said, "Return fire." Then, "Sections. Report," and the reports started coming in. "Hull breached, sector 11. Contained. Hull breached sector 12. Contained. Sector 6. Fine."

He slowed down to sing. Why didn't Abram jump? He could take the Alliance ships somewhere safe?

"Keep moving." Auburn prodded him from behind. "We've only a small window before they lock the whole ship down on us." She pushed them both against the wall and fired back the way they had come. "Or we get killed." A blaster beam sizzled past close enough to feel the heat.

"They have to stop firing on the ship." Ean tried to stop again, to sing. Rossi grabbed his arm and dragged him.

They turned another corner. A door at the far end opened.

The lead soldier tossed a small disk down the passage. It rolled to the end and stopped as a team of Roscracians poured through the door. Ean didn't see what happened because Orsaya's team turned into a passage halfway along. No one followed them.

Orsaya's people knew where they were going. They must

have had this route planned out long before they'd arrived on station. How long had Orsaya known she would need this?

He stopped halfway along the passage, gasping for breath.

The soldier behind them walked on his heels. "Keep going, or we'll be trapped in here. If that happens, they'll pick us off like target practice."

Rossi shoved him forward.

The lights went out as the doors at either end of the passage clicked shut. After a few seconds, Ean's eyes adjusted to the dim emergency lighting.

Admiral Markan had locked down the station.

Despite Rossi's pushing him from behind, despite the guard in front pulling him, Ean couldn't move. He leaned against the wall and dragged in lungfuls of air.

Another Gate Union ship fired on the *Lancastrian Princess*. Ean rocked under the blow.

Abram should have listened to him. If he had, right now he would be inside that protective field.

"We've two minutes if we're lucky," the guard behind Rossi said.

Rossi shoved Ean hard. "Unlock the doors, bastard."

How did Rossi know Ean could unlock the doors?

"Galenos is bluffing, Wendell," Markan said through line five.

"He doesn't need to bluff. All he needs to do is turn that device on. And remember, we can jump, but you're on station. You can't."

The station *could* jump. It had ten lines, even if they were atrophying. If Ean could force the *Eleven* to fire a pulse, everyone would jump to their designated spaces, and Ean could sing the station into the *Eleven*'s fleet.

Another blast rocked the *Lancastrian Princess*.

Rossi shoved him again. "Doors."

"You could open them yourself." He was a ten, too. Ean had no breath, wasn't sure Rossi even understood him.

Rossi slammed him back against the wall and closed a fist around his throat. He had strong hands. "Open the doors, or you'll never sing again."

Orsaya was too far away to save him. Ean held up his hands, then indicated that he needed some voice.

Through the lines, the *Lancastrian Princess* was doing another damage report. "Hull breached, sector 5. Contained."

Rossi loosened his grip. Slightly.

Ean sang the doors open just as Admiral Markan's voice came through the loudspeaker. And the lines. "This is Admiral Markan to the rebel soldiers. Surrender now, and you will be treated leniently."

"Rebels," muttered the soldier behind Rossi. "This was our op. He takes it over and calls *us* the rebels."

Despite the doors being open now, they didn't move. Ean, in the middle of the group, couldn't see what was going on at the front, but he could see flashes of light, and the cooked-flesh smell was strong again.

The *MacIntyre* fired on the *Lancastrian Princess*, which moved behind the *Wendell*.

"Six twenty," Wendell said through the comms to MacIntyre, and the *Wendell* moved one way while the *MacIntyre* went the other, firing as it did.

Ean had to get those comms to Abram and Helmo.

"Go, go," Orsaya yelled then, and they ran out into another scene of carnage. Did anyone ever get used to dead bodies?

Someone pushed him down from behind.

A crackle of lightning passed above his head. Finally, someone was using a Taser.

A soldier behind Ean turned the Taser-firer's face into charcoal. She hauled him up. "You are not worth all of this."

Through the lines, Wendell was talking to Captain MacIntyre about the *Wendell*. "Galenos has destroyed the weapons boards."

Abram had ordered all the weapons taken out as well. Wendell didn't mention that. He'd probably brought along replacements.

Orsaya's people shot anyone in their path.

Through the comms, Markan was preparing for sustained fire on the *Lancastrian Princess*.

"*Burnley, Xavier, MacIntyre, Rasjeet.* Combined ten-second pulses in a 7-4-3 sequence. I want that ship so hot, it melts."

Ean forced enough breath into his lungs to sing Markan's line open to the *Lancastrian Princess*. As the words came through, he saw Abram and Michelle jerk around to stare at the comms.

Michelle smiled.

"They'll move behind the *Wendell* again as soon as we start firing," Captain MacIntyre said. "*Xavier* and I won't be in a position—"

"Captains, the Alliance has claimed the *Wendell* as its own. Fire on my count. One."

Helmo was already moving his ship.

Why didn't they jump?

"Move," a soldier told Ean. It seemed the only word they knew.

A platoon of Markan's soldiers disgorged from a lift at the end of the corridor. Orsaya's people turned into another side corridor.

This part of the station was old. It reminded Ean of the secondary yards at Ashery. The walls were scuffed and the markings faded. The two people they saw wore maintenance overalls or civilian clothes.

In front of them was a blank wall. No doors; no lift. Ean hesitated, but was carried forward in the rush as Markan's people rounded the corridor behind them.

He stepped into empty space.

WHEN Radko had first shown Ean around the *Lancastrian Princess*, she had pointed out the jumps and told him that most soldiers used them in preference to the lifts. It was the first and last time Ean had seen them. He'd forgotten they existed.

Until now.

He watched the floor numbers fly past with horrifying speed—11, 10, 9. He hadn't realized there were so many floors on Confluence Station.

Around level 6, he started to slow down. The time between levels 5 and 4 was longer than that of 6 and 5, and the time between 4 and 3 longer still.

Through the station lines, an aide reported to Markan. "Orsaya's going down to the old shuttle bays."

"We've got that covered. Get someone down there and arrest them all."

Through the ship lines, MacIntyre was warning Wendell to jump, "Just get the hell out of here."

Ean had slowed down so much that between level 2 and level 1, he had time to read the huge warning stenciled onto the wall.

EXIT IMMEDIATELY.

He planned to.

"Bend your knees for landing," Orsaya said.

How had he caught up with her?

He dutifully bent his knees but still hit hard.

He forgot all about exiting immediately.

Something else Radko had to teach him when he got back. If he survived to get back.

Rossi and Orsaya grabbed an arm each and dragged him out.

"Markan knows you're coming," Ean gasped as he ran. "He says he has it covered."

Orsaya called behind, "We're expected, people." She didn't ask how he knew.

They stopped at last at a dilapidated shuttle bay that looked as if it wasn't even used anymore.

"Thank God," Ahmed Gann said as he waited, gasping, beside Ean. "I can't run any farther."

Ean couldn't either, but it was reassuring to see someone who was as unfit as he was.

"In here?" Orsaya asked Ean.

He shrugged. He wasn't sure.

Orsaya looked at her soldiers, who nodded, then waited.

"There are people following us," Gann pointed out.

Orsaya held up a hand for silence. She waited until their pursuers came thundering around the top of the passage—which wasn't that long, but it felt as long as going through the void—before she keyed in the door code.

They waited agonizing seconds for the triple locks to open the door.

Through the lines, Ean could hear preparations for departure.

Helmo, and whoever was in charge of Gruen's ship, calling in the line nines. Abram calling the media ships, telling them to get ready to jump.

They wouldn't make it in time. Why had they left it so long?

Markan had new orders for Captains MacIntyre and Xavier. "Coordinates 174-189-262. I want both of you firing on any shuttle that exits."

Ean started to sing, an open message to all the lines. He was here, and they should jump together. They should jump now.

The attacking soldiers kept up their relentless run.

The air lock finally opened.

They came face-to-face with guards in Roscracian uniform. All of them holding blasters.

Orsaya's people dived for the floor. Guards dragged Ean down as the lines responded, and jumped.

Ean expanded his song to include the lines he'd recognized earlier as those of the station. The lines of the station answered and stayed with them.

In the forever of the void, Ean had plenty of time to wonder if he was dead yet, for surely the Roscracians would have killed them by now. He also had time to check each of the lines and ensure they were all right. Even the new ones.

"Station lines?" and the lines sang a yes.

The second line eleven was stronger here. Ean stretched his song to pull that in, too.

It tried to come. It couldn't.

Even its song was muted. Lost.

Ean strengthened the sound, but it still wasn't enough.

Line nine on the new eleven-line ship was a tiny thread, barely there. More badly damaged even than the *Lancastrian Princess*'s six had been after Rebekah had tried to destroy it.

Nine was the line that moved a ship in and out of the void. No wonder the ship was stuck.

He tried to fix it. Couldn't.

He widened his song, searching for anything that could help.

He found it. Dozens of new lines from the linesmen who'd been on Confluence Station for the last six months.

All the way up from one to ten, strongest at the higher levels. Ean took every line he could and sang and sang. Gently at first, using the lines the others gave him to strengthen the tiny thread of sound, knitting it back together until the nine at last had enough sound of its own to take what the others offered.

FORTY

JORDAN ROSSI

ROSSI WAS SURROUNDED by the confluence.

It was the most glorious music he had ever heard. It was love. It was beauty. It was joy.

Lambert's voice interwove through the lines, bringing them together, pulling in every line he had. Including Rossi's, and every other linesman on the station.

Rossi gave his gladly.

It lasted forever, and it was over in a second.

ORSAYA'S people dropped to the ground. One of them grabbed Gann and pulled him down, too.

Rossi noticed that in a half-detached way, even as he watched them pull Lambert down—not that Lambert needed any help because he was already falling.

Then his own face hit the deck—he hadn't realized he was falling, too.

The soldiers inside the shuttle bay mowed down the ones outside, and vice versa. By the time they realized they were killing their own team and turned aside their weapons, it was too late. Orsaya's people picked off the rest.

Two guards seized Lambert and pulled him in and onto the shuttle. Another two seized Rossi's arms. They almost jolted his shoulder out of its socket as they pulled him along.

They strapped him into a seat.

A guard slipped into the pilot seat and started preflight checks. Another strapped herself into the comms seat.

"Get me Wendell," Orsaya ordered. "And a safe path to Wendell's ship."

Stupid woman. Didn't she realize the station had jumped?

Stupid Lambert. Didn't he realize the danger in moving a station? Particularly one where the lines hadn't been primed. Particularly one where extra sections had been built onto the shell. He was just lucky they were alive.

Not that Rossi felt very alive right now.

The lines were clear. He heard Markan ordering, "Fire on the shuttle as soon as it exits."

Markan hadn't realized yet that his message wasn't going anywhere.

"Go," Orsaya ordered her pilot.

"Fifteen seconds for the air to recycle, ma'am."

Orsaya nodded, but she looked twitchy.

Someone shoved an oxygen mask over Rossi's face, and he realized his heart was trying to beat alien time again. Line time. Two sets of line time.

Wendell came online. Rossi heard line five before the comms came on. "Orsaya, you can't let Lambert control things like he does." He was the calmest Rossi had ever heard him. It was almost scary. "Kill him before he does anything else. At the very least, gag him."

They exited the shuttle bay to, "This is Commodore Galenos from the *Lancastrian Princess*, to Confluence Station and Gate Union ship *Wendell*. Surrender now, and we will not harm you."

Orsaya shook her head. "That man has cast-iron balls. He's surrounded by enemy ships and he still thinks—"

"Orsaya," Wendell cut across her words. "Have you checked your screen yet?"

The proximity alarm started wailing. The pilot swore and

moved his hands swiftly over the board. "What in the nine hells would come this close to a station?"

"Another shuttle," someone said, while the woman at the comms brought the viewscreen up.

Rossi craned his head to look.

"What in the hell is that?"

FORTY-ONE

EAN LAMBERT

THE VIEW ON the screen reminded Ean of his recent space-walk, when he'd been so close to the Galactic News ship that he had no idea if he was up or down.

It was a ship.

The noise of the lines overwhelmed him. The beat of the second eleven was subtly different from the beat of the first.

"God," said the comms-person, and for a minute she sounded like Losan. "Get away from it."

"It's huge," someone else said.

"Are you seeing this?" Orsaya demanded of Wendell.

"Oh yes."

The proximity alarm got louder.

The pilot swore as he powered the reverse thrusters. "We'll hit the station at this rate. For God's sake, someone, get me a clear space."

"On it," said the comms-person.

Ean sat back and listened to the lines. It was different being inside the shuttle. In here, he felt safe, surrounded by the lines, snuggled up against the security of the bigger ship—now with its full eleven lines. Not that they were in perfect health, but they were okay, although line one was quiet. He whispered a special welcome to line nine, which had come back from the dead, or wherever lines came back from when they were so damaged they were almost the equivalent of dead. The deep, resonant line sounded in his head.

The shuttle crawled on.

"Have you gotten me a space yet?" demanded the pilot.

"It's not as easy as you think. There's a lot of junk out here."

There were a lot of ships. Ean could feel the lines.

They slid slowly past a gaping hole in the side of the ship.

"Holy Jackson and Philtre," one of Orsaya's people said. "Did you see that?"

The metal was serrated, as if a gigantic shark with particularly large teeth had taken a shuttle-sized bite out of it.

"I hope a weapon did that."

"A weapon with teeth," someone murmured uneasily.

The underside of the ship was pitted and scored. Even discounting the bite, this ship had been in the wars.

"Got it," the comms-person said. "But you're not going to like it."

"Get me away from this ship."

"Coordinates 172-184-267."

"I'd like to get a bit farther out."

"Not going to happen," Comms said. "You want to see this." She put it up on-screen. "I'm taking this from Confluence Station. They're otherwise occupied at the moment and haven't noticed we're patching in."

She panned 360 degrees.

The Gate Union ships had gone. Ean could have told her that. The station had jumped along with the *Eleven*'s fleet. He recognized the shapes of the ships he knew. Even better, he could place them against the lines in his head. The *Lancastrian Princess*. The *Wendell* and the *Gruen*. The media ships. The *Eleven*. Confluence Station. He recognized the lines.

And here, in the first quadrant, another alien ship similar to the *Eleven*, only four times the size.

"Holy—" Ean wasn't sure who'd said it.

Behind the new eleven was a fleet of smaller ships. Alien ships. Row on row of them. They filled the screen.

Even Orsaya was speechless.

Gann was the first one to break the silence. He gave a humorless laugh. "Imagine Markan if you'd brought that out before his coup," he said to Orsaya.

Orsaya nodded, and Ean got the feeling she wasn't even thinking of the war right now. "Impressive." She shook her head and visibly pulled herself together. "No doubt Roscracia would find a way around it."

"I just hope there's no one left alive on there," Comms said. "Or if there is, that they know we're friends."

Ean didn't think anyone was alive. The line ones were too quiet.

MARKAN finally stopped trying to call ships that weren't there and called Wendell instead.

"Fire on that shuttle."

"I don't have any weapons." Ean might have imagined that Wendell's voice was extra cold, but he didn't imagine—through the lines—the look Wendell gave the comms at Markan's request. He was getting used to dipping into the lines he wanted to see/ hear while tuning out the rest.

Markan snapped off the comms with more force than needed. "Organize two armed shuttles," he told someone near him.

Ten thousand kilometers farther out, a ship flicked out of the void. Ean didn't see it on the shuttle screen, it was too far away, but he saw Wendell's and Markan's reaction to its arrival.

"Magnify," Markan said.

Someone did.

It was a massive Alliance mothership.

Motherships were the biggest ships in the fleet, the size of a small moon. One of them could reduce a planet to scorched earth in a few hours.

"Bloody hell." Markan leaned on the comms until the shuttle crews he had just dispatched answered.

"Destroy that shuttle. Ensure everyone on board is dead, especially Lambert."

"And Orsaya?" his aide asked.

"Lambert is the only one who can control those ships

right now. Get rid of him, and we'll have the upper hand because we have all the tens."

Abram was ordering armed shuttles out, too. Ean could see from the distances that the Gate Union shuttles would arrive first.

It was time to even the odds.

"Markan is sending out armed shuttles," he said.

Orsaya gave him a sharp look, as if she knew he wasn't telling the full truth. "How many?"

"Two."

The pilot was already recalibrating the controls. "Get me a path through this junkyard."

It might as well have been a junkyard. All the line ones were poor. There was nothing alive left on the ships. Right now, it was a good thing because the alien lines were stronger than those on the human ships. If they'd been fully active, Ean doubted he would have been able to even pick out the lines of the *Lancastrian Princess*, let alone lines he knew less well, like Confluence Station.

"Make toward the *Eleven*," Orsaya said, then to Ean, "You can get us in behind the protective barrier the way you did with Lady Lyan's ship."

Once inside the barrier, she was safe from both Markan and Abram. Ean didn't want that. "I have to sing."

She nodded.

Ean took a deep breath. He wasn't just going to sing the *Eleven*'s defense down, he was going to open every channel he could to Abram.

Something hit the shuttle on the port side and knocked him against the wall.

"Damn," the pilot said, and pushed them forward so fast their gravity increased momentarily. They went so close to the new eleven, Ean was sure they scraped against it.

Markan's shuttles must have been fast.

"Get among the smaller ships," Orsaya said. "It will be harder to hit us there."

The pilot nodded, then slowed to an almost stop as a laser beam went past and heated the damaged hull of the confluence ship.

"Nice flying," said half a dozen voices.

"Thanks." The pilot was too busy sweating—and swearing—to bask in the praise. "Someone get me a fast way out of here."

Ean was glad the confluence ship didn't have a protective field like the *Eleven* did.

The field. He'd almost forgotten. Dodging laser beams could do that to you. He sang a quick command to the *Eleven*'s line eight to turn off the field and only when he was done he remembered he'd meant to open lines to Abram as well. Would Orsaya notice if he sang again?

The pilot opened the throttle, and the shuttle surged across space between the huge confluence ship and one of the smaller ships. The shuttle rocked, and moved off track as something hit it from the starboard side. Something else hit just after from the port side.

The comms-person said, "Alliance shuttle. Armed."

"We know that," the pilot said.

"Incoming."

"Incoming from this side, too," the comms-person said. "We're sandwiched in the middle."

The pilot did something else with the controls that made Ean's stomach flip, and flip again.

"Nice flying," everyone said again.

"I can't keep this up," the pilot said.

They made for the next ship. Like its parent, it was scored and burned although it was whole.

"Incoming."

They dived behind the smaller ship. Then behind another.

The third had a huge metal bite taken out of it. It was a wonder it could fly.

"I don't know who these guys were fighting," someone said, "but I don't want to meet them."

"They're as battered and bedamned as we are," Ahmed Gann said, looking at the next ship they passed. This one was whole, but the exterior was burned and the outer metal scored.

He sighed. "Too little too late. We got the ship even if we can't use it. Still. I'm glad we'll die rather than watch our own side destroy us."

It was interesting he didn't say the Alliance would destroy them.

"Don't be such a defeatist, Gann." Orsaya glanced back at Ean. "We still hold the wildy."

The wildy was a wildcard in an old card game played on the Yaolin worlds. Rare and precious, it could turn a low hand into a winning one—or a winning hand into a losing one—depending how you played it.

She opened a channel to the *Lancastrian Princess*. "Galenos, before you continue shooting, let's remember who I have on this shuttle with me."

She waved her blaster in Ean's face. "Say something to your friends, and make it short," and pushed the blaster into the side of his cheek.

What did Abram and Michelle need to know most? Politics.

"There was a battle on the station," he said. Would she fire if he said the wrong thing? "Orsaya and Ahmed Gann against the rest." The last was muffled through the hand Orsaya put across his mouth.

He thought about biting her.

"Our own people are trying to kill us," Orsaya told Abram. "Maybe you could do something about it. Then we'll talk some more."

Ean heard the amusement through the *Lancastrian Princess*'s lines, smelled it even as a cinnamon redmint fragrance, as Michelle said, "And there she has us," and could see both Abram and Michelle shaking their heads over it.

Abram's voice didn't show any of that amusement when he said, through the comms, "Acknowledged." He opened a line to Confluence Station. "Admiral Markan. The shuttle is under our protection. Call your shuttles off, or we will be forced to attack them."

"What the—? Galenos, keep out of this."

Their shuttle nosed out from behind the ship. Two Gate Union shuttles fired on it simultaneously. This time the shudder on the starboard side flipped them over.

"Starboard engine gone." The pilot edged back.

Abram was already on the comms to Markan. "Fire on the shuttle again, and we will fire on the station."

A mothership firing on a station would probably obliterate everything in the surrounding space, too—including the shuttle and all the alien ships—so Ean was relieved to hear Abram open a line to the *Gruen*, and say, "Aim for the station and prepare to fire, then hold until I give the order."

Why hadn't he pulled the weapons boards out on the *Gruen*, too? Or was it a bluff? The station was part of the *Eleven*'s fleet now. What would the *Eleven* do if one of its ships fired on another?

Then, back on the original line, Abram said, "Confluence Station, prepare to be boarded. Shuttle, be ready to return to the station once we have control."

It was quiet in the shuttle. Rossi's and Ean's gasping breaths—both lines eleven were strong at present—were the only noise under the everyday mechanics of circulating air and heating. There was a slight off noise in the air-conditioning. Someone needed to fix line two on this shuttle.

The two Alliance shuttles zoomed past them, lasers firing. On-screen, they joined battle with the Gate Union shuttles. The lights from the lasers flickered on the hull of the ship they were sheltering behind. It looked like lightning in space.

"Time to talk," Orsaya said to Ahmed Gann. "Remember that without Lambert, those ships out there are useless debris. Ask for everything we want and more."

She looked consideringly at Ean. "I don't want you interfering." She gestured with the blaster she held. Two soldiers came over and strapped his arms securely to the seat.

Ean struggled. "I haven't done anything to you."

"I want to control this particular conversation, Linesman."

When they were finished, he couldn't move from the shoulders down.

He should have sung the line open. He opened his mouth to do so now, but another soldier shoved a gag into his mouth. He thought he would choke and had to turn his face away.

Beside him, Rossi's amusement came clearly through the lines.

Orsaya nodded at Gann, who took the comms and flicked it on. "Lady Lyan, Commodore Galenos. Ahmed Gann here, currently on the shuttle. We have a deal to offer."

Ean smelled the redmint cinnamon of Michelle's amusement again as she said, "Gann."

"We have the only means of controlling those ships out there," Gann said.

"You're holding a Lancastrian citizen captive. A member of my personal staff."

Michelle could consider everyone on the *Lancastrian Princess* her own personal staff, but Ean smiled just the same. Not that anyone could see it under his gag. Once he would have hated to be considered part of the Crown Princess of Lancia's personal staff. Now? He was glad to have found a place among people like Michelle and Abram and Radko. They were "of his line."

He had to find a way to help them, however. They had helped him, and if anyone deserved to get out of this alive, it was his friends on the *Lancastrian Princess*.

His gaze fell on Jordan Rossi, who didn't have to sing to the lines. He thought at them. Ean should be able to do that, too.

He tried, using the techniques his trainers had attempted to teach him at Rigel's. Nothing. But then, he'd never been able to communicate without sound. He tried harder. The lines couldn't feel him. And why would they want to? It would be like forcing his thoughts on them instead of working with them.

Those old trainers would be laughing now.

Through *Lancastrian Princess* line five, he heard Abram call the mothership. "*Excelsior*, dispatch a party to take and secure the station."

Soon after that, they saw on-screen a dozen miniwarships—each one as big as the *Lancastrian Princess*, each one bristling with weapons—drop away from the mothership and make for the station.

Gann didn't notice although Orsaya's shoulders twitched once, and she didn't relax until it became obvious the ships weren't coming to the shuttle.

Ean let himself flow with the lines. On board Confluence Station, the first *Excelsior* arrivals fought pitched battles with Admiral Markan's people. By the time the *Excelsior*'s soldiers had finished pouring onto the station, Markan was outnumbered five to one. The fight didn't last long.

The main calls through every comms were for medical

staff to deal with heart attacks. Confluence Station seemed to have an epidemic of them.

The two lines eleven waxed and waned in strength. Ean needed to sing to them, to calm them, but he knew Orsaya wouldn't take his gag off.

Ean tried thinking at the lines again. There had to be a way, because every linesman but he could do it.

Afterward, he lay, exhausted, and listened to the sounds of the shuttle, which was so quiet he could hear the air-conditioning again. Even Jordan Rossi had stopped laughing at him and was listening to Michelle and Gann with all his attention.

Maybe Ean should be listening, too.

"So you are proposing a new political grouping? The Alliance, plus the worlds you bring in."

"As equals," Gann said. "Twenty worlds, along with whatever you have."

Ean could smell Michelle's perspiration through line one. This wasn't something easy she was doing here even though she sounded relaxed. "You could bring that many worlds in?"

"Twenty of the best," Gann assured her. "Plus we have the controller for those ships out there." He glanced at Ean when he said that. "Together, our new alliance will be the start of something powerful."

Ean was the only one on the shuttle who heard Michelle's soft sigh. There was a long pause, then she said, strongly, "The Alliance accepts you as equal partners."

THAT wasn't the end of it. Gann and Michelle talked for two more hours before Abram finally gave permission for Orsaya's shuttle to approach the *Lancastrian Princess*.

"Weapons down," Orsaya said quietly to her crew. "No sign of aggression." She looked as old and as wrung out as Katida had after line eleven had started giving Katida heart attacks.

"Thank God it's Galenos and Lady Lyan in charge," Gann said as the pilot took them into the designated shuttle bay. "I wouldn't put it past some of Yu's other people to double-cross us."

They only untied Ean when they had docked. Ean was still pulling his gag off when the air had recycled, and the escort of guards entered. Bhaksir's team was the escort crew. Radko wasn't part of it. Ean checked the lines to see where she was.

In the hospital, joking with the other patients.

Bhaksir bowed to Orsaya and Gann. "Administrator, Admiral. Lady Lyan welcomes you aboard and asks that you join her and Commodore Galenos for refreshments and further discussion. Your crew will be quartered and looked after."

Orsaya indicated that Ean should go in front of her. He stepped out into the corridor, blinking at the familiarity of it. The music of the *Lancastrian Princess*'s lines welcomed him. He was home.

He sang to the lines as he followed Bhaksir, and they came in strongly to welcome him back. All of them, including both line elevens. It was so strong, it forced him to his knees.

Behind him, Rossi muttered something uncomplimentary.

FORTY-TWO

✦

EAN LAMBERT

THE NEW ALLIANCE was formally ratified six weeks after Ean got back to the *Lancastrian Princess*.

Fifty worlds of the old Alliance—they'd been hemorrhaging worlds while Ean had been kidnapped, Katida told him—and twenty from Gate Union. The Yaolin worlds and most of those from around them in the Pleiades Sector, plus a small number of other worlds who had allied with Orsaya and whom Gate Union had kicked out. One of those worlds was Nova Tahiti, Ahmed Gann's home planet.

"We knew some of the power brokers were unhappy with the way things were going," Katida said. "But no one was expecting a coup."

Some of that was due to the linesmen, Orsaya told Katida over the celebration dinner the three of them shared the evening of ratification. They'd been able to hold the Roscracian faction off until Iwo Hurst and Markan had combined forces. Sandhurst had long been working toward taking over the line cartels; Roscracia was happy to help, provided the linesmen in turn supported him in his bid for Roscracian supremacy in Gate Union.

Ean still wasn't sure how he felt about Orsaya, but she and Katida got on well. He wasn't surprised about that.

Orsaya stabbed reconstituted steak with a force that should have dug a hole in her plate. Or bent the fork. "Until the confluence, Paretsky, Rossi, and Naidan kept Sandhurst in check. But once they went out there." She chewed with single-minded ferocity. "Redmond controlling supply of the lines, Roscracia controlling Gate Union, Sandhurst controlling the linesmen. We could see where it was going."

Most of the higher-level linesmen were still in the hospital after Ean's inadvertent use of their power.

Rossi, when he'd been asked about that, had snarled, and said, "Lambert has no finesse." Ean hadn't been meant to hear that, but everything came through the lines now, and Rossi's noise was clearer than others. Orsaya had also said privately to Katida—another thing Ean wasn't supposed to hear, but Katida had passed it on—that a lot of it had to do with having the confluence taken away from them. Many of them were exhibiting classic withdrawal symptoms.

Orsaya attacked another piece of steak. "That's why we became so interested in Ean Lambert," as if he weren't there.

Ean tried to act as if he wasn't.

"For six months, he was the only level ten doing the lines, and he was good."

Katida nodded.

"Lines that we had to retune all the time were fixed. We haven't touched them since."

Katida nodded again.

You still needed a linesman to keep an eye on them. Little things went wrong, like line six when Ean had first stepped aboard the *Lancastrian Princess*.

"I don't know why Rigel kept him hidden."

Ean did. Now. The other linesmen wouldn't have accepted him. He had to be grateful to Rigel for that.

"If Rigel had been a different person, we'd have used him to go up against Sandhurst. But Rigel." Orsaya waved a dismissive hand. "He'd be eaten the first day. And Lambert didn't seem overly political or ambitious."

"No," Katida said, but Ean thought she almost smiled.

"When Rossi came back talking about line eleven and behaved the same way he had at the confluence, it was obvious the confluence was another ship. We knew we needed Lambert to get that ship for us."

All three looked up as Abram stopped beside their table.

"Admiral," Katida and Orsaya said together.

Abram grimaced. Promotion wasn't what he'd planned, he'd told Michelle one evening when the three of them had been alone in the workroom. They had never formally told Ean he couldn't use the couch there, and it was the only place he felt truly at home nowadays.

"You can't refuse it again," Michelle had said. "That would insult my father."

Ean didn't think Abram would worry about insulting Emperor Yu if he thought it best for Michelle's safety, but Michelle had added, "Someone has to keep Katida and Orsaya in line, and if not you, who else?" Then she said, "Please. I agree with my father in this."

Even though that was what she said, Ean could feel through line one it wasn't what she wanted.

"If you don't want him to, then why ask him?" Ean had asked.

It was Abram who sighed. "You can't hold on to the past forever."

And Michelle had added, "He's public property as much as I am. You are, too. You won't have any choice in what you do, either. But unlike Abram, you and I will be together for a while because you've effectively linked yourself to my ship," and her smile showed just a hint of the dimple Ean was sure must have annoyed the geneticists so much.

The Alliance wouldn't let him go. Not with the knowledge he had. Before he'd met Michelle and the crew of the *Lancastrian Princess*, being tied to Lancia like that would have been unbearable.

"If the lines are here, I'll be here." It was more a promise to the lines than it was to Michelle. He'd be there for Michelle, too, because he wanted to be part of the different future she and Abram promised for Lancia.

"Thank you." Michelle turned back to Abram. "You have to accept this promotion."

Abram had just raised an eyebrow.

"I'll miss this," Michelle said.

Abram had sighed again. "So will I."

DINNER over, the three admirals left to do whatever admirals did in the lead-up to creating a new political union. Ean got himself another glass of tea and sat in relative peace, listening to the music of the lines. One hundred twenty-eight ships had come out of the void with the new eleven. With so many, he could only pick out the bad notes, but he took time to give special attention to his own eleven's fleet. All lines, including the now-mended media ships, were fine. They made a symphony in his head of life, work, and the stars.

On the wall, separate screens showed reporters Coral Zabi and Sean Watanabe covering the event. Déjà vu. It wasn't that long ago they'd done the same thing at the signing of the peace treaty.

The second meal shift arrived, mingling with the first, who stayed to watch the ratification ceremony.

Captain Wendell stopped at Ean's table, hesitated when he realized who was sitting there, and almost walked away. Then he shrugged and sat down.

Wendell's crew had fared the worst of anyone. They were from the Wallacian worlds, which had stayed with Gate Union. The union had put a bounty on their heads. If they were ever caught in Gate Union territory again, they'd be killed.

Yaolin and Lancia had both offered them citizenship. As yet they still hadn't chosen one over the other although, according to Fergus—and Ean had no idea where he got his gossip from—at Michelle's request Emperor Yu was already moving to decree they become honorary citizens of Lancia, whether they wanted it or not.

Ean nodded at Wendell, who nodded back.

"You're different from what I expected," Ean said, when the silence became too long and stilted.

Wendell could have learned his steak-eating techniques from Orsaya. He probably had. He swallowed his mouthful and raised an eyebrow but didn't speak.

"Through the lines, you're a cross between a—" Ean stopped. He had the command of Abram and some of the flair of Michelle. "Yet in real life, you're—"

"Human," Wendell suggested. "Ordinary."

"Not ordinary." Never that. "Different to the line view."

Wendell took a long mouthful of tea. "I expect the lines take on the characteristics of the whole ship, not just one person. And I have a very good crew. Or I did have until you started killing them."

Ouch. Ean was almost glad to see Fergus and Rossi making their way across. Not that he wanted to see Rossi ever again, but the New Alliance insisted *all* their linesmen be trained, and somehow Ean had become de facto line trainer, along with everything else. Sometimes he thought he'd be crushed under the weight of all he had to do now, but he wouldn't change it. He wouldn't change the lines.

All the lines surged with that thought.

Rossi staggered and collected himself. "Bastard," he greeted Ean, and Ean wasn't sure if he meant it for the inadvertent line surge or just meant it generally.

"This is it," someone from another table said, and everyone fell silent as the screens focused on the representatives from the seventy worlds.

It was longer than the last ceremony because this time a representative from each world stepped up to press their palm against the treaty as signature.

Lancia was represented by Emperor Yu. Michelle was among the watching dignitaries, and the camera focused on her a lot. Tall and beautiful, flanked by two equally beautiful but millimeters shorter women who could only be her sisters and two handsome but centimeters taller men who had to be her brothers. Michelle looked tired, and Ean could see by the body language of the other four that they didn't have a lot to do with each other or with their older sibling.

They watched the ceremony in silence.

Finally, the signatories stood together for the obligatory video at the end. Someone gave them glasses of sparkling wine. They raised their glasses.

Everyone in the dining hall raised their glasses, too. Ean raised his own empty tea glass.

"To the New Alliance," Emperor Yu said.

Every voice in the dining room echoed it. "To the New Alliance."

EAN was kept busy. Visiting ships, voice lessons, line training. Plus he had to do enough schmoozing of his own with the military who swarmed around him wanting to know about the ships.

It would have helped if Rigel's lessons had been more about how to deal with the military rather than about working with civilians.

The three linesmen spent a lot of time together.

He was grateful for Fergus, who knew everything and everyone, or if he didn't, made it seem like he did. Sometimes he was even grateful for the brooding presence of Jordan Rossi, who occasionally got exasperated enough to deflect some of their questions. Rossi was master of the barbed put-down.

Sometimes, too, Ean snooped too much through the lines—lines didn't have boundaries like humans did—and it helped to have Rossi's snarling, "Get out of my lines, bastard," to pull him back to civil behavior.

Every evening at 19:00 hours he, Fergus, Rossi, Engineer Tai, the medic, and Captain Helmo met with the three admirals—Abram, Katida, and Orsaya—for a private speculation about the lines.

On the third night, they discussed the likelihood of two elevens being found in the same region of space.

"Coincidences like that don't happen," Abram said. "They came together, or one came looking for the other."

"Or maybe they were simply routed, and this was the only place they could escape to," Katida said.

They were, as Ahmed Gann had once said, a battered and bedamned group of ships.

"However they got here," Abram said, "they came from somewhere. And they were fighting someone. We have to expect that one day, their own people will come looking for them. Or their enemies will."

Orsaya blew out her breath. "I'm not sure I want to meet a force that can rout ships like that so effectively."

Neither did Ean.

The initial Agreement of Worlds charter the member worlds had signed had made the ships the common property of a combined New Alliance fleet headed by Admirals Galenos, Orsaya, and Katida. Part of that, or so Katida had told Ean, was that no one wanted Lancia in charge, so they'd provided the equivalent of a committee to keep Abram in check.

Ean didn't ask why they thought Abram would be there. There was never any question of that.

"And the other part?"

"There are obviously aliens at war out there. We're your three best admirals to have in such a situation." Katida had never boasted about her abilities, but she was sure of them. "A war like that could even turn Gate Union and the New Alliance into allies in the future."

Or Markan could try to make a deal with some of the aliens.

What would the aliens think, when they finally did arrive, to realize that humans had collected their ships and refurbished them to suit themselves? Ean hoped they'd listen to reason.

The ships wanted humans. They'd told him so. They were looking for people to communicate with. Ean suspected a line's definition of "people" was different from that of a human's.

After that, Tai tried to describe line eleven. "It's huge and it's . . . You can feel it, and—"

"Hmm," Abram said. "Now describe Ean."

"Ean. He's not—"

"When he sings. What does he sound like?"

"Oh, that." Tai's voice hushed. "He sounds like space, and people, and— Have you heard him?"

The one thing he seemed to have in common with the other lines was that no one could describe them. Ean supposed that was because no one had the words to describe what lines felt like. But it was embarrassing, all the same.

Katida cut in. "There's a degree of ecstasy in both. One can only surmise both touch the same centers of the brain. Probably the nucleus accumbens."

Her voice was clinical. She sounded as if she had thought about it a lot. Or talked to some brain specialists about it.

The medic nodded slowly. "Maybe."

"Wonderful," said Rossi. "Now we have crazy Ean Lambert with direct access to our brain," but he didn't deny it. Ean wished he had.

Abram nodded, as if what they were saying wasn't unexpected. "So does Ean sound or feel like line eleven?"

Tai shook his head doubtfully.

"No," Katida said.

"No," Rossi said, a lot more explosively, as if it was sacrilege to even suggest it.

"So a different line then," Abram said. "Line twelve?"

That joke was beyond repeating. Abram should have known better.

"Or a ten so badly damaged it feels like a different line," Rossi said.

Ean *wasn't* damaged. He was a certified ten, no matter what Rossi said, and he could mend the lines as well as Rossi did, even if he did it differently.

"Or the only ten who hasn't been damaged by current line training," Katida countered.

Captain Helmo, who hadn't said a word until then, said, "I don't think there is any doubt. He communicates with line eleven rather than just reacting to it the way the others do. The ship treats him like a different line." He paused, and Rossi opened his mouth to argue with him. "My linesmen treat him like a different line."

Rossi closed his mouth.

MICHELLE arrived back on ship at midnight.

Ean was in the central workroom, telling Abram about Fergus's training. It was going well.

"So, officially a twelve," Michelle said.

She hadn't even been at the meeting. "Not you, too."

Michelle looked exhausted. The skin under her eyes looked blue and bruised. She carried a black-and-gray uniform shirt over her arm. Ean stood up. Michelle and Abram would want to talk. Abram left in three weeks. His replacement would be here in four days, and they hadn't seen much of each other since Abram had become an admiral.

"I'm going to bed."

"Wait." Michelle smiled, so that her dimples showed, and held up the shirt, then shook it out so that it was displayed for Abram and Ean. She'd added two extra bars on the pocket, below his name.

Ean buried his face in his hands.

"Try it on." She tossed it over.

Ean caught the shirt automatically, then didn't know what to do with it. A dignified exit was the best he could think of. "Good night."

He took the shirt with him, for what else could he do with it?

Through the lines, he saw Michelle settle back on the couch with a sigh while Abram got them both tea.

He looked at the shirt clutched in his hands. He belonged here. Whether they mistakenly believed he was a twelve or whether he really was one, surely this shirt meant he'd made a place for himself here. With the lines.

The two fleets made a chorus in his head. Of course he belonged. He was of their line. He belonged with them. Why would he think otherwise?

Yes. He belonged with them. He dropped the shirt on the end of his bed and settled back to talk with his fellow lines. It was time he found out more about them.

"So," he sang to line seven. "What exactly is it that you do?"

THE ULTIMATE
WRITERS OF
SCIENCE FICTION

John Barnes	Jack McDevitt
William C. Dietz	Alastair Reynolds
Simon R. Green	Allen Steele
Joe Haldeman	S. M. Stirling
Robert Heinlein	Charles Stross
Frank Herbert	Harry Turtledove
E. E. Knight	John Varley